PRAISE FOR JAMES A MOORE

"Gripping, horrific, and unique, James Moore continues to be a winner, whatever genre he's writing in."

Seanan McGuire, New York Times bestselling author of the InCryptid and October Daye series

"*The Last Sacrifice* is brilliant, devious, dark and compelling. This is epic fantasy at its very best. Highly recommended!"

Jonathan Maberry, New York Times bestselling author of Kill Switch

"Moore has laid the groundwork for a trilogy that promises to be loaded with terrifically grim fantasy storytelling. There is a lot of swift, merciless violence in this book, mingled with an undercurrent of very welcome, if very dark, humor. All of it together takes me back to what made me giddy about epic fantasy way back when."

Rich Rosell, Barnes & Noble Sci-Fi & Fantasy Blog

"James A Moore is the new prince of grimdark fantasy. His work is full of dark philosophy and savage violence, desperate warriors and capricious gods. Exhilarating as hell."

Christopher Golden, New York times bestselling author of Snowblind

"*The Last Sacrifice* is dark and violent with no punches pulled. The worl[illegible] focuses [illegible]ry."

"With *The Last Sacrifice*, James A Moore has triumphed yet again, delivering a modern sword and sorcery tale to delight old and new fans of the genre. With its intriguing premise, stellar cast of characters, and flavorful horror elements, this is damn good stuff."
Bookwraiths

"From living mountains to the secret behind the veils of a nation, Moore pushes and pulls the story through questions and answers, keeping the reader on their toes. For me, *The Blasted Lands* is more immersive and thrilling than some of the fantasy masterpieces. Moore shapes a story which appeals to fans of all types, showing how fantasy can be a grand equalizer."
Literary Escapism

"The end of the book had me on the edge of my seat, wanting more. I will definitely be reading the next book in the Seven Forges series as soon as it comes out."
Avid Fantasy Reviews

"*Seven Forges* is an excellent, enjoyable, and thoroughly entertaining fantasy debut into a new world of swords and sorcery, complete with romance, intrigue, and danger."
Attack of the Books

"Wow, that twist. In some ways I think I should have seen it coming, and I kind of did, but *Seven Forges* just lulled me into security and BAM! Craziness!"
On Starships & Dragonwings

"James A Moore dedicates *Seven Forges* in part 'to the memory of Fritz Leiber and Robert E Howard for the inspiration.' Moore is far more than an imitator, though. He does some fresh, counterintuitive things with the genre conventions. More than once, he startled me into saying out loud, 'I didn't see that coming.'"

Black Gate

"I thoroughly enjoyed *Seven Forges* although I was left speechless by the ending and left wondering for days whether there was to be another book in the series. There were so many threads of stories left open that I need to know what happens next."

The Bookish Outsider

"Moore does a fantastic job of building worlds and characters in *Seven Forges* as we hop on board the train that is about to meet its doom."

Troubled Scribe

"The race of the Sa'aba Taalor are the newest and freshest I've read in decades. Where many writers will have gods who are nebulous and unreachable, many of Moore's gods respond immediately. I think I like his creatures the best – the Pra Moresh. Here Moore's horror roots allow him to really shine. His descriptive prose and keen eye for the horrific proves that he's a master architect of the gruesome and prognosticator of fear. If you have yet to try these, then do so on my word. You'll thank me for it."

Living Dangerously

BY THE SAME AUTHOR

The Tides of War series
The Last Sacrifice • Fallen Gods

The Seven Forges series
Seven Forges • The Blasted Lands
City of Wonders • The Silent Army

The Blood Red series
Blood Red • Blood Harvest • Blood of the Damned

The Chris Corin Chronicles
Possessions • Rabid Growth • Newbies

The Serenity Falls Trilogy
Writ in Blood • The Pack • Dark Carnival

The Griffin & Price series (with Charles R Rutledge)
Blind Shadows • Congregations of the Dead • A Hell Within

Alien: Sea of Sorrows
The Haunted Forest Tour *(with Jeff Strand)*
Bloodstained Oz *(with Christopher Golden)*
Buffy the Vampire Slayer: Chaos Bleeds
Cherry Hill
Deeper
Fireworks
Harvest Moon
Homestead
Under the Overtree
Vampire: House of Secrets *(with Kevin Andrew Murphy)*
Vendetta
Werewolf: Hellstorm
The Wild Hunt

Slices *(stories)*
This is Halloween *(stories)*

JAMES A MOORE

Fallen Gods

TIDES OF WAR, BOOK II

ANGRY ROBOT
An imprint of Watkins Media Ltd

20 Fletcher Gate,
Nottingham,
NG1 2FZ • UK

angryrobotbooks.com
twitter.com/angryrobotbooks
No gods no masters

se, Inc., New

places, and
are used
fictitiously. Any resemblance to actual events, locales, organizations or persons, living or dead, is entirely coincidental.

US edition ISBN 978 0 85766 711 3
UK edition ISBN 978 0 85766 546 1
Ebook ISBN 978 0 85766 712 0

Printed in the United States of America

9 8 7 6 5 4 3 2 1

This one is for Tessa,
who always makes me smile,

and for Tim Lebbon, who reignited
my love of dark fantasy.

CHAPTER ONE
SUNRISE

Brogan McTyre

Brogan McTyre knew he was sleeping. It was only in his dreams that he had time to grieve.

When the He-Kisshi came and took his family, stole them away to appease the appetites of the gods, he followed and sought to stop them. He failed, and his world changed.

In his dream he had time to think, to consider the world around him without feeling the pressure of keeping his allies alive and trying to stop the gods from destroying the world in a retaliatory tantrum.

Long enough then to lower his head and remember his beloved Nora's laugh, her kiss, the feeling of her breath when they embraced. Leidhe and Sherla, laughing at a secret jest between them, the sort it seemed that only twins could share. Time enough to mourn his son, Braghe, who would never grow old enough to shave, or ride a horse, or sharpen a knife.

He understood that what he saw was not real, could

not be real, and did not match with his last memory of slipping into a fitful slumber along the rocky edge of the Broken Swords, amidst chunks of rough crystal the size of his head.

The fact that he knew it was a dream changed nothing. In that moment, everything he experienced was his reality.

He stood along the spine of the mountains, facing north. To the south the range continued on almost to the sea. To the east the black, raging storm clouds hid half the land away and shattered the peace with a thousand tongues of lightning. To the west the lands were clear and pristine, but foreign to him: Mentath, the country he'd fought against in his youth, was a place he never wanted to see again.

The female voice that spoke to him came from Mentath and spoke with barely suppressed hatred. "You are hunted, Brogan McTyre. You, who have enslaved a people and angered the gods."

"It was enslave them or kill them. They deserved worse than they got." In the real world he might have felt guilt over the words, but not in his dream.

"The gods do not agree." The voice trembled with rage and the storms lashed out to the west, mirroring that fury.

Not to be outdone, Brogan raised his axe above his head and roared back, "The gods took my family from me! They deserve nothing but death and destruction!"

"Blasphemy!"

To the west something twisted within the cloudbanks. A great, hunched shape that slithered through the storms and hid itself in the corner of the eye. Below that form the ocean surged over the land devouring all that it touched, threatening to reach all the way to the mountains.

Winds roared across the plains and reached out, whipping his hair in a frenzy. His clothes rippled in the charnel gale, and the scent of carrion forced itself on him.

Brogan was not afraid. He should have been. He knew that, dream or not, he had actually angered the gods. He understood that their rage would end the world.

"Tell your gods I'm coming for them! Tell your gods that I'll see them dead for what they did!"

"You who end the world would make threats? The gods will have you one way or another, Brogan McTyre. We prepare for you. We will cut your heart out and offer it to the gods. If they are merciful they will let us live. If not, in whatever comes after this world, we will find you, and make you suffer."

The wind woke him. It blew across his face and pelted him with a fine, gritty hail.

Brogan rolled over and pulled his cloak closer around his broad shoulders. There was absolutely nothing glorious about sleeping in the mountains as winter crept closer.

For one moment he was at peace, and then the truth rushed in as brutally as the tide in his fading dream.

Nora. Braghe, Leidhe and Sherla. Their loss was a weight on his chest that would likely never leave him.

It was also a hot blade that burned inside, a glowing ember that wanted to ignite and burn the world.

He opened his eyes as the wind shifted and he felt a

warm breath touch his flesh. Warm enough that it was something other than the wind.

His hand clenched around his axe's grip and he looked up toward the source of that warmth.

Harper Ruttket smiled at him. It was not a pleasant expression. The glint in the eyes and the curl of his lip, reminded Brogan far too much of a predatory animal.

He tried moving the axe, but Harper was wiser than that. The man's foot pressed down on the blade and kept it pinned there.

Sometimes he forgot that Harper was his best friend.

"It's morning soon. The sun is climbing and soon enough we'll be discovered if we're not on our way." If Harper was at all worried about the way Brogan tried to move his blade he hid it well behind that predatory smirk.

"I hate you, Harper."

"Of course you do. That's why you put me on the last watch of the night. Get up, you bastard."

The dream was gone but the reality remained. He was a wanted man. He and his friends were being hunted down for offending the gods. They had done so by interrupting the ritual sacrifice of all four members of Brogan's family. His family died, but the rituals demanded were not completed and, as they soon learned, the world was ending as a result of their actions.

The Grakhul were a people who served the gods, preparing the sacrifices and committing the ritual acts. Brogan and his companions had killed a great number of Grakhul, mostly men, and sold the rest into slavery, making them wealthy beyond measure. But they couldn't spend a coin without getting themselves burned at the stake or worse. They'd angered the gods and that was bad enough, but they'd also offended the Slavers Union by selling them the remaining pale-skinned people and lying about where they came from. The Grakhul were under the protection of the very gods Brogan had already offended. The messengers of the gods, the He-Kisshi, had, according to the rumors they'd heard, destroyed the home of the Slavers Union to show the dissatisfaction of the gods. The slavers would doubtless like a refund.

Brogan wasn't much in a mood to negotiate with the slavers, as he was already a condemned man in all five kingdoms. He was going to need that money to muster an army sufficient for his needs.

The only good news was that Brogan was a mercenary. He understood how mercenaries felt and worked. They would be loyal as long as the coin held out. They would also be loyal to their own before they'd be fair with the slavers. At least until the slavers offered more money.

He rose and looked down toward the east and the gathering storms that swept across the plains of Arthorne, hiding half the known world from view.

The winds howled. The rains drenched the plains and left a vast watery surface where once had been desert. To the south, where the land was higher, the waters had not completely taken over, but rivers and streams all flowed over their banks, lakes were larger than they should have been, and in some places the heavy caul of storm clouds obscured what should have been easily seen.

The day was only just beginning and there was so much to do. He had to gather an army. He had to plan how to fend off several armies that wanted them captured and offered to the gods of the Grakhul.

He had to leave behind his friends, if only for a time, and find the best possible answer for how to kill a pantheon of gods.

There was a voice in his head that told him his tasks were too great. He thought of Nora and his children, and crushed the doubts behind a veil of hatred. Fuck the gods. They'd pay for what they'd done.

If he could save the world in the process, he'd do so. If he could not, he'd be content to slay the gods.

To the east the sun broke the horizon. The northern areas were buried in storm clouds and lightning. The southern areas were bright and clear. Beneath his feet the Broken Blades – where once upon a time gods, or giants, had fought and died – held the light at bay.

To the northeast the darkness continued, save where tongues of lightning shattered the peace and stabbed into the heart of the land again and again in an endless fury.

The gods were angry and they wanted blood.

He knew just how they felt.

Myridia

She opened her eyes and squinted against the bright sunlight reflected down from crystalline shards.

She was chilled; the air held a note of frost, and Myridia was without a cloak. Around her the others were just as cold. They did not feel the chill in the same way as the savages around them. They stiffened in the cold, moved more slowly, until they warmed themselves by a fire or through activity. If the weather was cold enough they could freeze as solid as the ice, but their temperature was better suited to being in the depths.

The remnants of her dream were still there. She didn't think it was completely a dream. She suspected the gods had used her to convey a message to the leader of her enemies, the one called Brogan McTyre. She had seen him before, of course, when he'd captured all of her people that he didn't slaughter.

It had been a wonderful dream, screaming at him. In a perfect world she would be the one that offered him to the gods.

She intended to do all she could to make sure that happened.

Somewhere in the distance, the Night People were coming for them, but they had not arrived yet. And to ensure that they did not get close, she and her sisters would ride through the waters during the day, swimming and taking their other forms, breathing water and moving at speeds that would shame most horses.

"Up!" Myridia called to the others, and they responded quickly, their pale skin made almost silvery by the light cast upon them. She stretched and savored the growing heat of the day.

Lyraal stood in one smooth motion, her eyes squinting against the sunlight. Her hands touched key points on her body, checking her weapons were in place and testing a few spots where she'd been injured in previous fights. The moves were entirely unconscious and Myridia knew it from watching her friend over the course of the last few weeks.

"We should go. We have a great ways to travel yet."

Lyraal's eyes assessed her. She knew the other woman was looking for signs of weakness. By Lyraal's words, Myridia was in charge. She made the decisions and led them toward the Sessanoh and the chance to purify that area for the sacrifice of the men who had offended the gods. That didn't mean she was above judgment. Lyraal watched her, and would also be the first to tell her if she was no longer fit to lead.

Behind them the sun reached the massive crystalline blades thrusting up from the mountains. Fiery light bounced across the ground in a myriad of hues, a reminder that gods had battled in this very area.

"The river calls," Myridia agreed. "We have a long ways to travel and we have dawdled long enough."

The Night People had followed them before and taken Garien and the other humans they'd traveled with for a time. Now Garien's troupe followed them, hunted them as part of the creatures they had tried to escape.

There was no one to blame for the delays except Myridia, who'd told herself that moving with the band of performers offered them all protection from their enemies.

She should have listened to Lyraal. They should have moved on and taken the rivers instead of riding horses. It would have been faster.

Myridia called out to her sisters again and they moved with her toward the river, gathering their meager supplies as they went. They did not need much. They had their weapons, covered in oilcloth. They had some clothing. Fish swam in the water and would be easily caught and consumed.

As the waters covered her legs, Myridia willed the

change and watched her skin harden into iridescent scales. Fingers and toes lengthened, and webs grew between the digits. Her eyes grew larger, her mouth changed shape. The sides of her chest once more revealed the gills that so often lay hidden and protected.

A moment later she was under the cool, rushing water and swimming hard to the west and south, following the river's course. Not far behind her, Lyraal sang a song of rage and sorrow into the waters and followed.

They would reach their destination. They had no choice. The world would end if they failed.

Niall Leraby

Niall smiled. He couldn't help it. After the gods knew how long, they had outdistanced the rains again. More than that, they had outrun the clouds. The skies were blue and clear, though a look behind told him that the calm would not last. The storms were there, raging in the distance, but they did not move as quickly as he and his companions.

Still, as Mosara, his mentor, was fond of saying, one should always look to the light if one wished to avoid getting lost in the darkness.

A little light. A small blessing. For the moment he was dry, and his clothes were dry, and he did not smell of damp and mildew.

Tully rode the horse next to his. They were both sore from the ride, but grateful for it as well. Neither was much of an equestrian. Tully had never had a need, and Niall always preferred to travel in a wagon rather than to actually ride on one of the beasts. Still, one adapted.

They'd been in a wagon and then they'd walked for days and now they rode, courtesy of the slavers who rode with them. Well, they were slavers, but currently they had no stock to sell. That had been taken from them by the He-Kisshi.

Niall and Tully both knew the creatures far too well. One of them had chased them, fanatically. It had come for them with a thirst for vengeance, ever since they'd killed it.

Killed it. He-Kisshi, as it turned out, lived up to their reputation for being undying. The damned thing had been strangled, burned, cut, and beaten repeatedly but it wasn't until Stanna, a giant of a woman if ever he'd seen one, had come along and cleaved away the head of the thing that they knew it was dead. Even then they'd burned the vile hooded skull just to be certain.

Stanna rode ahead of them now, talking with Temmi, the young woman he'd seen grow from a giggling, happy girl to a solemn, bitter survivor of the He-Kisshi's endless attacks. Her entire family had been killed by the nightmare monstrosity. He'd been worried for a time that she might not recover with her sanity intact, but it seemed that the redheaded giantess was good for his friend. They had become companions, and when they stopped each day to settle their camp, the slaver taught the younger woman how to fight and defend herself from attackers.

Riding at the end of their column – a larger party than he'd expected – was another of the slavers, a man named Lexx, who was long and lean and bore the scars that he, too, had received from the He-Kisshi. The damned things seemed incapable of leaving anyone unmarked by their presence. The beasts had nearly killed the man. He was intact now because the slavers paid for him to be healed by sorceries that few could hope to afford. The scars he suffered were copious, but he could walk and he could see from both eyes though one had been torn free with a whip, according to Stanna.

Lexx saw him looking and smiled thinly. He was not a pleasant man, and there was something about him that made Niall leery. Still, they traveled together. Niall smiled back and nodded before looking back toward Tully.

Tully was still a mystery to him. They'd have never met if not for the Undying taking them as sacrifices – again the thought of his young neighbor Ligel, also taken for sacrifice and killed when they made their escape, came to him and twisted his guts with guilt. He doubted he would ever be free of that, especially since they were headed for his home, and he would see the boy's family soon enough.

He looked toward the south, the direction they headed, and the sun lit Tully's fine blonde hair and pale blue eyes. She squinted against the glare, and for a moment he thought she might actually smile. That was a rarity with the woman, though, to be fair, she had little reason for being of good cheer.

They had survived much, yes, but she was still wanted in her own town, and likely still hunted by the very people who'd raised her. He didn't know all the details and she wasn't much in a mood for sharing any news with him.

Some people have more secrets than others. He accepted that.

"We're attacked! Get your weapons!" He recognized Stanna's voice, but the words made no sense. Who could possibly want to attack them in the middle of nowhere?

Niall looked around, his face set in a scowl of concentration, and spotted people heading toward them. They rode hard, each and every last one of the attackers leaning over their horses and charging forward with every bit of speed they could get from the frantic-looking animals.

Were they truly attacking? He could not say, but he also could not take a chance. That much he had learned since being attacked the first time by the He-Kisshi: not every person he met would be a friend, or even indifferent. Some of them just wanted to kill.

Tully shook her head and said, "Not on this stupid animal." She dropped from her saddle and landed easily. Then, as the animals started to get nervous about the approaching group, she slipped away from the trail and the horses alike.

Niall thought about the damage he could take if the horse threw him and quickly followed suit. Some of the people around him were trained to ride the beasts into combat. He'd let them take the lead.

By way of weapons he had two, his walking stick and a decent-sized knife. He chose the stick for the present. It was sturdy wood and could take a blow from a weapon if it came to that.

An arrow hummed past his ear. At least, he thought it was an arrow. It was fast and noisy and probably would have killed him if he hadn't been damned lucky. Whatever the case, that was enough for him. Time to get off the road.

By the time he'd made the decision the new group was among them, swinging weapons and screaming like maniacs. If they were trying to communicate an idea, he had no notion what it was. If they were trying to kill Niall and his friends, they seemed to have no need to talk about it. They just hollered and screamed and whooped.

A horse came at him. Whether the rider was male or female did not matter. All he saw was the enormous shape of the animal, someone atop it, and an arm swinging. The arm was too long by far and he assumed a weapon was making the extra length. The staff moved without conscious thought. Mosara had always insisted that any fool who chose to be a gardener should know how to defend himself, because even in a place like Edinrun, someone walking alone risked being attacked.

The hard wood shivered in his hands and the rider was past, nearly unhorsed by the blow. Niall staggered back to keep his balance and narrowly missed the next horse trampling him.

He heard Stanna screaming, not in fear, but in rage. He could see her up ahead as she grabbed a man off his horse and threw him to the ground like he weighed no more than a cloak.

Tully made no noise, but he saw her moving, darting past the horse that almost crushed him. Her arms were too fast to truly see, but the charging horse let out a shriek and reared up, and the next animal in the charge was suddenly bleeding from the neck. The rider let out a scream that was louder than the horse's and flailed his arms as he was thrown at Niall.

Sidestep and swing. The rounded end of his staff

shattered the bones in the man's face as he fell. He did not get back up.

Niall tried to look everywhere at once, and to remember to breathe. His heart hammered, his arms shook.

Somewhere behind him someone screamed. He didn't have time to look. The next rider was coming. Ultimately all he could do was slip to the side as the rider steered and the horse charged. It was simple enough math: if one of the damned things ran him down he'd be broken if not killed. He'd rather not, really.

Stepping aside he saw Tully throw a blade that stuck in the side of the rider's skull. He went down and the horse charged past.

As it did so, the rider flopped to the ground.

Next in line were two horsemen riding a dozen feet apart. They covered the road entirely, and between the two of them they held a length of chain that rattled and hissed with each stride of the horses.

Tully saw it at the same time he did and dove for the dirt off the path. She cleared it with ease.

Repetition. That was what Mosara had always emphasized. Even as he moved his staff into a guard position, Niall knew he'd done the wrong thing. He should have jumped. The move was purely automatic.

The horses and their riders and that heavy chain between them? They didn't seem to care why he stayed in the same place.

The chain drove his staff backward and he felt it slip from his grip before the hard wood smashed into his chest and struck a glancing blow off his skull. After that the chain hit him in the stomach and lifted him from the ground. He barely felt that part. He was already sliding into darkness.

Beron

Beron looked across the plains and smiled tightly. They were close. He could nearly taste the blood of his enemies.

His smile faltered. No, no blood. They were to be taken alive. He might well have their tendons cut to stop them from escaping, but Brogan McTyre, Harper Ruttket and the rest of their ilk were worth the most if they were alive.

"Well, a little fun then," he said aloud. "I have branding irons."

"What's that?" Levarre looked his way and scowled. The man was not as happy as he had been, though he had plenty of reasons to smile.

"Be calm, Levarre. I was only considering the methods I'll use to torture McTyre and his friends."

The other slaver nodded.

"We are doing a good thing. The gods want the bastards, and we want the bastards, and we'll have three times our investment returned to us, even as we save the world." The air was preposterously cold and rain had fallen for days on end, still Beron was cheerful. "We have the upper hand."

"They are not ours yet, and if we fail, what of Ariah? What if he is disappointed?"

"Then we take care of the matter as we need to. But our new god is pleased with us. We gave him over a hundred beautiful women to satisfy his needs and we offered him three of the Undying as sacrifices."

Rather than please his associate, the words made Levarre flinch. Beron scowled.

"You felt all that I felt, Levarre. Ariah gave you weapons of power to show you that his word is his bond. He has made you a priest in his name. Celebrate that notion. We are no longer merely slavers looking to reclaim what was stolen from us. We are the messengers of a new god who will help us save the world."

"What of the other gods? What will they do when they find we have turned our backs to them?"

Beron spit, his broad features moving into a snarl of barely contained rage. "I owe the gods nothing. They punish us for what was not our doing. I will offer them only contempt, and if I must I will offer them the tip of my blade."

"You've gone mad, Beron."

"No. I have found an opportunity. The very same one you accepted. If you do not see yourself as part of the new regime, give me your weapons and I will offer them to another who is wiser and braver."

The words were a calculated risk. Levarre was a large man and he was a very capable fighter. He was also proud to a fault and just as greedy as Beron. There was the chance that he would attack. There was also the chance that he would see reason. Beron's hand rested on the hilt of his new sword; the black blade seemed nearly to vibrate at his touch.

"Do not belittle me twice, Beron."

"Then do not give me reason." Beron moved closer and placed a hand on the other man's thick shoulder. The muscles under his skin were as hard as stone. "The gods are ending the world. They destroyed our city and sent their Undying after us. We fought back and we got aid from a different source with similar goals." He paused to let his words register. "We are surviving, my friend. We are surviving and we are trying to right what the gods have set wrong." He shrugged. "If we can gain more than we risk, that is merely an added incentive."

Three riders came toward them from the foot of the mountains, clearly defined in the light cast from the rising sun. They were the messengers sent to gather intelligence. They rode hard and fast, and circled the two men once as their horses calmed.

Lommen spoke first. He was always the first to speak, and seldom one to have much information. On the bright side, he was stupid and best used as a human shield. "It's them. Brogan McTyre and his associates. Not all of them, but a good number."

The second rider, Ellsworth, added, "They are twenty-three in number. Twice that many are supposed to meet them but haven't arrived yet." He shook his head and spat. "They're recruiting an army. If we're to stop them we should do it soon." Ellsworth was worth the money he was paid. He was also thorough.

The third rider waited for the other two to finish. Unlike them, Harron was a mercenary. He was also a useful double agent, having just spoken to half a dozen of the men with McTyre. Had he been given the chance he would have gladly killed McTyre. Not because he disliked the man, but because his loyalty was strictly to coin. Like Beron, the man was from Kaer-ru. Mostly the people of the islands who came to the mainland were of a mercenary mindset.

Harron sat astride his charger and drew out his sword, a heavy cleaver of a weapon. He rested it across his thighs. "The rest of their riders are coming from Torema. The numbers are a guess. They called all of the riders with them when you bought the slaves. Those men are gathering as many mercenaries as they can." His voice was low, and deep, and carried all the inflection of the wind. He didn't care what was happening. He cared about coin. He was, in short, exactly the sort of mercenary that Beron liked best. Beron had more money than most. He could afford to pay more.

Harron pointed with his chin. "We can head off the newcomers. Or we can attack the group there. Either way, I'd do it soon, if I was in charge."

Beron looked to Levarre. His companion looked back and sighed. "We get McTyre now, we don't have to worry about the rest of them."

"Just what I was thinking. Harron, get your men. Let's finish this. Levarre, gather the rest. We'll discuss tactics on the way."

The one thing he knew was already taken care of was the horses. Their hooves had been covered in cloth. It would fall apart sooner or later but for the moment the coarse fabric muffled the sounds of the approach.

Within five minutes everyone was ready. Those who had not gathered their supplies already would go hungry later, or would buy supplies. He was not paying his people to be lazy. He knew a few of the mercenaries were caught off guard, but only those who had not worked with the slavers before.

Beron and his closest companions, including the leaders of the mercenaries, rode together.

"They're up in the mountains?" Beron asked.

Harron nodded. "There are easy enough paths to follow, but they have an advantage right now. They have the height and a good number of archers. If we attack quickly we might get them unawares, but I won't hold out a hope of it."

"And this is the best time to attack?" Levarre didn't sound convinced.

"They are still waking. The sun is up over here. It is in their eyes if they look this way."

Levarre was not a fool. He was also not a coward. He was simply nervous. Angering gods could do that to a faithful man. But he would follow Beron's lead. Beron did not tolerate people who would not obey. They tended to die, and badly.

True to that point, the heavyset man nodded his head and then checked his weapons. He bore a long dagger and a short sword with markings identical to the ones on the hilt of Beron's weapon; gifts of their new god, Ariah. Beron didn't know if there was anything mystical about the weapons, but he knew they were sharp and that the tip of his spear had cut into a member of the Undying with ease.

There were stories about the Undying. He had met the vile creatures himself. They were the stuff of nightmares. They were the Undying. And yet they had captured three of the vile things and delivered them to their new god, along with many, many slaves.

He closed his eyes and for a moment remembered the madness that was Ariah's form. A god? Perhaps. Whatever the thing was, they had made a bargain.

Would Ariah be able to kill the Undying? He had

no idea, but at least the damned things were no longer going to chase him and his followers. The rest might, but not those three.

"Stop your dreaming, Beron." Levarre's voice cut through his thoughts. "It is time."

And so it was.

CHAPTER TWO
TRAVELING TO NEW PLACES

Interlude: B'Rath

B'Rath watched the sun strike the crystal shards along the Broken Blades and cast prisms of light down across the land. The sky where he traveled was cloud covered, but the rains did not bother him. He was on a mission of the gods and that seemed to offer some small protection.

When he took his family from Saramond he had one plan in mind – to get away from the city before the gods and their servants destroyed everything. Somewhere along the way the He-Kisshi – terrifying things – had taken notice of their small caravan and tried to steal the wagons and supplies for the pale women they'd freed from the slavers.

B'Rath was a shrewd bargainer. He convinced them to let him keep what he had in exchange for taking care of the sick and wounded among the pale women.

In exchange, the servants of the gods seemed capable of keeping away the worst of the weather. The area was still flooding. The waters were low enough that the wagons were not affected, but the people walking were in a current that covered them to their ankles.

The only good news about that was that the pale women seemed to thrive in the rain and water.

They were an odd lot. They were called the Grakhul, and they seemed to suffer many tragedies as they roamed. First, from what the women had told him, they were captured and sold as slaves. Before even that, the savages that took them killed all of their men.

He looked into the back of the wagon he was driving. Four of the women were there, all of different ages. Though it was hard to tell them apart for all of that, he could see that two of the women were older, but their faces betrayed little to show it, and their bodies were lean and hard from being forced to walk for several weeks as near as he could figure.

All looked younger than his thirty-four years. A few wrinkles on otherwise smooth faces. Bodies that were not quite as vibrant as they had likely been in their youth.

One of them, a younger woman named Eliam, looked his way. "All is well, B'Rath?"

Her voice was soft and sweet and carried an accent he could not place. He knew most of the accents from the Five Kingdoms. Before he ran away he'd managed the largest stables in Saramond. That meant dealing with travelers from every land. Still, these women were unknown; their language was as alien to him as their He-Kisshi protectors.

"I am trying to understand where I am supposed to take you, Eliam."

She nodded, and lowered her head. He thought the

gesture was both an apology and a gesture of thanks. Whenever they spoke of where he had to take them, the women made the same response. Eliam, one of the few he could actually speak with, had said before that they understood his sacrifice in going with them instead of with his own family; there had come that point, however, where the choice was to abandon the women or accompany them. Rather than risk the ire of the He-Kisshi, both against him and against his entire family, he had chosen to continue on, tending to the sick and injured as they traveled.

They gods were already angry. Why make the situation worse?

"There is a place where the mountains are cut. Where the waters reach from one side to the other. We must go there."

"Harlea's Pass. I know it." He nodded. He had never been there, but the name came because the smaller of the two moons, Harlea, lit the entire passage every night as she rose. At least that was the story. He had never seen it happen, but had heard from many travelers about it.

B'Rath squinted at the mountains and the light shining down. "You see how the waters are moving here? I think that means we're getting close to the pass. Do you think we should continue on? Or should we stop and eat?"

Eliam smiled. "If you are hungry we should eat."

"Not me. We have many mouths to feed and most of your people are walking."

"They will leave us soon, those that can. They will move on to the pass and swim the rivers to get to where we need to be."

"Swim the rivers? Won't they drown?"

"We are not like you, B'Rath. We swim as well as the fish."

He had no idea what she was speaking of, but he had to admit that most of them seemed strong enough to risk the currents if they had to.

"I prefer a good wagon, myself."

"I love the waters." Eliam sighed as she spoke, a sound that made him think of young lovers separated by fate.

"Will you not swim with the rest of your people?"

"I am to remain with you as long as you tend to our wounded. I am to speak for you so that the rest can understand."

"You are stuck translating my words." He nodded. "I'm sorry you can't swim, but I rather like the company." That was the truth of the matter; he missed his family and he suspected that his idiot brother, Uto, had already buried their mother. She was not well when they parted, and though she put on a brave face, he knew the wasting illness was killing her. His children, his wife, they were with Uto and probably safer. He prayed they were safer.

This, what he did? He did because the gods asked. He was faithful, even when the gods terrified him, and just now they were scaring him constantly. The pale women did not scare him. They were at least human. The He-Kisshi were the servants of the gods but they were terrifying. He had seen Saramond, his home, destroyed by savage storms, torn asunder by wind and rain and endless volleys of lightning. Though he had not encountered them, yet, he knew that there were armies of people out in the storm-soaked areas looking to find the people responsible for what was happening. He also knew too many who would hang a man first, and consider his innocence or guilt later.

So, yes, he liked the company. He liked any companions at all that seemed calm, and good, and human.

The rains came harder. Not stinging and cold as they had been, but constant. At least there was no hail. His father had always told him that a blessing was easy enough to find if one only looked. The rain was not a flood. The water that fell was not frozen. The women with him were grateful for his aid and not hungry for his blood. There were enough of them that they were safe, at least. Only a truly mad person would look at a gathering the size of the one with him and consider attacking.

From all sides the noises came, high-pitched keening sounds that rose into the skies and very nearly seemed to summon more rain.

"It is time for them to go." Eliam's voice was a soft, lonely whisper.

She moved from the canopy where the wounded rested, and slid closer to him, looking out at the rain and the white shapes of her fellow Grakhul.

"They sing," she said. "They call to the gods and ask for speed and favor."

The closest of the women to him nearly doubled over, looking toward the water at her feet as it rushed past. Her fair hair fell, covering her face, but he could see the changes elsewhere on her body. The skin on her arms seemed to wrinkle for a moment, and then it coalesced into a fine sheen of scales. Her arms and legs grew longer, her fingers and toes elongated. A moment later she looked up toward the skies again and her mouth opened wide, calling out in a screech that seemed impossibly high and loud. Her eyes were wrong, wide and bulbous, larger than they should have been. Her teeth and jaw line were different as well, warped out of proportion. Her nose seemed almost the same, but because of the spreading of her lower face, the shape was wrong.

The song that the rest of her people sang grew that much louder as she joined them. Not in perfect formation, but nearly as one, the Grakhul who were uninjured turned away from the wagons and supplies and ran toward the right side of the small supply train.

B'Rath could see no difference in the terrain. It was too wet. But the Grakhul were not as limited. They dove and splashed into the river that moved to that side of the wagon, were caught in the hard current, and disappeared without surfacing.

He knew he should have been horrified. He had seen women become something else, something that looked dangerous and very nearly predatory. Instead B'Rath was awestruck.

It is not every day that one sees a miracle from the gods.

"Your people..."

"Yes, B'Rath?"

"Your people are truly blessed by the gods?"

Eliam looked at him for a long moment, her eyes studying the lines of his face, the features that made up the sum of his parts.

"We are chosen. I do not know that the words mean the same thing."

His heart beat harder in his chest than it should have, as if he'd run a great distance. "I have never seen such a thing."

"That is just a part of our world. We can live in the waters. We can dwell on the land."

"I grew up near the sea. I was born in Adimone. A sea town. I have always loved the waters."

"And yet you lived far away from it?"

"My chances for a good living were not near the sea. My family moved, and I went with them."

She nodded her head. "That is much like life for the gods. It is not what I want, but it what is best for my family."

"What do you want for a life?"

"What I am doing right now. I want to see everything. I want to see the mountains, and the lakes, and the places that my eyes have never even noticed, that my ears have never heard about."

B'Rath smiled and nodded. He understood wanderlust. When he was younger he always wanted what was beyond the sight of his eyes.

"Then we shall see all that we can while we get you and yours to the Mirrored Lake you have spoken of."

"You are a good man, B'Rath."

There were things he had done in his past, places he had been, and occurrences where he survived by wits and a dagger. Those things stopped him from being a good man. "No," he spoke in a whisper. "Faithful. I am faithful."

They rode on in silence for almost three hours, and the currents of the water proved him right. Harlea's Pass became clear to them. The vast arch of crystal-coated stone was impossible to miss as the waters pushed and rushed through the opening. There was nowhere else for the waters to go, save through the cavernous hole in the mountains.

B'Rath stared at the waters warily and slowed the wagon.

"Why do we stop, B'Rath?" There was a note of despair in Eliam's voice.

"The horses cannot make this passage, Eliam. They will drown. I cannot take the wagon through here without it capsizing. The supplies will be lost. More importantly, the others in the wagon would be thrown into the waters and if they are too sick to travel as the others have, they will suffer along with the horses and with me."

Eliam looked at him, her dark eyes wide and her mouth barely holding back a quiver that was both fetching and heartbreaking.

"You look like you are ready to cry, Eliam. What troubles you?"

The blade in her right hand drove deep into his turned chest and found his heart. B'Rath might have screamed if he'd been capable, but the pain was too large. Heat spilled across his ribs, and then his belly, in the cold weather, and he stared into Eliam's eyes without comprehension.

"I am sad, B'Rath, because the gods say you have served your purpose and should be freed of your pain. Your world is ending, and they would not want you to suffer."

The words made sense, he supposed, but he would have argued them if he could.

Instead he simply stared into her eyes until he saw nothing.

The will of the gods is often beyond mortal comprehension.

The weakened and elderly among the Grakhul changed, though it seemed the transformation was painful. They slipped free of the wagon and followed the powerful currents.

Within minutes of the pale women departing, the wagon and the horses and the corpse of B'Rath were swept sideways and then hauled along by the deceptively powerful current.

Niall Leraby

He awoke to laughter. Which, considering how much every part of his body ached, Niall found rather annoying.

It took a few seconds to work up the nerve to open his eyes, but he was rewarded with a glare of sunlight that was enough to blind him for a moment.

Stanna leaned in to squint at him and was kind enough to block the sun in the process. "He's awake."

Niall tried to think of useful words to say and failed miserably. He tried to make a noise and managed only a low groan. A moment later Temmi was looking at him and shaking her head. He couldn't tell if she was disappointed or merely disagreeing about his state of being.

She cleared up the confusion by speaking. "You look

a mess, Niall. I'm glad you're alive."

He peeled his lips away from too dry teeth and gums. "Water?" It was more a squeak than a spoken word, but Temmi nodded her head just the same and handed him a full skin. "Don't drink too fast." He heeded her warning. Still, the water was sweet as it passed his lips, and felt good enough to make him groan in pleasure.

"What happened?" His voice now sounded too coarse, too deep, but still he could speak and that was a nice thing after the first attempt.

"In general, we were attacked." Stanna stated the obvious without hesitation. "In specific, you got run down by scavengers."

"Scavengers?"

She nodded. "Aye. They don't show up too often, but now and then they come around. They're mercenaries who couldn't find work. Lot of open territory out here and they'll do their best to catch people off guard. They caught us easy enough. I thought there were too many of us for them to try anything."

Temmi sniggered. "There you go, thinking again. Like you've any skill for it."

Stanna affectionately cuffed the younger woman on the side of her head and sent her staggering. Temmi was thinner than when they first met, her face all hard angles now, but at least she could smile. That was a lovely thing. The death of her family had left her sullen and, if Niall was being honest, a little scary to be around. Now she was more herself again, though very obviously changed by the experiences she'd endured.

Stanna looked his way. "The scavengers are looking for weak prey. They are not very wise. Slavers are not weak."

"Stanna, even if slavers were weak, only a fool would try to fight you," Niall pointed out.

She actually smiled. "You are wiser than you look." He had only to study her arms to know she'd crush him in a fight. Having watched her sever the head of a He Kisshi, he had little reason to doubt her combat skills.

"Don't tell him that. He'll get ideas." Tully spoke, her expression sour. "The scavengers tried to take you. Instead Stanna handled the matter." She shrugged. "Well, her and about ten of her men."

Stanna shrugged. "From now on we travel with warnings."

"What sort of warnings?"

Tully spoke before the other woman could. "The scavengers' heads have been mounted to posts. They'll be traveling along with us as a reminder to anyone who forgets what capable warriors look like."

Niall took the time to sit up and look around. Several heads had already been impaled and stood at attention, tied to the wagons around them.

"All the gods."

Temmi shook her head and spit. "Don't call on them. You don't want to get their attention."

"Or that of the He-Kisshi." Lexx's voice was a harsh bark, but he smiled as he spoke. "Best not to offend the Undying."

Tully shrugged, but her eyes went to the other slaver and she forced her face to stay neutral. Niall knew her well enough to know that she did not like or trust the man.

Stanna shrugged. "If they come, we'll kill them. I am tired of running."

"We're not running. We're headed for Giddenland." Niall ran his fingers over his face and felt sore spots. Touching his nose made him wince and his eyes water.

"You broke that right and proper," Stanna smiled. "Fixed it while you were out. Try not to touch it too much or you'll ruin that pretty face."

Tully snorted. "I think it adds something. He was too pretty before."

Stanna nodded. "Makes him look older."

Temmi looked around and squinted at the feel of air brushing along her face. "We should move on soon. The rains are coming and I've had enough rain to last me a lifetime."

Stanna smiled at the other woman. "Aye. Now that this one is done napping and we've taken care of the warnings."

She leaned back and stretched her body and Niall watched, unsettled by how tall she was and delighted by the play of her form under her clothes. He made certain to look away quickly, lest he offend.

"Can you ride, Niall? Or do you prefer a wagon?"

"I'll ride." He thought his body would prefer the wagon. He also suspected the slavers would take it as a sign of weakness that he could ill afford to show them after being knocked senseless by his own stick.

Stanna leaned down and grabbed his walking staff. "Yours, I think."

"Yes. Thanks." Stanna nodded as she moved toward her horse. Tully watched him as he looked after the slaver. Temmi watched the slaver too.

Lexx moved past them both, his eyes looking to no one.

He was an odd one. Niall didn't much like him. He suspected the feeling was mutual.

Brogan McTyre

"Here they come." Harper spoke softly, his eyes watching the dark side of the mountains. "Hold. Hold... Loose your arrows."

He'd deny it, but Harper was good at taking command. There was no one Brogan trusted more along those lines except, possibly, himself.

The men rose and aimed and shot, dropping down a moment later. Behind them ten more men stood, and aimed, and let loose.

There were not enough of them to make a proper assault. There were barely enough for a proper defense, but they could manage this, at least, while the fools below tried to reach them.

Arrows sailed down the mountainside. Some hit stone and skittered in different directions, but others hit flesh. Slavers, and they were slavers, wailed and fell back, or made no noise at all as their lives ended.

Brogan watched on, his axe beside him, his bow at the ready. The snow had started ten minutes earlier, a thick, wet barrage of icy flakes, and he guessed it would be coming for a while. That worked to the benefit of him and his kinsmen but the slavers had vast numbers and he wanted them to give up before it got worse.

He also wanted his family back. The odds were roughly the same, so he stood, took aim, and let loose an arrow that sailed true and buried itself deep in the heart of an enemy.

It was his turn to squat again, and to find another arrow. He only had seven of the damned things. He almost never needed them. Mostly when he fought it was up close and personal.

In the time it took him to notch an arrow, draw and let loose, Harper had struck four men dead. There were none of them he could see that kept up with his friend. Had there been time he would have simply watched and tried to understand how the man could move that quickly. Instead he shot, missed and crouched.

Below them the slavers came on, most of them wearing hard leather instead of metal armor, and all of them looking as scared as he felt. Slavers did not normally look afraid. They traded in fear as easily as they traded in bodies, but anyone in their position would have been just as worried. They could not take the time to use arrows of their own as they scrambled to find a way up the mountainside with weapons and shields that only worked in close quarters.

Brogan let loose and saw the arrow hammer into the side of a man's head. The thing punched through his ear and stuck in the wound. The poor bastard was alive. He reached, slipped on the icy surface under his feet and screamed as he bounced back down the mountain.

Still they came closer. Still they came. The Mentath had been the same way; the bastards used numbers to make up for their weaknesses, if they had any. He couldn't seem to recall any of them lacking the skills needed to kill.

In those days Brogan had been ordered to serve his king. Now the same man wanted him captured and executed.

Aim, breathe, release. The arrow caught one of the men in his armpit. He screamed a great deal. Brogan was still reaching for another arrow when Harper's next round took the man in his throat and stopped the infernal noise.

"Fuck! They've got dogs!" Bump's voice cracked as he yelled. He shook his head, spat and threw down his bow in a fit.

Sure enough, the sound of dogs scrabbling through the darkness became clear as the animals came closer. The damned things growled and panted and whined and made their way higher.

Harper took two of them out in short order. One was a clean kill and the other was wounded and screamed its agonies into the cold air.

The third of the animals made it to the top and charged Sallos Redcliff without hesitation. Sallos dropped his bow and put up his left arm as the hound tried for his throat. The arm shook and Sallos screamed as the beast's teeth sank deep into his flesh and started chewing. The whole of the dog shook and shuddered as it tried to pull Sallos to the ground. "Get offa me you bastard! Get off!" Brogan moved, grabbing the animal by the scruff of its neck and hauling for all he was worth.

Sallos screamed again and used his good arm to cuff the brute on the side of its face, hammering one of the animal's eyes.

It yowlped, and let go its grip, and wriggled, and tried its very best to bite Brogan as he spun with his whole body and threw the damned thing through the air and over the ledge.

"Move, you damn fools! Out of the way!"

Brogan barely managed to dodge as Bump and his horse charged at the edge of the mountain. His heart hammered hard and his eyes flew wide. The man had lost his mind.

Yet instead of going over the crest himself, Bump dropped from the horse and rolled across the rocks, scrabbling desperately with his gloved hands.

The horse, surely panicked, leapt into the air and fell down the other slope of the mountain, with a loud whinny.

There were several screams from below and Brogan dared a glimpse. The horse rolled and flopped and smashed into half a dozen of the slavers who, to their credit, did their best to get over the sudden appearance of a large horse plummeting into their midst.

Harper stepped closer to the edge and took full advantage of the chaos, pulling his bow taut and releasing in a flurry.

From somewhere down below came a bellow to retreat. No one needed to call out twice. Easily half the slavers were already running, tumbling down the steep side of the mountain.

Bump stood up, slapping at the dirt on his thighs, laughing out loud and grinning like a fool.

"You damn near killed me!" Mosely, Brogan's cousin, was not at all amused.

Bump shook his head. "Missed you by half a foot at least."

"And you've as good as killed your horse, you damn fool!"

"Not my horse." Bump looked at him very seriously. "That particular animal belonged to Davers. Half blind and slow of foot. I was doing it a mercy, really."

Davers looked his way, shocked, and Bump started laughing all over again.

Brogan cleared his throat. "It's all well, lads. Not the part about the horse, but we'll make do. Bump will take Davers on his saddle. No one has to walk." They were about to part company, and if he were honest the horse he rode might have made a good replacement, but he felt he'd need the animal even if he wasn't likely to ride it to his final destination.

Harper sighed and looked down the side of the mountain, where the slavers were still descending, despite barked orders from at least one person down below.

"That was a lot of arrows."

"You could always climb down there to get them."

"No, my friend, I think I'll have to survive without. I don't feel like being captured and tortured today." He smiled and looked at Brogan with a quick sideways glance. "Or any day, actually."

Mosely was still glowering at Bump. The shorter man, surely half the weight of Brogan's cousin, seemed little impressed by the stormy expression.

"Watch over them, Harper."

"Best I can." His face was unreadable as he looked at Brogan. "Try not to be gone too long, eh? They're in this for you, not for me."

"Not any more. They're in this to stay alive now, because of me."

"Don't be an ass. They could hide a lot easier without chasing across half the kingdoms to find you. They could lie about being there and most would have no reason to doubt them. It's me and you, we're the ones everyone saw and everyone knows. And maybe Mosely and Laram, but only because they came home with us, didn't they?"

Brogan looked at his bow and picked it up. The axe and the sword found their ways back to where they belonged on his person.

"Look out for them just the same, Harper. And for yourself." He shook his head. "I'll do all I can to be swift about this nonsense."

"Not nonsense. Be swift, yes, but don't doubt. This is the only chance we have, brother."

Brogan nodded and looked north toward the home he had left behind. The others had to go south, had to move away from the armies of Mentath and Stennis Brae alike. He had to go in the opposite direction.

"We meet again in Torema?"

Brogan nodded. "As soon as I can get there."

"And if Torema is unsafe?"

Brogan shrugged. "Head for Kaer-ru. We'll need a ship before it's all over with in any event."

"I hate ships. I hate the ocean."

"Too big. I understand." Brogan nodded. "Go anyway. We'll still need a ship."

"Aye." Harper would not look at him. It was a simple fact. The man did not like to part company. One thing to spend a few days alone in a house when the snow fell too hard to let a person travel. Another to be parted for a long while. They were grown men. They had different parents. They were brothers just the same, and Harper hated being away from all that was left of his family.

"Watch over them, Harper." He was repeating himself

but some things needed to be said twice.

"Have a care, Brogan. Look twice before you take a step."

Brogan nodded and moved to his horse. Time to go.

He was looking for power and there were only a few places in the world where he might truly find it, according to the Galean witch.

He intended to find those places.

He rode down the side of the mountain with ease. There was little to it, really, for a man with a well-trained warhorse. Brogan's had been trained very well indeed. He saw to it himself. No fear was left in the animal that he had found, at least none for natural things. The animal had shown a few skittish steps when the He-Kisshi attacked, but then so had Brogan.

Still, it was an odd thing to place his person on the Mentath side of the mountains. The Broken Swords were massive; they broke the continent in half, albeit unevenly. They thrust high enough into the air that breathing became a challenge for people from the lowlands. Being from Stennis Brae, that was not a problem. Brogan had lived high enough into the mountains that he never had a difficult time with breathing even the coldest air.

Most of the day was wasted climbing down, and when he was finished the sun was setting and his horse was tired. He took the time to groom and tend to his animal. It was only fair. They worked together, after all.

Many of his associates named their animals. Brogan did not. Give a beast a name and others might learn it and call the animal closer. Also, names held memories and responsibilities that he did not approve of. The animal was just an animal, not a person. They worked well together because he had trained the brute to obey. That did not mean he wanted a sentimental attachment.

Why? Because he'd had horses cut out from under him too many times. He saw what it did to the foolish and unwary, who were not prepared for combat's results.

Worst situations? Brogan had watched his animal die once, and had then eaten the meat of the thing rather than starve to death. Name an animal and that was a harder choice to make.

The sun set and while the air was cold it was much warmer than in the mountains. He settled for the night and wrapped himself in his cloak, resting as best he could against an outcropping of dark brown stone. The axe stayed near his hand. The sword he sheathed.

With sleep came dreams. No voice challenged him this time around.

With dreams came family and moments of peace.

The next day he traveled alone, walking as often as he rode. There was no trail, and much of the time he was forced to lead his horse to avoid calamity on the narrow, stony paths he could find. Moving north through the foothills. By noon he realized that he was being followed. By the time the sun set again, he knew who was following him.

He made his camp and when the fire was large and warm and inviting in the chill air, he moved away from it, circled around and crept up on Anna Harkness's location.

Anna Harkness was one of the most striking women he had ever met. She was, in point of fact, the first woman he actually noticed since Nora's death at the hands of the Grakhul. He was aware of other women, but he did not notice them for their appearance, not until he met Anna. She was traveling with him and the rest.

She was also traveling with her very jealous husband, Desmond. Or she had been. Desmond was nowhere to be seen.

Anna let out a gasp when Brogan walked into the ring of light around her small fire.

"Why are you out here, alone, and following me, Anna? Desmond must be furious."

"Desmond is always furious." She waved the comment away as one might a pesky fly. "Desmond constantly assumes that every man wants me."

Brogan did not answer that comment. He was smarter than that.

"I'm here because you will never remember everything you need to remember in order to achieve your goals."

"What do you mean?"

"I know why you've gone off, Brogan. You have to get beneath the mountains. You have to find the Fallen Gods."

"Aye."

"And what are you supposed to do after you find them?"

"Gather their hearts."

Anna shook her head, and a small smile moved over her heart-shaped face, and sent the rings of dark curls around that face rocking back and forth softly. Brogan looked away, lest she distract him, though it was already too late.

"You are to gather the heart of their power. That is not the same thing. You'd spend hours or days looking for a heart and never find it."

"So why you? Why not Darwa?"

"Because Darwa must prepare for if you are successful."

He leaned back. "If I am successful?"

Anna shook her head. "You could fail, Brogan McTyre."

"Not if I'd like to live. Failure will not happen."

"You see? You and Desmond. The both of you. You act as if thinking it makes it a truth."

Brogan shrugged. "I will believe in failure only after I fail. Until then I believe that I will succeed. If I do not do this, doubt slows my arms, blurs my eyes and makes my knees weak."

Anna listened to every word and smiled softly when he was finished. "Usually, when I yell at Desmond about being too sure, he simply says that he will not fail. You at least have reasoning behind your foolish words."

"If you're going to follow me, we may as well stay by the same fire."

Her eyes narrowed a bit. This close in, near a bright fire in the darkness, he could see the few silvery hairs that mingled with the black. He could see the fine crow's feet around her gray eyes. They did not detract from her beauty in the least.

"To what end?"

"I'll not worry so much about someone finding you in the night if you are near the same fire."

"And what do you think someone would do to me?"

"If they caught you asleep? Anything they desired. If they found you awake and tried to attack? I suspect they would suffer greatly, or die."

She stared at him a moment longer. "Well, I do like sleep."

"On my honor, I'll not try to have my way with you." He stared into her eyes and did not flinch. As striking as she was, she was not Nora, and for now at least the loss he felt outweighed foolish desires to be closer.

Also, Desmond would cut his manhood away. Or die trying.

She stared back, studying him with an intensity he actually found uncomfortable, until, at last, she nodded.

Within ten minutes her fire was extinguished and her supplies were stowed with his. She did not have a horse. Anna had walked down the mountain after him, never bothering to hide. Her horse was with Davers.

"I'm still having trouble believing Desmond agreed to this."

"He didn't have a choice."

"Really?"

"Either he lets me do as I need to do, or he accuses me of cheating. I told him once that if he ever accused me of cheating on him, I would surely cheat on him as soon as I could because I'll not be punished for a crime I have not committed."

"He seldom wins arguments with you, does he?"

"He never wins arguments with me."

Brogan nodded his head. "That explains a great deal."

"Keep that sort of logic to yourself, Brogan McTyre, or I'll wither your penis." He stared at her long and hard and finally she responded, "The only way you'll know if

I'm telling a truth is to test me."

In the long run, it wasn't a test he wanted to attempt.

Beron

The rains caught up with them, which did not put Beron in a good mood. He'd known the respite would be brief, but he was tired of being wet, tired of wringing out his clothes and tired of looking for high ground so he could avoid drowning while he stalked Brogan McTyre and his people. Oh, and he was tired of failing to get anywhere along those lines.

Earlier they'd set up another raid, careful that they approached without horses or dogs. The finest cutthroats among his people were promised a proper reward for each and every one of McTyre's men they captured and for McTyre himself the prize was preposterous.

They found a camp that was empty of any people at all. Just a few tents and a fire that was burning down to little more than ashes. From what they said, no one had been there for hours.

Beron left his sword sheathed. His hand found the handle of his whip, however. He raised the whip over his head and promised a flayed back to the next person who failed him.

Not a single person there was foolish enough to think he was bluffing.

Three trackers were trying to find their enemies. They were very good at their jobs. He reminded himself of that fact as he waited for their return.

In the meantime, it was raining hard and they headed south again, as there was nowhere else to go that did not involve riding up the side of the steep mountains or riding back to Harlea's Pass, and he had no desire to waste the time. The water was cooler than it had been and that was a relief, but he had doubts it would last.

The rain was out of season and the gods were at work, making certain that the land was a misery even before they ended the world.

Time was becoming a serious concern.

Even if he captured all of the bastards, it would take time to get them to Mentath, where a reward would be waiting.

"We've soldiers approaching!" The voice belonged to an old-timer named Roy. The man was not in his prime any longer, but he was loyal and he was an excellent watch.

With no hesitation at all, the older man pulled his short bow and settled a few arrows nearby. He did not draw the bow or notch an arrow, but he could with ease, and Beron knew the man was fast.

The soldiers wore the colors of Stennis Brae. There were roughly fifty of them, enough to be a problem if they decided it was time to cause trouble.

The man in charge was lean and hard, with dark blond hair and a full beard. The men with him looked as grim as he did, and not a one of them was unwounded.

Beron said nothing, but he rode to the front, along with Levarre and four others.

The man watched them and nodded. "Well met."

"I suppose time will tell." Beron kept his gaze leveled at the man like a weapon. Fear and intimidation were tools of the trade. He would offer the man nothing.

"We seek a fugitive from our lands. A man named

Brogan McTyre."

"You are hardly alone." Beron shook his head. "Should we find him we'll take him to Mentath, alive and bound. We've been promised a handsome reward."

"Bounty hunters?"

"Hardly. We are slavers. McTyre and his filthy curs sold us a false bill of goods. We intend to be compensated."

"Whatever Mentath offers, Stennis Brae can match."

Beron shook his head. "Doubtful. They offer us three times the sum we paid. We paid a great deal for the slaves we received."

"We want Brogan McTyre and his people alive. Bring them to us and the offer Mentath made will be honored."

Levarre smiled and spat. "It's a point of pride then? Whoever gets these bastards to offer over for sacrifice? Perhaps we should offer to the highest bidder when the time comes."

Levarre was always too fast with his tongue. Still, it was a lovely notion. Start at three times and see how high the offer would go. The problem was, the Marked Men of Mentath were not the sort who would tolerate a change in agreed-upon tactics. They were reputed to be hard killers, and most of the soldiers in Mentath were already known to find torturing their enemies a lovely hobby.

What could the Marked Men do? Beron had no idea, but he'd heard they were unstoppable in combat and he didn't much like the idea of fighting against people he could not kill.

"You've seen the traitor?"

Beron nodded his head. "We have."

"Where?"

Beron allowed a small smile that did not reach his eyes. "We're slavers. Nothing without a profit. Why would we foolishly offer you a target to hunt when we could make a better profit by keeping our tongues?"

"Because my name is John Leeds and I follow Ulster Dunally."

Shit. Second to the king of Stennis Brae and a legend when it came to combat. The sort of man, according to the tales, who had killed hundreds in his time. Hundreds. That was the problem with most of the people from that area. They thrived on warfare.

"My name is Beron, first of Kaer-ru and then of Saramond. Leader of the First House of Slaves. I remain unimpressed by your lineage."

Leeds stared hard at him and shook his head. "Do not make this personal, Beron. I seek Brogan McTyre. I'll have him one way or another. If I have to crawl over your remains to find him, I will."

"No. You will die trying." Beron shrugged his heavy shoulders. "I have four times the men that you do. And that is being kind." In truth he had ten times, but not all of them were ready for war.

"Stennis Brae is not a pack of slaves for you to shackle."

"I do not care about your country. We sell no slaves there."

One of the riders came closer to Leeds and whispered something too softly for Beron to hear.

Leeds stared at Beron. His expression was harsh. "There is a charge against you, levied by the scryer who was with us. A claim that you have taken the Grakhul people as your slaves."

"That would be the very people that Brogan McTyre sold me. I no longer have them with me, as you can see." His hand moved to the hilt of his sword. The look on the other man's face was enough to let him know he would not talk his way out of the situation. The kingdoms were looking to appease the gods by any means.

"Beron of Saramond. You and your men would be wise to surrender."

"Instead I'll give you one chance to run. Ride back to your king and leave here. We'll let you keep your lives."

"That cannot happen."

Beron nodded and drew his sword. Rather than speak, he let out a piercing whistle and the men with him formed into a rough wall behind him.

"So we fight, Leeds."

The man nodded and called out. The men with him formed into a wedge shape behind him and prepared for battle.

Beron muttered softly, "Ariah, I give these fools to you, in your name. Guide our weapons."

His right hand held the sword. His left gripped the spear the demon had offered him. His knees worked at the sides of his horse and the animal moved forward into a fast trot.

Leeds came for him, swinging his sword in a hard arc. The man was skilled and fast and Beron barely knocked the weapon aside with his own blade. Then he shoved the spear tip toward his enemy and saw the point slide past armor and drive deep into the man's chest.

John Leeds let out a soft gasp and fell from his horse. The spear came free as he dropped.

Behind him another man bellowed out a command and the rest of the men from Stennis Brae charged.

The slavers moved forward as well, and Beron rose in his saddle, screaming Ariah's name as his battle cry.

He could not say that the weapons in his hands were better than any others he had ever held, but they were good weapons and he used them. The second man bared his teeth and came for Beron, holding a pike and aiming for his heart.

Beron twisted as their horses came closer and the tip of the weapon cut into his shoulder instead of his chest. The pain was a deep, fiery flash. The spear in his hand slid a bit with the impact. It hit the man in his stomach and skipped across the armor. They were close enough that the sword did its work just the same, and hacked into the bastard's face. Flesh and bone split and then the soldier was howling in pain.

Levarre rode up on his side and moved past, screaming Ariah's name. The dagger and the sword in his hands seemed to shine with a dark light of their own, but that could have simply been Beron's imagination. Whatever the case, he let out another bellow and charged forward as the men behind him came on.

The enemy did not look comfortable. They shouldn't have. They were vastly outnumbered and Beron used that fact to his full advantage.

Interlude: Ariah

Ariah moved through his endless forest of blooms and plants, touching this blossom or that leaf, caressing the thorns that were too soft to ever hope to cut his flesh.

Somewhere beyond his prison the slavers had made sacrifices in his name and with each person they killed, he felt his power grow. The spirits bound to his name did not dissipate or move on. Instead they were drawn to his location, dragged through the endless darkness between the realms and forced to come to him.

Gods ate their sacrifices. Demons did not, or at least he did not.

His followers slept, content with their actions. He was content, too, but he did not sleep. He never slept. Instead he moved to the He-Kisshi in his possession and the Grakhul women that had been brought to him as sacrifices.

The Undying were currently flayed open and left on the ground, their hides held by thorns as thick as daggers that cut into the leathery surface of their bodies.

He had no idea how the Undying worked until he opened their bodies and pulled out the barely living creatures inside of them. The humanoid shapes within did not survive long away from the living cloaks of the He-Kisshi.

Several of the women stared at him, horrified. He did not hide his true shape from them. They dealt with gods and sacrifices, so they were used to the more visceral parts of his form.

"What are you doing? The gods will be angry." The woman that spoke was older than most of those around her. The human eye could barely tell her apart, but Ariah was not human and he saw things differently.

"They are already angry. And I have been punished for a very long time. What will they do? Imprison me?"

"The Undying are sacred!" She protested even as he

touched the first of the hides and felt it try to pull away from him. Even dormant, the things understood that he was an enemy.

"Not to me." The woman flinched at the tone of his words. One of his many hands reached out and gripped the Grakhul's chin firmly. "Your kind has told countless lies. Did you know that? The people of the Five Kingdoms mostly believe that the He-Kisshi are called Grakhul, because your kind have spread that lie. They spread it because words, especially names, sometimes have power and better to risk all of your kind than even one of the Undying."

He leaned closer to her and she stared into the closest of his multi-faceted eyes. "Nothing to say to that? Very well, I will speak and explain. The gods did not create you. They altered you to suit their needs. That is a complicated trick, to be sure, but even I can do that and I cannot do what most gods can do. I cannot create."

"I don't understand." She spoke with muffled words, as he still had his grip on her chin.

"Be patient, and I will show you.

"The He-Kisshi were created by the gods. They were formed from the nothing, given shape by the gods as surely as if the gods decided to have children. They were born into your world because the gods wanted voices to work for them.

"They are amazing creations. They are truly undying. Burn them away and they will reform. Cut them apart and bury them in a dozen different places and as soon as the parts are back together, they will rise again. You know this. Some of your own sacrificed yourselves that these might have bodies again.

"But while I cannot make life, I can change it." Ariah shifted then, became smaller and paler until he looked like a male of the Grakhul. Not just any male, but this one's life mate. A small blessing or curse depending on perspective. The woman whose chin he held saw him and blinked away angry tears, wounded by his gesture. "You see, this is why I find your kind so fascinating. I give you a face drawn from your best memories and you hate me all the more for it. I wonder if that is a choice, or if the gods reshaped you so that you have to be loyal to them."

She said nothing, but continued to glare.

"Be lucky that I am feeling the time alone. I'll not kill you just yet, but soon enough I might change my mind."

He sighed.

"Or I could change you so that you obey me as you have your gods."

She remained silent.

"Very well. Let me show you something. While mortals could not kill your He-Kisshi, I could if I worked hard enough. I would rather not expend the effort, at least not in that way. There are twelve of these creatures. I have three of them. One fourth of their entire numbers. I will make them my servants. I will offer them back to your world, but first I will change them to suit my needs."

"The gods–"

"Will do nothing!" She flinched as he roared, but her face remained held in his grip. "They have made their prison well, but they have not stripped my power from me. That is beyond them. I am trapped here, but I do not wish to be seen by the gods and so I have stolen away their ability to see here. Even your He-Kisshi cannot let them see into my realm. Here I am the god."

He sighed and let go of her chin.

"I cannot create, but I can change things as I must."

He moved away from where she stood watching. There had been several attempts by her and her sisters to run from him and so, eventually, he simply had his vines wrap tightly around the lower halves of their bodies. She continued to work at the thick plants and they continued to remain unmoved.

"Look upon the children of your gods and watch how I make them my own."

He touched the first of the heavy forms and the He-Kisshi shrieked, a sound that was completely unnatural, a hiss of ice on a hot skillet, a roar of a bear and a howling wind all rolled into one horrid cacophony.

The flesh that he touched blackened. It did not burn, but it changed. The fur that covered the flesh fell out and the hide thickened even more.

"Each beast must have a name. You were Lidin-Throm, child of the gods. Now you are Ahbra-Sede, the first bloom." The flesh-cloak rose and shuddered. Ariah caught the thing in his hands and smiled, moving closer to his captive audience. "Should it be your honor to bear the first of my children?"

She shuddered and shook her head, whispering prayers to the gods.

"They cannot hear you here. They cannot answer you. Only I can offer you mercy." He moved past her and looked at one of the others. She was younger, barely entering the first blossom of adulthood. He smiled and cast the cloak at her.

Ahbra-Sede took her as the He-Kisshi had always taken a host, and the wretch screamed her agonies into the air.

The insect that Ariah grabbed was small and hard-shelled. He held it in his palm and changed it, made it something different than it had ever been before. His smile was wide and chilling to the woman he spoke with. "I cannot leave my poor child defenseless against the He-Kisshi." He moved his hand to the cowled face of the thing he called Ahbra-Sede and blew his newly changed pet into the thing's maw. The woman watched, horrified, as the beast swallowed the offering.

Ahbra-Sede staggered and reeled, shivered and changed. Whatever was happening was painful and the woman once more made a prayer to the gods that could not hear her, begging that the creature be granted mercy.

Ariah smiled indulgently as he touched the second of the He-Kisshi. "I told you, they cannot hear your words and pleas. If you would like mercy, you should pray to me."

She did not listen. So, when he was done altering the third of the He-Kisshi into one of his children, he settled the living nightmare on her shoulders and let it take her. "You were Bogrun-Nissht. Now you are Derhe-Sede, my third bloom." He fed the seeds into the creature's mouth and continued his manipulations of spirit and flesh alike.

"We will have fun, my children, and you will get me from this place. It is a time for gods to fall, and demons to rise."

Without a word the newly reborn children moved toward the hidden doorway between the worlds, an exit denied their creator. He nodded, satisfied with his plans.

Then he looked to the Grakhul left to him and shook his head. "What shall I do with you?"

They did not answer him.

After a time he smiled. "I know just the thing." The changes he made were painful. All of the Grakhul screamed as they were transformed, and Ariah listened, pleased.

Niall Leraby

"That stick of yours is impressive." Stanna looked at Niall as she spoke and with a frighteningly fast move she grabbed his walking staff and held it in her hands. She wasn't really that much taller than him. It was the muscle tone that unsettled. That, and the scars, and, all right, her frightening proficiency with weapons. And if he was being honest, yes, she was bigger and stronger than him.

She held the staff in the flat of her palm and frowned as it wobbled this way and that, staying in place only because she rolled the palm of her hand to make sure it stayed where she put it.

"The balance is bad. Too heavy on the one side and nothing to counter it."

"Well, it is a walking staff."

"Exactly the problem. We have to find a better weapon for you."

She stood up and took his staff with her. "Come with me."

What choice did he have, really? He'd had to find a proper stick in the first place and now she'd gone and taken it. Niall rose, frowning, and followed.

Stanna led the way to one of her wagons. There were several in their little caravan and as far as he could tell they all belonged to the slaver. He supposed being a slaver probably paid better than being a gardener's apprentice.

Stubble was growing on the sides of her head, and as she walked Stanna ran her fingers along the stuff, mumbling to herself.

Not far away, Temmi watched as they passed and called out to Stanna, "You look wrong with that much hair."

"Yes. I am aware. I'll be shaving it away soon." She smiled at the other woman and spun Niall's staff in her hand effortlessly.

She dropped his staff to the ground when she reached the third wagon and started moving a dozen different weapons out of her way. Finally she pulled out a deeply polished staff that was longer than his which had a weighted metal ball on one end and on the other a long blade that looked wickedly sharp.

"Here. Feel the balance." She tossed the weapon toward him, taking care that the pointy end was not aimed in his direction. He caught it and looked at the piece. It weighed almost the same as his staff. A little more, but not much.

"Well balanced, yes?"

He looked her way and nodded. "Yes, actually. Impressively crafted."

"Good! Now defend yourself."

Her foot caught his old staff and she flipped it into the air, catching it with ease. While he was still being impressed by her ability to raise the thing into the air, Stanna swept the heavy end of the staff toward Niall's skull.

He barely got the spear up in time to stop the strike and, as it was, he had to backpedal to keep his balance. Stanna came at him again, moving forward, her eyes locked on him, her expression pure murderous intent, and Niall let out a squawk as he defended himself a second time, the impact of the blow running up his arms.

He got a better grip on the spear and slid into a defensive position. Stanna brought the head of his walking staff down toward his skull, and he blocked her, stepping in close and bringing the weighted ball of the weapon around in a hard arc.

The slaver blocked his move effortlessly, and shoved him backward with her superior mass. He stumbled, almost caught himself and landed on his backside in the dirt.

The spear bounced away from him and Niall tensed, expecting to break his arm deflecting the next blow. Instead, Stanna walked past him and grabbed the spear. She tossed it to him again.

"Excellent! Now stand up and do it again." Niall looked at the woman as he caught the spear and then started standing. She didn't wait long but came at him again with the walking staff. Niall jumped out of the way and got a death grip on his spear.

"What are you doing, woman?" He dodged to the left as she came at him again, and barely missed getting his ribs swatted for his efforts.

"Teaching you how to use a spear. Come at me, Niall. Make me know I am fighting a man."

He shook his head and advanced on her, the pointy end of his new weapon aimed at her face.

Stanna slapped the spear aside with his staff and moved in closer as he recovered. Her hand caught him in the chest and sent him sprawling. She'd knocked the wind clean out of him and he grunted, gasping on the ground as she stood over him.

"Stand up again."

He nodded and got to his hands and knees, still gasping. She waited patiently until he was actually standing and then she attacked, the staff hitting his spear hard enough to sound like a tree falling in the woods. He kept his grip and then grunted as she smashed into him with her shoulder.

Still he stood. This time around he'd braced himself. She brought a flurry of attacks down on him and he defended as best he could, using the spear much as he would his staff, pleased by the balance it offered.

Five minutes passed before she stopped attacking him, and Niall was winded, panting and sweating by the time they were done.

Stanna may as well have been taking a stroll for all the effort it seemed to take her.

"Better. We will practice again tomorrow."

She threw his staff into her wagon.

"We will?"

"Yes. In the meantime you should find a cover for your blade. And oil. It will need regular sharpening, of course."

Niall eyed the woman for a moment and nodded, doing his best to smile. Oil? Where was he supposed to find oil?

He had not spoken aloud, still Stanna said, "Ask Temmi. She has oil and a whetstone, both." She turned on her heel and started walking. Niall watched the way she moved, predatory and sensual all at once, and tried not to stare. "Go saddle up. It's time to ride. We'll be at your city soon enough."

That put a smile on his face. Edinrun was home. He'd never much cared for it when he was there, but after being taken by the Undying, and escaping being a sacrifice to the gods, he was thinking that his family's estate just might be the best place in the world that he had ever seen.

Tully was climbing on her horse at the same time that Niall managed to work his way up onto the animal that Temmi had procured for him. Her exchange of services for coin had worked out very well indeed when it came to translating for Stanna. The animals were not the largest or the fastest, but they were mostly tame and well trained. So far, the thing hadn't bucked even once while he was on it. He'd seen a man thrown before, and never wanted to be in that position.

Tully shook her head and looked at him. "I do not know about our companions."

"What do you mean?" He offered a frown of confusion.

Tully scowled. "They're slavers, for one. Not that they've tried anything foolish, but you never know. And Lexx, for the other, he keeps staring at you and at me when he thinks we're not looking."

That earned a nod. "Thought it was my imagination."

"No. It's very real. I thought it was just his eyes. I don't know what happened to him, or how he was mended, but his eyes are broken when you look at them. They've been broken and fixed, but not fixed right."

Indeed, that was the case. His irises looked like broken plates badly reassembled. Likely there was a Galean healer in the mix somewhere; otherwise the man would have been blind.

He nodded, and Tully continued. "Also, they are heading with us to Edinrun, and that is fine, but they travel without slaves. What are they going to sell?"

"Oh, well, they were going to sell slaves. Turns out the slaves they were going to sell belonged to the Undying, so it was best to let them go."

Tully thought about that for a moment as they both started their horses on the path, a distance behind the slavers, actually. They'd catch up if it looked like they had to, but Niall, at least, was fine staying away from the rotting heads that adorned most of the wagons.

"That makes sense, then," Tully said. "But in any event, I don't like Lexx and I don't trust him."

"Stanna seems all right."

"She's not interested in you."

He felt his face flush. "I never said she was."

"Just as well. She's interested in Temmi."

"Seriously?" He looked ahead and saw the two of them riding side by side, engaged in a conversation.

"Oh, yes. She wants Temmi."

"Does Temmi know?"

"Of course she does. She's much smarter than you are."

"I'm plenty smart."

"Can't see what's right in front of you. If you could you'd have known Stanna isn't interested in men."

"Well, maybe she likes men and women."

"Might be, but she doesn't like you in any event."

He looked at Stanna again and couldn't decide if he was disappointed or pleased. Like as not she'd kill him if she was a rough lover. He'd known a lady back home, Daureen, who had a penchant for biting and hitting during sex. She'd been fun for a while, but one can only get battered so many times...

"What are you going to do with the spear?"

"Apparently I'm supposed to use it as a weapon."

"Don't be an ass. I'm asking a legitimate question."

"Stanna decided I need a better weapon than my stick, so she's teaching me as we travel."

Tully nodded. "I prefer my knives."

"You see, that's the problem. I am horrid with blades. I've cut myself almost every time I've even used my shears for cutting and pruning." He held up his left hand and pointed to a scar on his palm. "You'd think after two years as an apprentice I'd get better, but no, I did this only a few weeks before the Undying showed."

"And you want to use a spear with a blade like that?"

"Not particularly, no. But it seemed safer than arguing with Stanna."

"A solid point, she'd break you over her knee."

"I'm not a twig." He tried not to sound offended and failed.

"It's a matter of scale. Next to me you are large and even fairly well muscled. Next to Stanna you are a twig."

"Fair enough."

"What will you do when we get to your home?"

"I'll make sure that you and a select few are invited to stay at the family estate until you can find out what you want to do. As I will tell my parents that you saved my life, which is true, they will be most grateful and will accept you eagerly."

"Family estate? I thought you were an apprentice gardener."

"I'm apprenticed to Mosara, who is the gardener to the royal palace. It's very prestigious, I assure you."

"Does that sort of thing pay well?"

"If it didn't, I'd be forced to stay in the family business."

"And what is the family business?"

"My father buys things. Beyond that I'm not entirely certain."

Tully shook her head.

"What?"

"If I had a family business. I'd know more about it."

"What does your family do?"

"If I had a family I could tell you. I was taken in by a guild. They taught me a trade."

"What sort of trade?"

Tully took one of her blades and tossed it into the air, catching it without bothering to look closely. "It involves knives."

That was the end of the conversation for a while. Instead of speaking any more, Tully worked on oiling and sharpening her blades. After a while she even showed Niall how to sharpen his new spear, though that was more challenging than he expected while riding on his horse.

Bron McNar

In Stoneheart, the castle that was the heart of Stennis Brae, King Bron McNar played host to the rulers or delegates of all five kingdoms. Three massive hearths burned brightly and offered warmth to the room that was normally chilled, even in the heart of the summer, while numerous torches lit the great hall. The table was set with platters of meat and fruit and breads. Several cheeses sat on a large plate in the center, and Bron found himself nibbling a good deal more than he should have.

It was wrong to say that there were truly five kingdoms in the land. In truth the Kaer-ru were not a kingdom, but several island states. Just the same, they chose someone to speak on their behalf and that person was treated as a king by the king.

The official who spoke for the Kaer-ru was Jahda, a dark-skinned man of the Louron, who dressed in the loose-fitting clothes of his people and whose hair was always a sight to Bron, as it was incredibly long, and fell in thick braids down his back. The braids were not even and most were adorned with rings of stone or metal. The entire affair was then tied back to make sure it didn't interfere with his ability to move his head freely. The gray that was starting to show in that wild mess balanced out the occasional gold thread spun through this braid or that. Jahda, as always, had a soft smile on his face that mirrored the kindness in the man's soul. He was a good ruler, and wise. His people loved him. As far as Bron was concerned, the man was a wonderful example of how to lead.

Next to him at the table was Parrish, the king of Mentath, who had been a guest of Bron's for several days. Considering their bloody history, Bron found it interesting that he and the man were getting along so well. Perhaps it was the pending end of the world that brought them together. Parrish, along with several of his elite guards, were all Marked Men. They were considered the very finest fighters in Mentath. There were also rumors that through sorcery or other dark means, they had developed secret skills. He had no idea of the truth to that, but Parrish himself moved differently than he had once upon a time. He carried himself with greater confidence and certainly seemed convinced of his own invulnerability.

Bron had no notion if the rumors were true. All he knew was that Parrish and his favored were indeed marked. They sported strange symbols tattooed into their flesh and some of those glyphs seemed to shimmer and move when one caught them from the corner of the eye.

He watched as Parrish took a cut of meat from a roasted boar and settled back, his eyes moving slowly over the group.

The man next to Parrish was a well-seasoned fighter. He carried himself like one at least and he was wearing a sword that was not for show. It was hard and dark and the hilt was well worn from use.

The man himself had short, dark hair and a receding hairline. His face was clean shaven and his eyes were a very light brown. He did not smile. He had no reason to smile. Pardume had been crowned king of Arthorne only two days earlier. As most of Arthorne was currently being assaulted by the worst storms anyone had ever seen, he was effectively king of nothing. The gods had destroyed Saramond, the capital city of Arthorne, along with King Frankel, who had been a pawn to the slavers and his own vices. Even if the gods had not torn Saramond apart, had not sent endless storms to flood the plains, Pardume's kingdom would have been in a sad state of affairs.

No. He was not a happy man, but he seemed very determined.

Hillar was next. Not a queen but as powerful as any of the leaders, she too was treated as an equal. She was a force to be reckoned with. Torema was not a country, true enough, but if one counted all the port towns under Hillar's sway it had more people than most of the kingdoms. Torema was very nearly the heartbeat of all things in the Five Kingdoms. Every person that wanted to get anywhere else in the land eventually had to pass through Hillar's territory, or use her harbors to sell their wares, unless they wanted to risk all the dangers of landbound caravans.

Hillar's barons ran most of the seaports along the eastern stretch. Money was in constant flow through her territories – technically the property of Saramond and Giddenland but long since held in her sway – and if people were not happy, Hillar did not seem to care. Money bought answers. Those without money worked to earn it. Torema was nearly lawless, but Hillar made that lawlessness work to her advantage.

Hillar was not a woman to anger. She was handsome, not pretty. Her face was made up of hard lines and her hair was kept short and functional. She sported little by way of armor, but she traveled with an entourage that was both loyal and lethal.

Lastly there was Opar, the king of Giddenland. He was the very height of sophistication. He was intelligent and carried himself with poise. He sported a sword but wore no armor. Opar was handsome. He was lean and hard, yes, but it was rare that a woman looking at him wasn't enchanted by his wit, his charm, and his striking features. Sandy blond hair, green eyes, and a devilish smile. Of course Bron hated the bastard. He was too perfect.

Opar had won his place among the five kings by right of birth, and with a little help from his sword. Duels were an acceptable form of meting out justice in Giddenland, though few took advantage of that fact. Mostly it was the very wealthy who fought duels and remarkably few of them enjoyed the risk. Opar was very good with a sword. He'd been trained from the time he could walk.

Giddenland was the finest gem in the Five Kingdoms. The weather there was nearly perfect the year round; the people were educated and wanted for little. They'd built their world on slaves, of course, but that was their decision. There were still a few slave owners in Stennis Brae, but only a few. Most people agreed with Bron: slaves seldom made good workers. They'd work, yes, but there was nothing in it for them beyond food and a roof. They also paid no taxes.

"We are all here." Opar spoke calmly and smiled. "I appreciate the hospitality, of course, Bron, but shouldn't we discuss what must be discussed?"

Bron nodded and leaned forward in his seat. "The world is ending. The gods are angry."

"My latest reports from my homeland say that Edinrun has been driven to madness," Opar said. "The people I call my family and friends are currently killing themselves and each other, burning down buildings and quite literally painting walls and trees with blood." He looked at each of them. "I am awaiting confirmation from a source other than the scryer."

Bron continued, "I have a scryer that can confirm for you, I expect." He sighed. "We either find Brogan McTyre and his followers, and bring them alive to the Grakhul, or we all suffer the consequences of his actions."

Hillar leaned forward. "One of yours, yes, Bron? And you had him at one time. You let him go. That is what my scryers say."

Parrish actually answered before Bron could, and to his surprise, he defended the king of Stennis Brae. "Bron discussed that with me. The Undying took the man's entire family. All of them. Every last one. They were sacrificed before McTyre could get to them. I can understand everyone's outrage at the situation, but I'd have likely let the man go myself."

Hillar leaned back in her seat and placed her hands on the heavy oak table. "I would hardly say you are the best judge of anyone's actions. As I understand it you've broken from the gods and follow something different these days."

Parrish smiled. It was a thin curve of his lips and it never reached his eyes. "I follow the laws of the gods. That has never changed. I merely found other possible answers to my prayers, as the gods refused to answer them."

Jahda shook his head, sending a chorus of faint tinkling noises into motion as his hair moved. "There is no need for accusations of any sort. No one in this room has angered the gods. No one here is a price demanded by the gods. We should focus on Brogan McTyre and his people. That is enough for now." His words would have been harsh, but for the faint smile on his face and the kind tone. Not for the first time, Bron thought of his grandfather when he heard the leader of the Kaer-ru speak.

Pardume shook his head. "They need to be captured. Everyone here has heard of what is happening to my kingdom. Most of you have traveled at least part of your journey through the plains. The gods have ripped away a quarter of my lands. They are gone, destroyed by wind and storm and worse."

Parrish looked to the newly crowned king. "There is a great deal of my land that is useless to my people. Should your people need refuge, we can make arrangements." They all knew the land he spoke about. The area to the south was low hills and large grassy plains. The area could be inhospitable, but surely had to be better than the flood plain that was left of Arthorne.

Even as Pardume was nodding his thanks and preparing a proper response – the man was cautious, which was wise of him – the heavy curtains shook and the wind roared into the room. The thick glass of the windows rang out in musical notes as it fell to the ground behind those curtains.

Most of the people in the room, the entourages of the various rulers, tensed and prepared themselves for whatever might come past the dark blue fabric. None of them were quite prepared for the Undying.

The hooded shapes moved in from each of the six large windows, stepping over broken glass and looking directly at the large table where the rulers of the mortal realm feasted.

Bron stared at the closest of them. In response, the hellish thing looked his way, the dark opening in its hood showing a hint of the nightmarish teeth he knew hid in the depths. Hard claws clacked and clicked as they moved over the cold stone floors.

"I am Dowru-Thist. I speak for the gods."

Bron stood and nodded. He didn't quite bow. Kings do not bow, but he nodded and made clear he carried no weapons. "The gods and their servants are always welcome in Stennis Brae."

The He-Kisshi stepped closer, smelling of spices and charnel scents alike. "That is good. The gods are already displeased with you, Bron of Stennis Brae. You allowed their enemy to escape."

Bron clenched his teeth, but kept his tongue for the moment.

Dowru-Thist continued. "Brogan McTyre was held by you and then released. Had you acted properly, all of the strife the world is facing could have been averted."

"Had the gods not chosen to take the man's wife and all of his children Brogan McTyre might not have felt the need to steal them back."

The He-Kisshi stepped closer still, trembling with barely suppressed rage. "You dare to question the gods?"

Bron forced himself not to flinch from the vile thing. This near, its mouth was clearly visible, the rows and rows of sharp teeth, the dark things that moved among those teeth; long, serpentine tongues. The tiny, barely perceptible eyes that surrounded the entire hood-like mouth. How many vile black eyes? He could not say. They were obscenities, that was all that mattered.

"I do not question the gods. I make an observation. I could not punish the man for doing what I would have done myself."

It rose up, very nearly towering over him. "Would you stop us from taking your family, King Bron McNar?" The tone of voice was all he needed. There was a challenge in the words, but there was something more. The He-Kisshi spoke with many tongues and a wise man understood that some of those tongues told lies. Bron did not answer; he knew better.

"Would any of you fight back if the gods took your kin?" the He-Kisshi spat.

It was Jahda who answered. "We have done nothing to offend the gods. We have, all of us, been loyal and faithful."

Dowru-Thist looked in Parrish's direction. "Indeed?" Parrish, like Bron, was wise enough to not answer.

Pardume rose and lowered his head. "I am new to my throne. I know that my uncle was not a strong man. I will do all that I can to serve the gods."

"Your uncle has paid the price for his foolishness. Your kingdom, closest to the home of the gods, will continue to suffer as the gods continue to punish the world. That is unfortunate, but cannot be prevented." It was one of the other He-Kisshi that spoke. Surely the thing had walked, but it seemed to move too smoothly to actually take steps. "Know this, all of you. Should the defilers be brought to us and made to pay for their sins, all will be forgiven. All that has been ruined can be restored. If, however, you fail, the consequences are already known. Your world will end."

Hillar was the one who asked what all of them wanted to know. "You He-Kisshi, you are the ones who choose the sacrifices, yes?"

Dowru-Thist turned to examine her. It did not speak, but the hooded head of the nightmare nodded.

"Why did you choose to take his entire family? Why would you provoke a man so, when the plan has always been to take only one from any kingdom at a time in order to prevent this sort of anger?"

"We collect the sacrifices, but the choice is in the hands of the gods."

"The gods chose this?" She looked ready to debate with the Undying. Bron wondered if she would survive the discussion.

"You, Hillar Darkraven of Torema, you would question the gods?"

"I would understand why this is happening, that we might never have the situation repeated."

The Undying nodded again. "Consider this. Perhaps the gods were answering a prayer. Ask yourself who would benefit from taking a man's family away from him."

Hillar nodded and crossed her arms. Her brow knitted as she considered the words.

Dowru-Thist spoke again. "I come with glad tidings." There was a tone of sarcasm in the words, something that few would expect from the Undying. "The gods have offered extra time to you all. One kingdom has already fallen. Another now suffers from the First

Tribulation. But your kingdoms can be spared suffering for one month, if you merely sacrifice one of your children, each."

"Excuse me?" Parrish spoke again.

"One of your royal bloodline, one of your offspring. Offer one of your children, King Parrish, and Mentath is spared the tribulations for one month. Offer one child, King Bron, and your kingdom of Stennis Brae is spared for one month."

Hillar spoke. "We have long had arrangements. The royal families are spared from sacrifice."

"That is in the past, Hillar Darkraven. That was before one king took our Grakhul as slaves, one king let slip the people who had offended the gods, and one king offered himself to a demon in exchange for power." As it spoke, Dowru-Thist moved toward the window it had used to enter the room. The others followed suit.

"I have never violated any of the rules of your gods," Hillar maintained.

"The offer was made to all of the kingdoms together and now it is withdrawn the same way. One king alone would have ended the protection of your lineage. Three, however, is enough to demand sacrifices if you wish to stay the wrath of the gods."

"When would you need your sacrifices?" Jahda spoke as softly as ever, but his smile was gone.

"You have no children, Jahda. Of all the people here, you are the safest as you have no kingdom that you rule. But one of your islands could offer a sacrifice of a firstborn child to spare the Kaer-ru for one month. One week for travel. Two days after that to decide. On the tenth day, with the rising of the sun, one child must be offered to a pyre, still living, or the gods will forget all mercy."

"Mercy?" Bron spat the word. "What mercy?"

"You have been spared all that Saramond endured. We delivered the message to that city and its true rulers. All paid the price for the foolish that did not listen. You have received mercy so far because the gods know kindness in their way." Dowru-Thist shoved aside the heavy cloth curtains and looked back once. "Ten days. Find Brogan McTyre. Deliver him to the Grakhul who are spread across your Five Kingdoms, before the gods forget their kindness and tear your lands apart. Should you need more time, you know the cost that will be extracted."

The winds that roared into the room extinguished torches and nearly quelled the flames in the three hearths. Those same winds lifted the He-Kisshi into the air and cast them into the wintery air outside the castle.

Bron stared after the shape of the Undying. He barely breathed as he considered the options before him.

Parrish said what, perhaps, all of them were thinking. "They go too far. They make foolish demands."

Hillar kicked at the table and rocked it enough to scatter the platters of food across the surface.

The six most powerful people in the lands looked at each other and considered how little power they had in the face of the gods.

They were not amused.

CHAPTER THREE
STORM FRONT

Brogan McTyre

To the east the sky was a black caul, occasionally stroked by lightning and constantly dropping a heavy rain. Scintillating lights from the west shone through the depths of Harlea's Pass, allowing them to see what they could of the bad situation.

The vast wound in the Broken Swords was lined with heavy chunks of crystal. Some of the fragments were falling as the waters roared along the sides of the channel that was currently rushing from east to west, from Arthorne's plains to Mentath.

"Well, this is a problem." Brogan was eyeing the fast-moving waters and considering the best way to handle the situation. Somewhere, on one side of Harlea's Pass or the other, there was supposed to be a way to enter the hidden depths of the mountain. Whether or not that entrance was submerged was as potent a mystery as exactly where it might be hiding.

His horse was having nothing to do with it. Well

trained, yes, but not stupid. The animal snorted and stayed firmly on the southern side of the vast cavern.

Anna Harkness eyed the rushing waters and shook her head. "I'm not sure if there's anything I can do here."

He barely suppressed a desire to laugh. Best not to anger her. There was still the possibility that she could shrivel his manhood, and besides that he'd seen her perform magic before and had no idea what her limitations were.

"I can't even decide which side to try my luck with. I can probably walk the length, despite the river's flow, but it'll be damned hard."

Rather than answer, Anna moved onto a dry section of the crystals and crossed her legs, digging into her bag and searching.

"What are you...?"

She silenced him with a gesture.

He stared and crossed his arms. There was little he could do and he'd been told to hold his tongue, so he waited. While he was silent, however, he looked at the walls and considered where there might be a hidden passage. The fragments of quartz were not translucent. They were flawed and shattered by time. Those closest to the ground had been smoothed by years of water, but even they were murky and worthless in the eyes of any collector or jeweler.

Anna stood up and looked at the long tunnel dubiously. She sucked in a very deep breath and then exhaled in a hard rush, blowing dark power from the palm of her hand. The cloud did not obey the winds, which, like the waters, were flowing to the west. Instead, it defied the breeze and moved in an arrow-fine streak to hit the far side of the arch of crystal, approximately halfway down the passage through the mountain. Where it struck, the crystals blackened.

Brogan stared at the spot, awestruck. His arms fell to his sides and his mouth opened.

Anna tsked. "It's not that impressive. It's a parlor trick, really. The stones have been covered with the dust, but it won't last long. You should cross, and get to that spot before it's gone. I only packed enough to do that the once."

Brogan did not question. "Be careful while I am gone. The horse will help where he can; he's well trained, but he's hardly a defender of women."

"Then what is he?"

"A horse, you fool." The words were said without malice.

Anna, in response, made an obscene gesture that he would have expected from the likes of Bump, not from a woman as lovely as his friend's wife.

Ignoring her, Brogan lifted his axe and his sword in one hand and his bundled cloak and the hide of the He-Kisshi in the other, and started across the frigid waters, gasping as the cold sank into his legs and manhood alike. He gritted his teeth and began to wade carefully across the fast-running waters. The current was strong. He was stronger, but not foolish enough to test that thought for long.

One foot forward, then planted carefully, and then he moved again. The entire time he sensed Anna watching him, worrying her lower lip with her teeth. He did not have to look back to know it was true. He'd already seen the expression on her face a dozen times.

He stepped onto the dry land and turned to face her. By then Anna had crossed her arms over her chest and was frowning at him. "Best get going then. The skies won't get any lighter."

Had she been his Nora, he'd have made a comment to ease her mind. A jest, or a few words to let her know he would be safe. Those words were not meant for Anna. She was wed to his friend. It was Desmond's place to give her comfort.

Instead he spoke a hoarse order. "Stay safe, Anna. Desmond will kill me if you are injured."

"I've your horse. I'll be fine."

The horse snorted and stamped a hoof as if daring him to disagree.

Instead, he nodded once and looked for the flaw in the blackened area. She'd been right. Most of the powder had already been removed by the wind. There was some, however, trapped in the fine line that hid the opening.

It was made by someone's hands, though he could not have said for certain if they were human. Perhaps the pale Grakhul or the hooded He-Kisshi had reasons of their own for putting a door in the side of the cavern. Whoever it was had been gifted indeed.

The opening was hidden well. He could have looked for hours and never seen it. Only Anna's powder had revealed the spot. Even then, it took the blade of his axe being wedged into the fine opening before he could manage to force the spot open. The murky quartz came toward him a small amount and Brogan took advantage, working the blade in deeper until the heavy stone revealed an opening. It was not large. Brogan had to crouch to enter the tunnel that allegedly led to his prize.

Once he was through, the stone door swept back, perhaps pushed by the wind, perhaps weighted to close. In any event, he was sealed into the mountain in seconds.

Around him, the interior of the mountains was revealed.

There was little light from the east, but what was captured from the west was enough. It ran through the gigantic shards of crystal and glowed with enough ambience to let Brogan see. It would not last, of course, but he would take it as long as he could.

When he was a younger man his father had brought home a rock from the Broken Blades. The rock was called a "giant's tear," and Brogan had no idea why until his father struck the stone with a small hammer. One blow and the large stone fell into three pieces. Each section was filled with crystals, some clear and others a deep, blood red.

His father said, "These are rare, but not so rare that they have worth. They are merely pretty to look at." Brogan's mother agreed. She'd placed the three fragments around the edges of the fireplace and they cast brilliant light whenever there was a blaze.

The inside of the mountains was similar, but at insane proportions. Enormous shards of crystal thrust from every surface of the nearly endless cavern that made up the center of the mountain where he stood. The rising crystalline blades were rooted deep in the ground and above as well, and jabbed at the mass at the center of everything. They rose hundreds of feet into the air and came down just as far, penetrating the impossibility that he was staring at. All of the people in his hometown of Kinnett could have joined together on only one facet of the nearest crystal, with room for most of their houses to fit beside them. The mountains were gigantic, as befitted a burial place for giants. They were also hollowed out.

No, more likely they had grown around the figure he stared at.

The scope was impossible, of course. His mind hurt to look at the thing. He could recognize that what he looked at had been alive at one time. It was a skeleton. He stood near what might have been a forearm, or possibly a lower leg. He could not say. What he knew for certain was that there were two bones that were far too large for him to see them completely.

At least it looked like bone. When he dared touch it, his fingers ran over something as hard as the hardest stone he had ever seen. The surface was pitted and curved like old bone. He wished his horse had come with him, because he suspected he would be walking for a long while to find what he was looking for.

Far, far above him, barely visible through the thrusting blades of crystal, Brogan could see the arching curves of what could be ribs, rising into the top of the staggering cavern. When he looked, he saw what could be vertebrae in the distance. He had seen enough corpses in his time. He knew well enough what animals and men alike looked like when the flesh and meat were gone and all that remained was bone and gristle.

Whatever it was he looked at, it had once walked the lands. It had stood easily three to four times the height of the mountains.

That thought terrified Brogan McTyre.

If this was a giant, how vast were the gods? How could he ever hope to slay them?

The witch told him it could be done. He would trust the Galean. What choice did he have? His faith had to go somewhere and it would not go to the gods.

Myridia

Though they swam to get the distance they needed, Myridia and her gathered Grakhul did not sleep in the water. The currents were treacherous and the waterways unknown. They would likely get battered to death on stones if they tried to sleep in the newly formed river.

The seas were better for that. When they'd fled Brogan McTyre and his slavers, they'd traveled for days, far away from the grip of the undertow near the shore and they'd slept while traveling.

This was a different place. They were obligated to rise from the waters and camp on land.

The air was far colder now, and Myridia felt the chill try to bite its way to her core.

"Lyraal? Can you make a fire?"

The other woman nodded as she shivered and called to two of the others to help her find wood. It was not difficult. The area where they rose from the nameless river was covered in low trees and bushes, many of them dead and well dried. The land, she suspected, was cursed. She could not have said where the demons released by the gods had touched the world, but she could guess when she came across an area that was very nearly blighted. Of course, not every area near death was a sign of the gods' punishment. Some were merely not healthy. They lacked water, or the ground would not give the plants enough to eat. Here the ground was green, but it was not grass, it was fine lichen. Not all that different from the slick mosses she'd seen her entire life.

The others returned by the time she'd looked over the area. The land was too flat to allow for ambushes. It also offered little by way of shelter and the women had little by way of clothing.

Myridia thought for only a moment before unwinding the heavy oilcloth around her sword. She looked at the fine scales imprinted on the metal of the blade and ran her fingers gently over the pattern. It was a stolen blade. Taken from a blacksmith who had threatened her. Had he left her alone she'd have let him have his life, but the weapons were necessary, as the women had already learned.

Memni stayed in the water as the others gathered firewood. Someone had to, in order to make certain the waters were clear of threats. Several times she lowered herself completely into the waters and stayed below the surface longer than any human possibly could. Once the fires were set properly she'd be allowed to surface and sit with the others. Until then, it was her turn to stay alert for the Night People. They did not know that the shadow creatures could travel by water. They did not know that they could not. All they knew for certain was that the shadowy forms did not like the light of day, or a good fire.

The fire was for warmth and for more.

Memni's head came out of the waters and the girl smiled. "I hear the song!"

"What song?" Myridia was tired and had no patience for games.

"The song of the gods!" The girl pointed with her webbed hand, the thick talon showing clearly in the moonlight. She pointed the way they had come.

Lyraal looked toward the waters and then walked away from her fire, trusting the others to feed it and tend to it now that she had started the blaze with her flint and steel.

They did not disappoint.

Lyraal dove into the river and stayed under, barely even visible in the reflected light.

She came up a moment later and nodded, smiling. "She speaks the truth. There are more of us coming. Singing. We will soon have company."

Myridia smiled and nodded, silently thanking the gods. She did not know how many of her sisters were coming, but any and all would be welcome. They needed to gather their strength. They needed to prepare for the Night People and they needed to find the Sessanoh, which even now tugged at her insides and called to her soul. The Mirrored Lake had to be prepared. The sacrifices had to be found.

Now, maybe, they would have a decent chance.

The fire grew, casting flickering light in all directions, and Myridia waited within the ring of warmth the blaze offered.

Somewhere out in the darkness Garien and the Night People lurked. They were in the distance, she could sense that, but they would continue to hunt for her and the rest.

The He-Kisshi were gone, sorting out what had

happened to the others. Perhaps they would come with the travelers dropping in, but she could not trust in that notion. One way or another, she needed to speak with the He-Kisshi or with the gods themselves to find a solution to the shadow forms that were coming to take them all down.

In the meantime, however, "Lorae! Stand first watch on the plains. We do not want any surprises from the south or the east."

Lorae nodded and took her weapon with her. The short scythe was wickedly sharp, and the girl had taken the time to sharpen the outer edge as well. It would still thresh long grains, but it would cut flesh easily enough. When they had stolen their weapons each of them found what they could.

The sword in her lap was her weapon of choice. According to some a good weapon needed a name. "Unwynn," she sighed. "I will call you Unwynn." The woman who had sacrificed herself so that Myridia and the others could escape when they had begun their journey. She had been a brave leader and a strong warrior. She would be remembered, and if her name had power, perhaps she would not mind sharing it with a sword used to defend her people.

Her kin moved around her, settling themselves by the fire and gathering more wood for the blaze. They would want the light and the warmth throughout the long night, just in case the Night People showed.

For a moment Myridia remembered Garien's warm smile, his beauty. Then she shoved those thoughts aside. He'd have been a worthy mate, perhaps, but that time was gone. He was taken by shadows and had become one of them. Should she see him again, she would have no choice but to cut him down. When she stood again, Myridia wrapped her oilcloth around her body like a toga and walked down to the water's edge. Lyraal was still in the river along with Memni.

They had heard the song of their people in the waters. That should, if it pleased the gods, mean reinforcements, but until they were seen and identified, whatever came from upstream might have been touched by shadows and it was best to be wary.

It was over one hundred of her people who climbed from the waters when they saw Lyraal and Memni. They carried little with them, though a few had kept their clothes. Two of them dragged a heavy form to the edge of the river and pulled it to shore, panting and grunting despite their strength. Three more joined them and pulled the waterlogged shape into the dry area around the fire. She recognized all of them, of course. Not all by name, but their faces were familiar.

Despite herself, she felt tears sting her eyes. To finally know that others were alive and had escaped...

They were all sisters in purpose, of course, but her actual sister, older by four years, came toward her and they embraced. "Tyria! The gods are kind this night!" She wrapped her sibling in her arms and held her tightly, feeling the damp fall off her older sibling, feeling the cold of her flesh and the way her muscles shivered as they adjusted to being on land again.

"Myridia! You are so good to see! I thought you dead." She did not weep. Her wide, sweet face wanted to cry, but did not. Tears were for men.

"Did you escape them?"

"They sold us to slavers. The slavers grew wise and let us go before the He-Kisshi caught up with them." Tyria spat. "I hope the filthy city where they took us drowns!"

"You are here now. So many of you! I thought we'd never see anyone again." All around them the others came from the water and ran to meet each other. It was not much of a reunion in the grander scheme, certainly not all of the women and children of the Grakhul; still, it did Myridia good.

"We bring the body of Ohdra-Hun with us. He is among them and planning revenge."

Myridia saw the heavy thing and moved to it, eyes wide. Ohdra-Hun was among the harshest of the He-Kisshi, but he was also wise. If he were alive, she could have spoken to him, but for now he was merely an object that did not rot, and one they were tasked with by the gods.

"How is it that he is not here?"

"He took the shape of one of them. He rides with them. I do not know why, I only now that he will return to his body when the time comes." Tyria looked out over the plains. "Do you know how far to the Sessanoh?'

"No. We are getting closer. I can feel the pull. It draws us closer. We have lost so much time. I was foolish and walked with their people for a while, seeking protection in numbers."

"You are all alive. That says all I need to know of how well your plans worked." Tyria paused a moment and looked at her little sister. "Do you lead?"

"Yes. The gods alone know why. I will gladly step aside for you."

"No. You are here, you were chosen by Unwynn for

a reason. We will follow you now."

Oh, the desire to protest.

Instead she asked, "Do you have weapons?"

Her sister shook her head. "There has been no time to seek them. We have traveled fast and far."

"We have seen no cities here. We have no gold, no means of paying. What we have, we took." Myridia pointed to where her sword rested on the ground.

"We need to find weapons somewhere."

"More than you know, I fear. There are armies massing on the other side of the mountains. It is inevitable that they will gather here as well."

"Why do you say?"

"The gods are shattering the world, Myridia. The humans are going mad, trying to find the ones who started this. Their kings demand it and offer rewards. Every one of them that wants to live will fight for the chance to bring us the slaving bastards that ruined the last sacrifice. The gods say it must be them that die next, or the world will still end."

She had heard the same from the gods, but the thought that the humans sought Brogan McTyre and his band had not occurred to her. She had been too foolish, too smitten.

"There must be towns here. Somewhere. In the meantime we stay near the river, where our bodies can become weapons."

Closer than she'd hoped, the sound of horses and wagons came echoing along the river.

Tyria looked back the way she'd come and frowned. "That noise again. I haven't seen them, but I think some of the slavers might have changed their minds."

Myridia nodded at her sister's words but knew better.

The Night People were closer than they should have been. Close enough to be a problem. In the distance she heard voices that sounded like echoes.

From the east she saw the shadows. They moved like people. They walked like people. And horses and wagons. And oh, there were so very many of them. More than all of her sisters combined.

To the south they saw the lights of a city shining.

"There!" Tyria pointed to the distant glow. "There we will find weapons."

Myridia agreed. "Gather what you have, our journey this night is not done. We move for the city!"

They did not hesitate, her kindred; they obeyed. Within ten minutes they were on the move, jogging and fast walking for the distant city lights.

To the east the first of the storm clouds pushed over the Broken Swords and started creeping down the mountainsides.

To the south the city shone a path toward possible salvation. There was no choice at all, really.

CHAPTER FOUR
NOWHERE TO RUN

Harper Ruttket

"They're here!" Mearhan Slattery's voice broke the silence and Harper looked up at the woman. Her red hair was a mess and her face was drawn and all sharp angles. The scryer's words were meant for all, but she looked to Laram as she spoke. She'd betrayed them all, forced to by the gods, but none of them meant any more to her than she did to them. Laram was the exception. He'd planned to ask her hand in marriage before the betrayal. Now? Who could say.

Not that it mattered. There was killing to be done.

Harper rose from where he'd been sitting and raised his bow. He blew a harsh whistle and then used gestures to make his commands. The men with him nodded and obeyed, all reaching for their bows. They still had the advantage of height and they meant to use it.

From below them, the slavers came again. Not as many as before, but more than enough if the problems continued.

Brogan was off on his quest. The rest of the men listened to Harper, but they followed Brogan. It was a distinction that might have been lost on many, but not on Harper. Brogan was a leader. Harper was a strategist. Leaders were rarer things.

Harper looked over the side and down at the men coming his way. They were determined, say that for the bastards.

His first arrow split a man's nose and stuck a few inches in. The slaver screamed and rolled down the steep incline. Whether or not he lived was unimportant. He'd be out of the fight at the least. Bump let out a scream and loosed arrows as quickly as he could draw. Some hit their targets and others missed, but in any event the man caught the attention of their enemy and Harper was fine with that.

His second arrow took a man in the heart. That one was dead for sure before he flopped bonelessly down the slope.

Janned, next to Bump in the line of archers, took an axe to his head. The man who threw it hooted victoriously and Harper killed him for his troubles. Hard to make a noise with an arrow rammed down your gullet to the fletch.

Janned was dead. He had never been a close friend but they had long been allies.

Bump and Janned had been close. He let out a scream and ran from the combat, heading for his surprise for the enemy. Two others helped him haul the large shield of burning embers to the edge and throw it over. The coals weighed less than a horse, but they burned brightly as they rained down on the invaders.

The problem with the slavers was that they lacked commitment. They were being paid, yes, but as a rule they were best at intimidating their enemies.

Mercenaries were paid to fight as well, but they did it with more passion and more savagery. Harper had long since become numb to the number of men he'd killed and tortured over the years. Brogan would likely have been horrified and his body count was close to a hundred.

Three arrows in quick succession. Two kills, one man who would be suffering for a great deal of time as a result of the arrow in his testicles. He might live, but he wouldn't be happy about it.

Bump's coals were the trick, really. When a few of the men got burns they were annoyed. When one of them actually caught ablaze, the rest of them broke away and retreated. The man ran around screaming and swatting at his leg as the flames chewed away his leather and fur boots and made it to his leggings.

Harper considered ending the poor bastard's pain but decided against it. As long as he was screaming, he was keeping his fellow slavers from coming back up the mountain.

"Retreat, lads." He spoke softly. The men nodded and grabbed their belongings, already stowed and waiting. By earlier agreement they headed south along the spine of the mountains. As soon as they were clear of the slavers the plan was to descend and head east.

Sooner or later their reinforcements were supposed to show up. They would gather when they could; until then it was only the handful that were there and not a single soul more.

Brogan might have worried for Mearhan Slattery. Laram surely would, but Harper did not care. She would come of her own volition, because no sane woman would wait around for the mercy of slavers.

There was no mercy from slavers. There was pain and rape and, only if one were particularly lucky, eventual death. Most were not lucky. Slaves were how they made their wage, after all, and these particular bastards were down a king's ransom and looking for reimbursement.

They moved. Sure enough, Mearhan Slattery followed.

Beron

"Damn them all!" Beron roared the words and looked at the men coming down the mountainside. He couldn't afford to kill the bastards as cowards. He needed the warm bodies.

"There are twenty-five men or less up there and you stupid bastards can't reach the top of the mountain to hunt them down?"

One of the men – Durst? Dennis? Denst? He could not remember – shook his head. "They've poured hot coals down on us and they've thrown a fucking horse our way! We lost at least a dozen men to arrows just now. They have the advantage."

Beron sighed. The man was right, but he was also an idiot. Argus was supposed to be coming along this way, having lost his slaves to the Undying. While he was tempted to try killing the man for failing, he was rather certain the bastard would prove hard to kill and far too costly to take down in any event. Better to keep paying him.

Beron pointed with a drawn sword. "Take your fucking men two miles to the north. Climb to the top from there, and then chase the bastards down!" Beron's throat hurt from screaming. But the look on the fool's face was worth it. Beron knew exactly how scary he looked when he was angry; he practiced to make sure he was terrifying. It was how he kept everyone in check. That, and the money he paid.

Having been properly chastised, DurstDennisDenst nodded and then started calling out to his soldiers with a properly terrified expression on his face. He was wise. He obviously realized Beron was perfectly willing to gut him to make his point.

"Your war does not go well?" The voice was in his head. He felt each word in his sword hand and in his skull, a vibration not unlike the buzzing of a hornet. He looked around and as he did so, the world seemed to change.

Gone were the Broken Swords, replaced by a valley filled with an explosion of plants that were, in turn, buried beneath a million types of blooms. In the distance, trees offered thick, fat fruit if one could get past the dagger-length thorns.

"Ariah?"

The demon stood before him again, long and tall and lean and deadly. His human face was in place, for which Beron was grateful. Having seen the impossible shape of the demon once, he had no desire to see it a second time.

"Yes. I am here." He held a blossom that led to a thorny vine which seemed to be growing directly from the demon's arm. "You have done well and offered me sacrifices. I am pleased. Now, I reward you."

"Reward me? I have barely even begun to fight."

"Just the same. You are my priest and you have offered up prayers. Unlike the gods, I answer prayers." The demon's face pulled into a smile that was a lovely lie. "You brought me three of the He-Kisshi. I deliver them to you now, along with an army of faithful servants. They were the Grakhul women. Now they are yours to command in my name."

Just that quickly the images were gone and the mountains were once again in plain sight. Next to him Levarre was screaming. The man looked to the east and called for the slavers to unite and prepare to defend the camp.

Beron turned and looked in the same direction.

It was not a large army, but he suspected it would be enough.

The three forms at the front of the gathered force were once He-Kisshi. He knew that from the conversation with Ariah, but he suspected he'd have known in any case. They walked with the same otherworldly stride, and they were hooded things, their faces lost to shadow, their bodies seemingly covered in hardened black leather. There were three of them and they bore themselves with the same silent arrogance as the Undying.

Behind them came the newly reshaped Grakhul. It was fair to say he would not have recognized the vile things that came his way as the same women he'd meant to sell to the highest bidders. Those women had been pale and exotic and while not every one had been a beauty, they'd have fetched a sweet price on the bidding stands in Torema.

The things before him were still pale. That was nearly all they had in common with the Grakhul. All of them had mouths, but the lips were withered and drawn away from the teeth as surely as a dead man who's been too long in the desert. Their gums were dark gray. Their chins sharply pointed. The rest of their faces were gone, hidden behind masks of iron that looked to be riveted into the skulls where eyes and nose should have been. There were no visible slits to allow the things to see, but they seemed capable of sight just the same. The bodies were as withered in appearance as the faces. The skin looked mummified, and the hands and feet, bare to the elements, had the look of long dead things. As a man who had more than once nailed corpses to the outer walls of his home and spent time watching them dry or rot depending on the season, Beron was far too familiar with the sight.

Beron stared and did his best not to let his fear show. These were not natural things. These were purely the sort of creatures that he never wanted to be around. They moved when they should surely have been dead. They saw without eyes and perhaps even heard from the withered nubs that were their ears. The rich, silky hair that had been on the Grakhul – even when they were unwashed they'd had hair that could be groomed properly – was still there, but not all of it. A great deal had fallen out, or rotted away, or been torn from their heads – it was hard to say for certain. They were not bald, but that seemed more an oversight than something deliberate. The bodies had been tortured as they were changed. The scars showed where flesh and bone had been twisted like slightly softened wax or damp clay.

In the right hand of each of the creatures was a sword. Growing down the left arm of each, much as Beron had seen in the vision of Ariah, there was a thick vine covered in thorns. If he looked, he could see the roots of those vines riding up the arm and into the withered chests of the creatures.

Beron stared, barely breathing, as the things came closer. The three at the head of the columns did not speak, and he was oddly grateful for that fact. He suspected that their voices might be like Ariah's true face: something best never studied carefully.

The first of the cadaverous women came closer and stared up into Beron's eyes. He looked at the shaped metal that hid away half of the creature's face and swallowed his revulsion.

"But tell me what you seek, Lord Beron, and we shall find it for you."

"Brogan McTyre and Harper Ruttket. The men who captured you and sold you to me. I would have them brought before me alive. All of them, to the last."

The thing turned its head and looked to its followers. The scream that came from that horrid mouth was a dry mockery of a human scream, and it sent shivers through him. The creatures were either dead or close enough that they should have been unable to walk, let alone move as quickly as they did.

They had approached in columns, sixty or more to each line, following the cloaked forms. Now they broke formation and ran. They did not all go in the same direction. Perhaps fifty ran for the mountains, crawling like dogs, hands and feet seeking purchase as their swords were sheathed in a nest of vines. Still more turned to the south and east, screeching as they ran.

Around him the slavers and sellswords did their best not to panic. They stepped aside as the creatures scattered, moving in what seemed a random pattern. Only ten ran to the north, heading for the far edge of the mountains perhaps. In less than three minutes the iron-faced things were gone from the area, charging to follow Beron's orders.

The three hooded forms stayed where they were, not even bothering to look in Beron's direction. He looked at them because there was something off about how they moved; he had to take a moment but he finally understood: none of them touched the ground. They were several inches free of the dirt and runoff.

Levarre turned to Beron and asked, "What are they?"

Beron looked back, his face blank of expression because he did not know if he should laugh, cry, or scream. "They are the answer to our prayers."

Niall Leraby

Stanna called a halt to their ride and Niall looked her way, puzzled. They were within sight of the gates to Edinrun. He had been this far away on countless occasions, though normally to the west where the forest was at its heaviest. He could walk from here and be at the gates before the sun set.

He was about to ask why they were stopping when she called him over. He rode closer and Tully followed, a frown on her face.

"Niall, do they usually have the gates closed to your city?"

"No. Of course not." He had not truly looked aside from seeing they were closer. Now he did and he saw that she was right. The gates were closed. When night came and the city was in peril – which had not happened since Niall was a boy – they would sometimes close the massive gates and only allow people through the small doors. The small doors would not permit anything larger than a horse through. A wagon could not enter the city without being examined carefully. There was a reason for that, at least according to his father.

This? The main gates were sealed. The small doors were shut. There were soldiers along the edge of the wall, looking down. They were barely noticeable, but some had banners and that was enough to let him know the soldiers were there.

There were soldiers outside the walls as well. Riding on their horses, driving people away from the gates, near as he could tell.

"Well, we'll see about that." Without another word, Niall started riding again, heading down the main road and moving into a trot and then a run without conscious thought. His meager skills as a rider were barely enough to keep him in the saddle.

He had not meant to lead the riders, but they followed him, Tully and Stanna and the rest. Even Lexx, who seemed inclined to not care at all about what happened to the others.

As they got closer, the riders in front of the gates grew more alert. They were warriors of Giddenland, to be sure, at least if their coat of arms and their armor meant anything.

The doors and gates were barricaded from the outside. Trees had been cut down and cut to fit as braces, ensuring that whatever was inside the gates would not come out. Niall scowled as he came closer, his insides twisting as if grabbed by a vast fist.

Giddenland was a peaceful enough place, but over the years the royal family ensured the kingdom stayed that way by building a proper army, possibly the strongest in the entire land. King Opar made certain of it.

One of the horsemen came forward, his helmet down, his spear at the ready. Behind him, half a dozen more were already lined up and more were moving into formation.

Niall couldn't understand why at first and then he remembered the heads.

"My name is Niall Leraby, my father is Duke Andrew Leraby. Why are the gates blocked?" He tried to sound stern, but it wasn't something he was used to, and the way the soldiers formed up left him little to be confident about. The slavers rode horses, too, but the guards were armored, and they had greater numbers.

Stanna pulled up beside him. She did not speak, but she listened.

The man at the front of the gathered guards said, "The city is under quarantine, Duke Leraby. The people inside have gone mad."

"No. My father is the duke."

The man lifted his visor. His face was bruised, with one eye swollen nearly shut.

"No, my lord. I must inform you that your father has

gone to join the gods on the Final Battlefield. He was killed four nights ago."

Niall did not fall from his horse. He certainly felt as if he might, but he did not. The air was stolen from his chest and his heart seemed to beat too slow and too hard.

"My father, you say?"

The man nodded. "I am sorry for your loss, my lord. It is a grim thing; the city had gone mad. Whatever it is that takes place within the walls of the city, it is contained for now, but any who enter the city are driven mad as well."

Lexx spoke up, his voice as soft as ever. "It is the Second Tribulation."

"The what?" Niall asked.

"The Second Tribulation. The gods are angry and they are punishing the mortal world. Their sacrifices were interrupted. Until this is made right the world is in peril. The Second Tribulation is madness and the words of the gods say that, 'Madness shall hold the strongest minds prisoner within the greatest fortress.'"

Stanna stared at the man as if he had grown a second nose. "What are you saying? You've never been to a church in your entire life, Lexx."

Lexx stared at her for a moment and sighed. "Believe what you will. This is the Second Tribulation. The greatest city in the Five Kingdoms has gone mad."

"King Opar has ordered the gates sealed. That is all that is known at this time, Duke Leraby." The man looked at Lexx and frowned as he spoke. Niall understood the desire. There was something wrong with Lexx on a level that made him uncomfortable to be around.

Lexx, for his part, looked back at Niall and spoke softly, his voice barely above a whisper and heard only by his traveling companion. "You have a title and land. Your title was never enough. You should have stayed on the wagon and spared yourself everything that is coming."

Niall stared at the man without any comprehension. "What are you talking about?"

"You were paid your coin. You left it in the dirt when you tried to escape. You should have stayed on the wagon. You would have been spared all of this."

"Stayed on the wagon? What do you mea..." Comprehension sank in. "Were you there? Did you see everything?"

Niall was outside the gates of his home simply because the Undying had come for him. Thanks to Tully he'd escaped being one of the sacrifices for the gods. The only person who knew that was Tully. He'd shared the knowledge with no one else, not even Temmi.

The only other beings that knew of his situation were the Undying and their gods.

Stanna looked at Niall and frowned. "Did I see what?"

"Not you." He shook his head. "Lexx."

Lexx looked at him and shook his head. Then he lied, "I've no notion of what you speak. You are grieving. You should take a moment."

Niall mirrored the headshake. "How do you know about that? How could you know?"

Lexx urged his horse back a few steps, and Niall moved his horse closer. "You should calm yourself, young duke. Your grief has muddied your thoughts." Lexx's hand touched the hilt of his sword.

Things might have escalated, but the guard they'd been speaking to rode his horse between both of them, looking first at Lexx and then at Niall. "We've had enough bloodshed. Don't draw a weapon. It will not go well for you."

Stanna looked from Niall to Lexx and shook her head. "We leave now."

"What?" Niall turned his head so fast he pulled a muscle and felt heat run through the side of his neck. "We just arrived."

"Yes, and then the guards explained that the city is off limits. There's nothing we can do. There are other towns nearby where we can find an inn until whatever this is washes away."

Niall tried to find words and instead sputtered.

Lexx tilted his head and then shook it. "This will not get better until the right people are sacrificed."

Stanna shook her head and spat. "I'll not be the one to go after them. I've a mind to have good food and a damned bed." She wheeled her massive horse around and headed back the way they'd come, to the closest crossroads. There were towns down that way and likely the slaver knew it. As she approached the others she called out and explained, and the rest turned to follow.

Niall stared for a long moment and then also followed. His head hurt. His heart hurt. His father was dead and likely his mother too, and there was nothing he could do about getting into Edinrun, not if any who entered were struck with madness. Even at his lowest moment, the notion of losing his mind was not something he found attractive.

"People keep choosing to avoid their responsibilities.

We are all given duties by the gods." Lexx was speaking and Niall suddenly found his voice very tiresome.

"I don't wish to hear your philosophies, slaver."

"Not philosophies. Facts. The gods demand sacrifices. The sacrifices were taken. A gathering of fools interfered. And the next sacrifices refused their fates."

"What would you know about it?" His anger grew the longer the lean man spoke. Scarred, battered, but unbroken, the slaver looked at him and grinned.

"I was there. I saw what you did to the He-Kisshi. I saw how you and the little blonde girl ran. I have been promised retribution for all your sins."

"Enough!" That headache was still there, pounding at his skull. His father was dead. His mother was dead. His family was either all dead or locked away. Mosara, the best master an apprentice could ever hope for, was also likely dead. He'd been inside the city, tending to the royal gardens. All of them were gone. His world wasn't dying, it was already gone and this lowborn wretch wanted to mock him and make threats?

Lexx's face twisted with hatred. "It is enough. Come for me, little worm. Learn from your mistakes. I tire of watching you breathe."

Niall lifted his spear and jammed the heels of his boots into the horse's sides.

In a perfect world he would have charged valiantly forward and driven the spear's head into the bastard slaver's face. Lexx would have let out a scream and he'd have died right there.

Instead, his horse bucked hard and threw Niall from his saddle. He managed to hold onto the spear right up until the ground knocked it from his arm and loosened two of his teeth in his jaw.

Lexx dropped from his horse and came for him, a sneer peeling his lips from his teeth and his sword held tight in one hand.

"Truly, the gods are kind." The words were a harsh hiss. The sword's tip swept in a half circle and came back around to point at Niall's aching face.

For his part Niall was doing his best to move, but his body didn't seem to understand the simplest commands. His eyes worked fine. He could see the bastard coming for him. But he could not seem to breathe at all, and his arms and legs remained tangled and bent at different angles. There. A finger moved. If he could just have a few minutes, he would have a chance to kill the slaver.

Of course, the slaver had different ideas. Lexx came closer, the heels of his boots clacking against the cobblestones of the road leading to Edinrun.

Niall's anger swelled and he growled low in his chest, tried to force his limbs to move properly. They still refused.

"Come on then, you useless whoreson."

Lexx didn't seem to take offense at the title. Instead he moved closer and pulled back his blade just far enough to take proper aim. The tip would go right through Niall's eyes. He could see the trajectory. That blade would punch through bone and the soft eyeballs and probably, hopefully, would kill him quickly. The notion of being blinded for life was terrifying. To never see who he was speaking to, to never look at a beautiful woman, or a perfect bloom again.

Really, the day had started out so well and now this.

The spear that took Lexx punched through the back of his head and came out through his eyes.

Not at all prepared for the sight, Niall let out a scream and moved backward, his traitorous limbs finally moving.

The guard he'd spoken to before was looking down at him from his horse's saddle. He looked like a giant, especially since Niall was still on the ground, his head to the stones. He sat up as Lexx fell to his knees and then landed on his face a few inches from Niall. The eyes were gone. The bastard had suffered the exact fate he'd planned for Niall. Different method, same result.

His damn fool horse snorted and looked at him. He couldn't tell for certain, but it seemed like the beast was trying to apologize. He'd have none of that foolishness.

Niall rolled over and sat up, his head swimming, his jaw aching. Stanna was riding back toward him with Tully on her tail, both of them riding hard. The guards moved into formation again, their helmets hiding most of their faces.

The guard who'd killed Lexx dismounted and moved to his spear, pulling it from the dead man's skull.

"What happened here?" Stanna made no threatening moves, but instead asked her question as calmly as she could. She did not draw her weapon. She was not a fool.

Tully stared down at the dead slaver with wide eyes, but said nothing.

"The duke was thrown from his horse. This man," the guard pointed to Lexx's corpse, "was preparing to attack. I stopped him."

"Indeed you did." Stanna stayed on her horse and

waited for Niall to get up. "Are you coming? We've a ways to go."

Niall nodded and stood on slightly wobbly legs. The horse nuzzled him and rested its chin on his shoulder.

Niall sighed and petted the long face. "Yes. Let's get away from here." His voice sounded raspy and very nearly hollow.

Lexx's body rose into the air. It did not stand. It did not try to stand. It simply rose into the air, mouth agape and long hair whipping in a frenzy. A sound came from it that was far too thunderous to be a human thing. The arms and legs flailed, the sword dropped and was left behind.

Niall's horse did the only sensible thing, and bolted. The guards, Stanna, and Tully all had trouble controlling their animals. Niall had a moment where he thought he'd surely lose control of his bladder. And then Lexx's body, which had risen to a height of nearly seven feet, flopped back to the ground.

There was a blur of motion above Lexx's corpse, and that blur once again let out a peal like thunder and then rose into the air and soared to the west. Whatever it was, Niall could only see a distortion. Wherever it was going, he was grateful not to be heading in that direction.

The guard who'd killed Lexx looked around and gripped his spear. After a moment he relaxed a bit and shook his head. "Did everyone see that?" Several people muttered their acknowledgment and he relaxed. "Then be grateful. I thought perhaps the madness was spreading."

Niall had no answer to that.

Bron McNar

Bron McNar watched the dark clouds sweeping over the mountains. They carried with them a savage wind and a cold that bit deep, like a hound tearing at raw flesh.

The other kings watched with him. The Brundage Highway and the Brundage Cairns were swallowed by the coming storm. He could not see the actual event, but the clouds overtook where those landmarks to his kingdom rested.

Next to him Opar shook his head. "This is an ill omen."

Parrish cleared his throat, reached for the wine and said, "This is a storm. A vast storm, to be sure, but it is a storm. Stoneheart is as sturdy as castle as I've ever seen, and the mountains will allow proper drainage; there will be no floods here. We will endure, provided our host does not send us away."

Opar did not argue the point. Currently, at his request, Parrish was sending a small army to retake Edinrun. Parrish assured him that his Marked Men would not be affected by the madness and could, therefore, get him back his capital city. That left him with little will to debate the man who was his best chance at restoring his fortunes.

Bron chuckled as they watched the clouds rolling closer. They'd reached the edge of Journey End, the city he called home. Stoneheart was well past the walls and higher up, besides. The clouds obscured the Broken Swords, and the trees and plants whipped and swayed in the harsh winds.

"You're all welcome here. Besides, we have business to discuss."

"That we do." Hillar Darkraven looked toward the clouds and scowled. "This will not abate. We have to find them. We have to work together. I don't care much for glory. I'm too old to consider testing my strength against any of you. What we need is cooperation. Together we can offer a reward too sweet for any wretch to overlook."

Jahda nodded his silent agreement, his dark eyes taking in every detail of the storm. "The Galeans tell me the madness has taken Edinrun. The city is sealed against any fools who would enter. If this is the anger of the gods, then we must act quickly to avoid any more cities being swept away. We have lost Saramond and now Edinrun. This cannot continue. There are other towns, of course, but we need to protect the cities. Hollum is preparing to abandon itself and move south. There is no choice; the floods are too great and the storms threaten to sink whole buildings into the mud."

Pardume nodded his agreement and so did Opar.

"How do we stop this?"

"We find the bastards responsible." Parrish spoke plainly. "And we consider who we might have to sacrifice to keep our lands safe." Even as he spoke the winds slapped against the great castle and the clouds boiled past the heavy walls as if they did not exist.

"In all my life I never thought I might consider killing my own kin." Pardume spoke softly. "I have lost thousands to this madness."

Parrish spoke again, his voice as calm as still waters. "We have allowed this. We have accepted what the gods decreed and never once sought another way."

"What other way? What else is there?" Hillar cast her eyes toward him and shook her head. "We've doubtless all heard stories about what you've done to keep your soldiers at their best. Would you have us ask your demons for help? Would they have that sort of power?"

Parrish stared out the window and was silent for a long while. When he spoke, Bron nearly jumped out of his own hide. "I cannot say. I only know what you know. Demons have roamed these lands before, as punishments from the gods. We have lost cities. We have lost kingdoms in the past, but that was demons acting as agents of the gods. Now the gods themselves are the ones attacking. How can anyone know what a demon can do in these times?"

It was Pardume who spoke again. "Can you ask them?"

Parrish did not turn to face them. His hands were behind his back, and while he looked serene, those hands clenched together with enough force to whiten fingers. "Do you know what demons have in common with gods?"

Pardume frowned. "No. What?"

"Like the gods, they always demand payment. Like the gods, that payment is normally in the form of lives."

"We must consider all options, King Parrish." Hillar's voice was low and soft, choked with suppressed emotions. They all understood. The gods offered a delay if they sacrificed kin. If the demons could make a better offer, it had to be considered.

"I shall see what I can manage." Parrish spoke softly and studied the storm.

The winds roared and the curtains that blocked the open windows left behind by the He-Kisshi rippled and spilled frigid air into the chamber.

For a while they were all silent. Like Bron, they had to carefully consider their options.

When the silence grew too much for him, Bron left the great hall and moved toward the kitchens. There was food to be prepared and he was fine with that, but he was hungry and wanted to see for himself what fruit might be available, or even just a piece of good, hard cheese.

Before he reached his destination, Ulster Dunally stepped to his side, moving so quietly that Bron very nearly felt his heart stop when he spoke. Ulster was the very finest of his soldiers, trusted above all else. He was, despite the lack of blood relations, a brother.

"Majesty."

"Stop that shit. I'm dealing with enough of it already. Report to me. Have you caught the bastards?"

"No, Bron." He shook his head and his voice was low with regret. "I met up with slavers instead. They killed most of the men. Would have killed me, for that matter, if I hadn't been sick. Reeds took my place and died for his efforts."

Bron scowled. Reeds was a good man. The men he'd sent were among his best. "Why did slavers come for you?"

"They didn't. They came for Brogan McTyre, who seems to have offended the whole of the world."

"What did the man do now?"

"Apparently he sold them false goods." Ulster shook his head. "McTyre and his lot have a witch with them.

A Galean, or trained by one. I came back for more men. I've lost too many to them and I need hounds."

"You had hounds."

Ulster shook his head. "I don't want trackers. I have enough of those. I need war dogs."

Bron stopped in his tracks. "The problem with war dogs is they're trained to kill."

"Ours are trained to listen, too. They can be made to stop before a death occurs."

"You're very confident of that, are you?"

"Worst case, I'll kill the damned things before they can take a man's life. But we've lost too many to Brogan McTyre. I would rather not lose any more men when we can sacrifice a few dogs."

Bron nodded his head. "Have Red Lester gather them then. He's the best chance you have of actually getting the damned things to listen."

"Aye, Bron."

"Don't fail me, Ulster. I need this done the right way."

"I'll not fail you. I have too much need of getting payback on a few of the people with them that aren't actually part of the problem."

"You mean the witch?"

"That I do."

"They say salt is good for witches. Take some from the larders and then get on your way. The clouds are here. The start of the storm is too."

"I've been dreading it. The cold out there is already enough to scrub a man raw."

Ulster made a half-hearted bow and moved on.

Now the catch was what to do about the rest of it. The storm was here. People would soon be coming for shelter, if they could manage to leave their homes.

The anger of gods was a strange thing. He could not stop it without Brogan McTyre, the man he'd freed. But he could delay it. All he had to do was burn one of his children.

To lose even one to the gods... more than ever he understood why McTyre had defied the laws.

Niall Leraby

"What will you do?"

Tully spoke softly. She didn't need to yell. That was Temmi. Temmi was always loud when she was happy. Currently she was heading in that direction, and nothing could have made Niall happier, but the girl couldn't manage a whisper when she was cheerful and Tully knew Niall didn't need screams any more than Temmi had when the Undying killed her family.

Niall looked her way. He was struck again by her looks. Her eyes, the way she studied everything around her as if her life depended on it.

Not that it mattered. She wasn't interested in him.

"I'm not sure yet. I can't go home." He gestured toward Edinrun. "I hadn't thought beyond the city."

That was all he had to say. They had stopped only a short time after the fight. Stanna was still trying to work out why Lexx had gone mad. She couldn't understand it. He was not a man who fought without provocation, according to her. Now, he was dead. There would be no more fights, to be sure.

Stanna had told them all that Lexx was healed after a long time being ill and suffering infection. Temmi suggested his mind was injured and never healed properly. It made enough sense. The problem was sorcery was involved. There were enough people who could cast spells and protective runes. Niall wanted nothing to do with them. Tully shared his sentiment and once said you couldn't pick a pocket with a spell cast on it, not without having something horrible go wrong. As an experienced thief, she found that notion unsettling.

Niall paced and scratched at the back of his neck as if he had ticks. He didn't. He'd been raised by his parents, not abandoned. He'd lived in the same place all his life and never had troubles. If all of Hollum burned or sank, he suspected Tully wouldn't much care.

Tully's eyes grew wide in her head and her pale skin grew paler.

"Hide!"

Tully swatted Niall on his arm and started moving. There was a copse of trees not far away that might do the trick.

"What?"

Tully pointed to the sky and despite the growing clouds, he saw them. The He-Kisshi were coming. They'd discussed this before; both she and Niall were sacrifices. They'd escaped. There was a chance the Undying would come for them. No one understood how the nasty things tracked their sacrifices in the first place – the gods alone knew – but if they were after the two of them, they'd hide and try to spare the others the conflict. Niall moved toward the closest trees. If they were that far up, perhaps they would not see their escapees.

They needn't have wasted their efforts. The great winged shapes, six in all, moved toward Edinrun instead.

And Niall? Fool that he was, he moved after them.

"Where in all the hells are you going?" Tully's voice held a loud note of surprise.

"If they are lifting the curse I have to know."

"Well, why in the name of all the kings would they do that?"

"If they found the people that started this, the worst may be over."

He was hoping. Tully frowned. He was actually smiling.

"Niall, the rains are still coming. The gods haven't changed their minds." Lightning cut across the northern horizon, lit the clouds with white fire and showed shapes that might also be clouds or something far worse. Whatever the case, Tully had no intention of waiting around to find out for certain.

"But they might have, Tully. I have to know!"

Her expression said she thought him mad. But she was too, apparently, as she followed.

They didn't have far to travel. Stanna called after them but Temmi waved her to silence. A moment later they followed. Not the whole lot, thankfully, just Temmi and her pet giantess.

As they looked on with Niall, the Undying dropped from the skies and landed three to each side of the massive stone wall around the city. There were two doors, one north, and one south, according to Niall. Three of the cloaked demons settled near the northern gates and waited as the same guards approached them.

Fair to say the guards looked less confident this time around.

Tully and Niall stayed exactly where they were.

Temmi joined them and Stanna looked ready to go closer. Temmi stopped her with a shake of her head and a frightened look. She was a fighter, Temmi, but she was also wise enough to know how deadly even one of the Undying was. It was only the one that had wounded and then killed her family, after all.

Stanna said, "I can't hear what they're saying."

"Then shut it so I can. I'll tell you." Temmi looked at the other woman and scowled. Most men talking to Stanna that way would have likely had their faces shattered by her fist at the very least. With Temmi she stared hard, but finally nodded.

Temmi listened.

Finally she said, "The Undying want the gates taken down. They say the Tribulation is meant to spread."

Whatever the guards might have been saying was a waste of breath. One of the He-Kisshi stepped toward the closest log, a fifteen foot-long tree as thick as a horse's belly, and heaved it aside. The felled oak bounced and rolled several times, taking large divots of turf with each landing.

One of the guards reached for his spear, but the commander of the watch stopped him and motioned the rest out of the way. It wasn't cowardice. Niall knew that. The Undying were the Voice of the Gods. Every town, every city, every country had laws that said they must be obeyed.

It took seconds for the Undying to remove several hours of work. There was no doubt those braces required horses to move, a dozen men to lift, and that was after they'd been cut down.

While one cast aside the obstructions, another pulled

the gates to Edinrun open and stepped aside. The massive doors shuddered and slowly gave up their secrets. Niall stared, a dread filling him that rivaled when the He-Kisshi came for him in the woods.

Niall wasn't sure what to expect. Bodies stacked as high as the eye could see, perhaps. He'd heard stories of the plague that almost ruined Hollum a dozen years back. Thousands of bodies had been stacked along the walls and then burned in pits dug along the roads leading to the city. Tully'd seen the massive pyres, had smelled the burning meat. The taste of that smoke in her mouth was a memory she would never get away from and the source of several of her worst nightmares, from what she'd told him.

What he saw in Edinrun were roads leading into the city beyond the gates. There were no bodies. There was no sign from where they were that anything was wrong. That actually worried him more than anything else.

The Undying that had done nothing else pointed to the leader of the guards and spoke again. This time his words were loud enough for everyone to hear. "You are forbidden from stopping any from entering or leaving. You did not know before, but you do now. Should you try, your death will not be swift."

The guard dropped his spear, removed his helmet and backed away, ordering his men to do the same.

The He-Kisshi seemed pleased. They stayed for several minutes looking over the area, long enough to make Tully very nervous about whether they planned on hunting down runaways, and then moved into the town. Whatever the problem in the city, they apparently were not worried about it.

"Well. There it is. You can enter if you'd like." Stanna spoke clearly. "Myself? I think not."

Niall stared at the open gates for several moments, his eyes unblinking, his teeth clenched and grinding.

"No. I think not. There are other places we can be. We should find one of them."

Stanna nodded her head and moved back toward the horses.

Temmi followed behind her.

Tully shook her head and pulled at his sleeve. "Come on then. We need to be away from here. Before they come back out and decide they need something new to play with."

That got him moving.

As they started away they could hear the first noises from within the great walls that surrounded Edinrun. It could have been screams. It could have been laughter. Either way, it chilled Niall's blood.

Before they'd reached their horses the city guards came toward them on horseback. They had gathered their spears and their helmets and they looked plenty eager to be elsewhere.

"Bit of advice. Take to your horses and ride. What comes out of there is nothing you want to encounter."

"How do you mean?" Niall looked his way with a frown on his face.

"Whatever is still in there and moving is what's been killing everything else in the city, Duke Leraby. I've seen mad dogs with less desire for violence." Without another word the group rode on. They looked back several times.

Stanna spat. "Mount up! We ride!" She looked to

Niall. "Sorry for your troubles, but we're not here to save anyone. We're moving on. You can come with. You can stay."

Niall nodded. "I'll come with."

Tully nodded too. Staying would have seen him dead. Of that she had no doubt.

They rode to the west and then to the south. There were plenty of smaller towns where they could stay, and anything that got them away from the approaching storms was a benefit.

If they had to, they'd ride all the way to Kaer-ru and beyond. There were other places where they could be.

Interlude: Theryn

The rains did not stop. They grew worse, if that was possible, until the streets of Hollum began to flood. That shouldn't have been possible. The rivers had been low for months, and even to reach boats had required a ladder down to below the depths where the water should have been. It was the dry season. It was expected. So having the waters rise by almost ten feet was not a blessing. It was a curse. There were some boats, to be sure, but the rivers kept climbing and the waters grew more violent. Most of the small vessels would be sunk if they tried to ride the storm out.

The city elders fretted and fussed and tried to decide what should be done. The Union of Thieves took action instead. If it was something of value, it was collected. Sometimes taken by force, sometimes stolen in the night. Whatever the case, the Union claimed it.

Every boat that could float on water was seized.

Only the foolish protested. The Union was strong, had always been strong, and as they were taking care of the important people in the city, they had numbers beyond their usual.

City elders thought about strategy and how to move their households. There were slaves to consider. There was property that they would lose, no matter how hard they willed it to come with them. Houses that had held generations of wealth could not rise above the floods and become seaworthy, and so those generations of belongings had to be considered carefully.

Shopkeepers, blacksmiths, bakers, butchers, all knew better. What was there could be replaced; it would be unfortunate, but it could be taken care of. Those who were wisest paid the Union of Thieves to help them out. The Union was good at moving things that weren't easily moved. The slavers moved people. The Union moved possessions.

All of that, while the city elders contemplated and bemoaned the situation they found themselves in.

Hollum was still there, but the storms had grown to devastating proportions and Theryn, with the other rulers of the Union, got busy moving. It was twilight when the caravans started moving.

The people of Hollum fled the disaster. They escaped like the rodents that left Hollum. They were not proud. They were desperate. Desperate people seldom argue.

The city elders tried to take control of the situation. They demanded that people pay extra taxes. They told the leaders of the city guard to gather their forces and prepare to protect the goods they collected.

There were no wagons waiting to take their supplies.

The commanders of the guard nodded and bowed and then ran home to gather their families. The rivers rose and the streets of Hollum were swept clean of debris for the first time in decades. Some left before Hollum collapsed. Some did not. That is the way with disasters.

Those that left did not discuss locations. That decision had already been made. The Union of Thieves had no desire to go to Edinrun. Even before the madness that city would have never accepted them.

They rode for Torema. If ever a city and country had been prepared to embrace still more thieves and desperate people, that was the place.

Torema was to the south.

Theryn knew that Tully had gone south, too. He got that much out of Rik before she finished peeling his flesh away. Rik had underestimated her desire for revenge. He would never have the chance to do so a second time. She was not called the Blood Mother without good reason.

CHAPTER FIVE
ALONE IN THE DARK

Harper Ruttket

They were fast, they made obscene noises, and they took down the first of the horses like it was the tiniest of lambs and they were wolves.

The horse screamed as it died, alerting everyone else in the camp. The other side effect of the scream was that most of the other horses went into a blind panic, as did half the men.

Mosely said, "What are those things?" even as he pulled up his bow and took aim. He loosed an arrow into the side of one of the withered things and it hissed but otherwise failed to acknowledge that it should have been dead. The arrow had been true and pierced both a rib and its heart.

Laram called back, "Well, I don't fucking know what they are. Just run!"

Rather than listen, Mosely looked and tried to find a weak spot. He couldn't take out the eyes of the damned thing as the entire face hid behind some sort of metal mask. There was just that vile mouth screeching and biting air and the thin white hair above. The rest of the thing was almost as pale and looked like a starving beggar who'd gone without eating for at least a fortnight.

When the thing opened its mouth to scream, he shot and the arrow punched through the cheek of the face just under the mask and came out the other side of the mouth.

It kept screaming and it charged for him and that was the last of brave Mosely. He turned tail and ran. If it could be killed that was one thing. If it kept coming after it should have died, he wanted nothing to do with it. Sorcery was never a good enemy to run across.

He made twelve paces before Harper walked in the opposite direction, weapons drawn and face set with that nasty half-smile of his. "You've got a bloody axe, you weak bastard. Come use it."

Mosely flushed with shame. Much as he wanted to run, he reached for the axe on his hip and started back.

The thing with the arrow in its face came for Harper and swept one clawed hand at him. His left hand blocked with the hooked sword he carried; the hook caught the thing's wrist and with a flick of his hand the arm of his enemy was extended. The other sword came down and hacked the arm away just below the shoulder.

The creature screeched and Harper spun, using his right-hand sword to chop into the hamstring of the closest leg and down it went. It was alive, it fought. It reached for Harper and he stepped back with ease as it came for him.

Harper stepped back a second time and cut through the tendon on the one leg that still worked. It could crawl after him if it wanted, but the process would be slow.

"Grab your weapons! If you can't kill the fucking things, cripple them!"

One of the damned things came for Harper as he spoke and the man turned, parried the hand reaching for him and then ran his blade along the length of that arm. Muscle and tendon slid away from bone and as the thing fell forward, crying out, Harper hacked through its neck.

The next two approached with a great deal more caution.

"They can't kill us! They need us alive. Everyone needs us alive if they want to appease the gods." Harper retreated along the rough terrain as the two of them came for him, half slithering over the ground, moving their legs and arms in ways no human could without being crippled. They learned.

Mosely came forward and brought his axe down on the back of one of the beasts. It shrieked as the axe cut through the spine just below the shoulder blades and then it collapsed. It was still alive, still trying to move, but everything below the blow was motionless. The face of the thing turned toward Mosely and those teeth snapped again and again as it lunged.

Harper knew what was going through Mosely's mind. He punished himself regularly for being a coward, despite the fact that he almost never backed away from a fight. It was a struggle for him each and every time. Harper knew that, but said nothing about it.

Still Mosely swept the axe around and caught the thing in the mouth, shattering the jaw and sending teeth scattering over the rocks.

Harper moved like a dancer, cutting and dodging and blocking with that same smile on his face. He loved to fight. He lived to fight. That was the only time he ever seemed alive.

Mosely grunted and used the haft of his axe to block one of the things that seemed to come from nowhere and tried to eat his face. The hands of the thing grabbed his axe and tried to pull it from his grip. Mosely kicked out with one heavy boot and caught it in the knee, breaking the bones there. On most opponents it would have been enough, but the thing persisted anyway, leaping with its one good leg and pulling on the axe with all its strength and weight. Mosely was a big man but he was not braced for the action. He and the iron-faced beast went down together in a tangle.

The teeth came at him again. He shoved his forearm into the path of the biting creature. The heavy sleeve took the worst of the bite, though he felt the teeth worrying at his arm even through the layers meant to fight off the cold.

He couldn't drop the axe. He didn't dare. What if the scrawny beast turned it on him?

It tried. The iron-face pulled as hard as it could and it likely would have taken him, but Bump hit the fool thing with a hammer and shattered its skull from behind.

Bump didn't wait around. He was off already as Mosely tried to recover. The thing was not dead. He could feel it trying to move, but with most of its brains splattered across the ground and over Mosely, it was having troubles. Brogan's cousin grew pale and Harper knew he was close to vomiting, but he rolled away from it and tore his axe free.

Meanwhile, Harper was surrounded by four of the damned things. Two were down and cut to the crippling point. The others crawled over their fallen brethren and did their best to break the man's defenses.

Mosely followed Bump's lead and hit one of the vile things on the top of its head with his axe. The metal driven into the face did not yield. The skull did. Once again it continued to move, but its limbs jittered and danced and flopped.

Harper feinted at one of the things and it backed away warily. Five feet away, Mosely moved from one he'd downed, looking for the next. He didn't have to look far. It came in low and caught him at the waist, lifting his bulk with ease. Mosely was larger than most men. That ran in the family. The thing carried him off the ground and ran toward Harper, screaming the entire way.

Mosely tried hitting it in the back with his axe but he couldn't get a good angle; it was too close and he was too busy not panicking. His feet were off the ground and all he felt was air. He was traveling backward and tried to see where he was going, while calling out to Harper to warn him.

Harper grunted as Mosely ran into him. For one instant he thought the man would cut him in two and then the sword moved out of his way and he was smashing into Brogan's cousin.

They both went over. The thing drove them into the ground and ripped at Mosely, pulling his axe away. He screamed, cuffed it on the head and watched the blow do nothing. He'd punched larger men out with one blow but as he'd already seen the metal-faces felt no pain, or if they did, they ignored it.

Harper grunted and drove a dagger through the thing's skull. It flopped down over the both of them.

"Get off of me! Get up, damn it, there's more of them coming!" Harper's words were harsh but Mosely listened, rolling to his knees, grabbing his axe and looking around just in time for the next of the things to smash into him. Down he went again. This time his head didn't bounce off Harper but off a rock instead, and Harper heard the bone in his cheek break.

A moment later the things came for them again. Mosely reached for his axe, missed and fell unconscious. The tide turned. More of the damned things came, and try though he might, Harper could not save the boy.

Two of the things grabbed Mosely at the knees and shoulders and scuttled backward like crabs dancing with the tide.

Harper didn't have time to worry about that. More of the things appeared.

His swords rang out and drew blood.

For a time the only thing that mattered was the fight.

Myridia

The city was close. Myridia was grateful for that, because the cold was becoming more than a nuisance. Between the whole lot of them they might have had enough clothing to keep four people warm. They were over a hundred now, and all the moving in the world would only warm them so much, especially burdened as they were. Most of them carried food, or occasionally weapons, and five at a time carried the unmoving body of the He-Kisshi.

It would awaken eventually. Until then their duty was to keep it safe. They couldn't very well drag it across the stony ground, and so they lifted the shape and placed it on shoulders and walked it slowly across the terrain.

"This is not going as quickly as I'd hoped," said Tyria.

Lyraal nodded and said nothing. She carried her sword over her shoulder, and eyed everything around them. They had been too long without any sort of trouble and they longer they went, the more Lyraal grew agitated.

"There's nothing out here, Lyraal." Myridia regretted the words as soon as she said them.

"There's something. I can feel it in my guts. Something is nearby. I don't know if it's friend, or foe, or doesn't care. I'm not taking any chances."

In the distance the city stayed where it was. They'd walked for a day and a half and the damned place seemed no closer.

Behind them, Lorae cried out. She knew the girl's voice well enough to identify her instantly.

Myridia turned and Lyraal did, too. The great sword strapped loosely to Myridia's back came free, scabbard and all, with one shrug of her shoulders. Her hand gripped the hilt and she stopped herself from drawing the blade only when she realized what was happening.

It was the luck of the draw, perhaps, or the will of the gods. The great winged shape of the He-Kisshi was surrounding Lorae's body and she had time to cry out once more before the thick, furred hide covered her terrified face.

Very nearly as one the women stopped their moving and lowered their heads. It was a solemn thing. It was a joyous thing. To be in the presence of the He-Kisshi was always a sign that the gods were close. Lorae would be joined with the Undying. Her essence would become a part of it. In the process, she was sacrificed as surely as the humans. She lived forever, but she was never herself again.

Myridia clenched her teeth and held back a sob. She'd grown very fond of the child. They'd even practiced swordplay together a dozen times since fleeing their captors. Dead. Not dead. Either way, she would be missed.

The Undying fell to the ground and shuddered as it took Lorae's body. Myridia had seen one of the Undying take a body once before and had been horrified and fascinated. It spit out a corpse, withered and wet and steaming, and had covered a boy no older than ten. Smaller bodies seemed the preference of the Undying. A thousand small wounds covered the body it released. Flesh had rotted in some places, peeled back in others. The eyes stared blankly from the corpse. In a matter of minutes the boy who'd been taken rose as the Undying, covered in the furred, hooded form.

Now was mostly the same, though there were differences. This time the shape that rose had a hood that was slightly different in color, with fresh, wet fur slicked to the head. The body they'd been carrying had not had a head at all. The Undying grew a new one when it took over Lorae's form.

The He-Kisshi stepped toward Myridia, not looking around, not seeking who was in charge, but knowing that she was the one who spoke for the group.

"I am Ohdra-Hun."

She lowered her head and the others followed suit. "As you serve the gods, so we serve you." The words were a formality.

"Most of your kind come this way. They've been freed by the slavers. They will join you at the Sessanoh, if the gods will it."

"Do you know how far we must travel yet? We have come so far, and I fear we will not arrive quickly enough."

She looked into the great, gaping mouth of the Undying as it studied her with its tiny dark eyes. "Continue on your path. The gods have granted you extra time. The humans must make sacrifices of their own as atonement for their sins."

"What of the Night People, the things that follow us? They are bred of demons."

"What of them?"

"Do you know how we can stop them?"

Ohdra-Hun tilted its head and considered her words. The hands of the thing, nearly lost in the folds of flesh it wrapped around itself, clenched and released, fisted and relaxed as it thought, or perhaps even spoke to the gods.

Finally it said, "They are a threat, but the gods say you have what you need to stop them. I leave you now. I have… unfinished business with the humans."

"Thank you, Ohdra-Hun, for all that you have offered." Formality again. In truth it had offered little.

The He-Kisshi stepped closer, until she could feel the heat of its body. "It is cold here. Lorae leaves with me and asks a boon. She says she is filled with sorrow for leaving you. A parting gift, from her, and a thank you from the gods."

It spread its great wings and the wind caught it and lifted it high into the air. The wind was warm and it lingered around them. A hundred feet beyond where the last of them stood the air moved violently and snow fell from the sky. Where they stood, the snow did not fall and the air was warm enough that Myridia could no longer see her breath.

Around her the other Grakhul relaxed and a few even smiled as they savored the warmth.

Myridia nodded her head, gave silent thanks to the gods, and started walking. The warm air moved with them and kept the snow at bay. She did not know how long the blessing would last, but she planned to take full advantage. Unburdened of the Undying's form, they moved faster.

Beron

He looked at the body and nearly screamed.

"Why is this man dead?" Beron asked the men who'd brought it to him, the same ones that had failed him on two previous attacks, and pointed at the corpse. There was a deep wound in the forehead that ran down to the bridge of the nose and nearly split the face in two.

"We found him that way, Beron. Wasn't anything we did." The man was nervous. He had every reason to be.

"Meace, is it?"

Meace nodded. "Meace, the problem here is that there are twenty men we need alive. If they are dead, we can't offer them to the gods. If we can't offer them to the gods, they will keep up their plans to wash us all away, as they did Saramond. Do you remember Saramond? Do you remember when it was destroyed?" He gestured around them. The waters were not quite at flood levels but they were trying. The storm they had been riding away from was closer again and the rains spit and drizzled at them. Within two days those rains would surely be dropping lightning and shattering the peace.

Meace nodded. "Aye. We were told not to kill anyone."

"And yet, this man is dead." He looked hard at the slaver. The man had served him for five years or more. He was a good worker. A decent enough sort when it came to training and breaking.

"Yes. Well. Thing is, I think the man that did that was killed. Lawrence said he took an arrow in the throat after he threw his axe."

Beron leaned forward and smiled. "Excellent. Did that bring back the dead man?"

"Well. No, Beron. It did not. But we don't know for certain he's one of the chosen twenty."

One of the three hellish things that now walked with Beron and stayed with him almost everywhere he went, like his own personal Undying, looked down at the body. Something crawled out from the hooded face of the thing and buzzed away into the wind.

"This one is not among those chosen for sacrifice."

Beron felt his muscles relax. The thought that his stupid men would execute one of the chosen sacrifices and ruin his chance of gathering back his monies was one that did not sit well. Oh, and there was the entire end of the world issue to consider. That was still weighing heavily on his mind.

"Meace?"

"Yes, Beron?" Meace was nervous. Beron liked that. He wanted his men properly scared of him.

"I need you to find Lawrence. I need you to bring him to me."

"Right away. Absolutely."

Meace couldn't have moved faster if he tried. Beron saw the relief on his face. The man thought, rightly, that Lawrence was now going to be the target of his anger. Why? Because Lawrence had seen the incident and had not mentioned it to Beron. Lawrence would pay for that. Examples had to be made.

The cloaked thing looked his way.

"I can't remember your name." Beron was direct.

"I am Porha-Sede, the second blossom." There was something to the voice that made Beron uncomfortable. A hint of insects clicking over each other. A dash of the buzz of a swarming nest of hornets. The thing that had spilled from the hood had not returned. He couldn't help but wonder if more of the things crawled inside that dark space.

"Do the gods tell you which of these men we look for? Which ones are safe to kill?"

"No. Ariah does that."

"Excellent. Please, if you can, write a list of names for me?"

"Find me a scribe and I shall offer all that I know. I cannot write."

"Thank you."

"I am here to serve you, Beron of Saramond. You

have called, and Ariah has answered, in his wisdom. Together we shall see your quests through."

"Wonderful." Beron looked into that darkened hood. "You are a blessing, indeed."

The men started chattering closer to the mountains and Beron smiled as he saw the pale things coming back. They carried several forms with them. Not all of the people they'd been chasing, but Beron remembered the faces well enough, if not the names.

His smile grew.

From the other direction came horses. A great many horses. Men rode those horses and carried the black banners of the slave houses. There were wagons, too. Wagons meant more supplies. That was good. They'd been running low.

At the front of the line came Argus. Argus was one of only a few men Beron had met in his life who was physically larger than he was.

"Did you sell the whelps?"

Argus looked at him and spat. "Gave them to the Undying. Turns out the bastards are vicious."

Beron nodded his head. Argus was a businessman. He cut his losses.

"So now you're here and ready to fight hill men?"

"Now I'm here and ready to make money. I don't much care how."

Beron squinted. "Do you have more tattoos?"

"After meeting those things, I figured a few more wards couldn't hurt."

Beron chuckled. Argus had not met his new companions as yet.

Before the conversation could continue, Meace came

back with Lawrence in tow.

"I found him."

"I can see that." Beron nodded and smiled and Meace would have wagged a tail if he'd had one to wag.

"Lawrence, is it?"

Lawrence nodded. He did not look anywhere near as happy as Meace.

"Lawrence, why didn't you tell me that one of the men we have been chasing after was dead?"

Lawrence cringed. "Mostly because I knew you'd be angry. I'm sorry. It's just... Well, you scare the piss out of me."

Beron nodded. "I have been told I'm scary."

Argus said, "Well, you work at it."

Beron cast him a dark look and then turned back to Lawrence. "I tend to be scariest when I'm angry. Right now, I'm angry."

"I'm so very sorry, Beron. I have no just excuse."

Beron nodded and then pointed to Porha-Sede. "Punish him, won't you?"

Porha-Sede moved forward with that unsettling grace, his cloak-like shape opening and showing more darkness. "Do you want him alive?" That soft, sibilant voice.

"Make him an offering to Ariah."

"Excellent." The hood vomited out a cloud of black that buzzed and hummed and immediately covered Lawrence. The man screamed as he backed away. It was far too late, of course. The swarm of buzzing things landed on his body and hid him under their mass.

Despite himself, Beron watched. It wasn't that he had a problem with violence. He was far too used to violence to ever have issue with it. It was the bugs. He loathed them. They appeared somewhere between an ant and a wasp, with massive cutting mandibles and stingers in addition. They were as black as midnight, and glossy, and their bodies made a thousand tiny clicking noises that he heard even over their victim's shrieks of pain.

Meace backed away and then turned and ran.

Argus watched on, but his face was even paler than usual.

All around them the slavers watched, most of them losing their usual calm. It was one thing to kill a man and something else to watch him consumed alive by living nightmares.

Porha-Sede shivered and shook as still more of the things spilled from him. The sheer volume of insect shapes coming from within that cloak should have left it hollowed out, a rag on the ground.

For three minutes the forms covered Lawrence. Long before that time was over he'd stopped screaming and fallen to the ground. After they were done with him, the swarm moved back to their master and hid within the cloak again.

All that was left were white bones and those looked as weathered as driftwood.

The hood of the creature turned to face Beron. "Ariah is pleased."

Beron said nothing. He nodded instead. He wasn't sure he could actually talk at that moment without screaming himself. One thing to think of serving a demon. Another to see the dark miracles one of its creatures could perform.

Porha-Sede moved away, sliding toward its brethren.

Beron remembered to breathe.

Argus looked at him and spoke as if nothing was out of the ordinary. "I think I need more tattoos."

"They serve me."

The man looked at him and nodded. "I still need more tattoos."

"Right now we need to make sure our new captives stay locked in chains."

Argus spat and contemplated the bones nearby. "Now that I can do."

"Excellent." Beron thought about it. "And Argus?"

"Yes, Beron?"

"I'm glad you're here."

"Well, you still pay better than working as a tavern wench."

Beron laughed at that and shook his head. Argus was good for him. He helped keep Beron from growing too angry.

"We're bound for Mentath in the morning! Be prepared!" Several others repeated his command. He looked at the men who had been captured for him. Neither Brogan McTyre nor Harper Ruttket were among them. Still, it was progress.

Brogan McTyre

When the sun set, the darkness was nearly complete. The crystalline shafts that ran through the interior of the mountain still offered a faint glow, but it was not enough to let Brogan travel.

It was only enough to allow him see his surroundings. The vast skeletal form was semi-prone and the crystals pinned it in place like a hundred sword blades impaling a man. They came down from the ceiling of the cavern, from the sides and up from the ground, and it seemed that all of them made contact with that gigantic pile of bones. He could not decide if they grew into the form or from it.

With the darkness came sounds. There were things moving in the vast cavern. He knew it. He could sense them well enough and hear them as they slithered across the soft ground, but he could not see them in the growing darkness.

Brogan stood still for a while, his axe in one hand, his sword in the other, and he waited.

After nearly ten minutes something hard and cold touched his leg. Brogan brought the sword down six inches from his foot and felt the impact as the blade carved through something that made a cracking noise and then writhed and shuddered. Whatever it was, it had substance and weight enough to stagger him when it hit his leg, but it was already dying and that had to be enough.

Three more times during his first night he found things that needed killing. He surrendered himself from the notion that sleep would be possible and then continued on.

As it turned out, the first limb he'd encountered was apparently a leg. As he traveled he finally found the crotch of the giant's body and above that the hips and then the ribcage. He could only see them sparingly through the vast shafts of crystal that blocked most of his view. That was probably a blessing. Somewhere further along he suspected he'd find the head and for the life of him he could not decide if he wanted to see the skull of a dead giant. The sheer scale of the body was still overwhelming after hours of travel.

Even worse than that were his thoughts. When he was alone, Brogan considered too many things that were discomforting. He was haunted by his lost family, and again sorrow warred with rage with neither a clear victor, though both filled him with as many pains as if he had been impaled on the crystals that ran their course through his only companion in the mountain's interior. He considered the gods, and felt his anger grow warmer.

The notion of the body he walked along sent shivers through him and left his mind playing tricks. Truly, he was an insect beside it. What if the body moved? What if, after all of this time, it grew flesh and came to life? Surely the gods had the power to do that. Perhaps they'd bring it back from death just to crush him like an ant.

He contemplated the people he'd left behind to fend for themselves while he sought whatever it was that was supposed to help him fight the gods. That was a problem. He had endangered all of them. To be sure, they'd agreed to help him, but that wasn't the point. They were all at risk because he wanted to save his family.

Then, of course, he'd started the end of the world. No, that was the gods. They were having the sort of temper tantrum reserved for sleepy infants. But the end result was the same. The end of the world, if he could not stop them.

Yes, in the darkness, his thoughts were the sort he didn't want to have.

"I'm lost, Nora." He sighed the words. His eyes stung with unshed tears. Here, alone, he could finally say it. "I've gone and been a fool. I tried to save you, love, but I couldn't, and now look at the mess." The words echoed through the area.

He rested his face against his palms and tried to breathe without sobbing.

Nora did not respond. She couldn't. She was dead, after all.

Somewhere inside the vast cavernous space the wind must have been getting in. He felt a cold breeze blowing. The air was frigid already, but this was chillier still.

Brogan looked around and saw the faint movement of light pulsing through the crystal shards. Not like a flame. Not as bright as that, but more like the light reflected from a flickering candle. He could not hope to follow that shimmer, but he could watch it and he did, filled with a sense of wonder. Nothing moved. He knew he was alone, but the luminescence danced around him in counterpoint to the odd cold breeze.

"You'd have liked this, love. I never knew it was here." He thought of Braghe and the twins and knew they'd have been both horrified by the giant's remains and ecstatic about the lights. They'd have gasped and told each other a hundred tales.

The shards were wonders by themselves, vast as the skies, it seemed, and as he looked at the closest, he saw the glow move through it, highlighting the red hues and ignoring the paler areas. He followed the progression as it moved up toward the ribcage above him and touched the bone. In those spots where the light touched the skeleton it seemed, if only for a second, as if there was flesh again.

Several times he heard sounds in the distance, clicking noises and rustling sounds, but whatever made them stayed well distant.

Despite the odd disturbance, Brogan was drifting off into a deep sleep when the louder noises came from where he'd traveled. They were soft, but after the deep silence they may as well have been screams. Something had entered the same way he had. That someone, or possibly that group, now moved, seeking out something in the darkness.

There was only one thing to seek as near as he could tell. Brogan stood as quietly as he could and drew his axe, his sword. He did not hold them, but placed them within arm's distance.

The trick, according to his father, was to relax, just as one did when hunting. Make no noise that you did not have to make. He had traveled most of a day, near as he could figure, but he'd gone at a leisurely pace. Whatever followed him might try to come on faster. If it were human, it might take a while to find him, or it might go in the wrong direction. If there were hounds they'd find his trail easily enough.

Brogan frowned. No hounds. He'd have heard them by now. He'd never in his life run across a hound that didn't make noise. In the bundle at his feet the hide of the Undying he had captured and skinned shuddered and let out a noise like a sigh.

He managed not to scream.

Staying perfectly still was impossible and rather than try, Brogan let himself relax against the vast crystal shard that was nearest. The damned thing vibrated. It was not a harsh thing, but it was noticeable. He found it oddly soothing, like the sound of rain falling on the roof of his home.

Though he did not sleep, exactly, Brogan relaxed and drifted.

He came fully awake some time later when he heard the shouts from closer than he wanted to think about.

Whatever it was that cried out, there was more than one of them. He did not move. He did not need to. The things that were coming were likely after him.

There were more screams. And then there were other noises. Wet sounds, and the very distinct noises made when large bones are broken, enhanced by still more screams.

Somewhere along the way, Brogan raised his axe. Both hands held the haft and he kneaded the damned thing like bread dough.

When the noises stopped he swore to himself that he would stay where he was. He didn't need to see. Knowing wasn't important. He meant it too, right up until the time he moved carefully around the vast crystal column and started back the way he'd come. Because sometimes not knowing was worse.

Then again…

The carnage was impossible to miss. His eyes had long adjusted and he could see the shapes where they lay among the rocks and the dirt. They were broken. When Sherla was young she would make wooden figures. They were not very well crafted, seldom more than a few twigs that she tied together with thread she stole from her very tolerant mother.

His daughter loved to play with the damned things for hours. She would have conversations, give them names, move them about. She could have, he had no doubt, made armies and towns worth of figures if she'd had the time, the extra thread and no twin sister. Much as Sherla loved to make her dolls, Leidhe delighted in breaking them. She would always claim it wasn't her, even when she was caught in the act, and she would apologize if forced to, but everyone knew she never meant it. The little hellion simply thrilled at crushing those wooden shapes, as if she were jealous of them. Perhaps she was.

In the grander scheme of things, that memory was a small note in the book of recollections Brogan had of his lovely daughters. He likely wouldn't have considered it for many a year.

The memory was forced on him. The ruined shapes on the ground looked eerily like those broken stick dolls. The limbs were shattered and bent. The bodies twisted until the original shape barely existed any longer.

Each of the forms was a shadow in the cavern, but there was enough light to see the odd metal masks that each wore over their faces.

And there was enough light to see the thing that had shattered them.

If they were sticks, this was bone. It stood a full head taller than Brogan himself and was leaner. It was not skinny, but neither was it wide. The body was naked, but as it seemed only partially formed, it lacked any sense of awkwardness that might have come along. There was no sex to the shape. The legs were long. The arms were long. The body was long. The head was long and bore no face. That was the part that was the worst. There were no eyes, no nose, no mouth.

No. The creature looked down at the carnage it had wreaked upon once-living things and at that angle it had no face. As it stared, Brogan had time to study the entire form. He saw the bloodstains on the hands that reached all the way to the elbows. He saw the crudely formed hands themselves, which bore no fingernails and barely seemed to have joints enough to move.

And then Brogan forgot all about the hands when that blank face turned toward him. No. Not featureless. Not really. There was a rudimentary form of a face there. A hint of a nose, a slight curve where a mouth might be, and two deeply bored holes where the eyes should have settled.

Those two dark pits seemed to stare directly at Brogan. In the near darkness he could not tell exactly what color the standing figure or the corpses were, but all were paler than he was. Paler, save where the blood covered them.

That was enough. Brogan backed away, keeping his eyes on the tall shape. He made sure to know where it was at every second, because whatever it was, it had killed at least a half dozen things that looked like they'd been pulled out of nightmares, and it was looking in his general direction, as close as he could figure, and that was a notion that did not sit comfortably at all.

"I've no argument with you." Oh, how his voice echoed. Did he sound nervous? Of course he did. He could barely see his opponent and whatever it was, it had just torn several people apart.

It stayed where it was and looked at him, as still as a

statue. After he had moved back several feet, it stepped toward him but it did not move quickly. It merely started keeping pace. When Brogan stopped, so did the pale form. He saw the texture of the flesh and thought of the pale white trees of his homeland, the bark not quite as rough as many other trees, but often peeling like burned skin trying to heal. There were no peeled layers to this, but the texture was similar just the same.

He shook his head and contemplated his companion. If it wanted him dead, it would attack. If it wanted to follow him from a ways off, well, frankly, he wasn't so sure he minded the company so long as it didn't try tearing his body into a new shape.

He walked back to where he'd left his sword and his supplies and settled in. The air was still cold, so he wrapped himself in his furs and his tartan and he did his best to sleep while the pale sentinel watched.

It was not a restful sleep. It was haunted by thoughts of his family and by the thing that stared at him but moved no closer.

When the morning came, the light from the sun moving through the crystals once again made seeing an easier task.

His silent companion was still in the same spot. It looked in his direction, but once the illumination was strong enough, Brogan could see that his earlier estimation was true. There was no real face to the thing, but there were two deep holes where eyes should have been.

"What are you?" He didn't expect an answer. The thing had no mouth, after all.

He was not surprised when he got no reply. The thing

simply looked at him, as still as any statue.

"Fine then. You mind yourself and I'll have no reason to argue with you." Brogan gathered his things and started walking. He still had no idea what he was looking for. If it was a trinket, he'd never find it in the vast area.

Above him the remains of a giant remained impaled by a thousand crystal shards larger than all the homes in Kinnett and the king's palace besides. Next to that, everything else seemed trivial. Except that none of it was. The world was ending.

He had to fix that problem if he could.

To that end he started walking a little faster and did his best to ignore the thing that followed behind him.

Harper Ruttket

Harper shook his head and looked at the rest of his gathered forces. They were few in number.

"Well, that ended poorly." He spoke only to himself.

"Aye." Bump nodded his head. Not for the first time Harper wondered if Bump was truly the man's name. Someday he might even get around to asking, but at the moment it seemed a trivial thing.

They were together, and they eyed the slaver encampment. The gods might be angry with them but it seemed that surely something must be showing them favor to have allowed them to avoid capture for so long. There were over a hundred men in the camp, and by the looks of it fresh reinforcements had just shown themselves. The creatures that had chased them and captured a good portion of the party were nowhere to be seen and that was a worry. Like as not they'd be chasing after them again in the near future if they weren't already.

Mearhan Slattery looked at the gathered forces and shook her head. Somewhere in that collection of savages, Laram and others had been captured. Their fates were surely sealed. She looked genuinely worried about the man.

Harper said, "Unless Brogan pulls off the impossible, Laram is dead. You already know that. Why are you looking so worried?"

Mearhan looked back at him and shook her head. "I know he's soon to die. I don't want him to suffer. Also, I keep hoping that you and yours might actually manage to escape this madness."

The winds picked up and snow started drifting from the skies. The cloud cover was weak yet, but that would change. The gods had ordered the death of the world. The storms coming would not get gentler. If the snow came first, it merely meant they had to work faster to achieve their goals, lest a blizzard stop them from going anywhere.

"Are we going after them?" Bump scratched the back of his head as he stared at the forces gathered against them. Harper looked on, watching as more of the people in the camp began setting up tents.

"I just don't know. I hate the notion of leaving anyone behind, but we do them no good if we're caught."

"Ain't there others supposed to be joining us?" That came from Davers, who was wrapped as tightly in his cloak as anyone had ever been. He'd never been fond of the cold.

"There are. They might be on their way. They might have been stopped. Some of them came with us. You know we are wanted. If anyone recognized them, well, we might never see them again."

Bump spit at the ground and shook his head. "So. Go find the buggers."

Harper looked his way. "Come again?"

"You go find the fuckers that are supposed to be joining us. Me? I'm going to get our guys back." Bump didn't bother looking his way. He continued to study the camp.

"And how are you planning that?"

"I'm working on it. I need Sallos, Jon and Desmond with me." He paused a moment and then, "You all right with that, lads?"

Desmond hesitated. The other two nodded immediately but Desmond thought hard for a moment. Finally he nodded as well.

Harper looked at Bump and shook his head ruefully. "I'll say this for you, Bump, you're either fearless or deeply mad. We'll do it together. I don't want us weakened any more than we have to be."

"Then let's be to it. The port of Morella is waiting for us to buy a ship, as I recall."

Harper looked at the man for a long moment, then nodded. "I believe whatever those bastards are planning, it'll probably involve torture. Let's do this as quickly and carefully as we can."

Bump nodded and then started moving. "Come on, lads. No time like the present."

The three he'd chosen started after him, not a one of them looking very confident in his planning skills.

Harper watched them go and then looked to the rest of the group. "We'd best be off then."

Mearhan looked his way and shook her head. "Just like that?"

"Do you want Laram back? Or no? We haven't time to make elaborate plans. We go in, we find them. We leave." Harper stared into her eyes for a long while and finally she looked away. He did not gloat. There was no time for that. "Stay with the horses, please." It was a signal of trust. He hoped she understood that. By rights she should have been bound and gagged at the very least.

The horses were a distance away, secured, but left unguarded. There weren't enough of them left to post guards. Mearhan would have to do. Above them the clouds had already hidden the sun. It was not quite as dark as night, but it was heading in that direction.

CHAPTER SIX
SNOWFALL

Interlude: Roskell Turn

The Kaer-ru islands are not hard to find. On a clear day they can be seen on the horizon from the city of Torema. The city would not exist if it didn't service the islands and offer transport to and from the various ports.

Torema was a vast city, one of the oldest in the Five Kingdoms, and with a population that was larger than in any other place in the entire known world. Torema was built in layers, and unlike most of the major cities there were no walls or defenses around the area. They simply would not do much good. Anyone wanting to seize power in the city would have had to figure out where, exactly, the true seat of power was. There was a palace, of course, but though Hillar Darkraven was the nominal head, those who understood the politics of the city knew that there were others with almost as much power, and that those others tended to stay well away from the public eye.

The streets were uneven and mostly moved uphill

away from the docks and into the foothills to the west and the plains to the north. On the very best of days the city was dark with age. On the worst nights, the city was murky and fog-ridden.

The fog was indeed heavy when the boat arrived at the port of Morella, Torema's main docking area.

There were seven major ports in Kaer-ru and one smaller port that seldom got as many travelers. Few people wanted to travel to Galea. It was said to be a dark place, full of sinister intent. According to most, Galea was home to witches, demons, and monsters of all sorts. Most of the people who said that had never been to Galea, of course, but there were always exceptions.

The long boat coming in from Kaer-ru carried over fifty people. Most of them were passengers. They paid a few coins and they reached the mainland a few hours later. The same boat would likely not make another trip that night. The sun was setting. The darkness came, and with it the winds that blew from the north and the east. The cold winds were early. They weren't expected for at least another month.

At the docks four men grabbed ropes and tied the long boat in place. Boards were placed to allow the passengers to get from boat to dock and the men nodded at the newly arrived by way of greeting.

Few of the passengers seemed in good spirits, but there were always exceptions. Roskell Turn was not a large man. He was a half head shorter than average and he was slender. His skin was dark and his hair was darker. He dressed in loose clothing, the better to stay cool, and if the chilled air bothered him, he showed no sign of it.

He was engaged in a conversation with a woman who was taller than he was, with equally dark skin and a smile that was positively infectious. Daivem Murdrow was better dressed for the weather, with a heavy fur-lined cloak and warm leggings under her heavy tunic. She carried a short walking stick, and every time she moved her left leg the stick moved with her, tapping the ground.

"How long have you been here?" Roskell found the woman immensely fascinating. He paid attention to her every word, and when she failed to speak for too long he tried to find new topics of conversation.

Daivem smiled, fully aware of what he was doing. "For a few months. I have stayed busy, but I haven't had a chance to reach the mainland yet."

"In my entire life I've never gone to the mainland. Most of my kind are not particularly welcome."

"Your kind? Galeans?"

"Just so." He smiled and looked around the docks. There were few people around, well, few of good intent. Several were watching the two of them and the rest of the passengers, looking for easy marks in some cases, looking for actual prey in others.

Daivem shook her head. "Why so much fear of your kind?"

"We work with sorcery. That makes most people fear us, whether or not what we do is dark."

She nodded her head and frowned. "Ignorance is never a pretty thing."

"No, but sometimes it's useful. Three men who were considering attacking us changed their minds when you said where I was from." He spoke softly and remained amused.

"So why do you come to the mainland now?"

"One of my disciples called for me. She had a man come to her who wishes to stop all of this." He gestured to the gathering storms in the distance. Both of them understood that the clouds signified something other than a natural force at work. "She plans to help him and seeks my advice on how to best manage this feat."

Daivem nodded her head and the thick braids of hair running down her back moved and rattled.

"I am curious," Roskell said. "Both the people of the Louron and the Mentath braid their hair and almost never cut it. Why is that?"

"It's just 'the Louron', as it is with the Mentath. The names, I mean. For my people I think it's just a fashion thing. I have never cut my hair, but if I leave it free it's a cloud around my head, so at a young age I started weighing it down." In truth her hair was more a series of gathered dreadlocks weighted down by stones and baubles than it was a proper series of braids. They were uneven and would never come free. If she decided to loosen her hair she'd have to cut it away. "The Mentath? I believe their hair has to do with their honor. Once they are old enough to fight, they start growing their hair. As they get older the hair stays as a sign of their status. If they get it cut, they do so because they're being punished. My brother once told me that their enemies would cut their hair when they were defeated in combat." She paused. "My brother has also been known to lie if he found the lies amusing, so that should not be considered the absolute truth."

"A man who lies when he finds it funny?"

"Only to me when we were younger. He was the one who told me about this place, back before I ever thought I'd come to visit."

"So he's been here?"

"Yes, many times."

"But you have not?"

"This is my first time." Daivem eyed two men who were looking her way. She continued to smile, but Roskell was aware that she marked them. She was not a foolish person. Few he had ever met from Louron would qualify as foolish. They seemed, at all times, to study everything.

"So what brings you here now?"

Daivem looked around the area. Her hand waved toward the north. "The spirits call and I listen. It is what we do."

Roskell nodded his head slowly. "The gods are angry."

"Have they ever been cheerful?" Roskell gave her an odd look. He was trying to find a way to respond, when she clarified. "These gods, I mean. Have they ever been forgiving or kind?"

"Well, no."

"Then nothing has changed. They merely act from their typical anger."

"They are destroying the world."

Daivem nodded and looked at another group of men. This lot were drunk and staggering together in an attempt at a crude song. They could not seem to remember the words between them and she expected they would soon fight over that fact.

She was not wrong. A fat man looked to his friend and punched him in the face for saying the wrong words. His friend took that poorly and pulled a dagger from his belt.

"The world is still here. They have not destroyed it just yet."

"That is why I am here to help stop them."

"And how will you do that, Roskell of Galea?"

He looked at his left hand and the rings on each finger. The one on his middle finger held a dark red gem that flashed with each hint of light. "I have a ways to go. I have to reach the Broken Swords Mountains. I have to meet a man there. He is planning on fighting the gods."

Daivem nodded. "I wish him well. That seldom goes as planned. In my experience."

"You have experience with angry gods?"

Daivem tilted her head. "You might be surprised."

"Then you would have advice?"

"None that would make sense." Roskell was distracted by the violent fight between drunken friends. One of the men fell back with a vast bleeding wound on his face and the others argued as to what to do now that he'd been injured.

When he looked back, Daivem was gone.

"Pity. I was enjoying the company."

Beron

The Marked Men showed up just before the sun set. There were forty of them lined up nice and neat as you please, each on a warhorse, each fully armored and carrying enough weapons to intimidate a dozen mercenaries. They sported shields with the sigil of Mentath, three swords crossed under a skull wearing a crown, and swords and everything else one might need to ride into combat. They also moved in nearly perfect formation as they approached.

Beron hated to admit it, but he was suitably impressed. If he were being completely honest, he was even a little intimidated, and that was not an easy thing.

Argus looked at the people coming their way and spat. "Pretty lot, aren't they?"

"Well. Their tattoos are nicer than yours." Even as Beron spoke he felt an unease come to him. It had nothing to do with the strangers from Mentath. The sword at his side physically twitched. It moved of its own volition against his hip and he put his hand on the pommel, uncertain of what had just happened.

And again he found himself elsewhere. He knew he had not truly been moved, but it felt like he had. The air was warm and moist, the scent of flowers overwhelming, and once more the thin visage of Ariah looked at him. Ariah's left arm was buried now under a writhing vine that held a hundred red blooms. His right hand rested on a sword that was a perfect mirror of the fine blade he'd gifted Beron with.

"Why do you speak with the Marked Men, Beron?" Ariah's voice was still dark and pleasant, but there was an edge now, one that promised pain.

"We have an arrangement. I am to give the prisoners I capture over to them. Just the same, I did not call on them. I had plans to play with my freshly captured sacrifices first."

"They will lie to you. It's what they do." Dark eyes regarded him. "When you need me, call on me. My children are with you. They will act when you require it."

"They have offered me great rewards. If they have no cash, they do not take anything from me. Not this day or any other."

The demon shrugged and the vines drove roots into his flesh. "Unless you see the gold, they are lying. Remember that."

Without another word Ariah was gone and the cold sank into Beron again. He looked toward Argus and saw the riders had come considerably closer.

"Are you listening to a word I've said?" Argus was staring at him.

"I was thinking."

"Well, think a little less. We're about to have an argument with a large group of armored men."

And they were armored. There was leather and chain and plates of armor to cover all the vitals. They wore helmets that had shaped metal horns coming down on each side, the better to deflect a blow, and faceplates that had been lowered, leaving their opponents with nothing to see but the slot where their eyes should have been.

Beron waited to speak until the first of them had come to a halt before him.

She raised the faceplate of her armor and looked at him. "You've found some of them, Beron?"

"I have." He nodded his head and remained as neutral as he could.

"Are they alive?"

"Of course. I wouldn't bother with them dead. They're useless."

He still did not know her name, but he remembered their previous conversation. She looked far more intimidating sitting atop her charger than she did walking by his side. The others beside her, dressed in similar fashion, helped with that. One person alone seldom managed to look as properly threatening. Also, she was the shortest of the lot and astride her charger she did not look small.

"How many have you found?"

"At least five. I recognized them from when they sold me the new slaves."

She nodded her head and looked around the area. Most fighters were like that; they needed to assess everything constantly. "We can take them to King Parrish now, if you'd like."

"Do you have the gold to pay for them?"

That earned him a smile. "Gold is hard to carry over long miles." The bag she held out was almost the size of his head. "Gems. Not the full payment, but enough to slake your thirst, I should think."

She threw the pouch and he caught it with ease. It weighed enough to make his arm tremble. It only took a moment to inspect the stones. Even in the semidarkness he could see the quality.

"Argus. Show our guests to their reward."

Argus stared hard at him for a moment and then nodded. He gestured and started walking. Two of the horsemen broke rank and followed.

Beron looked at the woman and asked, "What is your name?"

"Morne of the Iron Seas."

The Iron Seas was the fourth house in Mentath. They were far to the west and home to some of the most brutal warriors in the kingdom. The land was supposed to be harsh and the seas there were not kind. According to what he'd heard, the Iron Seas had been seized from another race of beings long ago. The land was inhospitable, but highly prized. Most of the decent gems in the Five Kingdoms had been plucked from mines in the area. It explained why he was paid in gemstones.

"Well, Morne, it is a pleasure doing business with you."

"Our business is not yet concluded." She frowned as she said it.

"What do you mean?"

"I don't have my prisoners yet." She looked in the direction her fellow Marked Men had gone.

"You will. They are only moments away."

She smiled. "Are they?"

That was when Beron heard the screams.

Harper Ruttket

Harper looked at the gathered shapes in the near dark and nodded. "Now's a good time, I suspect."

He'd only held off because Desmond insisted. As the man was a terror when it came to his blades, it seemed best not to aggravate him too much.

He could see Mosely and Laram, Bos, Neely and Kano. The rest were surely there, but he could not spot them. The five he could see had been brutalized. They were bruised and bloodied but it looked like they were intact, at least.

"Let's be about it. The poor bastards are in bad shape." Jon spoke softly, but his face was set like stone. Jon, who had the best smile when he was happy but had stopped smiling after the raid in the north. Harper figured that as a sad turn of events.

Still, he nodded and the lot of them crept closer.

The edge of the camp was not well guarded. There were enough people there that keeping a watch should have been simple, but no. The slavers weren't worried about anyone attacking them. They were arrogant and lazy, near as Harper could figure. What sort of fool doesn't set a guard?

Desmond crouched low, his hands on the hilts of his axes. Despite his size Sallos moved silently, his eyes searching even as his feet settled effortlessly in the light snow. That was to their advantage, really. Snow seemed to suck away noise.

Harper got there first. He looked at Laram and the tight bindings on the man's wrists. His hands were turning purple from lack of blood.

"Not a fucking word," he whispered. And then his carving knife was working on the bonds and he was thanking the very gods that meant to have him for dinner for the fact the slavers hadn't used chains.

Laram snorted and huffed but said nothing. He rolled forward and shook his hands, slowly moving his fingers to bring them back to life. The rope that tied his hands had also been wrapped around his ankles after they forced him into a cross-legged position. It was obvious that Laram had tried to break the bonds but every move had only tightened the ropes. There was no chance of escape without help. Slavers were good at that sort of thing. The ground where he'd been sitting was dry, but the poor bastard was covered in a layer of snow that fell away as he moved.

Next to Laram, Bos and Kano moaned softly. Kano's left eye was swollen shut and looked to be bleeding. Harper gritted his teeth and suppressed a desire to growl. The blade moved, and Kano's hands were freed.

Bos was next. His skin was torn and scraped. He whimpered when the blood got to his fingers. They'd been left that way for too long, hands behind backs and tied to their feet. When the ropes slipped they were freed easily, but not a one of them was ready for a fight.

That could not be said of Mosely. Desmond's axe had cut his ropes and the big man was already standing, his round face set and furious. Not as solid as his cousin, Brogan, but he was a sight to see when his ire was up.

While Jon cut the ropes on Neely, Harper moved closer to Mosely. "None of that. I know you're angry, but we find the others, we leave here. There's too many for us to consider fighting."

Mosely's voice was hoarse. "There are no others."

"Come again, lad?"

Mosely looked at him. There were red welts around his neck. Not finger marks, but rope burns. Someone had caught him around his throat and half strangled him. "They only need the ones who stole the pale women. The others are gone. I don't know if they've been locked away or if they are dead, but they're no longer with us."

"We can still get them then." That was Bump speaking.

"No, Bump. I don't think we can. I think they'd slow us down."

"How do you mean?"

It was Neely that answered with his high, nearly girlish

voice. "First thing they did was drive nails through their heels. None of them're going to be walking anywhere."

Harper had heard of slavers doing that to runaways before. It didn't cripple them forever but it made the notion of escape nearly impossible.

Mosely spoke again. "That was the first thing they did. The rest we only heard. We didn't see."

Harper nodded and looked to Jon. "Get them away. Take the horses." Mearhan Slattery held the horses still. That much had gone well at least. "I'll catch up."

"What are you planning to do?"

"I'm going to find our lads and see what's what." Without another word he moved, sliding low and moving deeper into the camp. Mosely hadn't said where the others were, but he'd looked at the closest tent as he spoke. He would see soon enough.

It took only a moment to find the entrance to the tent. Longer to get inside, because he was alone and had no notion of what was in that little oasis, so he took his time looking around before entering.

There was a fire within. It was small but held the cold and snow at bay well enough. A hole had been cut to let the smoke rise and escape, but the air was still hazy from the residue. Easily half the tent was filled with supplies. Move men and you need wood, rope, dry goods, and fresh water. All of that and more was in the tent. Beside that, however, there was a man wearing clothing that was wet with blood. Mostly the clothes were brown, but from wrist to elbow the fabric was darkened with the red stuff that had leaked out of Harper's comrades. Most of them were dead. That was a blessing. They had not died easily.

The man was still working on the last of Harper's companions. It was hard to say for sure, but he thought maybe he was looking at Paddy.

Oh, how Harper wished he had time to return the tortures committed, but he did not. He stepped up behind his target, intimate, like a lover, and slit his throat in one hard stroke. The bastard gagged and reached to stop the blood from flowing. He never quite made it. When Harper cut a neck he made sure to do it right.

He did the same for Paddy, who was still alive despite the parts that had been cut away. Paddy might have thanked him as he died; it was hard to say as the poor sod had no tongue left.

In a perfect world he'd have stopped and sliced them all, but he had no time for that. The others were already on their way and he had to catch up. Finding weapons for the survivors was easy. They'd all been stowed in the tent. He took a cloak that had been cast aside when the cutting began and used it to hide his tracks best he could before he made new ones leading away from the others. It was a long, slow trek through the camp, around the edges and to the north before he wiped the footprints away again and headed south. It wouldn't confuse them for long, but he could hope it would be long enough.

Not but twenty minutes away by foot, still just within earshot, he heard the sounds of discovery. He didn't know if they saw the prisoners were gone or if they found the dead torturer. The result was the same in any event; screams and then people sounding the alarm.

Harper moved on, away from the death of five companions.

He did not scream. He did not curse. Instead he made a vow to kill as many as he could that decided to follow them.

Beron

He looked at the tent and the trail leading away from it. The metal-faced things Ariah had given him were still not around, but Beron had three of the demon's "children" with him and he intended to make good use.

"Find them. Bring them to me."

The dark thing nodded and then moved, rising silently into the air, while Beron and the Marked Men watched.

"What is that thing?" Morne stared into the sky as it rose and then seemed to simply drift lazily to the south and east.

"A gift from my new god."

Morne smiled and looked down at the markings on her hands. "So we're not the only ones."

"What do you mean?"

She showed him the markings on her flesh where they ran from the back of her hand and, as he had seen previously when she was not in armor, up her arm. "When you find your gods no longer serve your needs, it is time to find a new god."

Beron laughed and nodded. "Perhaps that is why they are so angry. New gods are coming along to take their places, yes?"

Morne looked around the area and shook her head, but she was grinning. "I expect that might be a part of it, but if they are going to take the place of the old gods they should get to it. There won't be much of a world left otherwise."

Beron chuckled, but imagined Ariah's face hearing that sort of thing. He doubted the demon would be so amused.

"So your new god gave you servants?"

"He offered help on finding my enemies."

She nodded. "Alive, or they do none of us any good. We have to ride. There are matters we need to attend to further to the east. But we will return." She smiled and offered a lazy salute. "Try not to lose them a second time."

Beron nodded but did not smile. The riders moved then, heading away from the camp in unison.

"I do not like her very much." He stared after their retreating forms.

Argus shook his head. "You are not famous for liking anyone, Beron."

"I like you well enough."

"Well, yes, but I'm paid to agree with you. Or at least to follow orders. She is giving you commands and you have never liked that."

"It is not something I will ever like."

"That is the thing about having the most money. It allows you to say whatever you please."

Argus looked at the clouds coming their way. They had almost covered the whole of the sky and the snows were falling harder than ever. "This new god of yours. Will he ever fix the weather, do you suppose?"

"I haven't asked him."

"Well, if you'd like to move on beyond this point, you should consider it. We're not going to go far if the snow is over our heads."

Beron nodded but did not answer. He was far too busy considering the possibility of new gods. He had accepted the terms of the demon Ariah, but hadn't truly considered the ramifications until Morne mentioned them.

If the Marked Men had also found a new god, what would happen when or if the old gods fell? A war in the heavens was not a thought he wanted to consider. On the other hand, a war between gods walking the earth was even more terrifying.

Harper Ruttket

Harper looked back the way they'd come and shook his head. They'd joined together again with relative ease and he now rode his horse again.

Desmond had looked his way with a question in his eye and Harper shook his head. He was alone; that should have said it all, but no one wanted to lose mates.

Bump unrolled the bundle Harper had made of swords and blades from the tent and everyone got something. It was the best he could do.

Desmond watched on, his eyes dark and murderous. That was the thing about Desmond. When he wasn't mad with jealousy from anyone looking at his woman, he was mad with the desire to fix everything wrong with the world. In fact, thinking on it, he was mostly just mad. His Anna kept him saner and she was gone just now, off with Brogan and looking for whatever he was supposed to find to kill gods.

That was a thought, wasn't it? "Let's be off, lads.

South, I think. Too many people around here for my comfort." He paused. "And too much fucking snow. I hate this. I want to be fucking warm."

Laram and Mearhan had looked at each other for a long moment and he'd half expected them to run into each other's arms, but instead, in the end, they'd nodded and looked at each other with a palpable longing.

He rather thought them fools for not acting on their desires. The world was ending. If they were wise they'd do what they could to spend that time together.

The snow was coming down heavier. He couldn't decide if that was a good thing. On the one hand their tracks would fade quickly. On the other, the things that had attacked them were pale, nearly white except where their faces were covered in iron, and he didn't much like the notion that they might use the snow as cover.

Giddenland was not that far, really. Though he had doubts of getting there quickly, considering the current weather. Davers kept silent watch. He rode near Harper and spoke not at all as he watched their surroundings and in particular the sky. Harper wondered, not for the first time, how the bastard could hope to see anything at all through the constant falling flakes. Still, Davers was one of the best at spotting the unexpected as far as Harper was concerned. He'd certainly caught a few surprises that had been laid out for them in the past.

Aside from Davers there were Tom Kind, Will Foster and Ogunt, a man who seemed to thrive on combat and loathe conversation. He and Ogunt got along splendidly for that reason. Tom and Will were doing a favor. Both of them had families and all three of them had heard about the troubles for Brogan and company and come running. They were being paid, but that was hardly the point; they were loyal friends.

Laram, Bos, Kano, Mosely, Neely, Bump, Sallos and Desmond were all there and would remain loyal, if only to save their own hides. Well, and because it was Brogan that asked.

There was the Slattery girl to consider, too. Laram was smitten. That didn't mean she could be trusted.

The rest of them, however, Harper worried about. Brogan would not, and so Harper worried for him. The mercenaries were just that, sellswords. They worked for the highest bidders. Right now Harper and the rest were able to pay, but if someone came along with more money, or if someone offered a bounty on their heads and their companions heard about it, everything could change, and very quickly indeed.

Davers snapped his fingers and pointed. Riders were coming. It was impossible to say who they were through the snow, but they were coming.

Whoever they were, they wore armor. The rhythmic rustle of metal and leather jingled and sighed as the people and their horses rode closer.

Harper gestured for everyone to stop and they did. If they were spotted, so be it. But there was no reason to make themselves known until they could see the strangers. The shapes moved by them, not close by, but near enough to be seen if they were careless, trudging slowly in the same direction. The strangers did not speak, but moved on, two columns of armored forms riding on warhorses, the sort of beasts that were trained in combat, and larger by several hands than the animals used by the mercenaries.

Near as he could tell, there were a few hundred riders moving past. It wasn't a comforting number, not in the least.

Finally a banner could be seen, three swords and a crowned skull. The Mentath, then, and likely led by Marked Men. There was every reason to believe they'd be hunting for Harper and the rest.

No one spoke. No one moved.

When enough time had passed, Harper led them to the south. They'd not risk running into a small army. They were wanted, after all.

Laram sat on his horse, head down, barely conscious by the look of him. Mosely was more lively, though his face was still swollen and one eye was puffed shut. Bos, Neely and Kano were like Mosely. They moved and they were alert.

None of them argued.

They rode well past the sunset and deep into the night before they found a place that looked suitably protected from the winds. There were a few hills and they found a spot between them that offered some shelter.

Most of the poor bastards looked ill-suited for anything but sleep, so Bump managed to start a fire and Desmond went off to find a bit of wood. They were hardly in the best shape in terms of supplies, but they'd make do well enough.

Desmond came back with enough wood to last a while and with a very plump rabbit besides. "Just looked at me, it did. Couldn't believe I was there. So I hit it in the head." His axe had taken the head clean off. Bump worked the fire and left cleaning the carcass to the proud hunter. Most of the rest were asleep or close enough that it didn't matter. They were alive. They were lucky, but they'd taken a few blows and most of them needed to mend.

Jon came back with more firewood. It was green and it smoked fiercely, but it was warmth and light in the darkness of unfamiliar territory.

When the shape came out of the falling snow, Harper was completely caught off guard. The cloaked form stepped to the edge of the fire's light and looked at them without speaking.

Sallos looked at the shape and didn't speak either. Instead he rose from his place closer to the flames and drew his blade.

When the stranger spoke, his voice set Harper's skin crawling. It was wrong. "You are wanted men. I am here to take you back. If you resist, you will suffer. If you come along I will cause you no harm."

Sallos nodded, stepped toward the stranger and brought his sword around in a hard slash. The shape was fast, but not fast enough. It stepped back and managed to avoid being skewered, but it lost a hand in the process. Sallos moved forward again and brought his sword around a second time, sweeping the blade with his whole body behind it.

The cloaked shape let out a warbling screech and clutched its bloodied wrist in a dark claw. The limb that had been severed twitched on the ground, and looked like nothing so much as a spider on its back trying to right itself.

Blood did not spill from the wound. Instead it bled darkness. Not a liquid that flowed to the ground, but a shadowy powder that fell to the snow and hissed.

Harper rose; Bump stood up. Desmond followed suit. Jon looked on, puzzled.

Sallos struck again, driving his blade into the shoulder of the shape. In response it screamed again and slapped Sallos aside.

Sallos was a large enough man that backhanding him should not have sent him anywhere at all, but he was staggered and knocked into the snow.

And the thing came close, screaming again.

It was not one of the Undying, not as far as Harper could tell, and he'd met all of them in his time, but it was at least as vile. What looked like a cloak from a distance was a dark, greasy-looking hide. Where Sallos had cut the thing that hide bled darkness.

And that darkness moved, slithered and spread across the snow. Not far away the horses started to panic. They weren't the sort of animals to be skittish, they were combat trained and usually very placid, but something had them on edge.

Harper was trying to understand everything happening. As he contemplated he drew his two swords and prepared for a fight. Desmond didn't seem to have that problem. He hurled the smaller of his axes directly at the thing coming their way and nodded to himself when the blade slammed deep into its chest.

It screamed again and this time the darkness vomited from that hood-like opening and defied the wind and all logic to attack Desmond.

He was a weather-tanned man, but that meant nothing in comparison to the blackness that swallowed his entire body. Whatever that blackness was, it covered the mercenary like a fine powder, coating each part of him. He didn't even have the chance to scream before he was buried.

Harper reached back to the fire and looked carefully at the burning branches. When he found one that was not completely set ablaze he grabbed it by the unburned end and pulled it free. Almost two feet of the stick burned.

Desmond screamed again and fell to his knees. Harper walked right past him, though it hurt him to do so, and shoved the burning stick toward the cowled thing. The fire pushed into that dark mouth and lit up the inside, letting him see that more things moved within. Those things, tiny as flakes of snow, caught fire as the flames touched them and they moved as they burned, spreading the blaze locked inside the cloaked form.

Whatever the hellish thing was, it rose into the air and let out a piercing scream that shook Harper's eyes in their sockets and half deafened him. Still, he looked on as the darkness inside that cloak rippled and burned and started falling from the hood and from the cloak itself, dropping and burning, a shower of tiny embers.

A moment later the cloak rose higher still and then dropped into the snow, smoldering.

Harper stared at his makeshift torch and back at the emptied cloak.

"That was just plain too easy."

He turned to look back and saw Jon crouching over Desmond. Without another thought he moved that way, still holding his torch.

"Is he alive still?" Bump worried his lower lip as he looked on. Put him in a fight and he was perfectly happy, but tending to the wounded, looking at the damage the living could suffer, and he felt a sudden desire to be elsewhere.

Desmond answered. "I'm alive. I don't know what they are, but these things are stuck to me."

Harper leaned in closer and held his torch where it could do some good. To be certain, whatever the things were, they'd dug in deep. All looked the same, small pebbles of darkness locked onto Desmond's skin. They did not move, they did nothing that he could see, but they were there and they apparently hurt.

"I could try to burn them off?"

"I just fucking saw what that did to that fucking thing. Do I look like I want to be roasted alive?" Desmond's voice carried an understandable edge of desperation.

"Well, no. Not really." Harper scratched at his head. "We could try to pry them out? Like ticks?"

"Gods, no." Desmond whimpered at the thought.

Jon asked, "Do you want us to just leave them then?"

"It might well be for the best, I think." Desmond pushed himself to his feet. He looked like he'd rolled himself in soot, but he was standing, at least. "Have we any spare clothes? I can't wear them too."

Harper shook his head. "No spare anything. If we're lucky we won't have to eat a horse before we get to Kaer-ru."

Jon took off his cloak. "Wear this for now. We'll try to do something about the state of your clothes."

The cold was biting and hard, and the bastard took off his heaviest protection without hesitation. Harper thought about it and retrieved the burlap he'd brought the swords in. Desmond put that on, too and then curled up near the fire.

While he did that, Harper put the torch on Desmond's clothes and watched as the small black things burst and popped and burned violently. It only took a few seconds for most of them to be burned off the clothes. The fabrics were scorched, but intact. Desmond's boots were barely harmed at all. But the flames that came from them would likely have been enough to blister flesh.

Within ten minutes Desmond was back in his clothes again, and looked mostly like himself. The small black things on his skin covered his hands, his face, his neck, and darkened his hair. His clothes looked unsoiled in comparison.

Jon studied his cloak very carefully when he got it back and Harper understood. Be they dust or something worse, he did not want the black things covering him as they did their friend.

Sallos had pulled himself from the snow and gone off in search of the fallen thing, but there was no sign of it. Whatever it had been, it had vanished.

Aside from a split lip and some bruising, he was none the worse for the wear. That was the thing about the people of Stennis Brae, they were built to take almost anything thrown their way. Probably why so many of the men became mercenaries. It was easier than honest work.

"Let's get some rest, lads. I'll handle first watch. And you after me, Jon, if you please."

Jon nodded and they did their best to settle in.

The winds howled and every time they did, the whole lot of them twitched. It was that sort of night. There might be some rest, but there would likely be no sleep except for those who'd been brutalized by the slavers.

Brogan McTyre

Three days passed without much happening. Brogan walked and explored, trying to find what was supposed to be easily found. He saw the vile things that had bumped against him in the darkness and was aghast. Too many legs, hard shells and pincers that looked capable of biting him in half. The only good news was that he was faster than they were. Perhaps they were starving. There wasn't much flesh around that he could see and the vast skeleton had long since been picked free.

He looked at the massive skeleton and, despite the time spent around it, still had trouble absorbing and keeping in mind what it was. The scope was simply too much. First there were the crystals adorning everything, half hiding the enormous shape, and then there were the bones themselves. The smallest digit of a finger bone was larger than three or even four of him. He wouldn't have been able to pull the damned thing with four horses.

That thought led him to wonder who had built a door into the side of the mountain and why. The door was certainly not for the giant to walk through. It was the size of a small man and built by someone skilled at concealment. It was there, and it existed, but he couldn't see why. Had someone made it just so they could come look at the bones of a giant or a god? Did the bones truly belong to a god? That led to other questions. How was the god killed? How had anything of that size ever walked the lands? How long ago had it walked if the very mountains had formed around the body?

Because he was tired of silence and his companion – still following at the same distance – never spoke, he talked out loud and wished for someone to speak with.

He stopped after a time and considered his meager supplies. He still had some hardtack, but his water supplies were running low and so far he had not run across much by way of water, save the odd pools that trickled down from the crystals above. He had tasted one and it seemed fresh enough, but the waters held a faint pink tint that left him uneasy.

Currently he had found what he thought to be the center of the vast cavern. He stood at the crotch of the giant's two massive legs. The shape above those hips sloped at an angle but far, far away, in the height of the vast cavern he could just make out the shape of a skull looking down at him, past the ribcage that was pierced by the largest of the crystal shards. It was hard to be sure.

"Am I really seeing the skull of that thing from here? Or do you suppose my mind is lying to me?"

He looked back to his silent companion. The dark pits where eyes might or might not be hiding stared at him from that blank spot where a face should have been. "Must be my mind. Your face is starting to look like a face." He snorted as he said the words. Maybe it was the light, which here, where the most crystal shards penetrated the mountain perhaps, seemed brighter. Here, in this place, the non-face seemed to have more angles. He could see the shape of a jaw line and cheekbones, and shadows fell where eyebrows might have been. None of them were prominent, but they seemed more obvious than before.

Brogan stared back at that distant spot where he thought, perhaps, he could see the skull of a god, and shook his head. "What am I supposed to do here? Am I supposed to climb this bloody thing and try to find whatever it is I'm supposed to discover?"

"I'm sure I have no idea."

Brogan turned, his hand already pulling the axe from his side, and bit back a scream as he looked at Anna.

"Gods, woman! You nearly got yourself killed!" His voice was loud, but despite his expectations did not echo back from the distant sides of the mountain's interior.

"The weather out there is getting worse. I'd rather be in here than facing the cold alone."

"You weren't alone. My horse was with you."

She nodded. "Aye, and I expect he's still out there. My best efforts to move him elsewhere did me no good."

"So you came to find me?"

"I told you, I'm not staying out in that weather by myself."

"Did the bodies not tell you it's dangerous in here?" He settled his axe back where it belonged.

Anna in the meantime stared at the nearly faceless thing and studied it like she might a particularly fat and slimy slug.

"They came through the bloody opening in the side of the mountain as if they knew where to look, and I suppose they did. I followed after them when the rains got too much and the freezing rains started." She pointed. "What is this thing, then?"

"I've no idea. He killed those things back there and then started following me. I felt it best not to argue the point with him."

Anna nodded. "Seeing what it did to them, I can understand that."

"What are they?"

"Never seen their like before. They might be more things the gods have sent after you, or they might be summoned things. Whatever the case, if you can be tracked, you can expect you will be."

Brogan pointed up. "Can you believe this thing?"

Anna scrutinized the giant from the new perspective, her mouth set in a soft pout, her brow knitted in concentration. Finally she looked his way and responded, "It was a god, Brogan. It was meant to rule this world at one time. There are a dozen different legends. It was a giant, or it was a god. It fought and was killed here. Maybe by the very gods that seek you now – or maybe it was one of them and died in taking this world. No one can say for certain."

Anna walked closer, her eye on the faceless thing. It looked at her but did not move, save to follow her with its gaze, as she got closer to Brogan.

"I can't make myself see it." Brogan shook his head. "I see it with my eyes, but my mind wants to believe otherwise."

"That's called wisdom. Sometimes it's best not to study something too carefully unless you have to. Some secrets, once learned, cannot be unlearned, if you see my point."

"Aye, I do. And I don't."

Anna looked away for a moment, once again studying the faceless thing with them. "The Galeans tell a story about a woman who grew too curious. She sought to understand the whole of worldly knowledge. First she studied, and when that was not enough, she summoned spirits and demons and demanded more information. When that wasn't enough for her she made demands of the gods.

"'What would you know?' they asked her and she said 'Everything. All there is to know.'" Anna paused for a moment. "It's said that the gods gave her what she wanted."

"And?"

"According to that particular tale she cut off her ears, that she might never hear anything else, and tore out her eyes, that she could stop seeing the truths they revealed to her. The knowledge was too much for her to hold inside and so she wrote as much of it as she could down on paper and gave it to the queen of her land."

"She wrote them while blinded?"

"That's as the tale is told, aye."

"So where is that paper now?"

"The Galeans say there were over one thousand books written down by the woman. No one could read them all, but they bound the pages and set them in a great chamber for others to see should they come seeking the secrets of the gods themselves."

"And where is that knowledge?"

"Those books are the foundation of the Galean beliefs. Wisdom from the gods, granted freely to one person."

"She shared the wisdom?"

"She said she had to get it out of her head and the only way was to write it down." Anna paused. "You understand why I say this?"

"I've no notion as to why. Tell me."

"Can you imagine how long it would take to write

out the wisdom of the gods? No one has ever read all of the books she wrote. There isn't enough time in a life to read it and understand it all."

"But she wrote it out?"

"She was changed by the experience. I do not believe she was mortal when the gods were done with her." Anna looked at Brogan and gestured to all that was around them. "I think this is like she was, Brogan. I think if you do this, you will be changed. You will no longer be mortal. Or perhaps I am wrong and this is a fool's quest that will lead to nothing."

"No choice. It's me and your husband, or the gods. One or the other must die." Brogan shrugged. "I've a notion that it not be me. I've no desire to appease the bastards that took my family from me." And he looked away. The wounds were still too fresh and he did not want to let her see them. Call it pride. Call it foolishness, but he wanted to be seen as strong, even if he felt weak.

"Well then, I suppose we should discover what it is you're seeking."

"And how are we to do that?"

"I have not read all of the books of the Galeans. I've only touched four of them." It was Anna's turn to look away. "Still, I read and I learned. There are others I would speak with who might yet give answers."

"How long were you in Galea?"

"Ten years of my life."

Brogan pointed to that vast area in the darkness above, where he might well have seen the head of a god. "I will look at that for a while. If you need to do something to make contact with your others, I will pretend I hear and see nothing."

Anna looked at him and slowly nodded her head. "It's not true, you know."

"What's not true?"

"Hearing the rituals will not drive you mad, or take your soul. As rituals go they're rather boring."

"Yes. Well, just the same I will try to decide if that is the head of a god and what it might look like." He shrugged. "It's not the words. It's the rest of it."

She stared for a moment, and then laughed. "Oh. You mean the part where I dance around naked?"

"Desmond would want me to look away."

"That's not true either. Desmond would probably prefer it, as I did many rituals around him."

"Well then, I might look around a bit." He nodded, and bit back on his possible disappointment.

Anna looked his way for a moment with a half-smile and then started pulling supplies from her preposterous bag.

Brogan spent his time looking around at the impossible skeleton, then looked back to Anna to see her adding several ingredients to a small copper bowl.

"Do you really think this was a god?"

"Well, it's either a god, or a giant, or both. Whatever it is, I do not think we've ever seen the like on this world in the time of humans."

"I wonder how long ago it lived?"

"I cannot conceive of that much time. Mountains grew around this. All that you can see was raised from the earth after this thing died."

At that, the faceless thing moved, sliding away from Anna and moving closer to Brogan again. The movements were not fast enough to cause alarm, but they were unsettling just the same.

"Who will you speak to, Anna?"

"As many of the Galeans as I can reach. They are, all of them, part of the knowledge I seek."

"What knowledge is that?"

"What else? What we might find here."

Brogan nodded.

Anna sat on the ground with her supplies and Brogan looked away. Far above him a dead thing seemed to look back. He wondered what, exactly, it might see from that height.

CHAPTER SEVEN
BLOODSHED

Niall Leraby

Stanna looked toward Niall, and her gaze was not gentle. "You never said you were royalty."

Her gaze actually made him feel guilty, though there was no reason for it. "I'm not. Not truly. I mean to say, my father is royalty. If my older brothers…" He broke off and looked down. "If my older brothers were still alive, I would not be considered anything but a gardener, which is what I have been training for since I came of age."

Niall looked her way and steeled himself. His feelings toward his family were complex. Mostly he loved them, but he wasn't overly fond of any of them. He would miss them, naturally, but they had not truly been a large part of his life since he'd apprenticed to Mosara. Was he grieving? It was all he'd done the last few days as they traveled. He'd done it to the point that Tully kept eying him like he might crumble and she was ready to catch the pieces. He was grateful and simultaneously annoyed by the expression. He had not been raised to accept pity easily.

Stanna scowled. "Yes, but you are now a duke, just the same."

"I am." He nodded. "I am a duke to an area of the city that has been driven mad. I suppose I might be worth a bit of money if I could get to it. If that's what you're after."

He regretted the words as soon as he said them. Stanna's scowl deepened.

"If I wanted money from you, you worthless fuck, I'd lock you in irons." With that she moved forward and Niall shook his head.

Temmi rode forward as well, trying to talk to Stanna. "He didn't mean it, Stanna. He's just a bit thick in the head, really..." He didn't want to listen to any more of the talk. The truth was he was being a fool and he knew it, but sometimes his mouth would not stop saying things.

Tully shook her head and looked at him. "You are not very bright."

"I'm getting that. I understand it."

"Go forward and apologize for the insult, before she turns back and cuts your fool head off."

Niall nodded and listened. He was still not great on a horse, but he knew enough to make the beast under him go faster. The ride got bumpier as he was trotted forward and he almost lost his seat when he slowed the animal down.

"Stanna, I'm sorry. I didn't mean that the way it came out. I'm at a loss to say anything wise these days. All I can think about is my family and there's nothing I can do to make them better."

Stanna eyed him dubiously. Her hand, he noted, was on the hilt of the sword she called the Bitch. Said sword was very large and, as he had seen for himself, very sharp.

She moved fast and grabbed his tunic. Her hand pulled it tight and Stanna lifted him halfway out of the saddle. "Speak to me that way again and I'll forget we're companions and friends." She did not talk so much as she growled.

Niall nodded vigorously. The idea of enraging her did not sit well with him. His life was in turmoil, but that didn't mean he wanted it to end just yet. Also, she might just maim him and that might even be worse.

Her hand released his tunic. Without another word to him she looked forward and he took the hint, letting the slaver ride ahead.

They had stopped a few times since leaving his hometown, but not for long. By dint of the fact that they needed a place to be and few of the small towns offered anything anyone needed, they'd agreed to move on to Torema. The city was large enough that they'd find accommodations and far enough away from Edinrun that they hoped to avoid the madness and the people who'd fallen to it.

On two occasions people from Edinrun had come upon them. The slavers they rode with took care of the matter both times. No one was locked in chains and the slavers didn't bother burying the corpses.

Somewhere along the way, as he was lost in thought, Tully found her way to his side again.

"There. It cost you nothing and might well have saved your life."

"There was always the chance she'd be less forgiving."

He looked toward Stanna again, as always fascinated by her. She was just so bloody large. He had never seen a woman anywhere near that size in his life and certainly not one so muscular.

Tully pointed to the horizon. "There it is. That has to be Torema, doesn't it?"

There wasn't much to see but a smudge on the horizon. "Well, we've entered the country. I suppose it's possible."

Rhinen, one of Stanna's men, nodded and spoke. "That's the place. We keep this pace and we'll be there late tomorrow." He spat. "And glad of it. I'm tired of riding."

"How large is the city?" Tully kept her eyes on the distant spot.

"Largest I've ever seen. You've got a dozen or more docks, and more ships than I have ever seen before in my life. Boats going to Kaer-ru and beyond."

"What lies beyond Kaer-ru?" Tully sounded like the notion pleased her.

"There's other lands beyond. I hear they have more kingdoms and wonders, the likes of which no one here has ever seen." Rhinen warmed up to the subject, or to Tully, Niall couldn't work out which, and felt his teeth grind against each other. The man was a slaver. Tully could do far better. Slavers might be people, and some of them, like Stanna, decent enough, but they sold others like property.

Tully chatted with the man and Niall listened without hearing. They were words about distant lands and near as he could tell, those lands would probably fall to the same angry gods.

He didn't mean to speak. He had no intention of getting into the conversation, but his mouth seemed to disagree with that notion.

"Do they have slaves over in these distant lands? Have you thought of trading over there?"

Rhinen, who had been speaking, looked his way and tried to keep a polite smile. "You disapprove of slavery?"

"I didn't say that."

"You didn't have to. I can hear it in your tone." Rhinen kept his voice surprisingly pleasant, but his eyes looked a challenge. "I've heard plenty of people protest it. I don't actually own any slaves myself. I just get paid to move them when Stanna decides it's time to move them. She got rid of the latest and that's her call. I just follow orders."

Niall blushed. "I didn't mean offense."

"None taken. I've a harder shell than that. But let me remind you, your dukeness, that the wall around Edinrun was built by slaves. They hauled the stones across miles of land, from the quarries to the city. They built the wall, stone by stone. They cost the royals of Edinrun a great deal less than hiring masons would have cost. That's why it was done."

Tully looked from Rhinen to Niall and waited for a response.

Niall shook his head. "I was not the one who paid for those slaves."

"No. I expect it would have been your grandfather, or, if he died young, your father. Back when rumors were buzzing around that Mentath planned to attack every land this side of the Broken Swords and it was all the fashion to use slaves to build vast walls."

Rhinen chuckled. "Way I hear it, the fine people of Giddenland decided to stop having slaves around the same time they realized they had to feed the poor bastards and care for them. Drained too much from the royal coffers."

"That's not true. I'm sure there were other reasons."

"What were they then?" Rhinen continued looking at him and so did Tully.

"I'd have to investigate."

"I'll save you the trouble. I already did investigate. Wasn't all that long ago that all five kingdoms were at war with each other every other day, and when they had villages they took over, they had new slaves. The slaver houses allowed them to sell those slaves for a profit. Those houses were in Torema and in Saramond. Those in Torema shut down when Edinrun freed their slaves and sent them to Torema. They didn't sell them. They gave them their freedom and sent them away. Said if they found any of the ex-slaves dirtying their doorways, they'd have them executed. That was all of forty years back as I heard it. Edinrun stayed nice, and clean as you please. Torema got all the wall builders sent their way. All of them. Hundreds died walking to Torema. Did you know that? They weren't given any food. They had no water. They just walked to their new home, with soldiers making sure no one got any ideas about waiting around in the forests of Giddenland."

Rhinen didn't raise his voice. He didn't have to. The area was silent of any conversation except theirs. Niall wasn't sure exactly when that had happened, but it had. Most of the riders were looking back toward them too.

Rhinen continued, his voice still remarkably calm and conversational. "Do you know Giddenland made a proclamation? They declared that there would be no more slaves in all of the country. What they didn't say was where those ex-slaves should go. Once again a lot went for Torema. It was closest, after all, and there is always work in Torema if one knows where to look.

"Now, my family, they were slavers in Giddenland and they were driven out of Edinrun. There was all kinds of taxes to pay if you owned slaves and didn't agree with the new rules. Some of my people went to Torema. Others went north to Saramond. My parents went north. I managed to apprentice with the slavers up there. Got good at transporting. Not so good at breaking. I don't like to hear people scream."

If he could have found a way to take his words back, Niall would have.

Rhinen continued remorselessly. "There are five houses of slavers in Saramond. Well, there were five houses. Now I expect that trade is done. No new slaves because of laws started in Giddenland. No new wars, really, so why would there be new slaves? Born of slaves? They could be sold. That's it. All of the older slaves were dying, and most didn't have children, or if they did, they stayed with the farmers and workhouses that kept their families.

"The first house of slavers spent a fortune buying the pale people. The ones you saw us with in Hollum. The Undying wanted them. They came and they got them and no one was foolish enough to offer any resistance." He pointed toward Stanna. "That fine lady, she has always paid me well for my services. I've been promised fair coin for this job, despite the lack of profit, and I've no doubt that she'll do right by me, and the others. She'll make no profit here. She'll lose a great deal of money. If I were in a place where I could say to her that I did not need the pay I would do so, but as it stands, we are likely the last of the slavers."

Rhinen smiled. It was not a harsh expression so much as a sad one. "Are there slaves and slavers in those distant lands, you ask me? I've no way of knowing. All I know is that Lady Stanna has treated me well over the years I've known her, and now we will part ways. She has no more work for me. So I go to Torema. There, I will try to find work.

"Unless the gods kill us all before that happens."

Stanna clapped her hands and smiled briefly. "I'd remind you I'm no lady, Rhinen."

"You are to me, Stanna. Anyone pays me is automatically royalty." He smiled at her and offered a salute.

Niall tried to find the right words to say. He didn't know if he should apologize or admit defeat or simply hide himself away. Tully was looking at him and her face was surprisingly neutral.

Up above them the clouds were coming their way, gathering slowly, but starting to form directly above them as if they were there to hide Niall's shame from the rest of the world.

Tully leaned toward him and said, "Why is it you want to anger our companions today? Have you a desire to ride alone? Or walk, for that matter, as the horse is only a loan to you."

"I'm a fool. My mind wants to linger in darker places."

"You've suffered losses. I understand that. I feel for you. So has Temmi. She lost everything. So has everyone here. I lost my safety in a town where I lived my entire life. Stanna lost her business, as Rhinen just pointed out." She did not yell. She did not have to. His shame was heavy enough and loud enough without screaming.

Rhinen looked his way and then reached out and cuffed him lightly on the shoulder. "You're hardly the first person I've argued with about being a slaver. Won't likely be the last. I come prepared for it these days."

"Your arguments are sound. I never gave much consideration to the idea before."

"There are wars, there are slaves. It's that or let the losers stay where they are, and no one has been willing to do that before. If there was money to be made transporting horses, or carrots for that matter, I would do the same job."

Thunder rumbled above them and Niall looked up just in time to see the shape dropping from the skies. He felt a huge knot instantly form in the pit of his stomach. Would this never end?

Even healed of its wounds, he recognized the Undying that dropped toward him. Ohdra-Hun lived once more.

"Don't you ever die?" He cried the words as he reached for his spear.

Ohdra-Hun's clawed hand grabbed him by the throat and lifted him from his horse. He was unseated with ease and the spear he'd sought fumbled free of his grip.

"I am Undying!"

Tully cried out and reached up toward him. He could see her eyes looking in his direction as he was lifted into the winds. He stared hard as she grew smaller and smaller and the horse and land he'd been touching shrank away as well.

Niall's stomach now felt like it was dropping and the fear he felt blossomed into a full panic.

Had he ever dreamed of flying? To be sure, but not like this. The air was so bitterly cold, and his eyes felt as if they had never known the moisture of even a single teardrop.

They rose into the clouds themselves and Niall could barely catch a breath.

"I have grown tired of your games, boy. You have escaped me too often."

"I've done nothing to you!" He screamed to be heard; the wind was shrieking around his head as they rose higher still. By the gods, the world in the distance was vast and he could see the ocean stretching away far to the south.

"You killed me." The voice came from that horrid maw amid a stench like death and decay.

"You took me from my home! You were making me a sacrifice for the gods."

"And now, I make you a sacrifice to my rage." The clawed talon that gripped his tunic released, and Niall scrambled, reaching for the hand, the cloak that whipped the air, anything at all that would stop him from falling.

He missed.

The ground came back to him quickly and he screamed the entire way down.

Tully

Tully's scream was the loudest. She had been right next to the poor bastard when he was hauled into the sky.

Temmi screamed too.

Stanna looked her way and her face became a mask of sorrow. She'd heard the stories from Tully herself and now she saw the end result of those tales. Niall and Tully, stolen by the Undying for sacrifice and escaping: how the very same thing had killed all of Temmi's family in an effort to get to Niall and Tully. It was the very stuff of nightmares, and Stanna's anger showed through the mask of sorrow.

"We've got to go after him!" Temmi's voice broke and she looked to the west and prepared to ride.

Stanna shook her head and caught the horse's reins. "No. We don't. There's nowhere to go."

Tully was not close enough to hear the conversation, but she was wise enough to understand. She lowered her head for a moment and then raised it and looked in the direction the Undying had taken their friend, while Temmi tried to argue the point.

Stanna looked at Temmi and scowled. "We've no way of knowing where they've gone. No way of knowing if Niall is still alive. No way of following them. That means we go on and we do our best to keep you safe and to keep Tully safe."

She turned to Tully at that thought and then rode close with her horse. "You, come on over here."

Tully looked at her and shook her head, uncomprehending.

"You ride in front of me from now on. You'll not ride alone. This way you can keep your eye out for that bastard thing and keep your weapons close. You see it, you hurt it. It keeps coming, I've been warned and I kill it. Again."

Tully managed to climb over easily enough with Stanna's help. A moment later the reins for Tully's horse were in the hands of one of Stanna's boys, the better to make sure they didn't lose any of the beasts.

"We ride! We're done being on the road. Off to Torema."

Stanna urged her horse to go faster, and her people followed suit. Loyalty was a hard thing, but even the least faithful among them knew they wouldn't get paid until they reached Torema and the banks there.

Tully rode in front of the woman, feeling small and insecure, but comforted by Stanna's presence.

Interlude: Morne

"Is it true what they say about Torema?" Broyton looked directly at Morne as he spoke. Broyton was younger than most of the Marked Men. He'd had a gift with the sword since before he was fully grown and when he asked to join their ranks, he proved it in singular combat with Cantin Hallsy, one of the captains of the elite forces. To the surprise of everyone but Broyton, he won the fight easily. He disarmed the captain and then gave him back his sword. The second attack ended the same way and Broyton was allowed to enter the black stone tower they called the Cauldron and prove his worth.

He was worthy, but he was also a pain in Morne's side. His questions were endless and normally revolved around what all boys his age thought of. That is, anything at all involving sexual relations.

Verden answered for her. "If you've heard rumors of

fantasies fulfilled, sexual desires sated, exotic women, men who look like exotic women, rare and precious foods from other lands, women from those same places, smiths that can make any weapon you can imagine, sweet wines, rapists, cutthroats, blackguards, murderers and the sort of people who'd kill you for as little as a copper, then yes, it's all true."

Broyton listened and went from looking excited to positively depressed. Morne made a note to herself to thank Verden for that later.

They'd ridden through the storm and made good time. Now they waited at the edge of the road leading to Edinrun, and prepared for war. They'd been commanded by none other than Parrish to come here and clean up the city and that was exactly what they intended to do. One hundred and ten Marked Men and two thousand horsemen. There was no city left to worry about from all they'd heard. The people in Edinrun had been driven mad by the gods. Those that entered were also driven insane. For most that was a problem, but not for the Marked Men or those riding with them.

They had protection from their own god. That was the claim and Morne saw no reason to doubt it. From the moment she had walked into the Cauldron and been tested, seen her new god and come out with the brands on her flesh, she had known the peace that comes from being among the elite and the chosen.

"You're young. You've likely never been with a woman." She looked directly at Broyton as she spoke. "You want to try new things. You want to hear about a thousand tales. Right now, we are busy. We have people to kill. When we are done, perhaps, we can take you to

Torema where you can finally have your every desire slaked. Until then, still your mouth about what you want from Torema and women in general."

Verden snorted laughter and Broyton blushed furiously. He did not like being told what to do by a woman. He liked it less when he'd been desperate to lay with her since they'd first met. Morne knew he wanted her. She didn't care. He could keep close company with his hand. Unless she was dead, he'd never have his way with her.

"It's time!" The call came from Cantin and a moment later they were mounting their rides and preparing. Helmets were put in place, visors were lowered. Whatever any of them might want to discuss was forgotten.

Around them, the stragglers who'd been on their way to Edinrun before everything went wrong looked on and then carefully backed away. They were not fighters, or even if they were, they were not Marked Men. The soldiers from Mentath were intimidating enough, but she'd seen the helmets that the other Marked Men wore and knew how intimidating they could be.

The locals parted like water around the troops as they started to move.

They rode in formation, as always, and as they rode the walled city came into view.

The walls were intact. From beyond them smoke rose here and there. On the walls themselves someone had meticulously hung bodies by arms, legs, or necks as they saw fit, and left the corpses and the living alike to rot and fall away.

Perhaps thirty people stood at the open gates, some

of them victims to the others, some active participants in atrocities best not studied too carefully. The signal was given by the captain, a silent gesture this time. And as one the Marked Men moved forward and charged.

Morne felt her heart pound and her blood sing with the possibilities of combat, life, and death.

Thirty people stood before the open gates. Two of them had the good sense to move out of the way. Horses knocked the others aside, and anyone who managed to stand after that was taken down by the long horseman's picks the Marked Men carried. Morne felt a woman's head shatter with her only blow as she moved through the gates.

In moments Morne and those closest to her were inside the city and looking upon the wreckage that had been one of the shining jewels of the Five Kingdoms. The academic knowledge in Edinrun was second to no other place in the world, and there was little doubt that all of that was gone now, ruined by the gods and whatever they'd done to the people. The roads leading to the city were marred by blood and bodies, but that wasn't the reason the Mentath were there. They had been given orders to take the city back from the mad and that was their goal. King Opar asked assistance from King Parrish and the Marked Men would do their best.

Theragyn, the lord of the Cauldron, demanded no less.

There were people aplenty moving along the roads. Most of them seemed dazed, or simply stumbled around, lost in their own thoughts, talking to themselves, or in some cases clawing at their own flesh. Morne's pick took care of three of them. When it became stuck in a skull she switched to her sword. Each blow was hard and broke bone or drew blood. The people behind her followed along and struck again at any she did not kill.

Each time a wretch died at her hands she called out to Theragyn and felt the power pulse through the markings on her body. It would not stay with her but she felt it. She knew it meant she had succeeded in her task.

The first few died easily. After that, the more dangerous inhabitants of the city of madness took note and started their own attacks. Some used weapons, but most attacked like rabid dogs, screaming and clawing and biting at whatever got their attention. The tactic was likely very successful on most.

The Marked Men were trained better than that. They struck down even the most savage assailants with relative ease, aided by their horses and their armor. The horses often forced the attackers aside and the swords did the rest.

Theragyn reaped what they sowed. Morne knew that, and reveled in the knowledge. Every life taken in the demon's name added to his power and he was a generous god who shared his bounty. There had been a time, not so long ago, when she feared what would happen to her in this world. That was no longer the case. She was skilled, she was powerful on her own, and she was blessed by her new god.

The arrow that came for her should have been her death, but Theragyn was a kind god. With his blessing she saw the shaft moving through the air and had time to escape it. Her eyes saw the beating of a fly's wings, could count the scars on a man's hand from fifty paces away, and her reflexes were very nearly as fast and sharp.

The madman that leaped for her with an axe in his hand could have been her downfall, but the same still stood true. Her blade blocked him easily and the man's throat opened like a blossom before her on the return stroke.

So it was with all of the Marked Men. Around her the armored soldiers they led did excellent work. They were trained well, they were armored and they were desperate. Only the finest among them would join the ranks of the Marked. Only the best would ever have a chance to enter the Cauldron and be reborn.

Broyton, a young fool in conversation, was a harbinger of death on the battlefield. Every person who came for him died quickly and those who tried to run were trampled under his horse. In that moment, she might well have considered him a proper mate, but she knew he'd speak sooner or later and ruin the perfection of his slaughtering skills.

The captain called out orders and they listened, wheels in an infernal killing machine, cogs in a weapon forged by Theragyn.

Verden stormed across the landscape, carving a bloody path through any meat that came his way. A spear broke against his breastplate and the man wielding it was nearly split in two by the return attack. Trained horsemen had every advantage over the mad and they used those advantages.

Around her the Mentath joined in savage, wondrous combat, all for the glory of their new god.

And older gods remembered how to be jealous.

Beron

Most of the people in Beron's camp trembled as he walked.

Five of the twenty that the very gods demanded had been in his grasp and they'd escaped. One of his new servants, a gift from Ariah, had not returned, and the other two were sent out into the snow to find what had been taken from him.

And Beron took out the losses on the fools who had failed in their duties. Three men had been set to watch over the prisoners and they got lazy. Silence had convinced them that they could wander off together and drink wine to warm up.

Now all three were staked in the snow, naked as newborns and freezing to death.

Beron stared at them for a long while, not speaking, just enjoying their moans, and finally walked away. There was something bothering him, something at the edge of his senses, and he hated when that happened. It meant distraction if nothing else, and he did not want to be distracted.

Time was too short to allow him to fall off track.

"Argus!"

"There's no reason to scream. I'm right here."

"Right fucking now I feel like screaming!"

Argus smiled and shrugged his shoulders. "It's your coin either way. How can I help?"

"Ten best trackers. You brought dogs?"

"A half dozen."

"Use them. Send the dogs and the trackers out and

find those bastards. I want them brought back to me. I want them in chains this time."

"Still alive?"

"What did I fucking say before? They're useless dead, so yes, alive." The man was still smiling. Sometimes he wanted desperately to punch him in the face.

"I already sent them, with orders to keep the fellows alive. Wouldn't want you to have to return your fortune to the Mentath. Kind of surprised they didn't take the damned gems back."

"I imagine they were distracted."

"One of the lads came back and said they almost lost the trail. It was a lot of Mentath that came by and a lot of horses. But they found the trail again."

"It was forty. Forty horses. If the dogs and trackers can't handle that–"

"It was forty came to camp. The rest rode right on past. Hundreds."

Beron spat. "Then maybe we'll get lucky and the bastards will start another war. We could use more slaves."

Argus chuckled, but nothing more.

Perhaps ten minutes passed before one of the dark shapes that had been gifted to Beron by Ariah showed itself. It moved so quietly that he didn't see or hear it so much as he sensed it. Glossy and black, the thing opened its arms and dropped a dark cloak across the snow.

"They killed Porha-Sede."

Beron looked at the shape and scowled. The cloak was all that was left of one of his Undying? "How?"

"Fire, it seems."

"Which are you?"

"I remain Ahbra-Sede."

The burnt, discarded thing in the snow before him twitched, and Beron wisely stepped back.

Ahbra-Sede tilted its head and then looked down at the remains. "It wishes to live again."

"And how does it do that?"

"The Undying can never be killed. They are Undying."

"So why does it reach for me?"

"There must always be a host, or the Undying cannot be reborn."

"So it could live again?" Beron smiled. Servants that could not be killed? What a lovely notion.

"Oh, yes."

Beron nodded and went to see his three naked fools. The knife at his side worked fine to cut through the bonds of the closest, a man whose name meant nothing to him, as he was already as good as dead.

While the man tried to thank him for releasing the restraints, Beron grabbed him by his closest leg and hauled him sputtering and screaming through the snow.

Argus was busy packing herbs into his pipe and watched with one raised eyebrow. "Going to castrate him or something?"

"Something. Watch and learn."

Ahbra-Sede watched on silently as Beron lifted the screaming naked man at his waist and threw him on top of the twitching cloak of black.

The cloak exploded into activity, wrapping itself around the fool and truly giving him reason to scream.

Beron and Argus both watched, fascinated, as thin, worm-like tendrils stabbed themselves into naked flesh and burrowed deep, reddening even as they pushed deeper. There were hundreds of them and they pulled the cloak in closer until it wrapped itself around the poor bastard. Beron stared, delighted that his pet would be returned to him, but from the corner of his eye he could see Argus, and the man looked horrified, something Beron had never seen before.

"Gods, Beron! What have you done?"

"I'll have my servant back! I'll find and hunt down all of those thieving bastards and this time I'll blind their fucking eyes and cut off their feet!"

Ahbra-Sede backed slowly away and shook its cowled head. "You do not understand…"

Beron scowled and looked at his Undying pet. "What do you mean? You said it needed a new body and I gave it one."

"Lord Ariah is powerful, yes, and he changed the Undying for you, but he cannot bring back the dead. That power belongs only to the gods."

Beron's scowl deepened. "What does that mean?" Next to him Argus cursed and grabbed hastily at his axe and the heavy short sword on his other hip.

On the ground, the condemned man screamed again but the voice was different this time, it was deeper and nearly deafening.

Beron's skin crawled.

Ahbra-Sede soared upwards, lifted on a blast of hot air.

The other shape rose from the snow, shivering and twitching, and in an instant Beron understood.

The things he had offered to Ariah had been changed. They were black and glossy, like well-cured leather that had been oiled and polished.

The thing that rose from the frozen ground now was brown and lightly furred and instead of pure darkness, the slaver could see a hint of teeth inside its hood.

Heat rose from the newly reshaped He-Kisshi, and the air steamed around it, half obscuring the horrific thing.

"Oh. Fuck."

"You dare much!" The voice roared from the Undying that had, true to the name, been reborn, once again returned to its proper shape.

Beron reached for his whip and snapped it several times as a warning. He couldn't get his foolish mouth to make sounds just then. He was too terrified.

"You would defy the gods? You would take another as your god?" The voice trembled, not with fear but with rage. It stalked forward and Beron stepped back. Beside him Argus kept his weapons lowered and also stepped back.

"You attacked us! What were we to do?"

"Free the Grakhul! Those you should have never taken!"

Sometimes instinct is all you have. Beron lashed out, his bullwhip cutting the air and striking the hood of his enemy.

The Undying caught the whip and ripped it from his hand. Beron yelped as his smallest finger broke from the force. The whip soared into the darkness.

That did not stop him from drawing the sword at his hip.

The sword shuddered, twisted, and turned, moving before Beron and placing itself between him and the He-Kisshi.

The Undying paused and seemed to study the blade. Without eyes clearly seen on the hideous visage, Beron could only guess.

"This is not finished, Beron of Saramond."

"Are you afraid of a sword then?" Beron grinned.

"I fear only the gods. I could kill you right now."

The sword wanted to fight. He could feel the way it pulled at him, nearly demanding that he engage the Undying. Ariah wanted the servant of the gods dead.

"Then come for me! Come and kill me if you can!" It was Beron's turn to roar and he stepped toward the thing, ready to slice it into bloody gobbets and feed the remains to his dogs when they returned. The very thought was giving him an erection.

Even as he screamed, he saw Levarre coming from behind, his dagger and short sword, gifted him by Ariah, held in hands that jerked and twitched much like Beron's did. The weapons wanted blood. They wanted the He-Kisshi.

Levarre charged as the creature looked at Beron.

And the Undying moved out of the way, sliding to the side with terrifying speed as it avoided the short sword's keen blade. Levarre compensated by hurling his dagger. The blade slid through the air and the Undying screamed again as the blade cut into its side.

The flaps of that leathery cloak opened and the creature rose into the sky, the winds driving with enough force to stagger all of the men and half blind them with air-blasted snow.

Black blood fell from the wounded beast and it pointed a finger at Levarre. "DIE!" One word and no more.

A second later the world exploded into white light and the hairs on Beron's body stood straight. He barely noticed. He was too busy being cast into the air and dropped a dozen feet away. His eyes burned, his skin burned, his muscles twitched and refused to obey.

Burnt ozone and roasted meat smells assaulted his nose.

The world faded and came back, vanished and returned, and finally Beron opened his eyes and could see, despite the dark blue aura that swam in his vision.

He saw enough. He saw Levarre's burned, shattered body and the field of ground around him that had been cleared of snow. He could only guess it was Levarre, for that was where the man had been standing, but what was left looked as if it had been torn apart by hounds and then burned in a funeral pyre.

Not far away, Argus was crawling on his hands and knees.

The He-Kisshi was gone.

"What happened?" Beron's voice was strained, and his lungs ached.

Several men moved cautiously toward them, eyes wide and faces made into masks of shock and terror.

One of them, Orton, spoke up. "Lightning. It came from the sky and hit… Well, it hit whatever that was."

Beron nodded and slowly, painfully, made his way to his feet.

Levarre was dead. His sword lay beside him, unscathed. The dagger a few feet away, half buried in melted slush.

Argus coughed and shook his head. "I'm done. I have always served you, Beron, but I'll not fight against creatures that cannot die."

Beron barely heard him. He was too busy trying to make sense of what had just happened.

Harper Ruttket

The sun finally broke through the clouds again, and Harper allowed himself a small smile. They'd moved on, riding through the snow and the cold, letting the wounded have the horses. In a few cases they had to double up, but the Slattery girl had stayed with the animals, and none of the soldiers from Stennis Brae had been waiting for them anywhere along the line. Being as she was scryer, he hadn't been certain if that would be the case or not. Desmond was not wounded, exactly, but the markings on his face, the strange pebbles that stuck to him, were a bother. They'd actually changed during the night –growing a bit, it seemed, though not much. Whatever the case, the end result was unsettling. He looked like a man cursed with lizard skin. Harper had heard of such things before, but never seen the like.

They walked and rode toward the sun where it cut through the cloud cover. The snow had stopped, and that, too, was a blessing. The cold bit, but it did not sink teeth deeply. They would survive. That was all that mattered just then. Fourteen of them and they were together. Between them they had weapons, water and food.

Bump had a look on his face that said he was considering making a rousing speech – he'd always wanted to make one, and Harper knew it – but the words weren't there in his head, or on his tongue. A good lad with an axe, but not much for speaking his mind in sentences longer than four words. Besides which, there was every reason to believe the man would end up laughing at himself before it was finished.

Harper had never much liked rousing speeches. The best rallying cry he'd ever heard came from Brogan when the widower said to kill all the pale-skinned bastards that had just slaughtered his wife. That speech amounted to a sword through a man's gullet.

He was still contemplating the fine art of making speeches when the thing they'd killed in the night dropped from the sky in front of them.

No. It wasn't the same, but it was close. This one was taller.

"Lay your weapons aside and come with me."

Harper contemplated which weapon to best shut the thing up. Two daggers wound up between separate fingers, ready for throwing.

It did not attack. It stayed where it was, roughly four inches above the snow.

They had no fire to use this time. They only had their weapons and all of them were cold and tired.

Still, Harper weighed his two longest daggers and held them at the ready. "Can't do that. We have places to be that do not involve being tied up and tortured."

The thing shivered violently and Harper saw something fall from the cloak into the snow.

"You will come with me. There is no choice. If you do not fight, I will not hurt you."

Desmond spoke up. "We'll see you dead first." He was covered in odd bumps, he was tired, he was half frozen, and yet his axes came into view and seemed to dance around his hands. He was a terrifying man when he wanted to be.

Jon had a javelin in his hand. He eyed the cloaked shape and Harper knew he was choosing the best place to hurl it.

Again the shape shuddered and the ground responded. It was subtle, but Harper felt it. The land under the snow moved and the snow shifted as well.

"What are you up to, you vile beast?"

"You killed Porha-Sede. I will not die the same way."

"We killed what?"

"The Second Child. I am the Third Child. I will have you as my prisoners."

Harper shook his head. "You make as much sense as a drunken slaver, lad. Go away before we have to get nasty with you."

The snow moved and bucked in several spots and for the first time since the thing landed Harper became truly uneasy. One thing to face off against a single creature, even if it was not natural, another to get a sense that you were about to be ambushed.

"What are you doing? Don't make us attack. Go on your way and we'll let you be." He spoke the words and tried to sound confident, but there was something going on that he could not see.

The shape shook again and whatever was happening beneath that dark cloak, a blackness pushed down into the earth.

"Enough!" Desmond hurled an axe and the blade sank into the cloak with a satisfying thunk.

"You are too late for that. I am properly seated and you will not move me." One of the monster's hands grabbed the axe and wrenched it out of its torso. There should have been blood, or at least, from what they had seen before, there should have been darkness. Instead the cloak fluttered open and Bump saw the dark black bark where flesh should have been.

The axe was cast aside and those hands, which also had taken on the texture of a tree's branches, creaked and moved into clenching fists.

That was when the ground erupted in a dozen places. The snow was shoved back and hard-packed earth crumbled away as thick roots came past the moving ground and struck at them, a dozen serpents of wood rearing up and striking.

Harper staggered back as the ground under him moved, but before he could compensate for the unexpected motion he was captured. A column of thick wood writhed and whipped around his right leg, pinning him as easily as he might grab a grounded fish trying to breathe and fight its way free from a net.

He stabbed at the thick wood and grunted as the blade dug in a small amount and the wood failed to give way.

Both blades struck repeatedly and had little impact. He looked toward the thing that called itself the third child and flipped the blades in his hands. One and then the other soared toward the hood of the creature. The first missed as it jerked to the side; the second, however, slammed deep into the opening.

The thing let out a warbling scream and threw its arms wide. Both of those clawed hands grabbed at the hilt of the dagger buried deep in whatever might pass for a face, and sought to pull the blade free. The cloak opened further revealing the deep, twisting roots that buried themselves in the ground and then came out and attacked Bump and his companions.

The root around Harper's leg contracted and he screamed as the pressure crushed the muscles in his thigh and calf and threatened to shatter bones.

Not far away one of the horses cried out as well, a sound that Harper would never forget. Thick roots crushed the animal and swept upward, circling around the two men riding. Bos and Neely both cried out and did their best to defend themselves, hacking away at the heavy roots with axe and sword.

The roots continued their greedy scramble and the hooded form doubled over, until, finally, it wrenched Harper's knife free from whatever face it hid.

It was over in seconds. All of them, fourteen travelers, and the thing had captured them as if they had no skills among them.

Hard vines encircled each of them and the cloaked form shuddered again. There was a great cracking noise and then the form drifted forward, leaving behind a freshly torn stump that bled red sap.

One of those odd, wooden hands held Harper's knife.

It moved toward him and shook with fury. "Vile human."

Bump let out a scream and hurled his axe in a move that was pure desperation. The blade sank deep and the handle vibrated and let out a loud warbling thrum as it quivered in place.

Again the creature screamed in pain, and this time it collapsed in the snow, shuddering and convulsing. Harper's knife fell to the ground and he reached, pulling his slender blade from the hilt and then hacking furiously at the wood around his leg while it was distracted.

The thing rose again and surged toward Bump, the man's axe standing still in the hood of the creature.

One hand grabbed Bump's neck in a parody of a lover's caress, the fingers scraping flesh away roughly.

The other hand was fast and drove a thumb into Bump's right eye, tearing the organ apart.

In his life Bump had endured cuts, bruises, broken bones and a thousand scrapes. One does not live as a mercenary without getting wounded. Harper knew that none of that compared to the pain as his eye was cut open. He tried to pull back but failed. The hand holding his face was too strong.

Did he scream? Gods, yes, until his voice was raw and his throat felt bloody. After that he didn't quite black out, but slumped back bonelessly, whimpering like an old man lost in nightmares.

Harper's blade finally cut enough of the root away to let him break free. Around him half his companions were wrapped in the roots of the demonic tree-thing. The rest were circling around, looking for a way to help their friends.

Mearhan Slattery was staring; her eyes wide, her skin paler even than usual. Laram, wounded or not, took at the thing with a roar, his double-bladed axe gleaming dully as it swept around with his full body weight and sank deep into the cheek of the second child.

The hooded beast staggered back and let out a gurgled groan, as, finally, the damned nightmare understood how to bleed. Laram hit it again, and a third time, his entire body into each and every swing of that axe.

Harper didn't have the sort of raw power that Laram

had, so he chose a different tactic. He ran for his arrows and did what he did best. The first arrow sank deep into the hood despite the beast trying to avoid it. The second punched through the back of the hood and shivered in the flesh beneath it.

One long limb reached out and slapped Laram aside as if he were only a child. Rough flesh tore his skin, left him bleeding, but Laram was back up in an instant and growling. His axe sank deep into the very arm that had attacked him. It was not severed completely but it was cut over halfway through.

The great cloak flapped as the winds came out of nowhere and knocked most of the free companions to the ground. The ground ripped and shook again as the roots lifted completely free, tightening their grips on the people who were pinned.

Sallos and Jon cut themselves free of the hellish tentacles holding them before the cloak and all of those dangling roots rose into the air and flapped away into the skies.

Harper's body shook with excess adrenaline and he watched the shape disappear into the distance, never once taking his eyes from it.

"What just happened?" The Slattery girl was speaking, but he barely noticed. When she repeated the question a second time he looked her way and shook his head. "We just lost half our people."

"Are we going after them?"

Harper shook his head. "No. We don't have the time. We have to move on."

Laram screamed, furious, and looked toward Harper. He was not disagreeing, just raging.

Bump, Bos, Neely, Kano and more besides. There was no time to go after them again. They had too much to do, too far to travel. There was the hope that they would not be sacrificed, not until all of them were captured. That was the only hope, really. The thing had taken them. He didn't know where; he didn't have any notion. They were gone. Did it work for one of the kings? Did it work for the slavers?

Harper spat into the snow.

"Gather your belongings. We ride."

Mearhan spoke, "But your companions–"

"Will have to escape on their own! The world is trying to end on us. We get captured, we get taken, then the world ends that much faster!" She flinched at his tone and Harper found he didn't much care. "Did you not say it yourself, girl? We are to be sacrificed! We ride on and try to avoid that!"

Laram looked uncomfortable with his words. Harper found he didn't much care. It was time to go, that was all. They had so far to travel and there were plenty of threats to face along the way, of that he had no doubt.

Brogan McTyre

"I don't understand." Brogan spoke carefully. Really it was a delaying tactic. He'd heard the words clearly enough, but he wanted to make sure of the meaning.

"You're hardly a stupid man, Brogan McTyre." Anna's eyes stared into his. Her voice was stern, but her expression was kind enough. "That head you've been admiring. They say what you need is up there."

"Did they by chance say how I'm supposed to get up

there? I don't see an easy path."

"There are... well, there are bones to climb and surely a few of those shards will work as a bridge to get part of the way from one point to another."

Brogan looked again, slowly considering the tremendous height of the dead giant before him. Scaling the sheer cliffs that thrust from the Broken Swords would be easy in comparison to climbing the bones of the giant. There were places where climbing would be easy, around joints, for example, but much of the skeleton looked frighteningly smooth. Also there was the sheer height. How high to the top of the mountains? Almost as high to the head of the dead thing he'd been searching around for a few days.

While Anna had performed her communications, he had looked around, finding small mysteries, but nothing that long distracted from the enormous thing that filled the mountains themselves. While he walked, Faceless, as he'd come to call their silent companion, often shadowed him and did nothing else.

Intermittently he'd hear sounds in the distance, echoes that traveled from the gods knew where and every time he paused to see if he could locate the source. They weren't just noises. They were stealthy noises, like whispers in the distance and the occasional clash of items dropped or struck against a surface.

He was worried about that, but felt no need to alarm Anna as yet. Whatever he was hearing would distract her from her tasks and she needed to accomplish those if he was to know what was needed to finish this business once and for all.

He looked at Faceless and said, "I don't suppose you'd

make the trek for me?" Not surprisingly, the thing gave no answer.

Anna slapped at his arm, only half playfully. "What you need rests up there. There's nothing for it. If you would have a chance to fight against gods, you must make your way up there."

"Did these voices tell you what I might be looking for?"

"Oh, yes. They say what you seek is the life of a god."

"Say again?"

Anna stared hard at him. "So, apparently gods never truly die. It's true his flesh has faded with time, it's true even that he is nothing but bones, but apparently the life force of a god is something that does not go away, even after thousands of years."

He pointed toward the skeletal remains. "So that is still alive then?"

"No. The body is dead. Look at it. It's dead. Or at least as dead as gods get, if what I've been told is true."

"So the life of a god is up there?"

"That's as I'm told, aye."

"Why hasn't anyone ever taken it before?"

"No one knew where to look. Well, that's not quite true. A man named Roskell Turn found the information in one of the books of Galea."

"And he never did anything with that knowledge?"

"But he did. He shared it with me so that I could share it with you."

"Why did he never come for it himself?"

Anna shook her head and the look she gave him was the sort his mother had cast his way when he was being foolish at a younger age. "I can't say. Perhaps he has no need for the life of a god."

"But surely if he knew–"

Anna sighed. "Brogan, before the gods killed your family would you have had any need of something powerful enough to let you fight gods?"

"Well. No. I just mean, if I'd known…"

"Would you have climbed to the very heights you must now climb just to have something you might never need?"

Brogan stared at the distance he would have to scale and nodded. "You've made your point." He looked up and up and shook his head, "It'll take days."

"Then I'd recommend we get started."

"We? No, no. Desmond will have my hide."

"It is neither Desmond's decision, nor yours." The look she cast his way brooked no argument.

"What if you were to fall?"

"Then I suppose I will fall. What if you slip and have no one there to catch you?"

"Then at least I don't take you with me." He glared at her, and she looked back, unimpressed by his attempt to intimidate. "Then at least Desmond doesn't experience my grief."

"And while I feel for you, Brogan, Desmond won't live to experience your grief unless we get done what we must do. We've already wasted enough time while you tried to suss out what you're supposed to look for. Let's be on our way."

He clenched his teeth. "You're a vexing woman."

She made an obscene gesture and headed for a thick chunk of crystal that ran at a low angle from the ground and aimed a distance toward the skeleton. It actually touched the thigh of the impossible thing. Annoyed by her, Brogan followed Anna just the same.

Faceless followed, too, once again at a distance.

"There might be things here, Anna. Things that will pursue us or try to attack. I have been hearing sounds."

"Aye, and so have I, you daft fool."

He stared hard. "You heard them?"

"I'm not deaf, Brogan. I hear as well as you."

"You didn't say anything."

"And neither did you."

Brogan thought back to her earlier words, ignoring the useless debate about whether she should have told him what she'd heard or if he should have told her. They'd argue it soon enough, he knew, if only to break the silences that grew between them.

Finally he said, "I didn't mean to start the end of the world, you know."

Anna shook her head and cast another withering look his way. "What did you think would happen if you angered the gods?"

"I was prepared to have them take me and spare mine. I would have accepted that. I would have done anything at all to keep my family safe." His teeth ground against each other as he walked.

"Be that as it may, your plan fell through. I appreciate you're trying to fix things. If I didn't, I'd not be here." As she spoke she started up the gentle slope of the crystal and Brogan followed. The surface beneath them was sheer, but lightly angled. Up ahead the shard had facets facing in different directions, but he didn't foresee any issues, at least until they reached the bones. Bones curved, at least mostly, and he wasn't sure they would find the surface so easy.

"I'm very aware of my failings in this. That's why I'm here, too. I intend to stop the gods. Having seen this," he gestured to the massive frame of bones, "I tend to think my chances are slightly less than good. Still, it's the only option that works for me. I'll not see my companions killed for what I did."

"They knew what they were doing. Desmond and I had a very long discussion about his actions when he came home."

"Oh, did you? How did that go then?"

"He ducked the pan I threw at his head. I was kind enough not to actually take a cleaver to him. He made a promise to me, and that promise included not getting himself killed on fool's errands, no offense meant."

"I can't disagree. Just the same I'm grateful to him and I intend to see him out of this alive and healthy if I can."

"You had best." She moved faster and he followed, and knew without looking that Faceless continued with them.

When they finally stopped for the night it was out of necessity. The sun had set and the vast crystals no longer reflected the glow into the area. They sat in a small circle and despite his initial worries, Brogan barely even gave their location a second thought. While he supposed there was a chance of falling to his death if he tossed too much in his sleep, it would have to be a very long and fitful toss before he would get anywhere near the edge. The translucent stone was vast indeed and at so gentle a slope that there was no true cause for concern.

Anna managed to get a fire started, though he was

sure he had no idea how. There was little by way of kindling or firewood and yet she did it. He thanked her for that and then thanked her again when she pulled a hard loaf of bread from her sack. It wasn't much, but it was a nice change of pace from dried beef.

They didn't talk much. There wasn't much to say.

In time they slept and when Brogan awoke it was with his arm around Anna's waist and with his body spooned to hers. He moved away as carefully as he could to prevent waking her. How they wound up together he could not say but he'd not give her reason to call him names or, even worse, to consider herself unfaithful to her husband. They'd done nothing. They were fully clothed; still for some of the people he'd known in his life the fact that they had wound up in a situation like that would have been enough to cause shame.

Faceless sat across from the dead fire and stared at him with those round pits for eyes. If the thing had any thoughts about what had happened, it did not share them.

This time, Brogan was grateful for the silence.

Interlude: Lowra-Plim

Lowra-Plim crouched at the tip of one of the crystals thrusting from the mountains. It needed to mend and it needed perspective.

It felt the gods, of course, as it always had, but they seemed distant.

Lowra-Plim mended as it waited. The wounds were slower to heal than they should have been and he understood the reason. Demons were vile things, diseased and corrupt. Their servants were much the same.

The He-Kisshi did not need to speak in order to be heard by the gods. They were the divine collectors, the voice of the gods, the eyes of the gods, and their most common method of punishment.

While Lowra-Plim mended, it heard the words of the gods and understood. The world was awakening to the peril. The gods were angry and they would not be appeased without blood.

The leaders of the Five Kingdoms had been told to make a sacrifice if they wanted to survive. Even now they traveled to obey or sent messengers to handle the matter. Some headed for Gaarsen, not to ask the gods for mercy, but to conspire with the wretched beast that lay under the nearby hills, the better to betray the ones they had already disappointed.

Snow settled on Lowra-Plim and half buried the He-Kisshi; still it mended and it was aware. The gods had their plans and it would be needed soon to deliver a message and to handle difficulties that were rippling beneath a seeming calm in the world on the western side of the mountains.

So far there was winter, ice, and snow. Soft and peaceful.

That would end soon enough and the gods would make their statement.

Bron McNar

Hillar Darkraven and Opar had returned home. There was no choice, really. There were kingdoms to run and, truly, there were people to kill.

Parrish and Bron, along with Jahda and Pardume, made the exceptions. They rode together, heading for Gaarsen. For Parrish it was going home. For the others it was an attempt to find a different path to redemption. They did not speak of the matter but ultimately they intended to talk with Parrish and possibly even with his new god to see if there was anything at all that could be done about the gods and their current destructive path.

Rather than ride their horses, they shared a carriage that was as merciless as the king of Mentath. The vehicle was drawn by nine horses and covered in a thin layer of beaten metal. Around them three scores of Mentath warriors rode in formation. Where he could see their hands and arms, Bron could see the same markings that covered Parrish's flesh.

Bron did his best not to be impressed. His people were of a different stripe. They fought hard and they fought well, but they did not wear the same sort of armor as Parrish's warriors and they were not known for their ability to ride in formation. They were known for ferocity and surviving the elements. The men around him were dressed in layers of armor, some plate here and there, scales in some spots, leather and chain in others. Bron found himself wondering how they managed not to fall off the gigantic horses they rode.

Parrish smiled in his direction. "We will be there soon. You look restless."

"No. Worried. We run shorter on time than I'd like." A lie. His concern was about what would happen if Parrish decided to attack his country a second time. The king was not showing all of his forces. He was practically bragging about his military – and Bron acknowledged it was a military guard and therefore meant to show the best example of Parrish's army – but there was no doubt at all in his heart that Parrish was holding back.

Jahda looked long and hard at Bron and then turned to Parrish. "What sort of deal did you strike, Parrish? How is it that you and your finest have these markings? What do they do?"

Parrish smiled thinly as he answered. "They offer protection. They are not like armor... No, that's not true. They are like armor for the mind. The Galeans are said, some of them at least, to have abilities to steal a man's soul or to make him see what is not there."

"And what do they cost?"

Parrish looked toward Jahda and his smile fell away. "What do you mean?"

Jahda leaned back in his seat, his dark face half lost in shadows. "Gods are greedy enough. They demand sacrifices merely to be allowed to live, as we can see. Demons are supposed to be worse. Demons, I have heard, demand blood and more blood."

"Who said anything about demons?"

"I did. Either you are dealing with a powerful Galean – doubtful – or you are dealing with a god – also unlikely – or you are dealing with one of the ten Imprisoned who are locked away in this world. Gaarsen lies near the desert. The desert in the southern parts of Mentath is known to be the home of two separate demons that were used to punish the people who once lived there, just as a third is said to dwell in the north."

Parrish too leaned far back in his seat.

Bron stayed exactly where he was, interested to

know where the conversation was heading.

"My ancestors were not always wise when it came to the gods, that's true enough. Half of my kingdom is dust and sand and little more." Parrish crossed his arms. "That does not mean I follow in their methods."

"Of course not." Jahda smiled. "If you did the world would be ending because of you. Your previous kings refused to offer sacrifices or follow other laws of the gods." He was silent for a moment and the smile faded, the man's eyes seemed droopy but Bron knew better. The nominal leader of the Kaer-ru was looking for just the right words.

Finally he said, "There are no laws against worshipping other gods. The gods we have are said to have killed the ones who came before them." He gestured to the Broken Swords, where the remains of just such a deity allegedly rested. "As there were no other gods, they would not need to concern themselves. And yet, here we are and you have obviously found a patron of some sort that is not mortal. My sources say that the slavers have found another to follow, a different patron if you will. And then there are stories of a small tribe of shadow people who wander the lands and seek to take sacrifices for their new master. They come, as I understand it, from a place that is forbidden by one of your barons."

Parrish did not speak for so long that Bron wondered if the man had been struck dead.

Finally, however, he responded. "As you say, there are no laws against it."

"You continue to obey the gods. You continue to make your sacrifices. Still, you offer only what you must. I think your fealty belongs to a different master."

"You keep using that term. I have no master."

"We all serve someone else, Parrish. At the very least we serve our people and do all we can to keep them safe."

Parrish nodded. "As you say, three times Mentath has been punished by the gods."

Jahda nodded. "Gods are fickle, it seems. One offense and nothing happens. The same offense in a different place and their wrath is vast."

"As you say, I break no laws."

The leader of the Kaer-ru nodded. "That is why we travel now, yes? We must explore options. And that is why I ask you what the cost? If I am to consider what is best for my people, I must know what price they might be asked to pay."

Bron looked out the window. The snow fell heavily but none of the riders seemed to care. Even as he considered that fact the wagon rolled into a heavy stream and the horses slowed down at the urging of the carriage master.

Parrish leaned forward again and looked at Jahda and then at Bron. "There is a price, to be sure. But here I am and I have paid it and I am still me. I still rule."

"What price?" It was Bron's turn to ask.

"Fealty."

"So you have no master but the master you serve." Jahda nodded.

"As you say, we all have someone we must answer to." Parrish pointed a finger toward Jahda. "Tell me this. What is a demon?"

Jahda answered, "I do not know."

"How did the gods become gods? How did they take

down the gods before them?" Once again he looked at each of the men with him. "No answer? Very well then. I will tell you. They found worshippers."

"What do you mean?"

Parrish smiled. "Demons. Gods. They are the same thing. Some have simply not grown strong enough yet. The demons were punished for thinking they could match the gods in strength. They have been imprisoned where they could do no harm. Locked away in order to keep them from causing grief. But here is something to consider. Every cell has a door. Sometimes that door is open enough to let people through."

"To what end?"

"To let the demons gather their strength."

Bron shook his head. "You say the demons are like young gods?"

"Exactly so. They are as hatchlings waiting to grow strong enough to fly, only when they finally fly, they will move to throw down the gods who are above us all right now, just as those gods slayed their predecessors."

Jahda nodded his head, a thoughtful look on his face. "What makes you think they've grown strong enough now?"

"They haven't, friend Jahda. But they are close." He placed his thumb and forefinger in a circle that was broken with a hair's breadth between them. "They are so very close and the wise, the brave, will join them before they overthrow the gods."

"Even if they do overthrow the gods, Parrish, what good does it do us if the gods have destroyed the world?" Bron shook his head. He had no desire for false hopes as the world neared its end.

"Demons cannot create. That is what makes them weaker than gods. They can alter what they see fit to alter but they cannot create worlds or people. They need followers who are already there. To that end they will fight to save the world from the gods. They will fight alongside us."

Parrish took a long breath and looked at each of the other kings with him. His eyes focused on Pardume for a moment.

"The gods have grown old. There was a time when they created all that they needed. They answered the prayers of their followers and they served us in much the same way that we serve our people. They were not always kind, but they were fair and they gave as much as they took. That time is long ago. Look back at the legends and you'll see I'm right. The giants are gone. The beasts of wonder that once roamed across the lands have faded. The gods no longer offer rewards to the faithful." Parrish shook his head and frowned. "They merely demand more of us. They are old, they are dying, but they cling to their power and fight for every last breath."

"Where do you get this knowledge, Parrish? From your demon?"

"No." Parrish shook his head. "From the gods themselves. From the Scryers, and from the Galeans who have read from their books."

"What have Galeans to do with anything?" Bron shook his head again. He did not trust the Galeans; they were quick to tell lies, and also they used sorcery.

Jahda held up a calming hand. "There are those who say the powers of the Galeans are learned because the gods once shared their secrets."

It was Bron's turn to lean back and cross his arms.

"So, the demons plan to take on the gods and take their place as the rulers of the world?"

Parrish nodded. "That is what they have always planned. That is why they exist."

"Then why don't the gods just kill them?"

"For the same reason you do not wish to kill your son, Bron. Some day he will take your place upon your crystal throne should we live long enough for that to happen. That is what he is supposed to do. The demons do the same. Some day they take the thrones from their parents."

"Kings do not kill their predecessors."

"Speak for yourself, Dog of Kinnett. I took my birthright when the time came." Parrish spoke softly, but Bron had no doubt that he spoke true. "It is time, my friends, that new gods took the thrones from the bitter, old gods we have served for all our lives. If we are wise and we are careful, this can all work to our advantage."

Parrish leaned back again.

"First, however, we must make you an acquaintance of a demon."

Bron said nothing more, but he thought, oh, how he thought about the possibilities.

CHAPTER EIGHT
PRAYERS

Myridia

In her dreams Myridia was back in Nugonghappalur. The sun was shining and the cold summer air caressed her skin as she waded into the ocean to fish. In her dreams Bellari was beside her, his handsome face looking at hers as she studied him and thought about the mating dance that would surely come. That Bellari looked unsettlingly like Garien made perfect sense in her slumbering mind, as such abnormalities often do when sleep has finally come and freed a soul from mortal problems. In those same dreams the world still made sense, and the gods were not angry enough to destroy it, and her body was not crushed under the weight of her responsibilities to the point where most of her muscles ached constantly.

In her dreams, happiness was still a real thing and her people were still alive and free from the wretched bastard that had brought her nothing but suffering with his actions.

Myridia woke to the sound of screams.

It was pure instinct that made her grab for the hilt of her sword.

Her hand found the grip and she pulled it close, rolled to her right and was standing in a heartbeat's span of time.

And it was only then that she realized she could not see. There was nothing to see, not even a hint of light. Everything was black. Her free hand rubbed at her eyes and nothing changed.

She shook her head. She blinked a dozen times, listened on as the sounds of combat rattled and clashed all around her.

"What in the name of the gods?" Her voice cracked as she turned and tried to focus her attention on the closest noises.

"Whatever makes you think the gods have anything to do with this, my little bird?"

Not long ago that voice would have made her smile, but now the opposite was true. Garien's words sent ice running through her.

Fear was not enough to make her stop. There was simply too much at stake, and so she thought of where his voice had come from and jabbed hard at that location with her sword, Unwynn.

"Oh, so close!" His voice was loud and filled with joy, and easily a foot from where she had struck. A step forward and to the right to compensate and she tried again. Only the air tasted her steel.

Garien's hand, colder than ice, touched her face briefly and as she swung she knew it was a mistake. The attack was too wild and she lost her balance. As she tried to compensate, her foot caught a rock or some other obstacle, hard to say in utter darkness, and her momentum did the rest. Her left knee crashed into a stone and if she had not been blind already the searing pain of that blow would have been enough to do it. Still she kept the sword.

"You're very good at this." The mocking tone meant nothing. The only important thing was that he spoke from close by and directly above her. Unwynn's tip caught flesh when she thrust it upward.

Garien hissed and she felt something wet touch her arm. It was as cold as winter water in a small pond, but it was thick. She swept the sword in a short arc and Garien cried out a second time.

Rolling to her feet was not so easy this time. The pain in her knee howled and her leg felt too weak to hold her, but she managed to get into a proper stance again.

No words. She did not have time for them and she needed to hear past the sounds of combat nearby.

The cacophony was there. She recognized Lyraal's battle cry and thought it was Memni's scream that came from a distance away. Swords clashed and clattered, amid a storm of voices.

Garien dared touch her again, this time his hand ran along her back. Instead of swinging the sword she stepped back and lashed out with her free hand. As she suspected he was goading her and all she made contact with was the wind.

"It's not too late, Myridia. You can join us. Join me." His voice was a mockery. He tried to sound promising and seductive, but she could hear the laughter in his tone, rippling just below the surface. The worst part was that she knew it was a ploy and that it was working. In her soul she was still mourning the man she had known and this thing, this spawn of shadows, was toying with her.

She knew better, but she took a chance and tried to cut the bastard in half.

And missed.

The Night People, she knew, were either demons or the spawn of them. They were infected with the vile power of the very creatures the gods had sent down to the world to punish humans.

"Why are you so angry? I've made you an offer, Myridia. We can be together. We can talk as we did before and we can do so much more. All you have to do is join me, come with me. And we can be together. And your people will be safe. No one is dead yet. No one has to die."

Oh how easy it should have been to strike him, but the voice moved too quickly. It did not circle her, but came from one place and then another with no logic and she could not chase it. The ground was too uneven, as she had already learned the hard way. A misstep and she fell again, and if she fell the wrong way bones might break. Her knee was still weak, still in pain, and warmth was running down her shin.

Myridia moved one leg backward and braced in a better stance for fighting. Her arms trembled with the weight of the sword, at first light and easy and now enough to make her arms weak.

A small noise, little more than the sound of a pebble moving, and this time when she struck out the blade cut deep and Garien cried out in pain.

"Bitch! Ah, damn your eyes, you c–" She turned her

body on one foot and whipped the sword around in a hard slash. Cloth and meat parted under the strike.

Garien fell back, and she heard his body hit the ground.

Slowly, carefully, Myridia set her foot back on the ground and braced herself in a proper stance. When he spoke again it was from a few feet away. He had learned that she could sting even without her eyes.

"We are not done yet, Myridia." His voice sounded pained. She did not dare let herself smile. Demons lied. They were masters of deception. The gods warned of that constantly.

Her arms ached, the muscles in her back shook with effort; still the blade stayed at a guard position and still she listened.

Slow, steady breaths. There was nothing to be done with the sound of her heart beating too fast.

Lyraal let out a scream of rage and not far away something shattered.

"I will have you." The voice came from inches away and yet when she lashed out with her arm, there was nothing,

"You will be mine." Again, this time the breath ran across her face and her left earlobe. She drove in that direction with her body and cursed as the rock near her foot caught her toes and twisted her leg.

Finally she spoke, a small prayer to her gods. "I would serve you, my lords. For as long as you need me, I would serve you, but now I need your help."

She moved at the sound of someone panting, and though she managed to avoid the worst of it, Garien's carving blade cut across her ribs. It wasn't the blade she used, but the hilt of her sword that crashed into hard bone and soft flesh.

Garien cursed again and fell. Myridia thrust with the point of the sword and Unwynn cut into him again.

"How do you do that? You're fucking blind!"

Another thrust, and another kiss of the point into the bastard's flesh. Garien hissed and scrambled away, forgetting his attempts at stealth.

"Leave now, go far away and I will let you be." Her words were false bravado. Still, she knew she had hurt the demon-pet.

Whatever it was he threw smashed onto her just above her right eye and it was her turn to cry out. She still saw nothing, but she felt blood run down her face and into her open, blinded eye.

The fighting continued. The screams went on, pain and fury and occasionally the maddening laughter of the Night People.

Her face ached, her leg throbbed, and her muscles twitched and threatened rebellion.

One breath, barely a sigh, and again she stabbed. A miss. Again she stabbed, to the left of where she had thrust before, and this time Garien cried out again. Rather than pull back she lunged and felt the sword drive deep. There was resistance, of course, but Unwynn was sharp and her arms were strong and her weight was enough to aid in the thrust.

Garien hit the ground. She heard him fall and roll and hiss his agony into the air.

Not far away her sister cried out, a sound she had heard many times in her life, but this was different. This was a long howl of pain. She heard it, but she could not see and could not hope to reach that far without injuring herself.

Garien whimpered and the sword found him again. The flat of the blade struck him and she pushed, slapping him across his body.

Myridia said, "Lift the shadows or die."

Garien laughed, but it was a weak sound. "I do not control the shadows, little bird."

Rather than listen, she struck, stabbing into him with the point again. He stopped laughing and groaned as he tried to break away.

No. She would not have it. Myridia stabbed again and missed again, and found flesh. He was wounded and could not flee as quickly as he wanted.

"I'll see you dead, bitch!"

The blade moved to the sound of his voice and she felt flesh part and the tip slice across bone. She could not see, but supposed it was his pretty face she carved into by the way Unwynn danced.

Garien wept and despite herself, Myridia smiled.

How far her prayers had to go she could not say, but it seemed they were answered at last. The darkness broke apart and through a gray fog she could see the ruin of Garien's pretty face and his bloodied form. He was trying to stand and holding his hand over his left eye.

No words for him. Myridia stepped forward and let out a whooping battle cry. Unwynn cut deep, hacking his left arm away from the rest of his body and cutting into his ribs before she wrenched it free.

Garien staggered away, coughing blood.

The darkness was still there, but not as complete as it had been. She looked carefully as she chased after her onetime companion. It was the same everywhere she looked, the shadows clung to her followers like heavy spider webs, only giving up their positions reluctantly. The gods fought for them, the demons fought against, and neither truly seemed to hold proper sway but at least there was enough light to see.

Lyraal cut her target in half. The sword she carried dripped with gore and she stepped past the closest enemy with a snarl and moved toward the next. Myridia followed her example and took five steps toward the nearest of the Night People. He was a giant, and in a time not so long ago they had shared a meal and laughed together despite the way the world was failing.

Ian, the strongman, slapped her back with one savage blow. He did not taunt as Garien had, he did not speak at all; instead he simply attacked. Myridia's knees wobbled and then gave out as she hit the ground.

Before she could rise, a booted foot stomped down on the hand holding Unwynn. She gasped and let her weapon go as the heel crushed her hand harder.

"There we go." Garien's voice once again had its previous mirth. "That's better."

She looked toward him and saw his smile as he loomed far above her. Even as she looked, however, he was fading into darkness again.

"What is happening? What did you do?"

"I wanted to see your smile. So I gave you a lie. Silly bird. Your gods don't care about you. They didn't clear your eyes. I did. The shadows belong to us, the night is our slave. I only took it away for a moment, so you could see your friends before we kill them all."

"No!" She tried to fight, to pull her hand free, but

Garien's heel crushed down all the harder and two of her fingers flared into explosions of pain.

"Welcome back to the darkness. All you have to do is join us and this all goes away."

"Liar! You follow demons, all you know is lies."

"Say as you will." Her eyes were once again useless, and then Garien pressed down again, until another finger snapped. "Tell me, Myridia, where are your gods now?"

Interlude: Lowra-Plim

The gods, it is said, can be fickle. Some prayers they hear and others they choose to ignore. Some prayers are not to their liking and others find them if not kind at least sympathetic.

Their servants, the Grakhul, asked for help and they did not seem to notice. After a time, they changed their minds.

They gave their orders.

Lowra-Plim heard the commands of the gods and obeyed.

It shook the ice and snow away and rose from its place at the top of the mountain. Wings spread and a summoned wind lifted it into the air.

Countless eyes roamed the landscape and saw the problem. Tainted humans had wandered into and then out of a demon hive. Whatever they had been, they were no longer.

A shift of the body and Lowra-Plim dropped from the sky, catching the wind and directing its fall from the heights. From far away Dowru-Thist called out to say it was coming as quickly as it could, but Lowra-Plim felt no need to wait.

The shadow forms were winning their battle against the Grakhul. How could they not? They created darkness and blinded their enemies. It could not say if they deliberately left the pale women alive but suspected the answer was yes. More meat to taint and offer to the demon that created them. The gods would hear of this and likely expect something to be done about it.

Lowra-Plim called the wind to stop its descent, and the air blasted the area around it, sending snow, dirt and small stones skittering across the frozen ground. The Grakhul struggled on, but many of the shadow people stopped and turned to see the interloper.

They did not seem impressed.

"Go back to your masters. Leave here and leave these people."

One of the shadow people spoke. "We seek these people. They are to join us."

"They do not want to." Lowra-Plim stepped closer to the tall shape.

The shadow-thing stepped closer as well, a sword held in its hand. Like the body, the sword flicked and warped as if being cast against a dozen different surfaces, stretching and adjusting as shadows do.

"I speak for the gods on this matter. Let the Grakhul go."

"The gods have no choice in this, Undying. They are abandoning this world. Other masters rise at last."

Lowra-Plim tilted its head and slowly nodded. The shadow offered confirmation. Without words it spoke to the gods. They did not respond immediately.

"I am given mastery over all that the gods command. The wind is mine. The waters are mine. I can shatter the earth or raise mountains."

The shadow smiled. "We cannot drown. We are not made of air, and we would survive the mountains as we have the cold."

Lowra-Plim stood taller and tilted its head the other way. "Can you burn?"

"Can we...?" It hesitated, and Lowra-Plim would have smiled if it could have. The He-Kisshi were undying, true, but in most cases they could be hurt by the very elements the gods allowed them to control. Boiling water still burned, flames still ignited flesh. Knives cut and swords wounded, but when they were doing the bidding of the gods, the rules were not the quite the same. That was why Lowra-Plim could hold a raging ball of fire in its clawed hand and feel no pain, and suffer no wounds.

The fire needed no source. It was a gift of the gods. He opened his hand and the flames rose, twisting around themselves. The light it generated was not as bright as the sun, but it was bright enough to make a person squint and it was far more than capable of burning away the shadows.

Lowra-Plim threw the blaze at the shadow that had approached and watched as the tongues of flame licked across the entire form, even as it tried to flinch away. The shadows retreated from the brightness and were cast across the ground instead of standing in the air. Under those shadows a man stood, and his eyes flew wide, his mouth even wider as the flames ripped through his flesh and clothes alike.

All around the area the shadow forms scattered as the conflagration grew stronger still, until the darkness was pushed back. Rather than letting them escape, the He-Kisshi moved to the closest and touched it with burning hands. The creature shrieked with two voices, one human and the other something that had never been alive in the purest sense. Still, it burned and it died.

The shadow people ran. They did not reach for their wagons, but instead fled the area entirely, desperate to escape the flames. Three more fell victim to Lowra-Plim before they were gone.

The Undying were given many eyes and they followed the trails that the shadow people took.

Far away, but closer now, Dowru-Thist spoke in its brethren's mind and rose over the top of the mountains. It dropped fast, and then corrected its course, heading for the runaway shadow things.

The Grakhul were injured and some were likely dying. Lowra-Plim looked for the one in charge and finally found her. It had not met her before, but only days earlier Dowru-Thist had talked with the woman. She was standing, she was shaken. She had been beaten down.

Myridia held her hand and looked at the broken fingers. She was not gifted with healing. It understood her pain, but couldn't make itself worry too much. There were other matters to consider.

"Dowru-Thist hunts the last of the shadows. You are to move on. There is a river that will guide you most of the way to the Sessanoh."

She looked at him with dazed eyes.

"The gods want you to save this world. You must do

this thing. If you do not, all is lost. Your people will die."

The woman nodded and stood as best she could. Her body was battered and her injuries were many.

"Go to the waters. Swim. The gods will help you mend. The time for distraction is done. The shadows will bother you no more."

"What are they?"

"A demon's playthings. They will be eliminated."

She lowered her head and her face became a mask of sorrow.

Lowra-Plim reached out with one talon and grabbed the woman's chin, forcing her to look into its face. "Enough. These are not your people. They are not for you. They are tainted by the enemies of your gods, and they will be destroyed. You are chosen to lead. Prove worthy. Go. Now."

Without another word, the woman turned and moved toward the river, pausing only long enough to grab her sword and scabbard.

In the distance, perhaps half a mile away, a ball of flames dropped from the skies and scoured the earth, burning away a shadow and the flesh that hid beneath it. The screams were loud, and pleased Lowra-Plim's ears. What made the gods happy made the Undying happy.

Beron

The tent stank of sweat and fear. There were too many men inside it and the heat was stifling, made worse by the brazier that held three hot pokers and a few pounds of hot coals.

The men before Beron struggled mightily, but they were held by too many for their desperation to matter. Each was bound at the wrists and ankles, their faces pressed toward the ground, their feet stripped of boots and coverings.

Around the left ankle of each man a thick metal cuff had been locked in place, and between those cuffs were short lengths of chain. The men could walk in a shuffle, but could most certainly not run.

The first of the men had sores all over his face, blistered flesh where something had been attached and either fallen away or finished whatever it was that needed doing.

Beron nodded to the man holding the runaway's left ankle and lifted his hammer. The thick nail was placed against the man's heel and he fought and bucked and begged the slaver to stop, but Beron shook his head.

"You took my prisoners and ran from me. You'll not be running again for some time."

By the time he was done speaking he'd raised his hammer, and as he finished he brought the head down on the nail held in his other hand. Three hard taps and the full length of metal was driven deep into flesh, chipping the bone.

Some men fainted dead away. This one was stronger and merely screamed. His entire body shook and the men holding him cursed as sweat broke out and made holding him harder.

Beron didn't waste time savoring his victory. They would not escape again, that was the only part that mattered. The second nail went into his other foot and drew a thick stream of hot blood. He looked to one of his followers and nodded. The man came forward with a hot poker. Best not to let the runaway bleed to death. If the nails had caused him pain, cauterizing the wound was worse.

For almost fifteen minutes Beron spent his time hammering nails into the heels of foolish people. They thought to escape from slavers. Worse, they thought to escape from slavers to whom they owed money.

Each of them had secreted their gains in their clothes or in their boots. The money was gathered and given to Beron. He didn't bother to count it. That would come later.

In the meantime, for the next day the nails would remain in their feet. Only after that time would Beron pull them out, just long enough for them to think they knew how much pain they could suffer.

When they had calmed down and recovered, at least in part, from what had been done to them, Beron crouched next to the one who had talked the most and made the most threats.

"Your name is Bump." He did not ask. He did not need to. The man had identified himself when he spoke to his compatriots. Rather, they had given his name when he spoke his words of encouragement, back when he was in the same tent that had held the last group of victims.

Bump nodded his head. "Aye."

"You are a leader among these men?"

"Not a good one, as you can see."

"You are the answer to my prayers. You are a man who can see his faults." Beron stared at the man, who managed a defiant look in his direction, albeit with only one eye.

"So, Bump. You are a leader and I will speak to you as such. Know this. I am being kind. I respect your skills. But I am also extremely angry over what you and your men did to me. You took my coin and lied about where the pale slaves came from."

Bump said nothing, but his stare did not change in the least.

"So now I will tell you what I am offering you as a mercy. Behave. You will stay chained together. If you try to run, you will not get far. Do you understand?"

Bump nodded again, while a few of his men whimpered.

"Now understand this. If you try to run, any of you, I will burn out your eyes with hot pokers. Do you doubt me?"

Bump shook his head.

"Excellent. I will close the tent now. Do not be foolish; this time there will be guards posted outside and if they should fail me, they will join you. They understand that."

Beron left the tent and gestured for Orton to take the brazier. There would be no accidental deaths or deliberate suicides. They would not freeze to death in the cold but they would certainly shiver and wish for heat.

Ahbra-Sede, who had returned after its retreat from the He-Kisshi, stood near the door and watched, waited, should any of the prisoners attempt to escape.

Demon, god, whatever he might be, Ariah was keeping his word. Even now Derhe-Sede hunted through the snow and headed for the next band of renegades. Soon enough, Ariah willing, he would have his revenge against Brogan McTyre and all the rest of his dogs.

They only had to be delivered alive. To that end, when he was rested and could enjoy himself properly, he planned to start the castrations in the morning.

In the meantime it was cold and the sun was setting, and there were guards to post and plans to make. If all went according to plan they'd be crossing under the mountains soon and heading for Mentath. There was a bounty to collect and a world to save.

Harper Ruttket

Harper and his companions rode at night out of necessity. The bounty on their heads was too high, and there were things out in the area looking for them. More of the pale demons with the iron masks, and possibly other, stranger creatures. He could not say. The hooded thing had been bad. It had been powerful. It had reminded him of the He-Kisshi, who were very likely even worse and also hunted for him and his.

They'd made it far enough south that the snow was gone and replaced by warmer weather, but there was no way of knowing how long that would last in light of the world ending.

Davers rode near him at all times, his eyes alert and his posture almost as relaxed as Harper's. They had that much in common and little else. Davers was from Hollum, and from where they rode it looked like that particular city had been swallowed by the storms.

"Where are they, Harper?"

"Which they, Davers?"

"The ones we're supposed to meet up with?"

"I don't know, and that worries me. We should have run across them a long while back." He frowned as he spoke. In truth worry was a bit of an understatement. The majority of the raiders who'd helped Brogan were in that group and they were supposed to be bringing backup. As he and a few others were currently avoiding Marked Men and soldiers from Mentath, pasty-skinned demons, the Undying, slavers, and whatever else might be hunting them down, he needed all the help he could get.

Davers said, "I don't like the way this is going. I mean, all right, it's the end of the world, but I'd still like a few things to go our way."

"Well, we haven't actually been sacrificed to the gods yet. That's a plus, I suppose."

Davers shook his head and forced a smile at the attempt at levity. A moment later he shook his head. "You smell that?"

The wind shifted as he spoke and his companion caught the odors.

Like a fool Harper took in a deep breath and immediately regretted it. Sometimes ignorance was preferable to knowledge. This was one of those cases. The stench of rotting flesh and roasting meat was closer than he wanted to think about. Mostly it was the rotting flesh. Mostly. The smell of cooking meat actually made his stomach rumble, despite the carrion odor. They had run out of supplies two days earlier and had failed at all attempts to find game to hunt.

What bothered him the most was where the stench was coming from. He was guessing, of course, but

Harper suspected they were close to Edinrun. The lights he'd have expected to see were not there. The sky was cloudy enough that the city should have cast a proper glow from torches and fires. Instead there was a pall of smoke over the area. That didn't bode well. That much smoke meant a great deal of burning. Judging by the carrion scent and the meat that mingled with it, he could guess what was burning.

They moved on cautiously, doing their best to make as little noise as possible. As they moved east the smell grew worse and the lights made themselves known. For all they could see, it seemed that Edinrun might well be on fire.

"This is a problem." Harper shook his head.

"What's the concern?"

"This is Edinrun, yes?"

Davers thought about that for a moment and then nodded. "Aye."

"That's where the lads were supposed to be coming from. Might be the reason we haven't seen them is that they were stuck in the city when whatever happened took place."

They continued on, silence growing into an uncomfortable dread.

When Davers spoke again, his voice was softer than usual. "You think the Mentath we saw before came this way?"

"We went south to avoid them, but it's possible. We're near the southern gates. If they approached the northern gates we'd have never seen them."

"That wasn't a big enough lot to take on the whole city, was it?"

Harper looked around and took in details. There wasn't much to see. The gates were not yet in sight, and all they could make out of the city was the wall that surrounded it and the layer of smoke above it. There were markings on the wall, dark stains that he thought might be blood. A lot of marks, a lot of blood. Not far away from the wall were two massive stacks that he suspected were corpses. They were a good distance away and they were no longer burning. They were stacks that had already been burned, judging by the smoke, and here and there embers glowed in the mountainous heaps. Not dozens of corpses, nor even hundreds. Likely thousands. Enough to make his guts try to pull deeper into his chest. Mentath believed in burning the dead. They also didn't leave their fallen enemies to rot on the battlefield, and that was one he knew from experience. Like as not they'd made a few bonfires and roasted the dead.

"We'll not be visiting Edinrun," he said eventually. "We move on. We go to the damned docks of Torema."

"What about the rest of us?"

"Nothing to be done about it. There's too big a price on us. They might be captured already. They might be dead – in which case we are well and truly fucked. I think the Marked Men are here and I think they've taken Edinrun. Whatever the case, there's death and little else here right now."

Davers looked at him and then looked away, his eyes wide and his mouth hanging open. "I've been to Edinrun. It's a vast city, Harper. Vast. With so many people."

Harper looked at the distant fires. "I see two huge

pyres, Davers. I'm guessing there's more."

Davers nodded and they signaled the rest to follow. No one argued. They were mercenaries, and they knew what death looked like. Harper suspected none of them were in a hurry to get reacquainted with it sooner than they had to.

Their circuit around the southern side of Edinrun was long, and along the way Harper counted thirty-seven additional funeral pyres.

He was grateful they traveled at night, as were the people who rode with him.

"What do you suppose happened?" Emmett was a capable fighter and loyal to a fault. As with so many of them he had offered his aid to Brogan.

Mearhan Slattery was the one who answered. Her voice was low and husky, her face was lost in shadows. "The gods happened. This is the Second Tribulation. They had the He-Kisshi bring madness to the city and if we're wise we'll be away from here as soon as possible. The Undying are nearby and coming closer."

"Why?" Emmett looked at the girl and frowned. He almost always frowned.

"People, I don't know who, could well be your lot, have interfered with the will of the gods and will now be punished for the efforts."

"What sort of punishment?" Emmett again.

Mearhan looked up at him and shook her head. "I don't wish to be close enough to know the answer to that. If madness and floods are considered the least of the tribulations, then I want to be well away from whatever comes next."

Harper nodded his head. "We should move faster

then. The road is mostly clear." To prove his point he urged his horse to a gallop. They moved quickly down the highway. Harper made certain to keep an eye on their surroundings, in case any of the madness had spread beyond the walls of Edinrun.

Tully

Looking down on Torema in the daylight, they'd seen the Kaer-ru islands in the distance. Now that they were in the city proper and night had come again, they saw only Torema.

The city was old. Surely older even than Hollum, and the streets wound into a serpentine maze that crept up hills and back down to flatter land with no consideration of where those streets might end. Everything smelled of the sea. There were other odors, to be sure, but most could only barely be found past the stench of fish at the docks and the constant wafting breeze that carried the ocean with it, along with the fog.

The slavers seemed relaxed enough. That was a good sign in Tully's eyes.

They were, as a whole, rather solemn. They'd been riding for days and all they had to show for it were saddle sores and the memory of watching Niall Leraby get carried into the sky by a nightmare. That very same creature was likely to come back, at least for Tully and possibly for others. Temmi had hurt it. Stanna had actually killed it, cut its damned head clean off and then burned the head. That should have been enough, but Undying meant just that.

And it wanted her. There were plenty out there that

wanted a piece of Tully. Mostly for imagined crimes, sometimes for real ones, but the Undying made the rest of them pale in comparison.

The name of the place where they stabled the horses was unknown, but the name of the inn next door was the Broken Bow. Tully had no idea who came up with the names of most taverns but they often seemed at a loss for cheerful titles in her experience. In this case the sign above the inn depicted a ship with a hole in the underbelly. She knew nothing of ships, but guessed that was something to do with the name.

The inside of the place was nicer than she expected. The wooden walls were polished, the floor was covered with rugs and the chairs were solid. The clientele looked like they understood what bathing was all about. That went a long ways for her.

Stanna sauntered over to the bar and loomed over the man who stood there. "You have rooms?"

He looked up at her and nodded, very possibly terrified to do anything else. "Aye."

"Baths?"

"Aye."

"Food?"

"Mostly fish. Have a roast going but it'll be a few hours."

"Baths and rooms first then. How many rooms do you have?"

He looked at the group with her. "Not enough for all of you. Five all told."

"We'll take what you have. Is there another inn nearby?"

He nodded again. "Black Wings is on the next corner.

They've good rooms, but no tavern."

"So we eat and drink here and my lads go over there to sleep."

"I'd be quick about getting the rooms. A lot of people are coming to town right now."

She nodded her head. "Rhinen, see to the rooms." She opened the purse at her belt and threw him coin enough to buy the damned place. He caught the coins easily and moved out into the street. Two men looked like they planned to follow him, but Sans and another slaver blocked them before they could leave the place.

There might have been a fight, but the slavers had the numbers. A moment later both of the men were dragged outside by eight men and, she had no doubt, were convinced to behave themselves.

The innkeeper looked on and nodded. "I might have two more rooms for you."

"They'll be left alive, but I'll take the rooms just the same."

The man behind the bar nodded. "Relax. Get comfortable. I'll have baths drawn up. There are only two of them, but they can hold three or more comfortably."

Tully settled herself in a chair and Temmi joined her. A moment later Stanna sat down with three mugs of ale. Tully drank deep.

Temmi spoke softly. "We should find a scryer."

"What for?" Stanna wiped a mustache of foam from her upper lip and belched softly. The mug was already empty. Rather than rise from her seat she gestured to the man who ran the place and he hurried over with replacements.

Temmi looked at Stanna and sighed. "Because I want

to know what happened to Niall. And I want to know if that thing is really coming back for us."

"Scryers work for the kings, yes?" Tully only knew what she had been told. In her entire life the only scryer she'd ever met had been Temmi's mother, and that woman had long since been retired from the job. Also, being dead at the hands of the very same He-Kisshi, she was in no position to offer aid.

Temmi nodded. "Except there is no king here. There are scryers, if you know where to look."

"Do you know where to look?"

"No. But I'll find one just the same."

"You'll need a guard."

Temmi shook her head. "I'll be fine."

"Yes you will, because Butch and Loro are going with you." Stanna's voice grew louder and at their names two of the slavers got up. Butch was a thin man with a very large mustache. Loro was short, swarthy and balding, with a beard he kept trimmed short and the worst teeth Tully had ever seen. "Lucky you. Loro is from here. He can probably point you to a scryer."

Temmi did not argue, though it was obvious she considered the idea.

Tully and Stanna shared a bath, while four of the men cleaned themselves in the next one over. It didn't seem possible to get as dirty as they had, especially spending as much time as they had in the rain, but there it was. The men looked, but that was all right. She looked right back and so did Stanna.

The water was still mostly clear when they got out and the next group didn't hesitate.

By the time they were dressed and back down the

stairs, Temmi and her escorts had returned.

"That didn't take long." Stanna sat down and pointed to the stairs. "Up there to the left if you want a bath."

"Soon."

"What did your scryer say?"

"Ohdra-Hun, the Undying, will be back here soon. He will come alone."

"Well, that last part is nice."

"He's no choice in the matter, the rest will be hunting for the same fool that sold your lot the false slaves. Seems he's the one that angered the gods."

"Not a wise man." Stanna gave Temmi her undivided attention. "What else did your scryer say?"

"Hollum is gone, washed away. Most of the people from there are heading here. The news of Edinrun has reached them and they are avoiding the city."

"Good thing I've rented us rooms, then."

Tully nodded enthusiastically. She also considered the price that was likely on her head among certain people heading here from Hollum. If the Blood Mother was alive, it was a certainty that she would offer a bounty on Tully. Theryn was not a forgiving woman, especially to thieves she believed had stolen from her.

Four men in leather armor walked into the place, followed by a dark-haired woman with short hair and a sword on her hip. She walked with authority. She walked like Theryn, and looked to be roughly as friendly.

The woman looked around the room for all of three seconds and then moved toward Stanna.

"You are as tall as I'd heard." It might have been a smile. It might just as easily have been a sneer. Tully could not decide.

Stanna looked at the woman and nodded. "You'd be Hillar Darkraven?"

"Aye. And you're Stanna, of the slavers."

"A few of my lads have told me the slave trade is likely gone. I'm inclined to agree." Stanna pushed her chair back and stood in one easy, fluid motion. She towered over the other woman, who seemed utterly unimpressed by her height. "But I'm still Stanna."

Hillar nodded. "So you are. I've need of a few good mercenaries and you seem like you might be in the mood for a new line of work."

Stanna smiled. "How did you know I'm in town?"

"Well, first, you came with over forty slavers in tow. Second, my scryer mentioned it."

Temmi immediately found the markings on the table in front of her extremely interesting. Stanna cast her a small glance and nodded.

"And what would you like me to do?"

Hillar pulled out a chair at the table and sat down, craning her neck to stare at Stanna until the other woman took a seat.

"Why does the woman who owns this city need mercenaries?"

"Because the Marked Men are coming and they seek war."

Stanna leaned back in her seat and gestured to the innkeeper. She wanted food. The man hastily brought it. He knew exactly where his money was coming from and he was glad to provide.

"Why would the Marked Men come here? No disrespect, but this is hardly the first place they could attack."

"They've already taken Edinrun." It was possible that Hillar expected that proclamation to make people shiver, but she was wrong.

"Edinrun was overtaken by madness. Anyone foolish enough to go in there is likely to go insane, and even if they don't, the area is being watched by the Undying, who don't like people interfering. It's the work of the gods, after all."

"So my scryer has said. But they've taken it just the same. As I hear it, they'll be coming here next, and they aren't interested in surrender. They want to destroy as many people as they can."

"To what end?" Tully could keep her tongue no longer.

The woman who apparently ruled all of the city did not look at Tully so much as studied her. "They've found a god they like better than the ones who are ending things. They are making that god happy with sacrifices. Lots of sacrifices."

Tully laughed. She didn't mean to, but it came out of her anyway, a wild shriek of amusement. "Are there no gods that don't demand sacrifices?"

"Not as I've seen. No." Hillar stared at her as if she might possibly be dangerous.

Stanna spoke up. "I can't say for my lads, but I'd fight for you. Of course, forty men aren't going to mean shit to the likes of the Marked Men. I'd suggest you hire more."

Temmi looked at Stanna as if she'd grown a second nose that was wandering lazily across her face.

Stanna ignored the look.

Hillar Darkraven shook her head. "You misunderstand.

I have an army. What I need are people to lead. I want you as one of my generals."

"By all the gods, why?"

Hillar pointed to the room full of men, including a few who were currently coming down the steps having washed the worst of their stench away. "Because as big as you are and as fierce as you are, you manage to command these lads. I know from my own experience how hard that is for a woman to manage."

Stanna shook her head. "There's no secret to that. Pay them a fair wage and they are yours to command."

"It's more than that. You know it, too. There's respect to consider. They respect you. I need generals who are respected by their teams."

"Last I heard generals commanded a tidy sum. I would need a very tidy sum to lead men I've never met."

Hillar chuckled deep in her chest and leaned toward Stanna. "There's nothing left out there. Not on this side of the Broken Swords. Everything is going to shit. All of it. The only way I get to keep what is mine is by spending. You'll have your money as I'll have the coins from every last refugee coming to overtake my city."

Stanna looked at the leader of the city and nodded her head. "We'll work out the exact wages. I'll be choosing my own as commanders. Need to see what you have by way of troops."

"In the morning is soon enough. You're welcome to stay here. Or if you like you and yours could be guests at my place."

"Tomorrow is soon enough for that, too, Lady Hillar." Stanna looked around. "We want food and rest for now. Tomorrow. Might come see you then if you point the way."

Hillar rose from her seat. "Halfway up the hill. Look for the palace. There's only the one."

Stanna nodded her head as the innkeeper came with cuts of meat and bread. "Aye. We saw that on the way in. I expect we can find it again."

Hillar waved casually and then she and her men were out the door.

Stanna took her knife and cut the bloody meat on the platter before her. Tully did the same as soon as the plate was set down. She was hungrier than she'd realized.

Temmi grabbed food as well, slapping the roast onto a cut of bread and chewing noisily.

Around them the men were being served and they too made their share of noise.

Stanna said, "Fancy that. I'm a general."

Temmi replied, "Do you suppose anyone's going to win this war?"

Stanna nodded again. "I expect the Marked Men will, unless the He-Kisshi get to them first."

Tully nodded her head. "I reckon there's a first time for everything."

"How so?"

"I'm hoping the Undying win their argument with the Mentath."

Stanna nodded her head in agreement. "Just so long as they leave a few for us to fight. Can't get paid if there's no work to do."

CHAPTER NINE
RIVERS OF BLOOD

Interlude: Captain Odobo of Corrah

The sea was calm, and Captain Odobo smiled to himself. Their passenger had paid in the coins of the gods and he was not foolish enough to refuse passage to the Undying. Four coins to take the cloaked shape from Corrah in the Kaer-ru to a place where the land was lost and the ocean stretched on for eternity.

The creature left them to themselves and they in return did little but offer it food and water as they followed the directions they'd been given.

There was little enough to see. The waters stretched on as far as a man could look and above them the clouds were almost as dark as night. By all rights the winds and the waves should have been crushing the life from the vessel and Odobo knew it, but the Undying had powers, and right now the water was serene and the air was a light breeze that pushed them in the right direction.

Lendre stood nearby and the expression on his first mate's face said that he felt exactly the same way. They'd served together for ten years and knew each other well. Lendre looked his way and nodded, offering a small, tight smile.

There was a chance on any given day that the people who hired them for trips into the ocean might well feed whatever lived beneath the waves, but not on this occasion. Not at this moment. The Undying were vile things, but they were also servants of the gods.

Odobo did not serve all the gods, but he offered endless gratitude to the nameless god of the sea. Not nameless, not truly, but the name changed as often as the tides, and so names did not matter.

The Undying sighed and that cowled face turned toward him. Deep inside the darkness that hood offered, something moved, shifted and then the words came. "She has ten thousand names. But you do not need to know them. Simply continue to serve her and she will treat you with kindness. You have offered her sacrifices again and again in the course of your lifetime. She is grateful for all that you have given her, even if you were unaware of what your actions offered."

Odobo nodded and bowed formally as acknowledgment of the words. He was not sure if the Undying could read his mind or not. He did not care. The nameless god of the seas had offered thanks and he could do little else in return.

"She has always been kind to me. How then, could I be anything less?"

Again that hood turned and he saw the endless tiny eyes around the edge, black glassy beads that he suspected saw so much more than he could.

"Would you see her?" So softly spoken, but the

captain heard and his heart soared.

"Is that permitted?" Did he believe in the gods? Of course, but the thought that he might be allowed even a glimpse of one, especially the nameless god of the sea, was more than even the most faithful dared hope for.

"Only the gods can decide, but we are here because I am summoned and must now do the bidding of the gods."

Odobo nodded his head and smiled. "If it is the will of the gods then I gladly comply."

The Undying stood on the deck where it had been squatting for most of the last few days and threw wide its cloak-like wings. The air changed in that instant, the wind rising and the waves swelling.

The ship beneath them was unaffected as the waves moved, swelled and rose into the air around them. The deck tilted a bit as the waves moved, but they were not swept up or crushed and that by itself was enough to let Odobo feel he had been blessed, for the gathering waves rose higher and higher, some towering twenty feet above the mast of the ship and others rising five times that height. By all rights they should have been ruined if even one of those waves came toward them, but the Undying kept them safe. Or the gods. He was not certain that there was a difference.

The waters froze around him. They did not become ice. They simply stopped moving.

Odobo felt his heartbeat increase as he looked at the waves and columns of water that had risen high around him. Lendre ran from side to side of the ship, looking over the bow, looking past the starboard side and the portside as well, his eyes bulging. He had a mad smile on his face and his hands shook and flopped like fish caught and left on the deck to die. He did not speak, but he laughed softly and constantly, barely even taking the time to breathe. Several of the other men on the deck had fallen to their knees in supplication.

Lendre saw it first and pointed, his voice too high and his words incoherent.

Down in the depths, under the impossibly still waters, something moved. It seemed to rise slowly or simply to grow. There was no way to know for certain. In any event, whatever it might be, it was vast, far larger than the ship.

There was a moment when Odobo was certain whatever was down there was going to keep rising and swallow his crew as easily as a shark might swallow the tiniest minnow. Instead it stayed where it was and something, a small sampling of it perhaps, rose to the surface.

The shape was humanoid. He could not say what it was made of, but it was darker than the water and devoid of true features.

The Undying sang a keening song that made Odobo's ears hurt and his eyes shake in their sockets.

When the thing in the water responded, the sounds were a hundred times louder. He fell to the deck of his ship and covered his ears, squeezed his eyes tightly shut and clenched his teeth.

How long did they speak? Odobo could not say. He was thrilled to be in the presence of a god, or even a servant of a god, but he could not look up and he could not truly understand what was said. All that mattered during that time was the discomfort and the feeling that if he did anything wrong he would be destroyed.

He dreaded the idea of being noticed.

Eventually the conflagration of sounds ended and Odobo dared look up.

The shape in the waters was gone and the waves were settling back into the sea.

The Undying faced him and gestured with its hands. "Did you see?"

"Was that truly her?" His voice trembled.

"One of her names. Each name has a different face."

Odobo nodded and slowly stood back on his feet.

"What happens now?"

"Now she will prepare for her part in what must happen." The Undying turned and looked back at the waters. "We should be away from here before she moves again. She will be relentless."

Interlude: Morne

All around Edinrun the dead burned.

Within the walls of the city the Mentath settled their tents and waited. There was some concern at first that the regular foot soldiers and cavalry might well go mad, but nothing seemed to happen. That was just as well. There was no benefit in separating the troops.

Just as well; it would have been a challenge to haul all the corpses without them.

Morne and Verden sat across from each other at a makeshift table and ate as they studied the maps. The food was standard rations. Nothing within the city was to be eaten, in case it might carry madness. A dozen teams had already gone out and retrieved barrels of water for men and horses alike. The maps were likely not accurate, but they would do in a pinch.

"We're to take Torema." Verden sounded a bit surprised by that every single time he said the words, and he had uttered them a dozen times.

"Torema is just a city, same as any other," Morne replied. It was a lie and they both knew it. The city was not like others. It was a massive, sprawling port. Worse, it was populated by the exact sort of people who would fight for what was theirs with everything they had.

Most places, an army showed up and the locals were likely to just surrender, especially in smaller towns. Most people weren't fighters. They might beat their chests and talk of how they would fight, but it wasn't true. Most of them took one look at an invader and offered no resistance, because most people didn't care as long as they were left alone.

That was one of the tricks that they'd learned from King Parrish. The smaller cities around his country had surrendered long ago for that very reason. A ruler could demand an army, but an army made up of farmers who needed to tend their crops tended to ignore the call to arms.

Parrish said he'd made it a point to never attack a village. They just rode past and concentrated on the capital cities. As a result Mentath was the largest country in the five kingdoms. The smaller areas around them, the ones that were settled but until Parrish had no true rulers, had been swallowed over the last two decades. The sole exception was Stennis Brae, which was the proving ground of all of Parrish's later attacks. His first mistake, and he admitted it, was attacking the smaller areas and claiming them as his own. Those that were killed could not fight back, but towns nearby could and did. And they fought hard.

"We've no choice. It's what Parrish wants. It's what Theragyn demands."

"This..." Verden gestured around them. "This was easy. No one fights well if they've lost their senses. Torema is different. You know that, Morne."

"That's why we're here, isn't it? To help decide the best way to attack?" Cantin Hallsy had sent his best officers to different areas to consider the maps and what strategies might work to cover the area. The captain had his own ideas, but he also liked to ask those under him to suggest the best methods of attack. They were well trained and the exercise made them better. There was a chain of command and they'd follow it, but even the captain understood that Marked or not, they were not indestructible. They were just good at their jobs. Always best to make the troops better.

Always best to be prepared if Hallsy got himself killed.

"I'm thinking fire." Morne ran her finger along the northern edge of the city on the map. "Winds from the storm front might well help the blaze run down the hills."

"I'm not sure if the storm front will do it. The breeze from the ocean in Torema is always strong."

"Well, I like the idea of a fire to soften them. We have oil." She gestured to the stacks of supplies they'd already taken from the city. Nothing edible, but there were always other things. "We hardly need to waste any effort. Crack the barrels and drop a torch or two, then retreat."

He opened his mouth to protest.

"Yes, I know, the wind, but there are hills that should block at least a part of that sea breeze of yours, and they'll help hide the attack until the blaze is going strong."

A large and rather heavy bell rang four times in the distance. Too many people used horns. The bell was their alarm in case anything unexpected happened, like an army coming along.

They were not that lucky.

The shapes dropped from the skies and landed near the command tents. Captain Hallsy had unwanted guests. A quick gesture was all it took and both of them headed for the command tents, with a score of Marked Men following along.

The argument had started well before they got there.

One thing to hear about them. Another to see. The Undying were nightmares made flesh and they stood apart from each other, each looking around at the surrounding soldiers. All save one, who stood before the captain.

Hallsy looked understandably nervous, but he didn't back down.

"We were asked by King Opar to take back his city, he said nothing of 'tribulations,' and he certainly didn't tell us the city was off limits by decree of the Undying."

The thing gestured with one taloned hand and Morne looked at the long claws, imagining that they'd rend flesh with ease.

"King Opar will be punished for his insolence." The thing moved closer to Hallsy, who stayed his ground but with noticeable effort.

"Well then, if you'd like we can leave straightaway."

"You no longer follow the gods." The words were a statement.

"We have always obeyed the laws of the gods. Mentath has kept with sacrifices and all demands."

"You are 'Marked,' with the words of the demon Theragyn."

"As our king commands."

The Undying came closer still, until the hood of the thing was inches from Hallsy's face. Hallsy stared with wide eyes, but did not retreat.

"Your king has broken with the gods. You have broken with the gods. Those who walk with demons are subject to the same treatment."

"You would lock us away? Where?"

Captain Cantin Hallsy made a single gesture with his hand. It was a silent command that the man had never once used in his long command. He demanded that his troops retreat.

Morne did not question, but obeyed.

She repeated the gesture to her followers and they turned on their heels and moved with her, back into the darkness, and toward the northern gate of the city. It was the closest of the gates and, just as importantly, it was open.

By the time she had reached her tent the screams had begun. She dared not look back, and she didn't need to. She knew the sound of Hallsy's voice, had heard him give countless commands. Whatever it was the Undying did to him, it brought out a sound she would never have expected and would likely never forget.

The horses had no gear but their bridles and that

hardly mattered. Saddles were nice, but could be replaced. It took an effort, but she managed to climb on the charger's back and then headed for the gate at a hard run. The horse obeyed.

The sky was cloudy, but both moons shone down. Emila was full and Harlea was close. There was enough light to let her see the shadow of something descending from above.

One of the Undying hovered in the air above the northern gates, and the horse that was so very well trained looked at the thing and reared back, slowing to a halt. She was lucky she kept herself seated on the beast's back. Several of the men behind her were not as fortunate.

There was a pit of shadows where a face should have been. The great cloak of the beast was open and shivered in a breeze that she felt blow across her body as she moved toward the thing.

"I will spare you the pain of trying to leave," it said. "The gods have made their punishment known. You are bound to the city you sought to cleanse of the gods and their influence."

"What do you mean?"

The voice was cold, detached. "The gods have spared your lives, as your captain requested. But you may not leave the city of Edinrun. Your fate is that of the demon you serve. You are removed from this world."

Morne shook her head and sent her horse forward. It hesitated, but she insisted and finally the stubborn gelding moved, treading at a light trot until it reached the open gates.

The horse stopped when its muzzle pushed against something.

Morne did not hesitate. She urged the horse to turn and then reached her hand out to the open gate. Her hand touched a barrier that was not there. She pushed, hard, and almost unseated herself. Behind her one of the Marked Men took a chance and fired an arrow at the gate. The missile slid through the opening effortlessly.

Morne hit the air and felt the impact run up her arm to her elbow.

The Undying spoke. "The gods are merciful in their way. Edinrun is safe from storm and wind, the madness has been lifted. You will remain here as your world begins to collapse."

"What do you mean?"

The head under that hood tilted to the left and the voice that came out had an edge of humor she did not like. "Am I not clear? You suffer the same fate as your demon lord. You are no longer a part of the world. You are separate. You will live here. You cannot leave." Without another word it moved, sliding backward on the breeze until it slipped past the gate and then rose on the air, unfettered, free of whatever barrier locked Morne into the city they'd cleared.

Morne did not panic. Panic was for the weak, and so she suppressed the tremble that worried her guts. Nothing was written in stone, not yet at least.

Still, she thought as she touched the air that would not yield to her, this is a problem that will require work.

Beron

They came at night, and they attacked with fury.

The hounds cut loose with an unholy racket, and

Beron cursed under his breath. He'd just, finally, managed to wander into a proper sleep and now the damned things were starting up. He could not ignore them. That would be foolish. They were well trained to behave themselves.

He crawled from his bedroll and rearranged his cloak around his shoulders. A moment later he was out of the tent and staring into the night.

That was when he heard the screams of people.

"What's happening?" He asked the question of the cloaked shape next to him. One of his two remaining servants. It had come back with one straggler from the list of men wanted by the Mentath.

Ahbra-Sede replied, "There are hounds circling the camp. They have started attacking."

"How many, do you know?"

"At least forty."

He scowled at the thing. "Get rid of them."

The hooded shape nodded and then rose into the air. As it rose, more of the vile bugs that filled it fell free and skittered into the snow. Beron made sure to avoid getting near the things. They were unsettling at best.

Beron let out a piercing whistle and waited as more of the men came from their tents. He'd have a chat with them soon. They should have been out with him when the dogs started their noise. Instead they stayed in their beds and pretended not to hear, or worse, actually failed to hear the sounds.

The arrow caught him in the meat of his shoulder and Beron let out a roar. He pulled it free easily enough. It was not barbed and he was grateful for that. Still, close enough that a few inches and it would have been buried in his neck.

Spear and sword. He dropped into a crouch and began moving. He would find out who was responsible and he would make them pay.

The colors showed up easily enough and Beron felt his heart sink. Stennis Brae. The bastards had come for him and his prisoners again. Surely they would be better prepared this time.

The hound that came at him was proof of that. It was a brute, four feet at the shoulder and moving too fast for him to see much beyond the teeth in that face.

The spear came around and he thrust, and the bastard moved out of the way. A second later the teeth he'd seen were buried in the meat of his calf and Beron bit back a shriek of pain and focused on killing the damned mutt. Flesh and meat tore in his leg and his spear came down on top of the mongrel, driving through the body and pinning the damned thing to the ground.

It let go of his leg as it died, and Beron gasped at the pain. He was bleeding and badly.

Another hound came for him but his own pet took care of it. The black-garbed thing caught the dog in its claws and hurled it into the air as easily as Beron would throw an apple. The hounds were everywhere and his own were penned up. He could hear them barking and growling in the distance.

Beron limped for the pens. Maybe they could even the odds. Another arrow hissed past him and Beron turned to look back. The soldiers were prepared this time, and they intended to take what they wanted from the slavers. Beron disagreed and meant to show them they were wrong.

One of his men called out to him, but whatever he meant to say was stopped by the arrow that pierced his lung. The man went down, grimacing.

The sword and spear gave him confidence, but that didn't stop his shoulder from bleeding and didn't take away from the blood flowing freely down his leg.

He didn't see the arrow, but he felt it. His cloak took the worst of the damage, thank Ariah, but the tip still settled like a fire against his left shoulder blade. Another stuck in his thigh and left the slaver terrified about his survival.

Give him a sword and he'd match anyone. Arrows were a cheat.

His cloaked monster came to his rescue, moving behind him and spreading its wings, letting the arrows hit it instead of him. He moved faster to get them where they needed to be. All around him others were fighting or dying. The hounds were everywhere and they were savage. One of his men went down with two hundred pounds of war dog ripping his throat away. When it was done it charged at someone else, but thankfully not toward Beron.

Fast-moving black shapes skittered over the snow and threw themselves at the enemy dogs. The animals were well trained, but in the end they were animals: when they were attacked by the unholy creatures, they fell away from the fight and tried to save themselves, ultimately failing. Each that fell collapsed in on itself as whatever the shapes truly were feasted on them and drank them dry of bodily fluids.

When the shapes moved on they were swollen red with the blood of their victims, but they moved just as fast toward the next hound.

Behind him the servant he'd been given let out a scream. He felt its collapse more than he saw it, but still he turned and looked. Close to fifteen arrows stuck from its back. The archers were coming closer, marching in unison. His men were not marching. They were running from dogs, and they were getting cut down by arrows. The warriors from Stennis Brae hadn't even drawn a sword that he could see.

He'd almost made it to the pens when the spear took him in his right arm. The head of the thing cut through the meat of his forearm and came out the other end. The pain dropped Beron to his knees, and he coughed once and then vomited out his last meal. His sword fell from numbed fingers and his spear dropped from the other hand.

Two hounds came for him. They were enormous, and they were terrifying. One lunged, ready to tear his face from him, but the sound of a man's voice stopped it.

"Do you yield?" The question was asked as casually as if the man speaking was chatting about the weather.

Beron looked at his reflection in the steaming puddle of vomit and then pushed back until he was on his knees and both arms were before him.

Ulster Dunally spoke a second time. "Do you yield?"

Beron did not speak, as he didn't trust his voice. But he answered just the same with a slow nod of his head. A dozen men with spears stood behind their commander and they were looking at him as he'd often looked at new slaves.

After a moment he finally managed words. "Aye. We yield."

The choice was simple: live or die. Dead men couldn't fight back, or escape.

He did not warn the northerners about the dead thing and how it would want a new body. He had lost, and he was not a good loser.

When the time came and the dark cloak peeled itself from the dead host, he listened on as a solider from Stennis Brae was taken. It was a small victory, but he took it.

In the long run that decision cost him dearly.

Interlude: Seeds

The last of the reborn died, torn apart by the hounds it sought to feed on. During the commotion no one saw it die, nor did they see it take one of the slavers and wrap him in its form.

The slavers and their victims were taken by force, restrained with chains and dragged away into the bitter cold. There were wagons and supplies – those were commandeered and used.

When the people had left and taken their hounds, their horses and their supplies with them, all that remained was debris.

It was there that the remainders hid away in the cold.

The He-Kisshi see much, but they did not look. The gods made demands and so they rose into the air on the winds they cast, and they soared off to follow those very demands.

The seeds that had fallen from Desmond's face breathed, their shells expanding and slowly cracking. The cold was such that they might never have moved at all, never have grown, but though the seedmaker was gone, the entity behind them, Ariah, was still vital and made certain its desires were satisfied.

Each seed was fed by the blood of hounds stolen by the insects that had feasted during the fight. The hard, black insects wrapped themselves around the delicate seeds, their legs interlocking until the seed was protected from the cold and elements in a hard, chitin crust. Then the stolen blood was released, and the seeds were fertilized in warm nutrients converted by the bodies of the insects.

When that was done the dark lumps rested in the falling snow.

And finally the Iron Mothers came for them.

When they had first been created, the pale-skinned abominations with iron masks over their faces had numbered over two hundred. There were fewer left now. They had found most of the humans who had triggered the end of the world and delivered them to Beron or followed them until they entered the city of Edinrun, where the Second Tribulation held sway. Those that entered were destroyed, marked as tainted by demons and eliminated instantly. They were quick to learn, but not fast enough to capture the humans that passed the walls of the city.

Instead they hid, and waited until the final fate of those people was known.

The demands of the gods would not be met. The world would end. That is what the Iron Mothers told Ariah, and that was what the demon accepted, though he suspected there were ways around the issue. The gods liked to eat too much to kill all of their cattle.

Of course, there were other worlds, other stars they

could find if they wanted to expend the effort. To Ariah's way of thinking the gods had long grown old and lazy, which was why he and his brethren made their own plans.

The Iron Mothers gathered the seeds and took them into their bodies. Some of them were still intact, had remained uninjured by their exploits, but others were scarred and battered and barely had the strength to move on.

Though it cost the demon greatly, Ariah offered his essence to the weakest among them, giving them life when death would surely have claimed them. To all of the Iron Mothers he gave his essence, strengthening them for what came next.

All of them moved together. Some ran on two feet, others ran on four limbs. It did not matter so long as they worked together to reach their destination.

As they ran, their skin hardened like a crust of bread. Under that flesh their new forms would fester, changing as a caterpillar changes. The metamorphosis would be slow, but it would take place. Transformation is often painful.

Still, as has been said before, the demons could not create life, they could only alter it.

Ariah stayed locked in his prison for now. Around him his plants grew, his vines moved, and the dead remained dead. Seeds, once planted, needed time to grow. Soon enough it would be harvest time.

Interlude: Daivem Murdrow

Daivem eyed the caravan coming toward her and let out a soft sigh. The wagons and banners bore the royal colors of Giddenland, which she only knew because she had studied a scroll in her brother's offices. Giddenland was the very place she had just traveled through as she walked north and west, following the call.

It was seldom she walked so far to follow a summons, but in this case the source of the call had soared through the air, carried by winds and worse, until it fell like a star.

Now, nearly close enough to see her target, there was this to consider.

The driver of the first wagon called out to a man next to him, who in turn used a horn to call out to the next in line even as the first pulled to a halt before her.

Daivem Murdrow looked around. There was little to see here but snow and ice, and yet here they were, stopping as if she might be some vast, insurmountable obstacle.

"What happened here?" the driver demanded of her.

Daivem looked around again. There was snow, more snow and something else. She frowned as she squinted against the white glare.

There were drifts in the pure field of white, but she'd barely seen them. Still, had she been paying attention she would have heard the sounds, otherworldly though they might be. That was the nature of the Louron. They heard and they felt what others did not. She had been so focused on the one voice that called to her that she ignored the softer, more plentiful voices.

The closest drift was far enough away that she barely paid it any mind. Still, she looked at it now and understood.

"Bodies have been burned, I think."

"Not the bodies!" the man's voice broke with growing tension. "What happened to the walls? What happened to the whole city?"

"City?" Daivem frowned and went over the map she'd tried to memorize on the way. There was something here, perhaps. Or there should have been. There was no terrain to study, only the endless snow. Still, she looked carefully and realized that there were more drifts of snow collecting against mounds of bodies than she had realized.

The dead did not frighten her. She was from Louron. She traveled between worlds, often on a search for the spirits that cried out the most. The dead held no secrets from her. They could not.

Still, this was different from most cases. The dead seldom spoke unless they had something to say. Mostly the spirits moved on unless there was violence. There had been violence here. There had been great violence. She frowned as she studied the dead. They had not moved on. They had been stolen away.

The dead here were gone, imprisoned.

"Where did Edinrun go?" the man yelled now, speaking slowly as if to a fool. Perhaps she was a fool. She should have noticed. She should have known, but someone was stealing the dead away from their ruined bodies.

Edinrun. She shook her head and pressed her lips together. What was wrong with her? How could she not see?

"The people of the city. They are dead."

She frowned and looked to the man who spoke to her. He was hard, a soldier, well trained and well seasoned like hard wood. He would fight and try to kill her if the command was given. He was not alone. At least a hundred more rode with him.

"I'm not from here," she said. "I have been on the Kaer-ru Islands. I'm from Louron."

That stopped him. Her people had a well-cultivated history of mysticism. It often did them well to be feared instead of only respected. Respect could be pushed aside more readily than fear.

The man nodded and, through the snow, she saw another man approach the driver.

After ten minutes of conversation the man who'd walked up vanished back onto the caravan and the rider turned to her again just as she was getting ready to walk on.

"King Opar would speak with you."

Opar, she knew, was the king of Giddenland. If he wished to speak there was little she could do except agree or run away. So far she had no reason to run. Her hand squeezed the wood of her walking stick and she nodded.

"I will answer any questions that I can."

The rider sighed and climbed down from his wagon and gestured for her to follow. He did not wait to see if she did so. That was always the way with armies. They assumed everyone would obey, especially any who were afraid to die.

Daivem was not afraid to die. It was not the way of her people.

The cold was harsh, but she was well bundled and had grown accustomed. The wagon she was led to, and allowed to enter, was wonderfully warm, and she sighed as she stepped inside.

It was not overly ornate, but the wagon was sturdy and comfortable. There was a small stove for burning wood and it kept the air as warm as the tropical islands where she was born and raised.

The man that faced her was handsome, and while his smile was friendly, his eyes bore the haunted look of someone well out of his depth.

"I am Opar. I am king here. Thank you for talking to me." He seemed genuine enough in his words, as if he did not know she had been given no options in the matter. Perhaps he did not. Perhaps she had made assumptions because she faced soldiers. In reality they had offered her no sign of hostility.

"I will offer any help I can, King Opar, but I am not from here."

"You are from Louron, yes?"

She nodded.

"Louron is not like other islands. I have visited the islands, but I could not visit Louron. It was gone the day I went to visit."

"We are protected." She did not clarify. Louron, the people of that place, her people, they were not anchored to one world. They moved between worlds as the Shimmer saw fit. The Shimmer was the gift that protected them and it also protected the lands where they lived. While there was a connection to the world of the Five Kingdoms, it was not as strong as it was with many other places. Likely because the gods here were so temperamental.

"I am trying very hard not to, well, not to panic. But my capital city is gone."

Daivem nodded again, studying the man's face. He seemed like he was close to panicking and she could understand that.

"If this is where it is supposed to be, then yes." What else could she say?

"How could that happen?" He stared hard at her. "How can a city disappear? I was told when we looked for Louron that the weather was wrong, but I just thought the boat's captain was a fool. But now this. I don't understand."

She did not want to do these things. She did not want this conversation, but she was here and the man was lost in dread over his people and his country.

"I cannot tell you what has happened, but I can try to find out."

"Can you? I thought to find a scryer or possibly a Galean."

"They would indeed be better equipped to help you, I think."

He leaned forward and stared into her eyes. He was handsome, but he was also the sort that seemed too intent on having his way to be worthwhile.

"I must ask this of you. Please."

She stared for a long time and finally nodded. "I will do this."

His smile was genuine enough. The relief in his eyes was likely true. Still, his eyes lied when he offered his thanks. There were hidden things that, she supposed, weighed on the shoulders of a monarch.

Without another word she rose into a crouch and let herself out of the coach. The man who had led her there began to follow and she looked over her shoulder at him. "You may follow me, but you cannot go where I am going."

"Where are you going?"

"To find your king's city."

He started to say something, but by the time words would have been heard, she was gone.

She had seen people taken by the Shimmer, of course. It was as common as a breeze where she was from, but it took effort so far away from home. She had to ask the universe itself for help. Happily, the universe was kind. It looked like a person simply fading away as they moved. It felt like waves of water rippling across the body, but there was no moisture and those waves were exactly the same temperature as the traveler.

There wasn't far to go. She stepped onto the Shimmer and saw the city. It still existed, but it was locked away. She could not say what exactly surrounded the city, but she knew that to touch it would be bad. If the Shimmer seemed, to her mind, like water, then what her mind told her about the barrier around Edinrun was closer to a wall of burning thorns. Nothing burned. Nothing was stabbed by the sharp edges, but her mind told her it would feel like flame and hooked points.

Would she be able to walk away if she risked contact? Probably. A short walk brought her to one of the gates; she could not have said which one. All she knew was that the gate was open and that the living and the dead alike pushed at that entrance and had no success moving it. They felt no pain as they tried to break through, but the energies were there and held them back.

The living wore armor different from the soldiers that she'd already seen. The dead were different. Most wore only what they believed they should be wearing. In most cases that meant the very things they had died wearing.

One last look at the barrier. Like the Shimmer, the power was pervasive. It was everywhere and had no flaws. That told her all that she needed to know.

Stepping back to the Five Kingdoms was as easy as exhaling. A momentary sensation of waves without water and she was there. Daivem had walked only a few yards, but now her distance was several hundred feet from where she had been. A dozen soldiers had gathered and were looking for her.

Daivem allowed herself a smile. Let them call and look. She walked to the king's wagon and opened the door.

He looked relieved to see her. "We thought you taken."

"I had to travel a distance." She did not clarify. "The gods have taken your city. It still exists, but it is no longer here. They have removed it and sealed it as one might seal a clay jar with wax."

Opar shook his head, eyes wide and mouth pressed into a tight line.

"Can you take me there?"

She shook her head and lied. "No." She could have taken him there. The Shimmer would likely permit it. But once most people traveled that way they came to expect it. She would not be in service to this man. She had offered him information and had granted it. There would be nothing else.

"I do not think the gods want you to go there. I do not think they would let you come back, even if you could travel to that place." She closed her eyes. "The people I saw within the city wore the colors of another land. The dead… the dead outnumbered the living by many. Your city is gone. If you have access to the gods, they alone could help you retrieve it."

King Opar slumped in his seat and nodded his head. "I am lost. I have no way of saving my people."

Once again Daivem rose from her seat. She stared at the man and wished she could help him, but her plans did not involve retrieving lost cities.

"I wish you well, King Opar. Seek the Galeans. They have many secrets."

The king nodded. "There is nothing for it. I must go to Torema."

If he was expecting a response, he was disappointed. Daivem slipped away into the snow and resumed her solitary trek, lamenting only that she could not take the warmth of the coach with her on her travels. The king and his retinue moved on, and she went in the opposite direction.

Twenty minutes after she'd left the caravan she cursed silently and turned back. The dead called. There were some among her people who could ignore that, but she was trained to listen and to give aid when she could.

At least the place where Edinrun rested was not quite as cold. Daivem walked a long, slow perimeter of the gate, studying the signs that made themselves available. The spirits of the dead were not completely locked away. She watched one move and writhe and push against the barrier until it slid free.

"How are you here?" The man's voice carried a note

of desperation. "Can you help me find my way back?"

Well, that was the question, wasn't it?

"I do not know. Tell me what happened?"

"The Undying came. They brought madness with them. I could not see. I could not think, not in the right ways. All I could do was, well, go mad."

"How?"

"How did I go mad? I couldn't think." The man shook his head and his bald scalp shone in the spectral light of a nonexistent sun. "I saw my wife. I couldn't speak her name. I could not touch her, I ran away from her and... I feasted." He wept and she understood. He'd been taken by unnatural hungers. She had seen it before in different places.

"How did you get past the wall?"

"I only had to think about it hard enough." He frowned "And push very hard."

"Can you bring others, show them how? If I am to try to help you, I should try to help as many as I can, for I will not be this way again."

The man nodded and worked his way back through the barrier at the gate. The living did not notice him. That was not surprising.

While he went on his mission, she prepared herself, sitting on the ground and muttering. The walking stick was key, of course. For as long as she had been practicing she had worked on that hardwood shaft, carving the designs that the wood said should be there and imbuing the deep mahogany with power.

Her hands moved through her pockets, rooted in the bag she carried at her side, and finally found the right collection of ingredients. This place was not filled with the ambient remains of endless lives passed. If she were in the area where the wretched dead had ended, she would have been able to use that to her advantage. Necromancy was always easier where the dead had been. Without that benefit she had to use the herbs and powders she had collected over the years.

They came to her. Only a few at first, but more and more as the dead realized they could get through the barrier and possibly find a way back home.

Daivem had known to expect many, but the sheer magnitude of the dead was unsettling. So many had been slaughtered in the city. Very possibly all of the city. It might well be that none had escaped the slaughter.

She looked at the gate, saw the living still trying to press through the invisible blockade to their freedom and felt a dark satisfaction. Let them suffer if they had done this thing.

When she was surrounded by the dead, Daivem stood and held her walking stick high over her head. The mutterings of the dead stopped immediately and they looked at her with a combination of awe and fear and, yes, hope.

"I am Daivem Murdrow. I come from Louron. I have been trained to walk the world and to deal with the dead. I am here to try to help you, but I can make no promises. Do you understand?"

The man who had spoken to her earlier nodded on behalf of them all. "We understand."

Her dance was not necessary. It did not change the magic, but it helped her calm herself and remember all the details of the ritual. Ritual helped, sometimes, and they were taught all they learned with dance and with words alike.

The Shimmer did not approve of unknown travelers. The dead were known to the Shimmer and always had been; that was an advantage.

The wood in her hand glowed softly, and the air hummed with power as she worked her will on the Shimmer, asking for help and giving direction when the help was offered. The rift she tore between the worlds was a dozen times her size. The air rippled where the opening existed, and a sickly light flickered along the edges, sometimes silvery and others a pale green that hurt her eyes.

Without words she told them to move and the dead listened. The pretense of human form fell away from them as they moved, swimming the ethereal currents as they reached for the realms beyond their temporary prison.

Daivem freed them, but she exacted a price. The cost of opening the barriers between the worlds was heavy and if she had paid it herself she would likely have killed herself. Instead she took from each of the spirits. A small bit, effectively the equivalent of a hank of hair, but that energy would never come back to them.

As the last of the dead moved through the tear in the universes, Daivem joined them, stepping back into the bitter cold of the apocalypse in the Five Kingdoms.

They were still there. She could feel them as they began to disperse.

"Will the gods be angry with you?" It was the same spirit, the one who'd been trying the hardest to escape and had succeeded better than most.

Daivem looked around and gestured to the north and

east, where the clouds towered the highest and where the winds sent ice shivers across every part of her skin that was exposed.

"They are already angry. What else can they do? Destroy the world a second time?"

He said nothing else, but she sensed his gratitude before he drifted away.

Peace. She simply could not leave them locked away, punished a second time for crimes they had not committed.

The silence was bliss. It also let her hear the summons that had drawn her in this direction in the first place. Through the savage cold she continued, drawn as always like a moth to a flame.

Brogan McTyre

Nora pressed back against him, her body warm and familiar, and Brogan pulled her close, nuzzling his face into her glorious mane of dark curls. His body responded as it always did and he wondered if they could have a little time without waking the children. He opened his mouth to call her name into that glory of hair and–

The elbow that hammered into his guts doubled him over on himself and woke him right up.

While Brogan tried to collect enough air to gasp, he assessed the situation. It wasn't Nora he was pressed against. It was Anna. His body was just as excited as it had been in his dream and he was pressed against her in much the same way.

She hadn't turned toward him, but he heard her words clearly. "We all have urges, Brogan, and you're a fine-looking man, but I'm married. You push that thing against me any harder and I might forget that. I think we'd both regret that, wouldn't we?"

He said nothing, but carefully rolled away from her.

There was no true threat of falling. They were higher up than he wanted to think about, but the body of the giant was vast and they had settled in a curve of a backbone that left them mostly safe from rolling and falling in their sleep.

Still, Brogan preferred to not look down. The height was dizzying at best.

Anna sat up and looked at her feet. Brogan stood and looked down on her, his skin flush with desire, his manhood at attention. He looked away and felt a wave of guilt. She was with Desmond, and Nora? Well, she was gone from him.

That was what started all of this.

"I'm sorry. I didn't mean–"

"I know." She waved the words away. Her voice sounded as flustered as his and despite the circumstances part of him was complimented.

The sun was up. Light was starting to glow through the Broken Blades and into the mountain's heart. Looking around, he could see how high they were. The skull that was their destination claimed most of the heavens from his perspective. The whole of their world was petrified bone and calcified gristle. Vast, blood red crystal ran from the side of the mountain and pierced the heart of the giant body below them. Climbing over that had been terrifying, sheer angles and shards of bone larger than houses, and gaps where fragments had fallen over the years. He had made many unpleasant sounds while moving over that area and so had Anna. Faceless said nothing, but simply kept pace.

The odd figure was where it had been the night before, sitting on the edge of the massive vertebra and watching silently.

"Are you ever going to say anything? Anything at all?" he asked it every day, at least once. It was meant as a joke, but only because there was no mouth to see on Faceless. No mouth, no nose. If the thing breathed at all, he had no idea how.

As always, he was greeted with silence.

He looked to Anna. "I'll be back." She nodded. There was no reason to announce his intentions. They both left the area when they had to take care of bodily functions.

Sure enough, Faceless followed.

When he was done with his business he looked at the creature again. Little seemed to have changed.

"What are you?" Brogan asked.

Faceless replied, "What are you?"

Brogan stared hard and slowly walked closer. There still didn't seem to be a mouth but he'd heard the thing reply.

"Just a man who needs to fight the gods." Brogan shrugged. "Which likely means I'm a man who will die soon."

Faceless looked up at the vast skull of the dead giant or god they were scaling. Slowly, very slowly, one of the half-formed hands pointed in that direction. There were changes now. The hands had individual fingers, though they seemed at the moment to be fused together.

"Why do you climb?"

"So that, maybe, I will not die before I stop the gods

from ending the world."

Faceless turned that mostly featureless face toward him and Brogan looked into the deep holes where eyes should have been. Once again, he felt a shiver. There was something inherently wrong about a faceless thing looking at him.

"Why didn't you ever answer my questions before?"

Faceless looked at him and strained, and the mass of fingers that had been stuck together split apart with a sound much like an axe splitting a log into firewood. Faceless moved his newly freed fingers and stared at them for several seconds before answering. They moved flawlessly.

Faceless said, "I did not know I could speak until today. I think I am changing."

"Well, yes, you certainly are."

A few minutes later they were back at what passed for their camp, and Brogan was packing his things away. Anna was not there, likely having gone to take care of her morning business. He tried not to think about being pressed against her, and failed. There was a momentary guilt again, at the thought that he was betraying Nora. The feeling was irrational; Nora was dead. Desmond was not. Desmond deserved better, surely, and Anna was not provoking his reactions. He was simply attracted to her.

He slipped his satchel over his shoulder and rolled the joint to make sure the bag was secured properly. The travel was going to get even trickier, he suspected, as they would be climbing inside of the skull of the giant and there was no way to know what they would find, what sort of surfaces they could cling to as they attempted to scale to the very top of the thing.

To keep his perspective about what was and was not possible, Brogan made himself walk to the ledge and look down. Reaching the very edge of the vertebra was challenging, but possible. The actual act of looking down was different. It was a staggering challenge. Around him the world was hidden away by a massive ribcage, the blood red shard that pushed through those impossible bones. Lower, there was a corpse that was too large to fully comprehend and far, far below was the ground.

Anna's voice startled him. "It's a very long way down. I don't recommend it."

His heart thudded hard in his chest and Brogan stepped back, nodding. "I believe it would be a bad way to go. It would also slow my plans." He looked her way. "Faceless can talk, by the way. Just doesn't seem to have much to say, really."

"What are your plans, exactly, Brogan? You find what you need from here. You go forth to slay the gods? Where will you find them?"

He looked down again and contemplated the distant ground. The sun casting through the crystals painted everything below him a dull red. "I believe I know the place. There was a spot out in the ocean, not far from where..." he swallowed "...from where my family was taken and killed. A vast stone archway sat in the ocean and seemed to cause the storms. That is the place where I will go. That is the way to them. I believe that." He shrugged. "Your Galean friend said as much."

"How will you kill them, Brogan?"

"However I can. If they do not stop this. If they do not listen to me, I will find a way or I will die trying."

Anna nodded. "So let's be about it then." Without

another word she started walking along the edge of the massive bone, looking up at the next bone.

"I think it gets harder from here," he said, as he followed behind her.

"In my experience things seldom get easier the farther you go." She looked over her shoulder at him as she spoke. He found himself wondering if she was talking about the climb or resisting their mutual attraction. Was it mutual? Yes, he believed it was. Likely it was a bit of both.

They climbed for a few hours before settling in to rest. Their progress was better than he had expected. The inner lining of the neck bones had many places where they could walk relatively easily, and where they could climb without too much risk. Best not to look down too often, as the height was terrifying, but it could be done. Faceless kept pace from a distance, as he always did.

"So this god," Brogan tapped the bone beneath him as they settled in for a bit more hard bread and cheese. "He was killed by another god and left here?"

"That seems to be the basis of most of the stories. And then the mountains either formed over him or were built around him as a funeral cairn."

"Do you think the crystals were actually a sword?"

Anna looked his way and shrugged. Her hair was a mess, and dust lined her face. There was little water to spare and what they had was saved for drinking.

"That they are strong enough is a given. I hit one of the smaller ones with a rock when I entered the cave and the rock chipped." She finished her small meal and then pointed to the gigantic blade of crystal that ran through the dead god's chest. "Look at it. That would have killed him if he were a man, but it is hardly the shape of a blade as you or I know it. The gods? Who can say what they think or how they act? They are gods, Brogan McTyre." She gestured to encompass everything. "We have climbed this body for days. We are still not at our final destination. The world outside is likely going mad, but we have spent our time climbing. The. Body. Of. A. God. That a thing like this can exist is madness. That it once moved and thought and walked across the face of the Five Kingdoms is enough to give nightmares. That it fought another and died here? That we would, for any reason, one day find a need to climb into the head of a dead god?"

Anna sighed.

"I suppose they must have been a weapon of some kind. There are pieces everywhere. Pieces growing through the mountain. When I think about where we are standing, how we got here and why, I want to scream, Brogan. This is not a place for mortals to be standing."

"This is all I can do, Anna." Brogan spoke softly. "I would not take back my earlier actions. If there was any chance that I could have saved Nora and my children, I would have taken it."

"I never said you should."

"Nor did you need to. We have already spoken of this. I'd have come to Desmond's aid just as quickly if it had been you chosen as a sacrifice."

"Desmond. Desmond has been..."

Her face in that moment was a mask of sorrow, He didn't know what had happened but something was bothering her.

Before she could finish the statement and before he could have responded in any case, the ground beneath them shook violently enough that they'd have certainly fallen hard if they had been standing.

Brogan started to speak, but the sound became a scream when the ground beneath them moved again.

No. Not ground.

The body they stood on, that they crawled over like fleas on a hound.

It was the body that moved. It shuddered and shook a third time and Faceless was bowled over and sent sliding violently.

"What is this?" Brogan reached for Anna as she tried to stand and fell down again. He did not touch her, as his body was thrown, and he rolled as helplessly as a newborn. There was nothing for it, they were simply insignificant in comparison to the shaking surface they stood on.

And then it was over. No in-between. The form beneath them shook and then it did not. All around them the echoes of movement continued. The inside of the vast hollow space was like a drum beating, echoes crashing off each other and dust and debris falling from above. Several shards of broken crystal plummeted from the ceiling far above but none could reach them.

Brogan clutched at his chest, his heart thudding like a bass drum. Anna crawled on her hands and knees not far away and Faceless came toward them, his head tilted as he looked at their surroundings.

Far above them the position of the skull had shifted and the chin of the vast thing pointed down. The mouth, which had been closed before, now hung open. Most skulls had open mouths, as far as Brogan could recall. Or their jaws fell away. If this one decided to lose its lower half, they were surely dead.

"If we wish to see what must be seen, I suggest we do it quickly." Anna's voice sounded as shaky as Brogan's knees felt. "Should rather not be inside that thing if it falls from its perch."

Perhaps another day of hard climbing. He did not believe they could reach the top of the skull by the time the sun faded.

"What caused that?" Brogan gathered his belongings again as Anna did the same.

"The world is ending, Brogan. What makes you think a mountain range is safe from that?"

A new sound came to his ears. Somewhere, far above, the wind had found a way into the vast cavern. The wind let out a soft, low, mournful howl that carried through the area.

Brogan had no answer for Anna's question and so he started climbing, more desperate than before to reach his destination.

CHAPTER TEN
DESTINATIONS

Bron McNar

King Bron looked at the iron and stone tower before them. It did not resemble anything from any other part of Mentath, but that it was considered something special was clear enough. Ten of the Marked Men guarded the entryway and none of them looked the least bit bored.

The massive structure looked as if it had risen from the ground. It had no bricks, nor stones that Bron could see. Instead the walls looked as if they'd been brutally hacked from one vast rock, and later marked with a thousand runes made of cast iron with a hint of rust at each, with every rune running from the crest down to the ground. Some of the markings were half-buried in the ground. No grass grew where the structure touched the earth and no other plants were close by.

The monolith steamed in the cold air, though there was no visible source for the heat.

King Parrish looked at the stone monolith and nodded his head. "This is the Cauldron. This is where the Marked Men are shaped, and where I was shown how we can all survive the coming conflicts."

King Jahda nodded his head and squinted as he studied the lines of the structure. He did not seem as eager as Parrish. Pardume looked on as well, his face not easily read. He was new to them and good at keeping his feelings hidden.

The night was cold, and as ever the snow was falling. Along the main pathways several braziers burned, keeping the air warmer and lighting the way. Mentath still had slaves, and several of the palace servants cleared the worst of the snow from the paths. While Bron didn't much care for slavery, the end result was he could walk up to the gigantic black stone edifice that, according to Parrish, might well save them all.

Also, it was Parrish's kingdom and he was a guest. Parrish might well be the sort who would drive spikes through rude guests. Probably not, but why take the chance?

Gaarsen was larger than he'd expected. His castle, his home, was impressive by any standards. Gaarsen was larger. There was a wall around the city but it was more decorative than anything else. Parrish did not seem concerned about invaders. Then again, that was probably because it was he and his people who had normally done the invading over the years.

There were three separate castles in the city. One belonged to the baron of the region, a man named Quinn, who was supposedly on his way to meet them. One was apparently where the military of the area trained. The largest belonged to Parrish.

"Why do you call it a cauldron?"

Parrish looked his way with a half-smile. "I don't. Theragyn does. He created the thing and so I suppose he gets to name it."

"What does it do?" Bron looked carefully at the vast iron edifice.

"Theragyn uses the Cauldron to test the people he deems worthy. Those that fail the test are never seen again. Those that pass his trials come back marked, as I am."

Pardume asked, "How many fail?"

Parrish looked at the other man and offered a thin smile. "Only three to date. I choose very carefully before I allow anyone into the building."

Bron stared at Parrish for a moment and nodded his head. The man was being honest. Or at least mostly honest.

"How did this start?" That question came from Jahda. The man was still studying the towering structure. He was tall and lean and dark. He seemed much less of all three next to the Cauldron.

"Theragyn answered my prayers." Parrish shrugged. "I was sore after my loss." He looked at Bron and offered that same half smile. "King Bron sent me home. He defeated me very solidly and he did it with fewer people and a much smaller army."

Parrish shrugged and looked at the Cauldron. "I was angry. I admit it. I begged the gods for a chance at revenge, but there was no answer.

"And then one night there was. I was walking along the pathway right here when the Cauldron slid out of the ground in a fountain of fire that burned away the plants in the area. The whole thing was hot, and the markings you see," he gestured to the iron runes, "glowed like they were fresh from a forge."

Parrish looked down at the ground and the toe of his boot scraped at the earth where nothing grew. "The man who came to the entranceway did not leave the Cauldron, but stood looking at me from the opening. He was the largest man I had ever seen and he bore iron armor and carried an iron sword. His face was..." Parrish frowned. "His face was not human. When he spoke I heard the sound inside of my chest, as deep and loud as thunder."

Parrish shook his head and walked to the entrance. Four of the Marked Men stepped aside as he came closer and the looks on their faces bordered on rapturous. His hand touched the iron edge lining the mouth of the Cauldron. His fingers caressed the metal as if it were a favored lover.

"He offered me everything I wanted. All I had to do was offer him fealty and prove myself by entering the building." That half smile again, and Parrish shook his head, the motion sending his many braids rolling across his shoulders and back.

"There were trials inside the Cauldron. I could tell you of mine, but I have learned this: each person goes through a different process. Each test is designed for the individual. The reward is always the same. We are marked and we are changed."

"Changed how?" Jahda again, who studied Parrish with his dark eyes. Like Parrish, he had a half smile, but his seemed infinitely kinder.

Parrish looked at the other man for a long time and finally shrugged. "Faster mind. Faster reflexes. Other changes that are harder to define."

Bron listened carefully.

Finally he nodded and asked, "How do we meet this Theragyn you speak so highly of? Do we merely walk into his Cauldron?"

Parrish nodded his head. "If you wish to meet him, you, too, must pass his tests."

Bron considered the options, his brow wrinkled with worry and thought alike. A chance to save his family? His kingdom? A chance to get out from under the demands of uncaring gods? Parrish seemed to be doing well enough, but the Cauldron was here and not in Stennis Brae. Would there be a greater cost? Would he be forced to swear fealty to Parrish? He wouldn't put it past the man to forget to mention a few details like that. That sort of action was well within the king's possible ploys.

Parrish was an ally for now, but as he had just reminded the assembled royalty, they had been enemies once. And more importantly, Parrish had lost to Bron. He was exactly the sort that would hold a grudge. He admitted as much when he spoke of praying to the gods for a chance at revenge.

Before he could answer, Jahda spoke. "I will not be joining you. I am very grateful for the offer, but before I can make that sort of decision I must speak to the other leaders of the Kaer-ru."

Parrish looked displeased.

"You traveled all this way."

Jahda smiled again. "Indeed I did. How else could I see what you spoke of, King Parrish? How else could I know what you offered and what is at stake? But I must speak to the other rulers first."

Jahda's words made sense. The difference was that Bron had to answer to no one. Bron had to consider the safety of his people. He also had to consider whether or not any actions he made might anger the gods even further.

In the end any chance he could take to save his kingdom was a chance that had to be taken.

"I would meet your Theragyn."

Pardume nodded. "Me too. I would meet this god of yours." The king of ruins and little else sounded eager. He wanted a new chance at being a king. He wanted to rule a land that was not drowning.

Parrish smiled. "Excellent," he said, slapping Bron on the shoulder in a comradely way. When Bron looked to Jahda, to see if the man might change his mind – for it is said that fear is the surest way to make a man seek companionship – he was surprised to see that the man was gone.

Parrish did not seem nearly as startled.

"Come, Bron. Come, Pardume, time to meet. And afterwards, we will feast to our successes."

Bron nodded and said no more. Pardume nearly led the way in his eagerness to make new friends.

Interlude: The Blood Mother

Hollum was dead. There was no way around that. The people of Hollum, however, continued on. Many had wagons, which lined the outside of the caravan. Others had horses. Most, however, had only their legs and whatever they could carry, moving along with a cart or drag behind them. There was some food, but as this was Hollum those who had it charged others dearly if they wanted to eat.

The rains sometimes fell as water and sometimes as sleet, but they fell constantly. That was the one thing of which the people seemed assured.

Sitting inside her wagon loaded with supplies, Theryn, often called the Blood Mother, nodded to herself and considered their progress.

Sitting with her were her three lieutenants. Naza's face was scarred from the one time she let herself get caught stealing. The burns had long since healed. The memories remained. Choto was a little heavy and looked ten years younger than she was, which had led more than one fool to underestimate her. Kemm, who was, perhaps, the skinniest man Theryn had ever met. But he was deceptive. He was far stronger than he looked, and faster, too.

The three of them had one important thing in common: they were faithful. They did as they were told and they never questioned the reasons. They were also rare in that they offered advice when it was wanted and their suggestions were usually sound.

Most of the people on the trip were worried about survival. Theryn and company were not. They were worried about profits. The simple fact was that Hollum was dead and they intended to move their operations into Torema.

The coastal city had to know they were coming. They would be prepared to resist a wave of new refugees. Just as Theryn and the other rulers of Hollum had been prepared.

There were other rulers, though currently they were pretending to be anything but in charge. Most of the merchants had little choice but to abandon a great deal of their wares. They had been prepared for almost anything but a disaster large enough to erase Hollum from existence. Truly, who could have been ready for that?

The slavers were done for. Most of them had lost their wares in the floods. Those slaves that didn't escape were few in number, and as dead slaves did little good, they either had to be fed or let free. Food was a precious commodity. Currently Theryn and her group were making a handsome profit on dried fish and meats. The merchants may not have had room for their supplies, but the thieves always found a way.

There had been a few desperate fools who tried to steal supplies from the thieves, but they soon learned that the experts in stealing were also adept at preventing theft.

The rest of the leaders were still in charge of their groups, but they had little true power. The supplies meant profit. Profit meant opportunity. Theryn and her followers had access to nearly everything, and they were the ones people came to for what they needed. Except the whores. There were always people willing to pay for pleasure, and Theryn was not known for trading in those particular joys.

Naza shook her head and sighed. "We are two days away, Theryn. Three if we go slowly. How do we plan on moving into the city without being seen?"

The Blood Mother waved a hand and shrugged her shoulders. "We will advertise our arrival. We have supplies. We have coin. We will be welcomed with open arms." She steepled her fingers in front of her face. "Well, we will be tolerated. Others will not be as lucky."

Kemm nodded. "I am hearing reports from a few of the scouts. They say we're being followed by a small group."

"And?"

Kemm spread his hands. "You said you wanted to know of anything unusual. This group comes from the west, and they are keeping pace with us."

"How small a group are we speaking of here?"

"Close to a hundred."

"That's your idea of a small group?" Theryn raised an eyebrow and stared at her subordinate.

"We are fifty thousand people, more or less. We are an army, whether or not we mean to be an army."

"Fair enough. Watch them. If anything changes, let me know. Make sure we keep close eyes and have extra archers assigned to the western side of the caravan."

The slender man nodded. "We could just have them killed."

"Why do for free what we might get paid for?" She shook her head. "Watch them for now, and thank you for the warning."

After a while in the comfortable silence, she looked toward her other aide. "Choto?"

"Yes, Theryn?"

"How fares Rik?" Rik had been one of her lieutenants until he let his affection for Tully foul up his position. The man was an excellent thief, and a good and loyal aide, but Tully had always been a weak spot for him. He adored the little blonde thief. Currently he was among them, but his arms were bound behind his back and his hands were tied together in a very deliberately uncomfortable position. He'd spent the last few days in the elements, with the rain as his only regular source of nourishment.

"He's fallen four times and been lifted back to his feet. Much longer and he'll be dead." Choto's voice offered no regret or sympathy for Rik. Like most of Theryn's followers they'd grown up under her care. Unlike most of them, the two had been lovers off and on for many years.

Choto could easily have lied to her or betrayed her. She had not. Very little happened that Theryn did not know about.

"Unbind him. Let him rest in one of the wagons. Bring him to me in the morning and we will discuss what will happen with him next."

Choto nodded and offered a very brief smile of gratitude. They both knew the way this balanced out. Rik had done a disservice and he had been punished. If she decided he was truly repentant, Theryn would let him back into her good graces. If he failed her again, or if he was not properly grateful, he would not reach their destination.

The city was going to be a problem. It didn't matter what she said, or what she believed, money be damned. There were thousands of people coming to Torema, and even if they were welcomed with open arms, there would be a problem with how many people the city could take in.

"Naza?"

The younger woman nodded.

"You and Kemm need to go to our wagons. Talk to the drivers. We are going to stop for one hour when everyone else does, but we are not going to set camp. We're going to ride tonight and through the day. We need to get to Torema before everyone else. Please make it happen."

Naza smiled and nodded. She understood. A smaller army would be invading first and that army would have money and supplies. The rest could come afterward if they were so inclined but they might not be as easily welcomed.

Interlude: The Iron Mothers

They paced the caravan from a distance. There were a great many people in that trail of horses, wagons, and pedestrians, and the Iron Mothers needed to be certain of what they were approaching before the time came.

They were spotted. It was nearly inevitable. Without a word spoken between them, the group broke up and continued on their way.

When night came and the caravan stopped, the Iron Mothers continued on, but they did not move forward. They moved around.

Over the course of several hours, they made their way to new locations near and far and waited for the right time.

When Harlea and Emila had started descending toward the west and the distant Broken Swords mostly hid their light, the Iron Mothers made their move. As they approached the caravan they tore away their iron masks and peeled the old, dying skin from their bodies, revealing new, fresh flesh that was several shades darker than the deathly white hide they'd sported before. Their hair fell out as they moved, and was replaced by different colors. They no longer resembled the Grakhul they had been, but instead appeared as human women of different ages.

Naked, cold, they made their way into the camp. One hundred and seven shapes moved through the thousands who were slumbering, exhausted, and sleeping as best they could in the elements.

It was survival at stake and so they did what Ariah commanded and took what they needed to camouflage themselves among the humans. Some of the people from Hollum died in the process. Those who woke too easily or had not reached a deep enough slumber paid the price for consciousness.

Wet, bedraggled, shivering, the Iron Mothers did their work and hid away the bodies of the dead.

When the sun offered its feeble light and warmth, the caravan started on its way again, puzzled more by the loss of over a score of wagons than any other deficits that might have been noticed.

There were some who called for loved ones and could not find them. A few made attempts and others did not, but the Iron Mothers had hidden the dead well enough to avoid easy detection, especially since the rains had come in and made a mud wash of nearly everything around them.

The Union of Thieves had moved on in the night. The Iron Mothers took their place and walked on, moving with the people of Hollum, heading for whatever might be the final destination of a river of the wretched and displaced.

Ariah watched on from his prison, seeing all through the eyes of his Iron Mothers, and he was pleased.

Harper Ruttket

"Tell me that's not a mirage."

Harper smiled. "It is not a mirage."

Davers smiled when he heard those words. He nodded and pulled out his pipe and tobacco. He'd been saving the last little bits until he was in range of a place where he could buy more supplies. In a short span of time he had a cloud of smoke surrounding his face, despite the constant drizzle, and he seemed content.

"This is madness." Constir was a good lad, but always impatient. These days he was quiet more often than not as the gravity of their situation made itself known in a hundred little ways. "I can see the tents lining the city from here."

Harper looked along the line of the city. Seen from their angle, which looked down on most of the vast cove that was the very heart of Torema, the easiest thing to see was the thick caul of smoke and fog over the entire area, but, yes, there were tents everywhere along the edges, and wagons as well. The road into the city was clearly marked under most circumstances but it seemed many people had decided that the road was level enough to let them settle in.

Harper had every intention of riding over anyone in their way. He wanted to reach the harbor before the night ended.

"Any news from the gods?" he asked of Mearhan, who looked his way and said nothing for a moment.

Her expression did little to make him happy.

"Speak, please, Mearhan."

The girl sighed and shook her head. "We are not fortunate. You saw the shape of Edinrun. Several of your fellows were there."

"And are they dead now?"

She nodded her head and said nothing. Truly, there was nothing to say.

"Well then, we'd best get about gathering a ship and a crew."

"To what end, Harper?"

He offered her a thin smile. "If we can no longer be sacrificed to save the world, the gods will be ending us all soon enough. That means we have one hope. Brogan must find a way to kill the gods, or stop them."

"I don't think the gods will approve." She was trying for levity, but he could see her desperation.

"They don't seem to approve of much these days."

"We've time being bought for us."

"What do you mean?"

"The gods made an offer to the leaders of the Five Kingdoms. Each must sacrifice a blood relative to spare us for another month."

"And do you suppose the rulers will listen?"

Mearhan nodded. "Most often, according to the gods, the people would rather accept a punishment than lose a world."

Harper thought about that for a moment. "And you, Mearhan? Do you believe that?"

She looked away from him, her eyes cast downward. "Well, I gave up you and Laram alike, didn't I?"

"Did you? You told what you knew. You did your

sacred duty as the voice of the gods."

"Do you see it that way, Harper?"

"There's no other way to see it."

"I expect you're the only one here who would agree."

Harper shrugged. "I'm the only one here who betrayed the gods for the sake of a friend."

"What do you mean?" He could hear the shock in her voice.

"Do you not know, then?" She shook her head and he clarified. "I'm the one who led Brogan and the others to the Grakhul and helped them avoid the deadly places. Most anyone trying to reach them would have been killed by the areas that are poisoned. No one can move there without withering and dying, but I was trained, wasn't I? I knew the right paths to take and I led them for Brogan's sake."

"Did you hope to save his family?"

Harper sighed. "I didn't think it was possible. I truly did not, but I hoped. I served faithfully for many years and I hoped. I thought, perhaps, that the gods would listen to my prayers and save my friend from losing all that he loved. I was wrong."

Mearhan did not speak further and neither did Harper.

Instead they rode in silence for a time, each lost in their thoughts. He could not have said what the girl considered, save that she was likely worried about Laram. She betrayed him because the gods demanded it, and she did so with a heavy heart. She was still here when she could have slipped away a dozen times for the same reason. She hoped, he suspected, that Brogan might yet save the boy she loved and that, somehow, they would find a way to be happy together.

As for Harper, he had other thoughts to consider. He prayed that the gods would forgive Brogan. He had prayed that, somehow, they would spare his family, and that had not happened.

And more than once, he'd wished that Brogan's life was not so very perfect. Brogan, who had a lovely wife, and three children so filled with joy that they made his heart ache when he saw the family together. More than once he'd let his jealousy into his prayers and now, though he tried not to dwell on it, Harper once again found himself wondering if the gods had seen fit to answer his prayers, but had chosen the wrong ones to answer.

It was said that the gods rewarded the faithful in their own ways. Harper had been a faithful servant for a very long time.

He found himself wondering if that was why he had chosen to help Brogan in the first place. Had he lied, Brogan would have known no better. He could have made up an excuse. He could have said that the way to the Grakhul was hidden until the gods needed him and Brogan would have never known the difference. It was plausible enough. The ways of the gods were mysterious and made more so by the Undyings' whims, and the often vague answers the scryers gave when they spoke on behalf of the gods.

Harper considered the fate of the world and wondered, again, whether he could have prevented any of the things that had happened.

Ultimately it was a question he could not answer. In the end, only the gods could say.

They made their way into the city with little trouble, but true to his earlier thoughts he had to demand a few people move their belongings or lose them. For so many people it was exhaustion that made them foolish. Or, perhaps, they had simply given up when they reached Torema and realized there really was nowhere else they could go to avoid the wrath of the gods.

Several times he saw gatherings of locals eyeing him and his group suspiciously. That was hardly surprising. They were armed men and one woman. They came into the city prepared for trouble and so many had come with little or nothing that he could see. Perhaps they were looking for easy prey and found none. Perhaps they sought only to keep the worst elements from the city. If the latter were the case, they were failing in their duties. How much worse than the very people who had triggered the end of the world?

"Do we stop anywhere, Harper?" Constir's voice was soft. The lad looked around with dread in his eyes. How could he not? They weren't likely to find a place to stop and rest. Likely the inns were all filled.

"We find a ship, Constir. That might well be the best place we are going to find for getting a good night's sleep."

"A ship?"

"We have tents, too. If you think you can find a street that will take them."

Constir snorted at the very notion. The streets around them were cluttered with every sort of nesting, from tents to bundles of cloth to, yes, still more wagons. If it hadn't been for locals likely dragging the stragglers out of the main thoroughfares, those would have been filled as well. Harper had no doubt of it.

Mearhan said, "We're followed."

Harper nodded. "Aye. Likely there are soldiers here to make sure we cause no troubles. I intend to cause no troubles, unless they are started by another."

Mearhan frowned. "Soldiers? I've seen none."

"You are looking for colors. The soldiers in Torema don't wear them. They all work for Darkraven. She has no army as you are familiar with. She doesn't need one."

Halfway through the city and long before the docks, Harper called a halt. Hillar Darkraven's castle was within arrow range of the courtyard where they found vendors aplenty. The smells proved too much. They were ordered to keep close, and Harper gestured for Mearhan to stay with him as he went to buy actual food and possibly a skin of wine. There was seasoned lamb on sticks and roasted pork with hard bread. He bought both for himself and for Laram's true love, and they leaned against a low stone wall within range of the horses and ate. Any pretense at table manners went away in seconds. The food was too good. There was no actual conversation, but anyone hearing their grunts of pleasure would have thought they were rutting with complete abandon.

When they were done Harper offered the girl wine and she took it. Like most of the wines in the area the stuff was nearly blindingly sweet, but it was refreshing after the long ride through a frozen desert.

The weather was better here, but he doubted it would last. All one had to do was look to the north and note the approaching clouds. There was simply no escape from them.

A minstrel sang not far away, telling tales of disaster and doom. There were no current tales of heroes to be had. The world was ending, after all, and Hollum was in ruins, along with Edinrun and Saramond. Half the cities in the known world were ruined and the last of the large cities, Torema, was likely not far behind.

People tended to be stubborn. For the moment there were few who were looking to the ships in the harbor, but that would change and Harper knew it. When the storms came, or the people from Hollum, if there were any left, then the people around him would look to boats and consider distant lands.

The drizzle became rain. Not heavy yet, but decidedly wet and irritating; the mood of the crowd reflected the change as those who could gathered their cloaks around them, or did their best to avoid getting soaked in the gradually increasing downpour.

He'd have been far more worried if it weren't for the fact that he was carrying enough to buy most of the ships on the water. Not that he intended to advertise that fact.

Mearhan started to speak and he looked to her. "A moment. I'm listening."

Not a dozen feet away a heavyset man was talking about the people from Hollum. They'd been spotted and were only a day or so away. He talked as if they were a great invading force, and there was likely some truth to that notion. Whether they meant it or not, if most of Hollum was heading for Torema there would be fights starting up. There was no space left in the city and the people coming likely did not bring great wealth to spend with them.

"What is it, Mearhan?" He smiled as he spoke. She was a not a bad person. She was merely in a bad situation.

"You've been spotted, Harper."

"What do you mean?"

She pointed with her chin. "Two men up there were looking at you and talking. They wore chains around their necks. Slaver chains."

Slavers carried chains for locking up their charges that got notions of running. It wasn't uncommon for them to wear their chains as belts, or draped around their necks, especially in crowded areas. The slave houses did not wear colors anymore than the soldiers in Torema identified themselves, but they all had their ways of showing their affiliations if you knew where to look. Harper was surprised only because he didn't expect Mearhan to know anything about that.

As if reading his mind, she replied to his unasked question. "Laram told me about it. He always told me about his travels."

Harper nodded. "You might need to go to the horses. You've done nothing wrong, but being seen with me might not go well for you. Tell the others that I was spotted. I'll meet you down at the docks."

"What will you...?"

"Whatever I need to do, Mearhan." He handed her the rest of the wine. "Take care of that. I'll meet you soon."

She looked at the flagon and in moments, Harper had faded into the crowd.

Simple truths: getting lost in a crowd is easy if you know how. Brogan would have had a problem. Harper did not. A slump of the shoulders, a hood slipped over the hair, a different gait and suddenly Harper was gone.

It was all illusion, of course. Harper was still there. But if they were looking for a tall man with the warrior's gait they weren't going to see him. At least not if he was good at his job.

Of course, sometimes good wasn't enough.

The mercenaries came for him as hard as they could in a crowd, which was hard enough to let him know they were approaching. The sounds of people protesting as they got shoved aside, or knocked half off their feet by the men pursuing him, were enough guarantee of that, even through the sound of the crowded streets.

The first of them who approached was cocky. He had a club in one hand, because Harper was surely meant to be taken alive, and he swept it over his head, letting Harper know exactly what he planned.

Harper's dagger stabbed into the meat of the man's armpit and left him yelping and falling back. That was a tender spot and it was known to bleed well enough. The heavyset bruiser fell away and left his club behind.

Harper let the club stay where it was and moved on, slipping between people when he could, rather than trying to force his way through the crowd. The rains fell harder still and Harper did his best to use that to his advantage, hunching over and keeping his head low as the raindrops splattered heavily.

Near as he could figure it was human nature in large groups; if someone pushed, people pushed back. If someone just breezed past, no one cared. That left a few of his pursuers wondering exactly where he'd gone while they were getting pushed or confronted by angry locals.

Not nearly all of them, of course. There were those who tried to push through the crowd and those who followed Harper's methods. They found him again easily enough.

They came for him hard, and fast, and despite his skills, a few of them moved past his defense. A blow across the back of his head had Harper falling to his knees blinded by the unexpected pain. He rolled as quickly as he could, tried to stand, and found himself facing a massive man who hammered him in his face with a fist that seemed made of stone. Harper fell back, dazed, and was caught in the hands of someone else, who pushed him back toward the same fist that had sent him stumbling.

His dagger fell from numb fingers as the fist crashed into the side of his head and dropped him to the street.

That was his saving grace. Rather than try to stand again, Harper moved between the legs of the people around him and crawled across the filthy cobblestones, amid a collection of protests.

One man tried to kick him and he caught the muddy, booted foot and pushed. The man let out a yelp and fell onto his back in the crowd, a heavy puddle splashing across several others as he landed. Harper continued on as the fellow tried to get back to his feet in the crush of people coming from all directions. The streets were overcrowded already, but the struggle only made the situation worse for everyone.

He had no idea exactly what happened to the man he'd felled, but there were screams, and profanity. His face bloodied, his ears ringing, Harper found an alley to slide into and stood as the people around him flowed like a slow moving river.

He shook off the worst of the impacts, and felt blood flowing along the left side of his face. Not a lot, but enough to remind him not to get cocky about his ability to be sneaky a second time.

A woman's voice called out, demanding that he show himself. He saw her in the distance, a giantess who looked fully capable of pulling his arms off as easily as he might tear the wings from a fly. He knew her from reputation, a slaver named Stanna. He had no intention of getting close to her.

The alleyway wended its way down toward the harbor and Harper took it, hoping to avoid getting seen again.

His face hurt. The side of his head throbbed with every pulse of his heart. Muddy waters washed down the alley with him, heading for the docks. The rains were coming faster now, growing into a torrential downfall that made seeing anything even a few feet away more challenging.

Harper nearly ran the rest of the way to the docks.

When he got there he found his people waiting for him, Mearhan included. Despite his fears, no one had stabbed her or cut her throat. As a scryer only a fool would maim or kill someone who could speak with the gods. Of course, no one around here knew her as a scryer, so he had to simply call her a lucky girl.

Two men who dressed in the clothes of the Kaer-ru stood with them, looking unfazed by the heavy downpour.

Davers nodded to Harper and pointed to the two men. At a guess they were from Corrah, where the fishermen were notorious for hiring themselves out to strangers. Both of the men wore loose vests and baggy shirts underneath them. Both sported fishing knives and a few more blades besides, because only a fool walked the streets of Torema without adequate protection. As was the case with most of the people from Corrah, they'd shaved their heads and sported a few markings on the left sides of their bared scalps. Harper remained clueless as to what the markings meant, but felt no particular need to ask.

"Harper, this is Captain Odobo and his first mate, Lendre. They have a fine ship, large enough for our crew and a few dozen more."

The shorter of the men, heavyset and muscular, nodded and smiled. "Davers Hillway says you wish to rent our ship?"

"No. I want to buy your ship and rent your services." He paused to let that sink in. "But I want to see your ship first."

"My ship is not for sale."

"I offer you fair value because the journey is dangerous. You can buy another when we are done, or you can buy the same ship back from me for the same price if you prefer. I offer this for your sake, in case the trip leads to your ship sinking."

Odobo listened and considered for a moment.

"Let's go see about selling you a ship then."

Harper nodded his head and with a gesture asked that the man lead the way. They moved on quickly, all the better to avoid staying in the pouring rain.

Interlude: Trant's Peak

Far to the north, well beyond the Broken Swords mountain range, and as far west as a person could travel, Trant's Peak stood alone, a massive sentinel of stone that was coated in ice and nearly always hidden by clouds.

Find a place in the world and tell people it cannot be reached and almost inevitably someone will go there to prove the naysayers wrong. Trant's Peak had been mapped long ago and most people were warned to stay away because the pale people who lived there were not friendly and had no desire to barter.

Both of those statements were absolutely true. They were not friendly and they did not barter. Though they usually left people alone, they did not like visitors.

At the base of Trant's Peak the pale people gathered, first by the tens and then by the hundreds. Their huts and homes were left behind to stand or fall as the gods saw fit. They had been summoned and told that the time had come for them to seek and protect their brethren.

The pale people had no horses. They had no supplies. What they had was faith.

The gods called and so they obeyed, moving toward the waters and diving into the bitter cold waves, their bodies shifting as the water swallowed them. Their flesh grew scales, and their fingers and toes grew longer and developed webs. Their eyes bulged in their faces and their teeth and jaws changed. The nails on their hands and feet thickened into black claws, and their eyes moved on the sides of their heads, sliding outward until their vision was widened by the change. No one snuck up on the people easily when they were swimming.

On the far side of the land their kind were called the Grakhul. On the western shores they simply called themselves the people, as they had seldom seen anyone else and considered most of the world little more than a place the gods played with.

The waves were harsh, but not as violent as they were on the other side of the Five Kingdoms.

They had their destination in mind. The Sessanoh waited, as it had ever since they'd left it centuries before. After longer than any of them had lived, the pale people were going home.

The gods made demands and they listened. There was little else for them to consider.

They swam as fast as they could and ate the fish that crossed their paths when they were hungry.

The pale people were always hungry. The gods had made them that way.

Amen.

Myridia

The waters roared down from the heights, and despite her best efforts to reach the shore before she plummeted into the ocean, Myridia went with the rushing torrent. She had practice, and so she turned her fall into a dive and directed herself, praying to her gods that the sea was deep enough to allow her to survive.

She cut into the ocean like a knife, slicing deep and moving away from the cliffs.

Myridia broke the surface of the water and stared at where she'd fallen from. The stone was rough and gray and rose almost two hundred feet. The land here was sheer, and the waves were treacherous. She had dealt with cliffs almost identical to these all her life, and she felt an odd sense of homecoming.

The world is often new and exciting, and sometimes it is simply mundane. She had not known for certain that the waters of the river would run to the ocean, but there had been a good chance and when the river broke into the cold, harsh sea she'd been relieved.

Even as she watched on, more of her sisters rode the descending river into the water, most landing easily and a few slapping the waves hard enough to make her wonder if they'd broken bones. They kept falling, in numbers that were nearly impossible to count.

The He-Kisshi had told them to follow the river and they had, and the end result was this. To the left she could see hints of architecture instead of simple stone surfaces, but they were higher still than the cliffside and she knew that reaching her destination was not a task that had been completed as yet.

Myridia did not wait for the others, but instead did what she needed to do. She started climbing the cliffs, her claws helping with purchase. The rains had reached the area and kept her flesh wet enough to stop her from shifting back to her more human form.

Near as she could tell none of the others hesitated to follow. If they wanted her as their leader, she would set an example. They had much to do and time was running short.

Lyraal climbed beside her, the woman's powerful hands and feet clutching the slick stone, her sword still tied across her back.

She offered a simple smile to Myridia and continued to climb.

It was exhausting work. They made their way carefully up the stone, and more than once a sister fell and had to climb again. Myridia did not go after the ones who slipped. That was not why they were here. They had to make preparations.

The sun set to the west, and their shadows hugged closely to the stone and then slowly faded into night. Still they climbed. The light of the twin moons was meager in comparison to the sun, but despite the clouds, it was enough. Had they returned to human form they'd have never had a chance, but in their water-breathing forms they were hardier and their eyes more easily adjusted to the darkness, just as when they were deep in the sea.

When she finally reached a plateau Myridia climbed out of the way and settled on the rocky outcropping. The wind was softer than she would have expected and she guessed that the gods continued to aid them when they could.

Lyraal stood over her for a minute and then settled on the rough stone with a soft grunt. Myridia barely noticed. She was looking at the stone above them, at the symbols and structures that looked so very familiar. She knew that Nugonghappalur was gone, but when she looked up it seemed the city where she was born and raised still existed.

There was never a sight that so quickly brought tears to her eyes. It was not home, but it called to her and soothed the emptiness that had been her constant companion since escaping the men who'd come to kill and enslave them.

Several of the women around her let out high, keening noises, singing their thanks to the gods. She was not alone in her love of the gods, not alone in her bittersweet joy of seeing the Sessanoh and understanding the name properly. Back in Nugonghappalur the view they had now would have been the view from the waters. They had another day of climbing ahead of them, but that was just as well. They would have time to recover from the shock of seeing the place that was so very much like their home and yet so obviously not what it seemed.

Here, as with Nugonghappalur, the presence of the gods was obvious. Here, their connection to the gods would once again be complete. Despite her exhaustion, Myridia joined them in the song of thanks to the gods.

Was there joy? Yes. Was there sorrow? Of course. Somewhere in the middle of that was her love for the very gods who had threatened to destroy the world and then tasked her and the remaining Grakhul with stopping them from ending everything.

She was not surprised at all when three of the He-Kisshi descended from higher up. Ohdra-Hun was among them.

Myridia lowered her head as a sign of respect. The Undying's open hood faced her and she knew that the He-Kisshi studied her.

"You have done well and the gods are pleased. Less than a day away from here the children of your tribe continue their trek across the land. They will join you soon."

Myridia opened her mouth to speak but Ohdra-Hun silenced her with a gesture. "Your tasks are not completed. The Sessanoh must be sanctified. Choose carefully among your followers and prepare them. Let the blood of the Grakhul be offered to the gods as a sign of your faith."

"How many?"

"Seventy-two. You must choose the ones who are offered, Myridia. As the leader of this gathering that task falls to you. Do not disappoint the gods. They are watching and they will judge your decision."

On the cliff west of her, the other Grakhul continued to pull themselves from the water and up the side of the cliff, the last stragglers finally joining her.

The He-Kisshi moved toward the edge with their odd, waddling gait, and then spread their wings and dropped from the side of the cliff before rising on the winds.

For a moment Myridia had dared think the worst of her trials had been finished, but now she knew better. She was to lead her people and that meant she had to make life and death decisions.

"Seventy-two." Her voice broke as she muttered the words.

Lyraal placed a hand on her shoulder and Myridia turned, pulling the other woman into an embrace and silently begging the gods to grant her the strength to choose who among her brethren should die.

The gods had made their decree and she would respect that, but for the first time in her life she felt the sting of what she and her sisters had done since they were old enough to offer the rituals and prepare the sacrifices.

They had killed so many over the span of her life, far more than seventy-two.

She did not say the words, she dared not, but she thought them. She thought to herself that at last she understood why Brogan McTyre had come to them and slaughtered so many of the Grakhul.

Killing others to prevent the pain of loss was a concept she could finally truly comprehend.

The gods demanded sacrifice. The gods offered her the wisdom to understand her enemies at the same time.

Truly, she was blessed.

Tully

"I had my hands on the bastard and he got away." Stanna shook her head. She was not as grim as she sounded. She was, in fact, rather amused.

Tully looked at her and shook her head. "You sound like it's a good jest."

"Tully, lass, do you know how many people I've caught with these?" Stanna held out her hands. Tully looked at them, suitably impressed by both their size and the sheer number of scars they were decorated with. It was easy to forget exactly how massive Stanna was, especially since she was usually sitting down. They weren't currently sitting. They were looking up the slope at the spot where the first of the Hollumites was finally visible. "The thought that I had Harper Ruttket in my grasp and he got free is very funny to me. And annoying. That was a good amount of money I could have made."

Temmi snorted. "Now she wants to be a bounty hunter and a general."

Stanna merely smiled.

They came down the gentle slope in wagons, not one or two but over a hundred, drawn by horses and loaded with every imaginable form of supply. Even as they watched, one of the runners hurried toward them, moving as fast as a street weasel could, and waving one arm.

Torema did not have an army. Torema did not have watchers. What Torema had were people who would do nearly anything if money was involved. Darkraven was paying Stanna and she shared the wealth. The street runners were some of the finest pickpockets around. Like Tully they belonged to the Union of Thieves. She made certain they offered the proper oath, and then, just to be safe, she made sure they'd stolen nothing anyway.

The boy stopped in front of Stanna, and like most people looked her over twice to make sure she was real. "They've more than I knew could come here."

"Speak clearly, boy."

"There's hundreds of wagons. Hundreds. Behind them, there's more people than I can count. They go on as far as the eye can see." The boy's brown eyes were wide. "They'll flood us like a river. They can't all fit here."

Stanna looked around and spat. Next to her Temmi did the exact same thing. Tully could not say that the two were lovers, but she wouldn't have bet against the possibility and expected to keep her coin.

Stanna said, "I was afraid of this. It's the whole city. How many people in Hollum, Tully?"

She shook her head and thought hard. "Impossible to know. You were there at the same time. The city was almost doubled from all the people leaving Saramond." Her stomach fluttered at the thought. "Must be over a million. I don't think we can stop them. I don't think all of Torema can stop them."

It was Temmi that answered. "So we push them east. Near the city but not in it. They'll move that way if they can avoid a fight and the other side of the docks has enough land they can settle their tents."

Stanna squinted at the sky above, where the rains were still falling, and then looked up the long sloping hill toward the masses that were starting to trickle down behind the wagons.

Finally she nodded. "I like it."

She gave a sharp whistle that was loud enough to make Tully's ears ring and several more runners came out of the crowds. Tully watched them all with a hawk's awareness.

One little boy started to reach out but her hand slapped him across the face and sent him rocking back on his heels. All of ten and already too aware of the world to be shocked into crying by a hard slap. He started to protest and she shook her head. "You made an oath. Want me to call you an oath breaker?" Oath breakers tended to get themselves skinned alive when they were found guilty. No one in the Union stayed ignorant of the penalty. When it happened the Union made a show of it and left the remains where they could be seen. Didn't matter what city one visited, that was the way of the Union.

He nodded his head and kept his hands where she could see them.

"Find the captains. Tell them to meet me right here, right now. Be fast and there's an extra five coppers for each of you."

They couldn't have dispersed faster if they'd had burning brands shoved up their bums.

"Look at them. They've an army that couldn't be stopped if they attacked." Temmi was looking up at the crowds again. They were half a league off and appeared for all the world like a wave of flesh coming to swallow the town.

The captains arrived. Not surprisingly a number of them were Stanna's trusted men. There were others, of course, as the slavers alone could not hope to hold the city.

"Lads. We are not fighting that." She pointed and they looked.

"Thank all the fucking gods." Rhinen's voice was loud and clear.

Stanna smiled indulgently. There were occasions where she'd have likely broken his jaw for speaking out of turn, but she wanted her men happy and that meant being tolerant.

The more Tully studied the other woman the more she admired her. She was capable of incredible violence, had actually beheaded an Undying with one stroke of her blade, but she also understood restraint, and reward, and methods of fostering loyalty.

"We're letting the wagons into town. They have merchandise and they can trade. Hillar Darkraven is waiting toward the city center. She'll deal with them. Sans?" She looked toward the slaver and he nodded, his thick mustache bobbing up and down. "I want you to lead them down. Anyone gets foolish gets an arrow in the face. No exceptions. We will maintain control, or I will know why we failed."

She was looking at Sans, but all the captains nodded their understanding.

"The rest of you will lead everyone to the east. They want to come into town; that's not an option. They go east. Anyone wants to argue too badly gets chained or killed at your discretion. Do not lose control of them. There are too many for that. Urge them along and be as nice as possible, but be firm."

Stanna looked to one of the newcomers, a man almost the size of her, with tattoos all over his face and arms and shaved head. He looked like a bull that had been covered in colors and then trained to walk like a man.

"Argus, you get to keep control over all of it." He nodded and smiled. It was not a pleasant smile and Tully knew that if she ever saw the man in a dark alley she'd cut his neck into a second smile before she'd let him touch her. He reeked of violence and the way he looked at most of the women, her included, spoke of how much he enjoyed dominating his partners.

Tully did not like being dominated. Not ever.

"I'll keep them moving east, Stanna."

The newly minted general nodded and then looked up the hill. "Let's get this done. Wagons down here. Everyone else east, dead, or chained. Anyone needs to be an exception, you bring them right here to me."

The captains nodded and headed back to their posts.

By the time they'd reached their destinations the wave of flesh was well on its way.

Tully stared. The wagons were coming. Somewhere in those wagons, she'd have bet every coin she could steal, Blood Mother Theryn was sitting and waiting, planning how she would take over the Union of Thieves in the area. Tully knew it in her soul, and the dread that notion created was an ice storm in her guts.

As she watched, the masses of soldiers and mercenaries gathered by Stanna did their part and rode up the hill, many on horses, more on foot and carrying spears and other weapons. The spears stood out. They were fine weapons in the sort of situation coming their way. Anyone charging would find out the hard way that a barbed point could gut a running fool with ease. More importantly, they looked intimidating. Smart people ran from that sort of thing as quickly as they could.

The first of the wagons came to a halt, and then rattled down the hill as the soldiers let them get past.

The people behind the wagons hesitated and then, thankfully, paid attention. The wall of soldiers was set up well and kept the peace as the refugees from the end of the world moved to the east and down the hill toward a far less populated area.

Temmi laughed. "I didn't think that would work."

"You suggested it." Stanna looked at her with a half smile on her face.

"Didn't mean I thought it would work out."

"Well, just the same, it isn't over yet." Tully shook her head and kept watching as the wagons moved to their left, wending their way through the soldiers and toward the city. Sure enough there was a fortune strapped to most of the wagons.

"You expect trouble?" Temmi was looking at her.

"I always expect trouble. I hope against it, but I expect it."

Temmi nodded. "There's a lesson I've learned these

last few weeks."

Stanna patted the hilt of her sword, the Bitch. The thing was impressive, and Tully considered whether or not she'd have the strength to pick up the damned thing, let alone wield it.

She thought she could lift it. Not much more.

"It's a lesson we all learn. My father was an excellent teacher." The way Stanna said those words made her doubt the man had intended to teach his daughter to be prepared. More than one man had made use of a daughter as a toy. She shook the thought away.

In the distance one group of refugees decided to fight. The skirmish lasted all of thirty seconds before it was put down. Spears went up. Spears went down. Swords did the same thing. After that the crowd followed directions and moved to the east and the ocean.

It was a long, slow process. Tully watched on and wondered how many of the people in the distance she had known back when she lived in Hollum. Best not to think about that. Best to be happier with her new life.

The clouds had come in and the rains had started, but long before the migration of Hollum's people was finished, the hellish part of the storm had reached the city of Torema.

They were soaked through by the time their work was done.

Stanna made sure to post soldiers along the edge of the city. A great number of soldiers. Almost all of them had spears, the better to intimidate anyone thinking of moving for the city proper.

CHAPTER ELEVEN
HERE IN THE DARK

Brogan McTyre

The chamber was immense, but in comparison to the inside of the mountain it seemed almost tiny. In the distance, through the open mouth and the holes where nose and eye sockets were, Brogan could see the faint light from the crystals as the sun glowed through them. He had no idea what time it was. It hardly seemed important.

This was supposed to be the destination he sought. There was nothing he could see that was very impressive.

How many days did it take to scale a giant? He no longer knew.

Brogan sat on the ground – or what most closely resembled the ground – and grunted. His muscles shook from the strain of climbing.

Anna seemed to be in the same situation.

Faceless, the bastard, was perfectly fine. Of course there was the possibility that the damned thing didn't breathe or strain muscles. It was hard to say.

It had continued to change; there was a face of sorts, rudimentary as it might be, and the hide of the thing had smoothed out as if a proper craftsman had sanded and shaved the rough, wood-like surface of the thing and then polished and lacquered it to a fine finish.

Anna looked up at the depths of the giant's skull.

"The sun sets soon enough. We should make camp and prepare for the morning. I think we'll need more light than we have right now."

He nodded his head. "I've doubts we'll get much brighter. None of the glow comes into this area like it did in others, but we can make a fire, I suppose, as long as we're careful."

She turned her head to study him. "Do you think we'll smoke ourselves out?" Anna's voice carried an amused note to it.

"Likely no. There's plenty of air in here." He smiled at her tone. "But one can't be too careful."

"One can. We have enough to do; I think we'll be safe from a blaze in here. Safe from smoke. I can feel the breeze blowing through here." Anna held up a hand. "It's constant and moves toward the mouth of the thing."

Faceless looked at each of them with his unsettling hollow sockets. Brogan knew he saw, but still had no idea how.

"Faceless?"

"Yes, Brogan?"

"Have you figured out what you are yet?"

"No."

"And does that worry you?"

Anna got that look on her face, again. She had been

fine with Faceless when he followed them but knowing that the thing could talk left her unsettled.

Brogan frowned. He wasn't quite sure when he'd started thinking of Faceless as a male. The notion made him uncomfortable, too. Thinking of Faceless as a male meant thinking of the animated shape as closer to human. He wasn't sure he liked that notion very much.

Faceless remained silent for a moment and then shrugged his shoulders. He was not familiar with the gesture, but he had seen both Anna and Brogan use it and had apparently intuited what it meant.

"I am not sure. I've never thought about it before. I merely am."

"You're changing." Anna spoke softly. "You have fingers now, and toes." She looked him over. "And if the rest of you keeps changing I will have to ask Brogan to help you dress yourself for my sake. I've no desire to see what is forming between your legs."

Faceless looked down and shrugged again, apparently not at all impressed by the penis-shaped lump forming where before he had been smooth and genderless.

"How long have you been here, Faceless?"

"I do not know, Anna. I have always been here for as long as I can remember, but I only met Brogan recently." He turned toward her. "And then you."

Brogan set to starting a small fire with tinder and flint. As she had before, Anna managed to rummage in her bag until she found a small bundle of wood. Brogan did not like to think about that. Sorcery in any form unsettled him. And yet here he was, working out the details of a sorcerous attempt to fight the gods.

What else was there? He was a man. The gods were

not mortal. He could die and if the gods could die they needed help to remember how.

"What is it we do here, Anna?"

She looked at him for a moment as she set the wood in place. The small stack of tinder was burning properly and if she did her part the fire would be enough to give them light for the rest of the evening.

"We're making a fire. I think you mean something else. Speak clearly."

"I've said what I want. Will we be able to do it? Truly?"

"The Galean I spoke with has shown me what must be done. I have what I need. You brought the final part of the mix." She pointed to the saddlebag, which even now pulsed slowly as the contents sought to escape the bindings.

"That?" He looked at the bag. "The hide of an Undying?"

"I do not question the Galeans. They had much longer than me to study the Books of Galea. If we are to succeed, we will need that hide. We will also need to find what it is we seek here."

"What do we seek?" Brogan looked around. "I see nothing."

"Not all things are meant to be seen. You can't see the wind, and yet it is a powerful thing."

"Still, how do we find what can't be seen? I can feel the wind. I can watch the path the wind takes. Here there is nothing."

Anna continued stacking wood around the small fire and it crackled and grew, taking on a proper life. The glow highlighted her face and gave her a warmth that was stolen by the darkness. Brogan made himself look away.

"All I know, Brogan, is that we are supposed to be here. We will find the source soon enough and we will do what we can to work magic. If all goes well, you will be able to meet with and face the gods."

"I don't care about meeting them. I want them done. I want them ended."

Faceless spoke up, his words once again coming from nowhere. "Walthanadurn."

"I have no idea what that means."

"It is a name. Walthanadurn was the name of the god that died here. We stand in his remains." Faceless looked down at his hands. "He is dead, of course, but I can hear him."

"What do you mean you can hear him?" Brogan felt his skin crawl.

"He is still here. He is dead, but no god ever truly dies. They simply lose their connection to the world around them."

Faceless stood and moved closer to the fire. For the first time there was a light within the sockets where eyes should have been. Brogan could not decide if that faint glimmer was a reflection of the fire or something else, but either way it unsettled him.

"What does he say?" Anna asked.

"I do not think the god appreciates our invasion."

Brogan shook his head. "He wants us gone, he can tell us so himself, and if he gives us what we need we'll likely be glad to leave." There were no noises, no voices. Like as not Faceless was addled.

Faceless turned his way. "That is not the wisest course

of action with a god."

Brogan shook his head and stood up. "So far I've not done well with keeping gods happy. They've failed to appease me too, so we're even."

The sound was so low that Brogan felt it more than he heard it. His bones seemed to shiver deep inside his body and his guts churned. The feeling faded almost as quickly as it had come around. Anna felt it too, he could tell by the expression of discomfort on her face. If Faceless felt anything, he gave no sign.

Faceless looked his way. "That was Walthanadurn speaking."

"What did he say?"

"He said you had questions and that I should answer them."

Anna frowned. "Of course we have questions."

"Why was he murdered?" Brogan asked. He couldn't imagine why a god would fight another god.

"He was sacrificed. He was the last god left in the world that came before ours. The gods had fought to see who would control all of the world and toward the end, the battles had ruined almost everything that existed. The newer gods came to Walthanadurn, and Sepsumannahun, his oldest child, demanded that he surrender. Walthanadurn drew his weapon and was killed for his efforts. This is all that is left of him. He says the other gods used the rest of his body to rebuild the world."

"If he's dead how can he speak to us?"

"As I said, he cannot truly ever die. The world is built from his remains. He is everywhere."

Anna said, "And the gods destroyed him as they

destroy this world, is that correct?"

Faceless looked her way. "I suppose it is. That might be why he is now restless."

"Restless?" Brogan frowned.

"He moved just the other day. Not much, but he moved." Faceless looked at them and shrugged again. "He is the spine of this world. What they do to the world hurts him."

Brogan considered those words carefully and did not like their implications. If a dead god felt pain long after dying, the possibility that his family still suffered was greater than he wanted to consider, and yet...

"He feels pain. Do all of the dead feel pain? Does my family suffer after being sacrificed to the gods?"

"There is no death for those sacrificed to the gods. They become one with the gods, a part of them."

"Do they feel pain?" he asked the question again. His heart felt heavy. His blood thick. His stomach churned.

"That is part of the offering. Those sacrificed suffer that the gods can be free of their own agonies."

Anna shook her head, horrified.

Brogan spoke calmly enough, though calm was the last thing he felt. "Does Walthanadurn still feel pain?"

"He feels what the land feels. The storms cut him. The winds caress him. The waters bathe him. He is the world and all that it suffers, he endures."

"Ask him this. Would he be freed from that pain?"

"Yes." Faceless nodded his head slowly. "He has suffered for as long as the land has been here and he would be free of that."

Brogan nodded and then calmed himself. He wanted to rage. He wanted to scream and cut and kill. That he had lost his loved ones was a horror. That they still suffered for the cause of the gods was more than he wanted to know.

"Then tell him to show me what I need to kill the gods."

Faceless stared long and hard at Brogan, his eyes once more nothing but pools of darkness.

"He has but waited for you to ask."

Interlude: From the Sea

Past the place where Saramond had been, the waters surged and rose in a wave the likes of which had never been seen by a human being. There were no human witnesses, but the gulls in the air and the fish in the sea saw and understood. The single wave rose higher still and charged at the land, smashing itself against rocks, debris and the few remaining structures from Saramond. The waters tore across the land, and those foolish people who'd decided they could survive the changing face of the area were slaughtered for their folly, crushed beneath the waves, churned along with sodden earth and bashed into so much shredded pulp by the force of the wave.

Oftentimes a wave loses power as it collides with the land, but this wave defied that notion, surging larger, pulling more water from the ocean even as it shattered land and tore a trench several hundred feet deep across the crust of the earth.

Three hundred miles away the earth shuddered and rocked. Where Hollum stood, buildings collapsed, torn asunder by the vibrations and the surges of water slamming into buildings already weakened by the flood. There were always some who refused to abandon what was theirs, and this was no exception. None of the stragglers survived the surge that tore Hollum apart.

That very same surge started to falter after hitting the city. Even the largest wave must eventually lose power, and this wave was headed west. To the south the waters dispersed, and by the time they reached where Edinrun had been the waters were less than a foot deep. What came across Torema several hours later was merely a heavy trickle that soon rejoined the sea.

What rode beneath that wave, what had brought the water to shore, was a different story entirely. It drove hard toward the distant Broken Blades, eager to reach the area and end the conversation between mortal and dead god. The waters that had found an escape route through Harlea's Pass rose to a height almost thirty feet above that passageway, and the force of the water surging through the opening in the mountains was enough to devastate anything on the other side. The waters blasted through the opening and washed away everything in their path, instantly raising the level of the newly formed river to well over the flood levels. The river had no choice but to once again widen and carve its way through the earth and down to bedrock.

As the behemoth surged along its course toward the Broken Swords it tore at the foundations of the land, shattering stone and breaking everything it encountered.

Saramond, already dead, was easily destroyed. The mountains were still distant, and they were much larger.

Inside the mountains Brogan continued with his plans.

On the mountain pathways soldiers and prisoners walked, and near the very top of the mountains Stennis Brae continued on, waiting for a king to return and for a sign that salvation was still a possibility.

Even the forces controlled by gods take time to reach their destinations.

Bron McNar

Bron McNar walked through the dark tunnels and did his best to understand what he was seeing. There was mostly darkness, with hints and promises of actual sights. There were scents that should not have been there. He had been to the ocean only once in his life but he knew what the waters there smelled like, and the breezes that blew across him sometimes smelled and tasted like those distant memories.

Somewhere ahead of him Parrish was walking, but he could neither see nor sense the man at all. Instead he was by himself, walking down twisting tunnels that should not have been possible within the Cauldron. Even if most of what lay within the walls of the building was hollow, he had traveled too far to be within the confines of the structure and the distances above his head were too high to be held by the monolithic structure.

Pardume was long gone, having entered the Cauldron before even Parrish. There had been no sound from the man, no sight of him since he'd stepped into the monolith.

The wind changed again and brought with it a staggering heat.

Bron stopped moving and looked around, annoyed.

There was a possibility that he was supposed to be afraid, and perhaps he was on one level or another, but this was his world that needed saving – his family, his friends, his bloody kingdom.

"Enough games! Show yourself to me!" His voice cracked – the dry air was torturous and the heat left his skin feeling roasted. His hand gripped at the only security he'd ever needed, the hilt of his axe.

Everything changed. The winds became a howling wall that shoved at him, cast him backward into hot sand and nearly buried him alive. The skies opened even higher, showing him constellations that made no sense, which had never existed in the skies he knew from home. The walls were torn away, replaced by distant mountains and jagged towers that made the Cauldron seem ineffectual and insignificant.

Bron forced himself to stand. If this was a test of some kind he would either pass it or he would die in the effort.

Almost as soon as he thought it, the winds faded down to a gentle sigh.

Around him, beneath him, everything calmed.

And in the distance he felt more than saw the presence. There was something on the horizon, but it was too large to truly see. His mind refused to accept the possibility of anything that massive.

"Why are you here?" The words rippled through him. He was staggered by their force, but he did not fall.

"Parrish says we have the same enemies. He says I should work with you. I came to discuss that. Nothing more." He found looking at the distant mountaintop was easier than staring at that impossible form, so vast and incomprehensible.

"I am a prisoner. I am kept here by the gods. I would be free."

"The gods shatter the world. They end everything because one of their sacrifices was stopped. I would see that ended."

"Then we do indeed have the same enemy."

"I am not Parrish. I do not need to be marked. I do not need to prove myself. I have a kingdom. I have soldiers. I'll join with you in a fight, but I am my own man. I am my own king and I do not need more gods." Bron kept the tremble from his voice, but it was not easy. Whatever he faced had changed Parrish and his soldiers. Perhaps it was not a god, but he suspected that here, in this place, it came very close.

"The mark is not only to identify. It helps me move from my prison here and see the world beyond."

"Do you not already do that with Parrish and his Marked Men?"

"They are not enough. I need more."

"And what do I get in exchange? What do my people get in exchange?"

There was a long moment of silence.

"If you join with me, I will spare your people from their fate."

"What fate?" His body felt cold. There was no doubt in his mind that Theragyn, the new god of Parrish's people, was speaking a truth. There was nothing the creature could gain from lying. It was as simple a truth as the fact that he gained nothing from lying to a dog, or to a loaf of bread.

"Even now the gods seek to shatter the mountains. They seek Brogan McTyre, and he is hidden away within the Broken Swords, seeking power he should not reach for."

"If I join you, my people will be spared from this fate?"

"Yes. But if you do not join me soon, it will be too late."

Before he could say more Bron was assaulted by an image of the mountains where his kingdom stood crumbling, shattering. The castle he had built and called home broke into fragments as the mountain beneath it crumbled, split and collapsed upon itself. He saw the devastation, felt it tremble through his body, and heard the titanic roar of stone shattering as a great force hard enough to liquefy stone slammed into the mountains.

Bron fell down to his knees, terrified and humbled by the image that overwhelmed his senses. This, he knew, was the end of everything that mattered in his world. The family he loved, the kingdom he ruled, the life he had built for himself since he was old enough to walk, and to fight, and to stand on his own. The images faded. But the memory did not.

"You can stop that from happening?"

"I can save your people. The land may be impossible to protect."

A man who is king must first follow the needs of his kingdom.

Bron looked past the mountain that held his attention and forced himself to see the vast presence in the distance.

Bron's voice trembled and he no longer tried to hide it. The notion that his world was so fragile was always there, but now he understood the concept more readily and his pride seemed a trifling thing in comparison. "I will serve you in any way I must. You have only to tell me what I must do."

The world he'd been taken to faded away and was replaced by the walls of the Cauldron once more. The scent of the ocean returned, and the dry heat of the area offered its own satisfaction.

"But come to me and kneel. Offer me all that you are and I will offer you back a world more to your liking."

When Bron walked forward again it was with greater purpose.

Interlude: Jahda

Jahda walked the edge of the world, and took vast strides across the distances. Had he been truly in the Five Kingdoms he would have traveled much slower, but he walked the pathways offered by the Shimmer and each step he made was more like a hundred long strides.

There was no time.

The world was ending, after all, and he wanted to make sure his fellow Louron were well away before the gods finished their punishment.

Not that he needed to worry. There were other places for them to go.

Other worlds. He shook his head at the thought. He'd been happy here, but that was something that was changing. Peace was what he wanted. This? This was endless destruction.

He stepped away from the Shimmer and looked at the world he'd chosen to call home, settling his feet carefully in the heavy drifts of powdery white. The entire area was a wasteland of ice and snow. Where he stopped was the very easternmost edge of the Broken Swords, and he stared hard farther east. He could not see Edinrun, though he knew it should have been within his view. Distant, yes, and there was the snow to consider, but still, he should have seen it. Edinrun was a vast city with a wall that was constantly lit by torches lest anyone try to surprise the people there. It was missing.

Impossible, of course, but as a Louron he understood where it had probably gone. The walls between worlds were there, but with the right knowledge, or the help of the Shimmer, doorways could be opened and walls could be torn down.

Further away, impossible to see even from the height of the mountains. Torema stewed in its own air. He loved the city despite its many flaws.

Further still lay the Kaer-ru islands and home. It was time. He would be moving on. All the Louron would be moving on, or at least those who listened to his advice.

"You are a very difficult man to find."

He was not easily startled, but Jahda jumped a bit and his hand gripped the walking staff he carried much harder. He was first and foremost an Inquisitor, though he had not served in that capacity in years. He was capable of defending himself from most attacks.

The man Jahda found smiling at him was as short as he himself was tall. Dark hair, dark skin, a bright smile and fine clothes that should have seen him frozen to the ground rather than kept pleasantly warm. Up close those clothes were fraying at the edges. Closer still and one could see the stubble on the stranger's face and the exhaustion he tried to hide with his grin. The cold seemed to have no impact on him and his hat kept the worst of the snow from brushing across his broad features.

"I am often on the move. And yet you have found me. How may I help you?" Jahda managed a smile of his own, but it was difficult. The man was Galean and oftentimes those people had their own agendas.

"I am Roskell Turn. I am a Galean and I must ask for your assistance."

"Truly?" Jahda smiled more brightly. It was rare that a Galean asked for help.

"Indeed. I must reach the heart of the Broken Swords." Roskell pointed his hand toward the north. "The very height of the mountains, and I must be there within the next few hours. There are only one people I know who can manage that feat and I am not numbered among the Louron."

"What makes you think the Louron could help you?"

Roskell smiled. "In this world or the next, only the Louron can walk along the Shimmering Path."

"Others can walk it with our help."

"And now you understand why I have sought you." That smile again, one part friendly and two parts mischief, but he found himself liking the Galean just the same and he always trusted his instincts.

"Why should I help you, Roskell Turn?"

"Because I want to see the world saved, and according to one of my disciples the man who is hiding inside the mountains is our best chance of that."

"What is the man doing?"

"Trying to fight the gods."

"Gods cannot be fought. That is their greatest gift. No mortal can reach the gods. No mortal can touch the gods. No mortal can harm the gods. Is that not so?"

Roskell nodded and his smile stayed in place. "I have read the Books of Galea. I am one of few who has read over half of the thousand volumes. Along the way I learned that there are ways to break the rules if one is bold enough."

"And do you think this man is bold enough?"

"I have not met Brogan McTyre, but I understand he was mad enough to challenge the gods, and now he is mad enough to fight them. I think he will do all he can and I think that works to the benefit of everyone."

"He is supposed to be captured on sight and brought in for sacrifice."

"Have you ever known the gods to want to fight on a level field?" Roskell gestured again at the mountain range. "Or are they more likely to attack as a pack of dogs would, and to worry their opponents to exhaustion?"

Jahda chuckled at that. The legends of what lay beneath the surface of the Broken Swords were varied, but most claimed it was a dead god, or a dead giant, and that the giant was slaughtered, not killed in honorable combat.

"True enough, one supposes. How am I supposed to help you?"

"You can get me to the place I need to be and I can help Brogan McTyre find a way to fight the gods."

"Wouldn't it be easier to simply surrender him to the gods and be done with it?"

"It would be easier to feed a pack of hungry wolves than to fight them, but within days the same problem arises again."

Jahda studied the younger man for a few moments then smiled. "I will take you to find Brogan McTyre."

The Galean bowed and lowered his head. "You are a good man, Jahda of Louron."

"I have been called worse."

He gestured the other man closer and then called on the Shimmer. As the way between worlds opened he placed his hand on the other man's arm. "Do not let go of me. Do not walk away. The Shimmer is not always kind to strangers."

Roskell nodded his head and took a solid grip on the coat Jahda wore.

A moment later they walked into the Shimmer and Roskell let out a gasp of fear.

"Look to me, Roskell Turn. Do not stare too closely into the Shimmer. You might not like what stares back."

Without another word they were on their way. The Galean was terrified, and he trembled. In order to ensure that the worst did not happen, Jahda ran, taking vast strides, and when the Galean could not quite keep up he half-lifted the man and forced him along.

"What am I looking for, Roskell Turn?"

He said nothing, but instead the Galean's fingers touched Jahda's brow. An instant later Jahda understood what the other was seeking and it was his turn to tremble.

"You ask much of me, Galean."

"How else can we hope to save a world, Jahda of Louron?"

They ran through the places that hide between worlds and the Shimmer kept them safe even as it showed its newest visitor hints of a thousand endless horrors.

Harper Ruttket

The ship was of good size and Harper nodded his head. This close in, the harbor stank of dead fish and rotting vegetation. It was not as lovely as it seemed at a distance. Still the vessel he stared at was impressively large and seemed well tended, with three masts and enough space to accommodate as many as a hundred men comfortably. It would do.

"This will do."

Captain Odobo nodded and smiled. "How much do you offer?"

"How much do you ask?"

The price he expected was preposterous.

"I could build a dozen ships for that."

"You will not have time to build a dozen ships, and I must pay my crew."

"Does your crew live like kings?"

"I cannot offer my ship and my services for less."

"I can always find another ship."

Harper let his mind work on the haggling while he looked around. It was a good ship. Never much of a sailor himself he had made it a point to study ships on the occasions when he sailed and he had asked all the questions he could think of. That was the thing about a mercenary's life. You never knew what information would come in handy.

"Let's see the inside then. If you want me to pay a fortune I should see what I am buying."

"You will never find a better ship," Odobo promised.

They walked up the gangway and stood on the deck.

The wood was well tended. The equipment Harper could see was in excellent shape.

Odobo led the way into the bowels of the vessel and Harper studied everything. Part of him hoped to find flaws. Part of him was pleased when he did not.

They discussed prices and terms for several more minutes. Harper let the man win the war for a good price. A happy captain meant a safe journey.

"We will need to travel fast, and we will need to travel far."

"Where do you wish to go?"

"When I am certain I will let you know; for now keep the ship safe from strangers and load up with supplies. No one wants to starve on this journey."

"I have been to other lands, Pressya and to Lomorride. I have even sailed the edge of Bright Hook and Star's End. Wherever you want to go, we will get there."

"Excellent. I've no desire to pay enough to own a fleet of ships and then get sunk."

Odobo laughed.

Harper looked the man in his eyes. He did not smile in return. Instead he offered over one-tenth the cost of the ship. "You receive the rest after we launch. No one climbs aboard the ship that is not your crew or mine. There will be people seeking passage. You are no longer a passenger ship. Do you understand?"

Odobo smiled and nodded. "I am the captain. You pay my way. Yours is the only voice I'll let have say above my own on your ship."

"Good man." Harper smiled. "Buy your supplies, we'll be leaving fairly soon. We only wait on a few more people."

Harper gestured to the rest of his people. "In the meantime, we'll be finding places to settle in. The city has no spare rooms."

Odobo looked out at Torema as it rose slowly over the bay. From the lowest parts to the highest there were trails of smoke where fires burned. Those streamers married together with the clouds that spanned on as far as the eye could see. Rain came down and washed constantly into the harbor and still more people were coming to Torema to escape the ruination of all that rested behind those clouds.

"Do you suppose this is the end of the world?" Odobo spoke softly, and looked at Harper.

"It might be." Harper nodded his head. "It might not. We will see what can be fixed."

Interlude: Stanna

Torema was a mess. The city was flooded by waters and by people alike. Stanna looked at Hillar Darkraven, the woman who ruled over the city, and kept her face neutral.

"You did an excellent job of handling the newcomers, Stanna. Thank you for that." Stanna nodded her head. Darkraven continued. "Not as well when it came to finding Harper Ruttket."

"I saw him. I reached for him. He broke free. There were too many people in the way and if I'd pursued him then it might have caused a riot."

"A riot? Really?" The woman's voice was mixed with frost and doubt.

Stanna set her hilted sword on the table with a loud

thump. "Normally, I draw steel, people tend to notice."

Darkraven nodded and chuckled. "Point taken."

"If he's in the city your spies will find him soon enough. If he has left the city he'll likely come back." She gestured out the window that led to Darkraven's balcony. The view stretched out to look down at the harbor and the rough seas. "There is nowhere else to go."

Hillar Darkraven's good humor faded as she too studied the view.

"Have you ever been to Kaer-ru?" The woman's voice was soft and husky.

Stanna nodded. "Aye."

"Are there islands out there that could hold more people?"

"Do you think to invade?" Stanna frowned.

Hillar Darkraven pointed one scarred hand toward the north. "We just had several inches of water running from up north down into the harbor for over five hours. Half the people from Hollum likely got themselves washed into the sea, Stanna. Every report I hear is that the situation to our north is only getting worse and the only thing south of us is the water and the islands beyond."

"There are other lands."

"I'd not start a war."

"As you have already seen for yourself, money speaks where even swords are silent. Torema has the banks for most of the land. I have a fortune I'm planning to withdraw in the next day or so."

"Are you planning on leaving?"

"Not if I don't have to, but if I do, I'll be gathering

a ship and my closest companions. We'll find another land." Stanna shrugged. "I like you well enough. We could travel together."

Darkraven chuckled. She and Stanna had much in common, not the least of which was a highly developed sense of gallows humor.

The world seemed determined to end. They both intended to survive that possibility.

Stanna said, "Should I be looking into ships?"

Darkraven answered, "We have plenty." She gestured to the docks. "I own most of that."

Stanna smiled. "Well then, I suppose I should stay on your good side."

The other woman looked her way for a moment and then back out at the waters. "It never hurts."

"They'll come for the city. The refugees. They'll want solid buildings instead of tents."

Darkraven nodded. "And what do you plan to do about it?"

"The lads are building a barricade wall made of spears and pointed sticks. You have recently purchased most of the available lumber in the city. I expect the bills will be coming soon."

The woman shrugged. "Long as the wall serves its purpose, all is well. I've certainly got the money to spare."

"The soldiers will do their part and the men building the wall know what the stakes are." Stanna sighed, took her boots from the table's surface where they had been resting and, because she liked Darkraven, she even wiped the worst of the mud from the table's edge. "I suppose I should check on them. Time to change the guards in any event. Men get coin, they want to spend it."

Darkraven smiled and Stanna knew why. The woman owned a part of most of the taverns and whorehouses. That was why she was as powerful as any king.

Stanna frowned. "What do we do if any of the other kingdoms show up here and ask for mercy?"

"The same as we did for Hollum. There are places on the sidelines. If they want more, we'll have to draw swords and finish them."

"Do you think they'll come?"

Darkraven smiled. "Of course they will. There is nowhere else to go, as you already pointed out."

Stanna nodded. "I suppose I'll be buying the rest of the lumber on your behalf."

"Buy the spears and the swords, too. Soldiers need weapons to work."

Stanna nodded. "Shovels. Ditches don't dig themselves."

Darkraven shook her head. "Running a kingdom is hard work."

"Well. Costly at the very least."

Stanna left the room and then the palace. She had work to do and less time than she wanted to consider.

Interlude: The Iron Mothers

The Iron Mothers did not speak. If truth be known they had no vocal cords and no need of speech. They were not social creatures. They were Iron Mothers, and they had their own needs and desires that the humans would never understand.

Ariah did not make them to be friendly.

The sun set on the area near Torema that some were quickly calling the Hollum Slums. The rains were constant, the mud was thick, the desperation of the people in the area was heavy and even though they did not care, the Iron Mothers sensed the need and hunger of the locals.

The people of Hollum wanted land that was dry and buildings over their heads. Instead they had tents or lean-tos and little else. The stench of raw sewage was everywhere and most of the refugees had taken to letting the rain wash away their wastes.

The Iron Mothers still did not care. What mattered to them was the very efficient barrier that had been placed between the people of Hollum and the city. They needed the hard structures too but for entirely different reasons.

The good news for the Iron Mothers was simply that they were not human. There were a lot of guards, and those people were armed with swords, and shields, and other means of repelling human forces.

Through the continuously pouring rains the Iron Mothers gathered together. Most had found clothes, but few had found much by way of true protection. Since Brogan McTyre had defied the gods the Iron Mothers had gone from being Grakhul, to enslaved Grakhul, to sacrifices to Ariah. From that point on they had been altered by the demon, used as hunters and gatherers of the twenty who were sought by the gods and then, finally, they had come to serve the purpose for which they had been truly created.

They gathered the seeds, they planted the seeds within themselves, and they let the seeds grow. Those seeds had been born of Ariah's Children. Grown on the body of one man, fertilized by the blood of hounds and humans alike and then finally placed within the Iron Mothers to incubate properly.

It is said that demons cannot create. They can only alter.

Ariah found his way around that problem. He altered, and then let the humans create. Human life, human blood, had changed what he shaped. Now, the seeds came closer to fruition, and his offspring needed only the right conditions to finish their metamorphosis.

The Iron Mothers joined together, a little over one hundred women who were not dressed for rain and cold, who stared at the gathered soldiers and considered their best way past the barriers.

The soldiers stared back, saw pale women who reeked of desperation. Some of them might well have considered a trade – the women coming through the barrier in exchange for a good rut – but few of them considered the idea for long. The captains were loyal to Stanna and General Stanna would gut anyone who broke her orders as easily as she gutted cowards.

Fear is often the best motivator after greed.

A few of the soldiers made their comments. They gestured to their privates and made lewd offers to the Iron Mothers. The women did not understand or, frankly, care. They had an imperative to answer to and that was all that drove them.

They could try to fight their way past swords and barriers or they could go out of their way and seek an easier resolution. Fight or flight.

Sometimes combat is easiest. Other times...

As one, the group turned and started moving down toward the waters of the harbor. The construction had not yet reached that far and it would take them out of their way, but their burdens were precious to Ariah and therefore precious to them.

The rains fell and the cold crushed the spirits of workers and stragglers alike, as night grew deeper still.

Within an hour the group had found their way past the barrier and into the city proper. The path they chose required that they wallow through streams of water that had already been tainted by the waste of a thousand people or more, but that did not matter. They climbed from their stream and the rains came down hard enough to wash away the worst of the filth.

The streets of Torema were grossly overrun with people and their belongings. There were few spots that were not already claimed by the desperate and the angry. The Iron Mothers did not care. They moved past the huddled masses and further into the darkest places.

Not every one of the Iron Mothers managed to find a place without challenge. Several of them were faced with opposition. Some carried sticks; a few had daggers or even axes and swords.

What not one of them had was skin as tough as steel or claws that could rend flesh, or the strength to break bones. The Iron Mothers had all the tools they needed to protect their unborn children.

They used those tools to their advantage and a score of people died trying to stop them.

When they had found the proper places, the Iron Mothers did what they had to do. They entered the final stages of their life spans and began the metamorphosis.

The waters were an issue, and so they scaled walls and found places under roofs that were already dripping a constant stream of rain. With fingers and toes that could carve through hard wood, they dug into mortar and stone alike, and gripped the surfaces of the walls.

Once in place they opened their mouths and let the glands that grew there do their jobs. Fine silk spun out from distended jaws and painted over their wet bodies, coating flesh and the closest surfaces alike. When they had finished covering their bodies, they used the wind to help them spread the silk over their heads and faces until they were completely hidden away from the world around them. The silk was strong, but as the weather continued the fine strands grew harder still, until they were tough enough to resist even the finest edges.

They had done what they were meant to do, the Iron Mothers, and so they rested in their cocoons.

And while they rested, they changed one last time, making way for the children they carried and loved on behalf of Ariah.

And Ariah saw what his Iron Mothers had done and was pleased by their sacrifices.

Interlude: The Waters

The great gaping wound cut into the earth by the sea took its toll, even as the source of that wound barreled relentlessly toward the Broken Swords. The land, broken and misused, shuddered and shook and then split. Where Saramond had been, the great fissure snapped open and hurled rock and mud high past the surface of the waters.

The waves caused by the explosive earthquake were vast, and ran both north and south. The fissure opened in those directions as well, and the land that had been one became three. To the north a thick finger of land split away and broke apart along the lines of the Three Serpent Rivers, and became a wedge as the rift grew stronger. The land that had once been ruled by the Grakhul, already damaged, collapsed completely into the ocean. Several hundred miles of coastline to the north sank into the waters with a violent splash that sent still more waves rising and roaring across the land.

To the south the same occurred. A massive break in the continent ran nearly all the way to Hollum before it stopped. The land there sank more slowly, but it sank just the same. The coastal towns in that area had been hit hard, but until that moment they had survived the worst. That was no longer the case. Adimone, a large town that had always been faithful to the gods, was not spared, nor were the other, smaller villages that dotted the eastern coast of the land. Though many people had moved on, the stragglers were consumed by the sea and drawn away from the land in one titanic surge that swept in and then back out as if a giant were swallowing a vast gulp of the ocean.

When the waters returnedthey did not bring with them the bodies of the dead. Those corpses were gone, devoured by the goddess with a thousand names. The time for patience was over and the gods were hungry.

Further west the first wave that had sloughed across the land continued to build in force. Whatever it was that drove that wave surged forward and pounded across the land, shattering stone and crushing all that stood in its way.

It would not be stopped.

It was divine fury and it had been cast at the form of a dead god in an effort to stop the impossible from happening.

Still, in this, even the actions of the gods took time.

CHAPTER TWELVE
THE COST OF DOING BUSINESS

Brogan McTyre

Brogan stood as still as he could while Anna moved her fingers over his bared flesh, making the markings she said would aid him with the course they had chosen.

Faceless watched on, seemingly fascinated.

Brogan tried his best not to consider the situation. Currently his friend's wife was squatting before him and her left hand held onto his thigh while the right painted markings across his lower stomach. They both did their very best to ignore the erection that pointed in her direction. She did not look at it and he did his best not to think about any of what was going on. He had not expected that having his body painted by someone could be so very… sensual.

As if his world could not have been made more awkward, Brogan heard the sound of voices approaching. He was naked as the day he was born, and his weapons were a dozen feet away from him. His body was smeared in different dyes and his hair was knotted at the top of his head, giving the paints time to dry on his face, neck and shoulders.

"You cannot possibly be serious." His voice actually cracked and he looked toward his axe.

Anna said, "Don't you dare move. I invited them."

"What are you talking about, woman? Invited who?"

He saw Faceless from the corner of his eye. The creature had no mouth and yet he would have sworn it was smirking. There was no proof, of course, only that feeling of being laughed at.

The two men who stepped from the shadows seemed to genuinely walk out of the darkness as if they were leaving a tunnel. For a moment their skin wavered and their features seemed as if viewed from under the surface of a moving stream. A moment later they were in the vast chamber of the dead god's skull and covered in snow that was rapidly melting in the presence of the fire.

They were island men, and completely unknown to him.

The taller of the two looked his way with wide, surprised eyes. The shorter stared a moment at his naked form and then stepped closer.

"You have already begun?"

Anna looked toward the man and nodded. "I have. I wasn't sure if you were actually going to reach us so I got started. I've followed your instructions as carefully as I could."

He looked at Brogan and said, "I am Roskell Turn. It's a pleasure to meet you, Brogan McTyre."

He quickly went back to looking over the markings already placed on Brogan. Without any additional words he reached into the pot of paint that Anna had prepared from her bag of impossible supplies and then touched Brogan's cheek, his chin, the area above his left nipple and then a spot near his left elbow.

Happily the presence of the new men had apparently taken his mind off Anna and his body was finally behaving itself.

"Who are you and why are you painting my body?" Brogan looked longingly at his axe again.

Faceless looked at where he was looking and started to reach for the weapon. Brogan couldn't decide if he should stop the creature.

The man smiled and repeated his name. "I am Roskell Turn. I am a Galean and Anna told me what you were doing," he continued. "She asked for my help in preparing you for what must be done."

As he spoke the stranger dabbed here and there, and once wiped away part of Anna's paint. He looked at the woman and spoke softly. "A few minor adjustments. Perhaps they would not matter but why take chances."

She nodded, apparently not at all offended by the strange man playing with her canvas. Brogan was still trying to decide if he were offended. Probably he should be but he'd hold off until he got a response from Anna.

"Do you have the Undying's hide?"

Anna nodded to the heavy satchel that carried the burden and Roskell in turn moved toward it.

"It's heavier than you'd expect." The man grunted as he pulled along the burden and Brogan felt a little better about how much he'd strained and tortured himself while carrying the damned thing.

"It also has teeth and will try to capture you if you are

not careful." Brogan spoke carefully so as not to mess up the drying markings on his face. Anna had already yelled at him for that twice and he didn't want to dare a third fit.

She shot him a murderous warning with her eyes, but calmed when she saw that the marks had not been damaged.

Faceless offered him his axe. "No, thank you."

The glossy hands of the creature took a firm grip on the weapon and he stood perfectly still.

The other man looked at Brogan and spoke softly. "By all rights you are supposed to be a sacrifice."

Brogan stared hard. "Is this an argument we're going have? Naked or not, armed or not, I'll defend myself."

"I prefer not to fight you, Brogan McTyre. As I have come to understand it several of your men have already died and the sacrifice would no longer be sufficient for the gods. That leaves us little we can do except hope that you can accomplish what you are trying to do here."

"And how would you know what I am attempting?"

"Roskell told me."

Anna spoke up. "And I told Roskell. He's here because he was the one who told me what must be done and I wanted him to make certain I did what he described properly. We're only going to get one chance at this, Brogan McTyre." She already sounded angry.

"I'm not debating your decisions, Anna, but it might have been nice if you'd told me we could get unexpected company."

"I'd fully thought he'd have to climb up here as we did. If I'd known there was a short cut we might have waited."

"I could hardly wait any longer. The gods have begun their attacks in earnest." Roskell spoke as he unfolded the hide of the Undying. When it started to writhe about on the floor he cast a thick gray powder over the skinned shape and it came to a very sudden stop.

"What did you do?"

"It's sleeping. Even the He-Kisshi must rest."

Brogan nodded his head, suitably impressed.

Without another word the man dragged the cloak around until the dark fur rested on the ground of the skull and the tendrils and wet interior faced the ceiling far above. More of the gray powder was spilled on the inside of the thing and then he crouched over it, carefully studying the details and minutiae.

The other man came closer and looked at the shape as well, as if they had found the most amazing new plaything. Brogan shook his head and looked down at Anna, who still had her hand on the inside of his thigh but was now painting the back of his leg.

Roskell Turn dipped two fingers into the pot of herbal paints and began making markings along the top of the hooded form. The teeth of the thing were obvious and looked as deadly as a few hundred daggers all neatly lined together.

When the vibrations ran through the body they all stood inside, Roskell and the other man were justifiably horrified.

Faceless spoke to him. "The gods are retaliating."

"To what?"

"The gods are gods, Brogan. They know what is happening here and they would stop it."

"What are they going to do?"

"Whatever they can to stop you. Already they are attacking, but it takes time to bring together the force they need."

"What are they going to do? Send an army?"

"They do not need an army. They are gods. What are they going to do? They are going to destroy all of us if you do not do what you must and very soon."

The taller of the strangers was looking at Faceless, studying him carefully, and all the while listening to the interplay of words. His face was a mask of curiosity.

Brogan looked at Anna. "Almost ready? We are apparently doomed."

"Don't make light of it, Brogan."

"I'm naked and defenseless, surrounded by strangers, a sorceress, and a thing carrying my axe. What makes you think I'm in a jesting mood?"

"We are ready here." Roskell nodded and stepped back from his work. Without waiting to be asked he moved over to Brogan and dipped his finger again in the mixture, which was now running dangerously low.

"No talking," Roskell advised. "We must finish now."

There was silence as the pair finished making their markings.

"What happens now?" Brogan asked the words as both stepped away.

Roskell and Anna grabbed the He-Kisshi's hide and moved it up to place it on his shoulders.

"The Undying are connected to the gods. They are a conduit. If all goes well, you will be connected with this god. Not those who have taken his place, but just this one. If I am right, that connection will grant you certain abilities."

The thick, heavy hide tightened itself around Brogan's neck and he let out a noise.

He wanted to ask what happened if Roskell Turn was wrong, but he never got the chance.

Interlude: Daivem Murdrow

She followed the carrion birds. Sometimes they knew best. Also, the crows were easily seen in the nearly endless field of white. Well, sometimes, at least.

Daivem Murdrow walked on through the snow and listened. The time she had was quickly running to an end. The waters were building, and she could feel them. She had done services for the dead and they had returned the favor, warning her about the great wave of ocean coming her way. It was not meant for her, but it came nonetheless and she had little choice but to finish her task, or be done with it.

The voice that cried out for her was strong and she intended to listen if she could.

The clouds had long since eaten the sky and the snow was falling so hard that seeing anything even ten feet away was a challenge. The only good news was that she did not need to see in order to know where she was going. She only had to listen.

The wails of anger were as harsh as the winds that cut at her exposed flesh in the cold of the storm. Whomever it was who had died out in the wastelands around her was furious to the point of madness.

She walked and she shivered until, at last, she located the source of the rage that burned so brightly and made her walk so far.

That he was dead was impossible to deny. He seemed to have fallen from a very great height and shattered on the ground, but if he had fallen from a mountainside that mountain had moved on.

Daivem carefully removed the snow from the frozen corpse. It was broken and bloodied and if there had been a face it had been pulped beyond recognition even before the cold and wet got to it.

As often happened the spirit was tied to the corpse and not at all pleased.

Daivem nodded her head and spoke softly. "You would be gone from here. Yes?"

The only answer was another scream that no one but a trained Inquisitor might ever hear.

Without a body the spirit would either disperse or go away, but this one seemed to want more. For that reason alone, when she freed the essence of Niall Leraby from his remains she carefully bound him to her walking stick. It was a temporary solution, of course. But it would do.

"Yes." She listened and she nodded. "Yes, I can find them for you." Her smile was warm. "Of course I will find them. It is what I do."

She left the body where it lay. It was only meat and bone and without the spirit locked into it, there was little purpose to it, save to feed the crows that had already been feasting on frozen bits.

Beron

The behemoth surged and pounded toward the mountains, but was not seen by even those who were currently on their paths.

All they saw was the water, an endless wave that hammered toward the Broken Swords at a speed they could not hope to match.

The soldiers looked to their leader. Ulster Dunally in turn looked at the water surge coming their way and called out, "Run and ride! Get up the trail and go higher!" They were fortunate in that they were already near the top of the mountain. There was no careful thought given. There was only retreat.

The men in charge of the prisoners did their jobs. They took control of their horses and they rode, urging the powerful animals higher and higher toward the crest. Those caught in the wagons screamed and roared and prayed as they saw fit but there was nothing they could do.

Beron had never felt so helpless in his entire life. He was chained in place and locked inside a slaver's wagon – one of his own, actually – and there was nothing he could do but hope they did not lose purchase and slide back down the mountain toward the monstrous wall of ocean that was hammering toward them.

"Ariah. I have failed you, but I would serve you still if you will allow it."

He closed his eyes as he spoke and in an instant was once more in the garden of Ariah. The long, lean form of the creature was the same as before.

"You have not failed me, Beron."

"I haven't?"

"Not at all." The handsome face was amused. The vines wrapped around the demon's arm had swelled even more and thorns punctured his flesh bloodlessly.

"I am not done with you yet, Beron of Saramond."

"The world looks to be ending."

"I am not done with the world, either."

"Where am I to go? What am I to do?"

"You are already here, Beron. There is nowhere else to go for now."

"I thought…" He looked down at his hands. "I thought this was all in my mind."

"No. Not this time."

Ariah came closer to him, his serene smile in place, and touched the iron that locked Beron's hands together. The metal corroded and fell apart in seconds. As he watched, the chains around his ankles crumbled away as well.

"The world is changing. Beron. That cannot be stopped. But you are still my faithful follower and you will lead my armies across the face of this planet when I am freed from my domain."

"Your army?"

"They will rise soon enough. In the meantime, I need you to ride for Torema. There are people who are merely waiting for you to come to them and lead them."

"Ride?"

"I brought you here, Beron. Did you think I couldn't bring you a horse?"

"I never truly thought about it."

Ariah turned and walked. "I have a horse. I have your weapons. I have a shield for you this time, too. Try not to lose them. They are precious to me and hard to find from my current location."

He nodded to the demon as if the words made perfect sense. Ariah may as well have been explaining the basics of flying between Harlea and Emila. Beron heard but without much comprehension. He was still working out the details of being alive when he knew that the mountain he was standing on was about to be destroyed.

Ariah stopped before a table laden with fruit and nuts and even a selection of fresh meats. The sounds that Beron's stomach made would have intimidated the average bear. Ravenous was the only word that worked.

Ariah gestured for him to eat and Beron listened enthusiastically, nodded as the demon talked on, explaining in detail what was expected. He had to ride to Torema. There he would find his army waiting. In Torema he was to attack and seize control of the lands. The people there had to be made aware that they fought for Ariah or they died.

He'd had his fair share of dealings with Hillar Darkraven. He would make her see reason or he would cut her head from her shoulders and march it through the streets of her city.

Ariah continued, "More will join you. They'll have no choice. The time of weak people ruling is over with, Beron. You will be strong for me. You will gather allies and kill foes. There can be no mercy in this."

Beron nodded. "No mercy. None."

"Tell the slavers to join you or die, Beron. Let them know those are their only choices."

Sated for the moment, Beron looked up from his plate and stared at his host. "They join us or they die."

Ariah waited until he'd finished eating. It seemed he devoured a great feast, enough for a dozen men. Trays and platters were emptied of their offerings and little remained but husks and lengths of bone by the time he was finished, and yet he was still hungry.

"That's the way it is with demons, Beron. We are always ravenous." The words came from Ariah as if he'd asked a question but at that moment Beron was comfortably drunk on sweet wines and sufficiently sated that he did not care.

The companionable hand that touched his shoulder urged him quietly toward the first place they'd ever met. There, Beron saw the great steed that would be his and the weapons he'd carry.

"I will send you to Torema. Once there you will gather your army and seize the city. They will serve you or…?"

"Or they will die."

Beron felt feverish as he climbed the horse and settled his weight in the saddle. Once again his spear and his sword were ready. Once again he was given a chance to rule if only he could fulfill his part of the bargain.

He would not disappoint Ariah a second time.

When he rode forward the world around him shifted and, instead of standing on a mountain top or riding across a field of snow, he saw the ocean to his right and Torema proper before him. All around his position people sat in squalor. They looked desperate. They looked hungry. Hunger, he knew, could be a great motivator. It worked on slaves and statesmen alike.

Beron smiled as the people around him looked up at him astride the great war beast he'd been given by Ariah.

He gathered his thoughts only for a moment before he made his statement. "Torema has food and roofs and clean water. Who among you would sleep in a bed tonight and feast, and sup on sweet wines?"

All around the king of the slavers the hungry and the desperate turned and listened.

Interlude: Desmond

Desmond cursed and Bump crawled after him, not wanting to look back, hardly daring to slow down. The water was coming and there was no denying that sort of force. He'd lived through enough floods when he was young to know that water was more powerful than flesh when it set its mind to a task.

They'd scaled high and hard and even as he worried he saw Bump reach the pinnacle of the hill and start over to the western slope. Not that he could go very far without Desmond.

As if reading his mind, the shorter man reached down and grabbed his wrist, pulling.

"I'm coming! Calm down!"

"Not fast enough, you fool!"

Desmond dared a glimpse. The vast wave rushed forward and drove into the mountainside hard enough to make their bodies shake. Desmond fell on his ass and clutched at the closest rock for purchase. The stone did not slide as he feared it might and he stayed where he was as the vibrations continued. The water roared as it drove against the Broken Swords.

Still, for the moment they were safe.

Desmond called for Anna. Both she and Brogan had gone lower into the mountains looking for a passage that might not exist. If they were still low enough, they'd be drowned or swept away. The two of them moved down the slope, falling and rolling with very little control. Stones bruised Desmond's arm, and leg, and face. He groaned and did his best to stop. Whenever he thought he was making progress it was Bump's turn to run into him and knock him sprawling. Whenever he thought they might be safe from the impacts he was thrown again and often as not bounced off the shorter man.

Eventually the two of them rolled to a stop.

In the distance they could see the waters cutting through Harlea's Pass in a titanic wave that was unceasing. The mountain actually rumbled from the roar of that water.

Desmond lay back and counted the number of places he ached. It would have been much faster to count the spots that didn't hurt.

Desmond spoke mostly to himself.

Bump heard and responded, "What?"

"I said, I'm going to find my wife."

"Well, I'll not stop you."

"Good. I'd just as soon not drag your corpse with me."

Bump chuckled at that. It was a small jest but they were both alive and that seemed to make everything just a little more enjoyable at the moment.

That was when the mountain cracked to the north of them. Full-on split down the middle, vomiting dust and giving off noises like thunder.

Desmond sat up, his pocked face set in a scowl of worry, and the world tilted.

The mountain surged again and both of them were up and running once more, heading to the south where the mountains had the good sense not to jump up and down.

Behind them, the mountains exploded.

Brogan McTyre

Brogan fell backward, his legs powerless, his limbs refusing to listen to his commands.

He wanted to not fall. He concentrated on that idea. It did not work.

If he ever hit the ground he could not say.

His senses exploded before that could happen in any event.

The eyes of a man are limited. The ears can hear a lot but not everything. The skin of a man can feel any number of sensations but those, too, are muted when compared to the senses of a god. Brogan learned that the hard way as his body dropped bonelessly to the ground.

He had no idea what to call what happened to him. His eyes saw more than they should have. He saw through the skin of the mountain to the world beyond. In an instant he understood the devastation that had already taken place and he was horrified. The land he had traveled most of his adult life was gone, broken and blasted and bloodied. The cities he had escorted caravans to were in ruin or overflowing with too many people. Two separate armies rode toward Torema from the north. One sported the colors of Giddenland and the other carried the tattered flags of Saramond. They were large armies, to be sure, but they stank of desperation and hunger.

Saramond was gone. The very land it had once sat

on was lost to the ocean's tides. Giddenland was still there, but Edinrun had been erased from the world. He knew where the vast city was. He saw the people locked within its confines and heard their desperate screams. They could not escape and the darkness that surrounded the city walls seemed filled with other things, best not considered too closely.

The structures of Stennis Brae still stood at the top of the mountains, but they were abandoned. There were no people walking the pathways of his homeland. They had all moved to the west, and most were as confused by that notion as he was.

Somewhere to the south of them Bump and Desmond sat on the ground chained together. Desmond's mind was only for Anna, and Brogan felt guilt though he had done nothing wrong. His thoughts, he assured himself, were clean enough. His body disagreed.

Further south he sensed Bron McNar and knew his king had done something horrible, but he could not quite see the man. All around where Bron should have been there was a vast city of people and either they were obscuring his new senses or something else was. In any event he knew the king was in danger and that there was nothing he could do for him.

At the southernmost edge of the land was a place that was considered holy by the gods. It was a place of sacrifice and unending potential. He hated it in an instant, knowing it for a mirror of the very spot where the Grakhul had killed his family. If he could have, he'd have wiped the place away like a bad memory, but he did not have that power.

In the wastelands to the south and east, and in several

other places, there were pits of darkness that seethed and boiled with furious hatred and desperate hunger. They were not completely a part of the world, but like the area where Bron McNar lurked, they were half-hidden and left a taste across his mind that was unclean.

Still his senses expanded further.

Torema was still there. The Kaer-ru abided. Both the city and the islands were crowded and overflowing. There were so many people and so little left that could support the growing populations.

He knew without trying to understand why, that Harper was there and so were several others with whom he claimed fellowship. He saw them, sensed that they were safe for the moment and knew that he would be seeking them soon enough, because to the east and sliding north, the towns along the ocean's edge were either torn away or collapsing into the surging waters. So many deaths, all brought about by his actions and those of the gods.

Guilt tried to crush him like a boot crushes an insect, but he shrugged it aside. Guilt was a useless emotion and could wait until after he had finished his bloody work.

To the east and storming toward him was a great and terrible beast. He did not know if it was a god or a servant of a god, but whatever the case it was coming toward him to stop him.

There was fear in the heart of the creature. Dread tainted its very being and desperation pushed it to attack the mountains themselves. He felt the waters bombard the skin of the Broken Blades and shatter parts of it. The mountain held, but near the base cracks started to form and the raging tide pushed through the rough surface and broke into the vast chamber where a dead god rested.

In that moment Brogan understood finally that what he saw was only a fraction of what Walthanadurn sensed. The god was dead, but could not truly die. The god existed but wanted something else. The god saw, and tasted, and touched, and smelled, and heard the universe around itself and wanted to either live or be free from the memories that drowned the vast corpse as surely as the waves were about to.

"NO!" Brogan did not know if he spoke or if Walthanadurn's fading mind did. In any event his body shuddered and he turned to look at the titanic wave crashing against the mountain. The thing that rode inside that wave grabbed at the crystalline blades piercing the Broken Swords and pulled itself up the side of the mountain, bringing a surge of ocean tide with it that shook the mountains of the range to their roots.

Brogan knew that if nothing was done he and his companions would be crushed.

He did not know if he was the one who reacted or if it was Walthanadurn, but he reached to defend against the vast power in that wave and–

Walthanadurn's corpse moved with him.

His hands reached, and the dead god lunged. The vast hands of the fallen god grabbed the closest shard of crystal, the very blade that had struck the god dead eons ago, and–

Outside of the vast hollow mountain, the waves bashed themselves against the stone, and the shell around Walthanadurn cracked.

Inside the cavernous heart of the mountain an impossible corpse shimmered. Light flowed from bones and formed the shapes of muscles, of organs, of flesh.

Walthanadurn stood, and the mountain above him exploded, hurling tons of rock and debris into the air, scattering earth and snow and everything that rested atop the mountain into the sky.

Brogan let out a roar as his body stood and grabbed the massive crystalline shard.

The dead god stood and looked around and found its enemy far below.

There had been a time when the nameless shape in the water had been kin to Walthanadurn. In those faraway times he had gifted his daughter with a thousand names and control of the seas. By way of thanks she and her siblings had driven their blades into his body countless times until, finally, he fell to the ground and died as much as any god can truly die. They had betrayed him. They had slaughtered him that they might take even more of the world and the universe for themselves.

He would have left, would have traveled the stars, but they denied him that opportunity.

Brogan felt a god's cold rage in his soul.

It was not as potent as his own fury, but it was strong enough and Walthanadurn reached out and drove the vast splinter of sword deep into his daughter, struck her with all the force that he could muster and impaled her on the weapon that had murdered him. The remains of Sepsumannahun's sword remained as potent as they had been millennia earlier.

In one simple stroke the dead giant drove the blade through the very center of his daughter's heart and killed her.

But gods do not die easily.

The vast shape that had shattered half the continent retreated, tearing the blade from her father's dead hands as she fled, dying, to the oceans she ruled.

Brogan looked down through eyes that should not have been, and saw the impossible body he inhabited. He stood taller than the mountains. He towered into the clouds and storms that reached as far as the Gateway that tried to hide his children from him.

No. Not his children. Walthanadurn's.

Except they were one and the same. They shared the same mind. The same bodies. Somewhere inside of him he lay resting and the people with him were scattered.

From his impossible height he considered that possibility. He was a god. He was Brogan McTyre. Both could not be true. The god was dead. Brogan was alive.

That would not be the case for long, because now that the god had finished killing its daughter and defending itself, it wanted to be dead again.

The glowing flesh and muscles that had surrounded Walthanadurn faltered.

For one impossible moment in time Brogan had been one with a god. That moment was passing.

The body of a dead god shuddered and began to collapse.

A corpse that towered three times higher than the highest part of the mountains looked across the vast worldscape and Brogan saw all that it saw even as the consciousness of Walthanadurn began to pass.

The voice spoke to him directly this time, not through Faceless. The sounds that had shaken his flesh previously were now a fading whisper.

"These last gifts I give to you, Brogan McTyre. I send you and yours to safety and I touch you with my power. You are not a god. You will never be a god. But as you have sought, so you have found. You may touch the gods."

The massive skeleton came apart then. The bones that should never have moved again tilted and slid to the side. The mountains were shattered around it. The hollowed world that had been its coffin was ruined and the giant that had rested in the heart of those hollow places fell toward the sea and the remains of ruined Saramond.

That was the last that Brogan saw before he hit the sand.

He closed his eyes for a moment, disoriented and lost in the sensations he had just drowned in.

When he could finally open his eyes he saw that he was, indeed, resting on pristine sand not far from a placid ocean.

In the distance he could see the mainland and the storms, but here, at this moment in time, the skies above were clear.

Five feet way Faceless lay prone. Closer to him Anna was curled in a fetal position and whimpering. Roskell Turn was in similar shape. Almost a hundred yards further on, he saw the taller man, who had failed to introduce himself, pushing himself up from the sand. His face and body were painted with the granules and he had a wild-eyed expression that Brogan could understand all too well.

They should have been dead.

They'd dared to touch a god and they should have been dead. All that Brogan had thought he knew was gone, replaced by the memories of walking in a god's steps and sharing his mind with a being of nearly infinite power.

When Brogan stood, his limbs trembled and his skin shook. His eyes seemed half blind. His ears struck mostly deaf. He could smell the sea but it seemed weaker than it should have.

"We are in Louron." The taller man spoke. Brogan looked his way and for an instant wished he knew his name. The information came to him without bidding. The man was called Jahda and he was as close to a king as the Kaer-ru islands had. He was from Louron, which was both of this world and not of this world. He and his people walked pathways unseen by most. Brogan had seen them for a moment, when he and the god were one. That sight was gone now, along with so much that he had known.

He wanted to weep. All that he had learned was already fading and that seemed horribly unfair when he considered all that he had already lost.

He closed his eyes and felt the body moving under him, responding. He felt the impact of a god's blade as it drove through the heart of another god.

Anna moaned and slowly pulled herself into a sitting position.

The cloak of the Undying that had been his only garb crumbled. The material fell away in ashen pieces and he knew that, at last, one of the Undying had truly died. The power of a god is enough to kill anything a god might make.

His voice when he spoke was hoarse. "Anna, I hope you've clothes somewhere in that bag of yours."

She chuckled and looked away from his naked body. "I can manage something, I expect." Her voice shook. He understood all too well why.

"Did you succeed, Brogan McTyre?"

He looked at Roskell Turn, surprised. "How can you ask? Did you not see?"

"I saw the shape we stood in move. I felt mountains falling. After that I felt nothing. I thought I was dead."

"Walthanadurn offered one last boon." Brogan looked at the smaller man and offered what he hoped was a smile. "He spared us and sent us here instead of letting us die with him."

"Why?"

"Because I helped him kill his daughter." Brogan smiled. It was not a kind expression and he knew it. It was the grin of a wolf that had finally managed to bring down its prey. "I have killed one of the gods."

Anna looked up at him, her eyes wide.

"They'll be so very angry."

Brogan nodded. "Perhaps."

"Perhaps?" Her voice strained and her expression demanded more from him. "What else would they be?"

"They might be angry, Anna, but for now, they are also very afraid."

He looked at his hands. They seemed unchanged.

"Afraid? Afraid of what?"

"I have what we sought. I can touch the gods now." He looked over at Faceless, who was beginning to stir, and at the axe he had used on so many occasions. "And if I can touch a thing, I can kill it."

Far to the north the Gateway remained. He knew that. He had seen it with the eyes of Walthanadurn. If they were in the Kaer-ru, then they would surely find a ship to take him where he needed to go.

"I'll have their throats in my hands, Nora." He spoke only to the memory of his wife, but others heard him. "I'll have their throats in my hands and I'll kill them all for you."

To the north the storms raged and lightning lashed down from the heavens to the ground and the godless seas. Brogan thought of the fallen god he had helped to fell and saw that it was good.

Amen.

ACKNOWLEDGMENTS

Special thanks to Marc, Phil, Nick, Penny, Mike, cover artist Alejandro and, well, basically everyone at Angry Robot for being such delightful Evil Robot Overlords. You guys make it look like I know what I'm doing.

We are Angry Robot.

angryrobotbooks.com

SKYFARER
JOSEPH BRASSEY
SUSAN MURRAY
THE WATERBORNE BLADE
SUSAN MURRAY
WATERBORNE EXILE

STEAL THE SKY
MEGAN E. O'KEEFE
BREAK THE CHAINS
MEGAN E. O'KEEFE
INHERIT THE FLAME
MEGAN E. O'KEEFE

CARRIE PATEL
THE BURIED LIFE
CARRIE PATEL
CITIES AND THRONES
CARRIE PATEL
THE SONG OF THE DEAD